THE IDEAL MAN

T.J. EMERSON

B

Boldwood

First published in Great Britain in 2023 by Boldwood Books Ltd.

Cover Design by Head Design Ltd

Cover Photography: Shutterstock

A CIP catalogue record for this book is available from the British Library.

Paperback ISBN 978-1-80415-171-6

Large Print ISBN 978-1-80415-172-3

Hardback ISBN 978-1-80415-170-9

Ebook ISBN 978-1-80415-174-7

Kindle ISBN 978-1-80415-173-0

Audio CD ISBN 978-1-80415-165-5

MP3 CD ISBN 978-1-80415-166-2

Digital audio download ISBN 978-1-80415-168-6

Boldwood Books Ltd
23 Bowerdean Street
London SW6 3TN
www.boldwoodbooks.com

PART I

1

COLETTE

My father is innocent. I want to tell that to the social worker sitting on the long white sofa. Madame Ponsolle. She didn't offer me a first name, although she called me by mine when I opened the door to her. A black leather satchel sits on the floor next to her feet. A clipboard rests on her knee, official documents attached to it. Boxes she must tick or cross. Larger boxes for her to write comments in.

My father is not a criminal, but she doesn't believe that. To her he is just another prisoner she has to deal with.

'Here we are.' As I hand her an espresso in one of our best china cups, I try to see what is on the forms attached to the clipboard but glimpse only part of to-day's date. Tuesday, 3 April.

'Thank you,' she says, taking the coffee. I've lived here in my father's apartment in Nice for five years, but Ponsolle still spoke English when she first arrived, obviously assuming my French wouldn't be up to standard. I'm happy to let her think so. She tucks her greying hair behind her ears before taking a sip of coffee. In her black cords, white shirt and grey cardigan, she looks plain and insignificant, but whatever this small, neat woman writes on her report could help to get my father out of Baumettes prison in Marseilles early. Or keep him there until the end of his sentence.

Dad got six years. By the time they sent him to prison, he'd already served six months on remand and that, along with the automatic sentence reduction they have in France, gave him five years to serve. Soon he will have a hearing to reduce his sentence by a further six months, and Ponsolle's visit is part of the preparation for that hearing.

I sit in the white armchair next to the sofa. My espresso cup rattles in its saucer as I put it on the coffee table. Last thing I need is caffeine. It's just after 2 p.m., but I was too nervous to eat lunch. My stomach is still a painful knot of tension, but I'm starting to feel hungry and faint.

Madame Ponsolle watches me fold my hands in my lap. Under her gaze, I feel like a teenager, not a woman of thirty. She's here to assess where Dad will be living if he gets released, and she's here to assess me too. I'm wearing navy trousers and a cream jumper, an outfit that hopefully makes me look mature and responsible. This morning I went to the hairdressers and had my blonde bob washed and blow-dried.

My preparation for today reminds me of Dad's trial. Sitting there day after day in clothes his lawyer recommended I wear. Knowing strangers were judging me and that this could influence the way they judged him.

'How long have you had this apartment?' Madame Ponsolle asks.

'Nearly seven years.' Dad bought this place not long before Mum was diagnosed with secondary breast cancer. He'd just sold the business and was heading for early retirement. They were planning to live here for a few years before buying a villa further up the coast towards Cassis.

Best laid plans. Five months after diagnosis, Mum was dead, and five months after that, Dad had a one-night stand with the wrong woman and our lives fell apart.

'And you live here now?' Ponsolle says. 'All the time?'

'Yes. This is home.'

A home that has become its own sort of prison since Dad went into his. One of six apartments in a sleek, modern block in the exclusive Mont Boron area of Nice.

Ponsolle glances around her as she sips her coffee. I can't imagine she makes many visits to this part of town – it's a bit posh around here. She takes in the spacious open-plan living area, her gaze settling for a moment on the long, granite-topped kitchen island that separates the sitting room from the kitchen. The place where Dad and I will sit and eat together when he gets out. Her expression is neutral, but I sense unspoken questions lurking beneath it. Why would a man with all this do what he did? Or did his money and privilege enable him to do what he did? I want to snatch the clipboard off her, tear up her stupid forms and tell her that he didn't do it at all.

I must hold it together for Dad's sake. Ponsolle works for the SPIP – Les Services Pénitentiaires d'Insertion et de Probation. She is a small part of a large and ugly system Dad should never have been involved with. One I need to get him out of as soon as I can.

'Colette,' she says, 'can you tell me what you do for your living?'

'I'm a freelance copywriter.' She already knows this, I'm sure, but I play along with her. 'Mostly for the travel industry.'

I keep my tone light and enthusiastic. As if my work is what I've always dreamt of doing. As if I'm living the life I was always meant to live.

'Interesting,' she says without conviction.

'Keeps me busy.' The hours are often long, deadlines tight and the money a lot less than I was earning back in London, but the job has allowed me to be here for Dad.

'You work from home?' she says.

'Yes. So, I'll be around when my dad gets out, to help him settle back in.'

She nods. 'Can I see the rest of the apartment?'

'Of course.'

She finishes her coffee and picks up her clipboard. I usher her to the hallway that leads in from the apartment's front door and show her my bedroom.

'You have a brother,' Ponsolle says when I show her the guest room, 'Patrick. Does he come to visit?'

'He lives in Sydney with his family, but we hope he'll come over as soon as Dad's out.'

I'm not lying to her. Not exactly. Dad and I do hope

Patch will come over, but we both know that's unlikely. An official assessment would describe my older brother as estranged. I haven't told him about this visit, or the possibility of Dad's early release. Our infrequent phone calls often end in an argument. I still can't believe I've had to endure all this without him. I still can't believe he thinks our father is guilty.

'Dad and I have a really strong support network,' I say. This is a lie. The truth is nearly everyone we know has abandoned him. I'm all he's got.

I take her to Dad's room and follow her inside. Will she note the king-size bed made up for his return? His favourite toiletries in the en suite bathroom?

She wanders around the bedroom in silence. Dad's Tag Heuer watch sits on the dressing table. He didn't wear it to his sentencing. All of his valuables have remained with me, waiting for him to return and claim them. If Ponsolle opens the wardrobe door she will see shirts and trousers waiting for him. She will see the Tom Ford navy-blue suit he wore during his trial. When I brought it back from the prison and hung it up, I cried. It felt like he'd shed some outer layer of himself when he went into that place. One he wouldn't get back for a long time.

Artificial birdsong fills the room. Ponsolle pulls a

slim black phone from her trouser pocket and checks the screen.

'Excuse me,' she says.

'Of course.'

After stepping into the hallway and pulling the door closed, I hover nearby. She's speaking French to a colleague, and I can understand every word. She's saying she won't be too long here. She's confirming she has the address for her next visit. When her voice drops, I lean closer to the door, certain she's talking about me.

'*C'est une fille à papa,*' she says. '*Absolument.*'

Une fille à papa. A daddy's girl.

Heat flushes my cheeks. I tell myself I have nothing to be ashamed of. Nothing at all.

* * *

Back in the main room, Ponsolle pauses at the kitchen island to jot something on her clipboard.

'You are visiting him soon?' She points her pen at the blue-and-white-check laundry bag that sits in front of the washing machine.

'I go almost every week.' Each time I visit, I pick up his laundry, bring it back here and wash it, ready to take it back the following week. That's how they do it over here. The irony isn't lost on Dad and me. He made his first millions transforming a small industrial laundry business in Manchester into a UK-wide success. Thousands of vans and lorries with the *Fresh As* logo on the side. Now I'm washing his dirty clothes once a week and driving them from Nice to Marseilles in my Renault Clio or hauling the laundry bag with me on the train if the weather is bad or if I can't face the traffic. Before Dad went to jail, I never used to be able to drive on the right-hand side of the road. On holidays, Dad always did all the driving and then, when I was married, my husband drove if we went abroad. I've had to learn, though. One of many new skills I've had to acquire.

'You have a close relationship with your father?' Ponsolle asks.

'Very.' I smile. 'My mum used to say I was a real daddy's girl.'

She shoots me a suspicious look, and I instantly regret the comment.

'We're very close, yes,' I say. 'Always have been.'

Very close. Two words that fail to express the connection Dad and I have. He was the parent I went to first with any problem, not Mum. He's always looked out for me and now I'm looking out for him.

Madame Ponsolle walks around the sitting room.

She stops to look at the collection of gaudy clown ornaments on the vintage oak sideboard.

'They belonged to my nan,' I say. 'Dad's mum. She died last year.'

Ponsolle says nothing. Not that I expected sympathy. Nana Gilligan died alone in a nursing home in Manchester. Dad was devastated. In normal circumstances he would have been by her side. I went to the funeral on his behalf, which was the least I could do.

I miss her. She was the only other person who believed in Dad's innocence. A mother knows her son, she used to say. Dad's guilty verdict and the prison sentence killed her. No doubt about it.

Ponsolle looks up at the family portrait that hangs over the sideboard. Before the trial, Dad put our family home in my name so I could sell it. He knew if he went to jail, we wouldn't have access to all his savings and investments, and he wanted a pot of money I could have access to. It hurt me to sell Riverbank Cottage, our large, rambling home in the Surrey village of Ripley. I packed up most of our belongings and put them in storage but had a few things shipped across, including the family portrait. In it, I am sixteen and Patch is eighteen. We have just come back from two weeks in the Caribbean, and we are all tanned and glowing and happy. Mum and Dad have their arms wrapped around one another. Mum, a former Miss Manchester winner, is glamorous as always. Once upon a time, we were a family people envied.

Ponsolle must have seen photographs of Dad before. I wonder if she can see the resemblance between the two of us? I've got his wide hazel eyes. Mum used to say I had more of him in me than her.

'Your father was a boxer?' Ponsolle says. She has moved on to the small collection of framed photographs at the end of the sideboard. She stares at the one of Dad at sixteen, winning a local lightweight boxing competition. My pulse races. I should have put that picture away.

'As a kid,' I say. She will think this is proof of a violent nature. My father isn't a violent man, no matter what was said at his trial. No matter what lies his accuser told about him.

Ponsolle mutters something as she scribbles on her clipboard. She thinks she knows my father, but she knows only a mixture of facts and lies. She will know he was born Alexander Philippe Gilligan and that he is fifty-three years old. She will know he is a dual national, born in Marseilles to a French mother and a British father. Does she know his father was a soldier from Manchester and his mother a working-class woman from Marseilles? Does she know Dad grew up in Moss Side in Manchester with nothing? Does she know he is self-made? A brilliant businessman? A man who once was the centre of a large network of family and friends?

My father is the most interesting man I know.

She moves away from the sideboard and when she reaches the French doors that open on to the balcony, she stops.

'*C'est beau*,' she says, her professionalism slipping for a moment.

'Yes.' Even on a dull day like today, the view is stunning. The villas, apartments and gardens of Mont Boron are spread out before us. Beyond them rises the bulk of Castle Hill and the terracotta rooftops of Nice's old town. In the distance, the Pre-Alps form a hilly backdrop to the city. To our left the Bay of Angels is steely blue and restless after this morning's rain. Mont Boron is in the east of the city and looking west I can see the curve of the bay. At night the lights along the Promenade des Anglais follow that curve. Lighting it up like a runway.

'Right,' Ponsolle says, her tone clipped and official again. 'I think I have everything now.'

I want to drop to my knees and beg. Let him out early. He doesn't deserve to be in there. He should be here, living in his home.

'Are you sure?' I say. 'If there's anything else I can—'

'There is one more thing.' She picks up her briefcase and slides the clipboard inside. 'You are involved with the Families for Justice organisation?'

A statement, not a question. My mouth feels suddenly dry. Why does she want to know about that? How is it relevant to the hearing? 'Yes,' I say. 'I first heard of them after Dad's trial. Their online community has been very supportive.'

When I first accessed the FFJ website and read the stories posted there, it blew me away how many people all over the world are wrongly convicted and imprisoned. The people I've met through the chat forums understand my helplessness and frustration. They understand the agony of knowing a loved one is innocent and being powerless to help them. Connecting with the FFJ community has often given me hope when I've most needed it.

'I read the page you set up about your father,' Ponsolle says.

'Yes, it's public.' I set up the page on the FFJ website to share what happened to Dad. It gave me some satisfaction to tell his side of the story . 'Is there a problem? Is that going to affect the hearing? Do I need to take it down?'

'You really believe he is innocent?' Ponsolle asks. Her tone is curious now.

'Yes.' Weariness washes over me. I've lost count of the times I've had to justify my decision to defend Dad. I long to remind her his case was not without doubt. Here in France, the average sentence for rape is seven to nine years, but in cases where there is doubt about consent, the sentence is less than that. Even the judge who handed out his sentence, an unsympathetic woman determined to make an example of him, had to admit doubt existed about whether his accuser had consented or not. Doubts that Odette, Dad's lawyer, was certain would get him an innocent verdict or at least the minimum sentence.

'You know the hearing is not about whether he did it or not?' Ponsolle says.

'Yes, I know.'

'He was convicted, and he has served his sentence.'

'I know.' Odette made that clear when I spoke to her a few days ago. The hearing is not a chance for Dad to plead his innocence again. To get out early, he will have to show remorse for a crime he didn't commit. He will have to rely on the good behaviour he's shown throughout his sentence.

'Okay,' Ponsolle says. 'I am done here.'

We say goodbye at the front door.

'It was lovely to meet you,' I say with a smile. I want her to see I am sane and responsible. No reason not to release my father and let him come home. 'Do you have any idea when we might get a hearing date?' I ask.

She shakes her head. 'We'll be in touch.'

I watch as she walks briskly down the stairs. Only when she's out of sight do I close the front door.

We'll be in touch.

After all these years in the system, I know they like to keep everyone in limbo. The prisoner is never the only person serving the sentence. Their loved ones serve time too.

What about the woman who put him in there? She's had four and a half years of freedom. If Dad gets his early release, maybe I'll feel we've got back six of the months she's taken from us. After the trial, I told Dad's lawyer I wanted to speak to the woman who had wrecked our lives. Odette put her hands on my shoulders, looked me in the eyes and said that under no circumstances could I ever do that.

That hasn't stopped me thinking about her, though. Where is she now? What is she doing with her life?

2

JANE

My husband wakes me from the nightmare. Wakes me and pulls my hot shaking body close to his cool still one. I tell myself I am safe. I tell myself I am not in a hotel room with Sandy Gilligan.

'Bad dream?' Michel says.

'I'm fine.'

'You did not sound fine. What was it about?'

I hesitate. The anonymous darkness surrounding us almost makes me feel safe enough to share my secrets. 'Can't remember. Being chased or something.'

Michel yawns. 'You are safe now.'

Am I? My pulse is racing, my body still convinced the dream is real. I snuggle into my husband. At six foot four, he is so much taller than me. When standing, we look an odd couple, but when lying down, we are a perfect fit. I rest on the shelf of his thighs, his knees slotting into the back of mine.

'Try to sleep,' he murmurs, his voice drowsy.

'I will.' Aware he has to be up early for work, I urge him to go back to sleep too. Within seconds I feel the first tell-tale jerk of his feet as he drifts away.

I will not sleep again tonight. In the nightmare, Sandy Gilligan was standing behind me with his lips close to my ear. *Nice to see you again.*

Years have passed since he last invaded my sleep. Why tonight?

Taking care not to wake Michel, I slide out of bed and creep out of our room into the hallway. My phone sits charging on the table next to the front door, its usual resting place. Within seconds I am online, typing *Sandy Gilligan* into the search engine. As soon as his name appears on the glowing screen, I delete it. After the trial, I vowed to stop looking him up online. For my family's sake, and my own, I needed to put him out of my mind.

I glance back at the bedroom door. No hint of my husband stirring. In my phone's settings, I find Google Alerts and click on it. In the box at the top of the screen I type his name again. My heart thumps. I turn the alert off then on again. Thanks to Sandy I have a prey's instinct and that instinct is telling me to be cautious.

After checking my phone is on silent, I leave it charging and pad along the hallway to the bedroom next to mine, where my son is asleep. It took a long time to get him into a regular sleeping pattern but finally, at three years and four months old, he sleeps through the night. I stand over his bed and watch him, soothed by his soft breathing. I plant a light kiss on his head, my lips hovering over his dark hair. Theo has my colouring, but his curls are courtesy of Michel. 'Sweet dreams,' I whisper.

Back in my own bed, I replay my nightmare over and over. I can almost feel Sandy's hot breath against my skin.

He is locked up now. That is all that matters. He is locked up and I have a new life with my family. To soothe myself I think about this life. I think of Draguignan, the quiet provincial town in the Provence-Alpes-Côte d'Azur region I now call home. A long way from the Cotswolds village I grew up in. I think of this apartment, rustic but modern, in a converted outbuilding in the grounds of the Hôtel des Arbres, a boutique hotel not far from Draguignan's old town. The hotel owned by Michel's family. The place where we live and work. The hotel courtyard boasts plane trees two hundred years old. In the summer, lavender blooms in the wooden pots between the trees and guests escape the sun beneath white parasols. The hotel's website describes it as a 'quiet idyll'. For me it is a safe haven.

I tell myself I have nothing to fear. I won't let anyone take away this new life I have made for myself. Not even Sandy Gilligan.

3

LYNNE

My dearest Sandy,

An early release hearing!! When I got your letter, I didn't know whether to cry or dance around like a madwoman, so I did both. I know it's not a dead cert, and I know you're still waiting to find out if it'll happen, but I've got a good feeling about it. Putting aside the fact you're innocent, you've had a clean record in there and you've got a life to go back to on the outside. I know you said we mustn't get ahead of ourselves, but the thought of us finally being together, after two years of writing to each other… it's almost too much.

I can't believe two years have passed since I

saw your picture in that Daily Mail article. As soon as I opened the paper that day and saw your face, I knew you were innocent. I also knew my life had changed for ever. I'll never forget the instant connection I felt to you when I looked into your eyes. I saw the kindness in them, and I knew you were a good man, and I knew I had to write to you immediately and tell you so.

I'm so happy at the thought you might get out soon. Colette must be delighted? I can't wait to meet her. Thanks to you, I feel like I know her already. I know you're worried what she'll say when she finds out about me, but from what you've told me about her, I think it's going to be fine. She loves you and she'll want you to be happy. I know the two of us are going to get on.

Things are fine here. Apart from missing you like mad as always. I'm writing this on Friday night, after a busy week at work. Honestly, Colchester General Hospital couldn't function if it wasn't for us in the estates department. We're in charge of looking after the buildings and the grounds, we make sure all the deliveries and even the patients get to the right place at the right time, but do we get any credit for what we do? Chance would be a fine thing.

I'm doing my usual Friday-night routine. Dinner, a long bath, comfies on and now I'm sitting on the sofa with a glass of red wine and this letter to write. One day soon, we'll be sitting on a sofa together somewhere, cuddling up and sharing the stories of our day. For now, I've got your picture on the coffee table to keep me company. You're a handsome man, Sandy Gilligan. I know you say you looked better before prison turned your hair grey, but I think the colour suits you. Shows off your eyes.

It'll be weird, won't it, seeing each other on the outside? Four times now I've visited you in prison and, obviously, you get to see me at my best. Hair done, face on. Soon you'll get to see the real me. No make-up in the morning, stretch marks, the lot. I've got more than a few grey hairs poking through the red these days. That scares me a bit. I keep thinking, what if you don't like what you see? I know you'll tell me not to worry about stuff like that. You're always telling me I'm gorgeous. I expect it'll be a bit nerve-wracking for you too. Neither of us is as young as we used to be. I can hardly believe I've just turned fifty.

This'll be a short letter. I know I could have

waited to say all this until we speak on the phone next week but writing you a letter always makes me feel close to you. When you said a few months ago that my letters and phone calls were the only thing keeping you going in there, I nearly cried.

The wine I'm drinking is a Merlot, by the way. The one you recommended. It's nice. I'm a Yorkshire lass at heart so I doubt I'll ever be a wine buff, but I know you love the stuff so I'm trying to be a bit more knowledgeable. Shared interests are so important in a long-term relationship, aren't they?

My neighbours upstairs, the young couple I told you about, are rowing again. Reminds me of my first marriage. The walls are thin in this block of flats. Not that I'm bothered what the neighbours get up to. It's not like I'll be here much longer. Who knows where we'll end up living when you get out? No point making any big decisions yet. We've got all the time in the world to work out the finer details. The rest of our lives.

You will let me know when you get a date for your hearing, won't you? It's torture sometimes, being at the mercy of the prison services. Not knowing when my letter will get to you and when yours will get to me. Not knowing when we'll finally be free to start our life together. We were made for one another, Sandy Gilligan, and woe betide anyone who gets in our way.

Yours for ever,

Lynne.

4

COLETTE

'For God's sake, Patch, he's our father.'

'I don't owe that man anything.'

I'm sitting at the kitchen island, staring at my laptop. My brother looms out from the screen, a set of shelves crammed with books behind him. It's just after 6 p.m. in Sydney and just after 10 a.m. here.

'If he gets his hearing, he could be released soon,' I say.

'And I'm supposed to drop everything and fly to the other side of the world to see him?'

I look at my brother's broad forehead and strong jaw and wonder if he realises how much he looks like his father. 'Give him a break. He's paid a terrible price for something he didn't even do.'

'A jury found him guilty. Why can't you accept that?'

'He's not capable of... you know he's not.'

Another silence. It's rare for me and my brother to have a conversation that doesn't end up in this same dark place. When Dad went to jail, Patch said he felt betrayed. He believes there are two versions of Dad and that all our memories of him are false.

'No doubt you'll be there for him,' Patch says. 'At his beck and call as always.'

Patch hasn't been to visit Dad in jail. Not once. I press my lips together. Remind myself my brother has always been jealous of how close Dad and I are.

'Jenny says Dad made his choices,' my brother says, 'and we've made ours.'

Fuck Jenny, I want to say. She liked Dad just fine when he paid for her wedding reception. She liked him when he gave Patch the deposit for their bungalow on the outskirts of Manly, one of Sydney's exclusive northern beaches.

'I'd better go,' I say.

'Colette. I don't mean to be... It just makes me sad.'

'What does? Dad?'

'No. You. You've wasted nearly five years of your life on all this.'

A sharp pain in my chest. 'Bye, Patch,' I say, and end the call.

* * *

Speaking to my brother leaves me drained and unsettled. His memories of Dad are so different to mine. It's not my fault, or Dad's, that Patch wasn't capable or willing to take over *Fresh As*. Dad wouldn't have sold the business if his son had shown any talent for it. Patch thinks Dad is disappointed he chose to become a physiotherapist and work for the health service, but I only ever remember Dad supporting him and trying to make him happy. My brother and I had every opportunity offered to us. Private-school education and university. A beautiful home and expensive holidays. Two parents who loved us. We couldn't have asked for more.

I hoped becoming a father might make Patch more understanding. Yasmin is four now and Bronnie is two. I've spoken to my nieces on Skype, but I've yet to see them in the flesh. Some days I wonder if Dad will ever meet them. He's encouraged me many times to go to Australia for an extended holiday, but I know how important my prison visits are to him. Apart from the occasional visit from Uncle Jimmy, his wayward younger brother, I'm the only person he has contact with.

Why can't Patch see Dad is innocent? I know many men are guilty of what Dad was accused of, and I know many women suffer terribly because of them, but my dad is not one of those men. Stories like Dad's are the exception. One of the 3–6 per cent of false charges. A tiny percentage but these cases do exist and they're devastating.

Don't get me wrong, my father is guilty of some things. Guilty of falling apart when Mum died. Guilty of working too hard at times. Guilty of women finding him charming and of the odd harmless bit of flirtation that used to make Mum laugh. And guilty of inviting his closest male friends to Marseilles for a boys' weekend five years ago, finding a young barmaid attractive and inviting her back to his room.

The voice of the prosecuting lawyer from Dad's trial pops into my head, uninvited.

The evidence you've heard here in this court shows clearly that Monsieur Gilligan does not understand the word 'no'.

My chest is tight, my breathing shallow. I head to the balcony doors and open them. Outside, I fill my lungs with fresh air. Mid-April and the temperatures are picking up. The breeze is still cool, but it carries the scent of orange blossom on it and hints at warmer days to come. I focus on the view, seeking calm. Our apartment block has a manicured garden at the front. A stretch of glistening green grass and numerous trees. Fan palms, two young stone pines and, at one end of the garden, an orange tree that trails over the wall. Beside the orange tree, a set of steps leads to a secure gate that opens on to the winding Boulevard du Mont Boron. The apartment building can also be accessed from the boulevard via the entrance to the underground car park and from a separate entrance at the front.

A shrill, yapping sound comes from the direction of the steps. Seconds later, a short, lean woman in Lycra leggings and a silver quilted jacket appears, a chihuahua clutched to her chest.

Kathy Cherish. The sixty-eight-year-old widow from apartment number 3. Ash-blonde hair in a soft pixie cut, large diamond on her ring finger. When we first moved in here, she told Mum people often mistook her for Helen Mirren. Mum and I had a good laugh about that afterwards.

'Ramona, darling, don't fuss,' she says as she puts the dog down on the grass. Before I can head inside, she glances up at my balcony. Her shoulders twitch the way they always do when she sees me. As if a shudder has just run through her.

'Morning, Kathy,' I say.

She nods in reply and tugs on Ramona's lead, dragging the scrawny creature across the grass. When she opens the door into the block with her key fob, a loud buzzing noise erupts.

I wonder if one of my neighbours spotted Ponsolle here last week? Have they all been gossiping about my official-looking visitor? Let them talk. It hurts, but I'm used to it. When the police came here to arrest Dad that awful June morning, everyone came out to watch from their balconies as the two male officers led him across the grass and down on to the road to their waiting car. Kathy, of course, along with Ronnie and Rose from number 1 and David and Jean from number 5. The other two apartments are owned by French families, the Corbins and the Beauforts. They only come for a few weeks every year and they keep to themselves. My expat neighbours have made their shock and disapproval obvious from the start and, with Kathy as their ringleader, they've offered me no support while Dad's been in jail. Not that I'd want to go to their book club or their coffee mornings. I'm not that desperate.

That's not true; there have been times I've been very desperate.

I know what Kathy thinks of me. I once overheard her talking to Rose when the two of them were out on Kathy's balcony, drinking Prosecco.

'Colette's ruined her life,' Kathy said, 'and for what? Honestly, Rose, she had it all. She worked in advertising in London and she had a lovely husband. Ever so handsome and nice too.'

In the distance, to the west, a plane takes off from Nice airport, lifting up into the grey sky and arcing over the bay. For a moment I feel homesick, and then I remember that what I feel homesick for no longer exists.

Kathy was right; I did have a different life before all this. A job in the media department of Gotu, one of London's biggest and hippest advertising agencies. A husband I met in my second week of university and fell in love with immediately, and yes, Liam was, is, that rare combination of good-looking and kind, but he didn't believe in Dad's innocence, and I couldn't stay married to a man who thought so little of my father.

There was a brief time, immediately after Dad's arrest when I thought: what if? Could he have done it? But as soon as I saw him at the detention centre in

Marseilles, and he told me what had really happened, my doubt vanished. No man has ever made me feel safe like he does. He's my dad. Simple as that. Even without the facts of the case to convince me, that would have been enough.

Could I have stuck by him if he was guilty? I don't think so. I'd have been heartbroken. And angry. I would have been so angry.

From inside the apartment comes the sound of my mobile ringing. Could it be Patch, calling to make amends? I don't have the energy for another argument. I hurry to where I left my phone, on the kitchen island next to my laptop. When I pick it up, I see the name of Dad's lawyer on the screen.

'Odette, hi,' I say when I answer. 'What is it? What's happened?'

'I need to speak to you about the hearing,' she says.

5

COLETTE

Hope. I've learned to be wary of it over the last five years. Warned myself so many times not to fall for it, but this morning I can't help myself. An hour ago, Odette told me Dad's hearing will take place the week after next, and I haven't stopped smiling since.

Thank God, I didn't let Dad down. Ponsolle must have thought me capable of coping with him when he gets out. After speaking to Odette, I was too excited to hang around the flat so I shoved my laptop into my backpack and walked from Mont Boron down to the port and along to the Promenade des Anglais. It's almost 11.30 a.m. and the promenade is busy with Lycra-clad joggers, rollerbladers and tourists, as well as locals out for a stroll, like me. All of us enjoying this beautiful spring morning. Cloudless blue sky and sunshine bouncing off the choppy blue water. A brisk wind is moving the halyards of the flagpoles that line the promenade and slapping them against the metal poles with a loud twanging sound.

I stop and look out over the bay. This is one of the most famous views of the Riviera, but since Dad went to jail, I've often felt trapped by the breathtakingly blue water. At times I've longed for the surly grey of the North Sea or the English Channel, but I couldn't leave him here alone.

Nearby, a young, pasty-skinned couple who must be British stop to take a selfie with the Mediterranean behind them. At times I envy the tourists. Before Dad's arrest I only saw the romance of the Riviera. Now I know too much about the reality. I know, for example, that today, like every other day, some tourists on this Promenade will get their bags and cameras snatched by a thief who will run with the stolen goods to a nearby road where a scooter and getaway driver awaits. Later in the day, prostitutes from Eastern Europe in revealing outfits will hang out here, waiting for business.

On a nearby bench, an elderly man in a black flat

cap is reading the daily regional newspaper, *Nice-Matin*. I'll never forget the first time the story about Dad appeared in that newspaper. The headline in French.

British man arrested in Nice on suspicion of rape.

Inaccurate from the start. My father is a British-French man, but they never mentioned that in any of their reports. As the investigation progressed, *Nice-Matin* followed the story. At home, in a box file, I have all the newspaper articles relating to Dad's arrest and the trial. I haven't looked at them for ages, but I still remember the headlines.

Man charged with violent rape of twenty-six-year-old English barmaid in room 303 of the InterContinental Hôtel in Marseilles.

Alleged violence.

Later, during the trial, came the picture of Dad on their front page, along with his name. The woman who accused him got to remain anonymous in the media, but Dad didn't have that luxury.

During my phone call with Odette, she said she felt confident the hearing would go our way and told me to stay positive. French prisons are notorious for overcrowding and poor conditions and this factor, according to Odette, will motivate the panel at Dad's hearing to get him out of there. I don't know how Dad has survived Baumettes. Only last month an inmate was stabbed to death in the exercise yard. Whenever I get upset about the danger Dad's in, he tells me he grew up in a rough neighbourhood and that jail isn't so bad. Despite his assurances, I've often seen him with bruises on his face and arms. He always tells me not to worry. He says that although he hates violence he can look after himself. I can't help feeling grateful for that.

If he gets out soon, I'll never have to go back to the prison again. Never have to queue with all the other female visitors to get in. Never have to have my body and belongings searched as if I were a criminal. During the hour I spend with Dad in the visiting cell, my chest is tight; there is never enough air. Relief overwhelms me when I leave, and then I feel guilty for feeling relieved. When I get back to the apartment, I always take a long shower, but I can never seem to wash myself clean of the place.

* * *

After leaving the promenade, I walk to the Place Magenta and claim an outside table under the awning of the Brasserie Le Magenta, one of my favourite cafés in Nice. They have good Wi-Fi too, so I often come here to work. The Place Magenta is part of a pedestrianised shopping area that includes the Rue Masséna on my right. When Mum was alive, she loved to visit Rue Masséna's designer shops, and we'd often have coffee here and watch the world go by.

'*Comme d'habitude*, Colette?' asks the gaunt middle-aged waiter in charge of this section of the brasserie.

'*Oui, merci*, Paul.' The waiter and I are on first-name terms now and he knows I always have a cappuccino and a pain au chocolat in the mornings. We chat about the weather before he scurries inside to get my order.

I'm grateful my French is good enough for me to get by over here. Nana Gilligan spoke to my brother and me in her native language when we were toddlers. She coached me through my French GCSE, and we always spoke at least some French whenever we saw each other. After Dad's arrest, the language barrier often frustrated me. Odette speaks perfect English, but I worked hard on my French, so I didn't miss anything that was going on. When the time came for me to speak up for my father's character in court, I was able to do so in French. I didn't want anything lost in translation.

Paul returns with my order. After thanking him, I take my first sip of coffee. Strong and delicious as always. I pick up the knife from my plate, cut a small piece from the end of the croissant and pop it in my mouth. Soft, buttery pastry with dark, bitter chocolate at the core. Christ, it tastes good. As I chew, I can't help wondering what Dad had for breakfast this morning. Guilt creeps in and my next bite doesn't taste as good. After one more bite, I push the plate away. Probably best I don't finish it. These jeans I'm wearing are a bit tight around my waist, and I've been meaning to cut back on the treats for a while. Dad hasn't commented on my weight, but during last weekend's visit he did say he'd be following a strict healthy-eating plan if he gets out of prison. He suggested we could do it together.

Two elegantly dressed women claim the table next to mine. After Paul takes their order, they light cigarettes and start an animated conversation. I can't help wishing I had someone to talk to. Someone to share my good news with. I did think about calling Patch, but I don't need his negativity right now. Most of my former friends have drifted away from me. Holly, my best friend from childhood and maid of honour at my wedding, had always told me how jealous she was I had such a great dad. She used to jokingly ask him to adopt her. When she found out what he'd been accused of, she didn't support me. She told me she had to stick to her principles and stopped returning my calls. I haven't made any new friends since Dad went to prison either. Not real ones. Now and then I go out for coffee with a few of the women in my Pilates class, but I refuse invitations to go for drinks or dinner. If they get to know me better, I might have to share what happened to him.

I hate to admit it, but the person I really wish I could speak to is Liam. Being divorced doesn't stop me missing him. An ache blooms in my chest as I recall our last bitter row. The one where he told me Dad was guilty, and I told him our marriage was over. The last time I looked up his Facebook page, he had a new profile picture. His shaggy black hair still low over his dark-blue eyes, his crooked smile as sweet as ever. Next to him, her blonde hair pinned up in a messy bun, was his new girlfriend, Amber, a ceramic artist who wears colourful dungarees and works part-time for a mental health charity. He looked happy.

I haven't had a serious relationship since my divorce. A couple of one-night stands with men on holiday here and a three-month fling with a British guy who was teaching at one of the city's English-language schools for a summer. I didn't enjoy the sex with any of them. All the stress of what was going on with Dad, I suppose.

I take my laptop out of my bag and open it up. The document on the screen is the copywriting job I'm supposed to be working on today – a website for the Sunset Aparthotel in Cape Town. *These stunning apartments overlook the iconic Table Mountain.* The last sentence I wrote looks at me accusingly, demanding to be added to, but I shut the document down and log on to the Families for Justice website. Now that Dad's hearing is going ahead, I feel confident Ponsolle didn't make any fuss about my connection to the organisation. Dad never asked me to get involved with FFJ. He once told me to take the page down but relented when I explained how much support I get from the people on here.

I update his page with the news of the upcoming hearing. Odette couldn't give me the exact date until she gets more information, so I write that the hearing will be coming up soon. I also post an announcement about it in the members' chat area. It isn't long before a couple of replies come in. The first is from

Karen, a woman from Melbourne I talk to now and again.

Stoked to hear your news! Fingers crossed for you, babe. XXX

Karen's brother, Alfie, is in jail in Bali for smuggling heroin. Karen has been campaigning for his release for three years now. The second message is from a young guy called Zac, who was arrested and jailed for rape in Benidorm, only to be released ten months later after a successful appeal.

Awesome news. Stay strong. Truth is everything.

There are miscarriages of justice everywhere if you're open to seeing them.

I reply straight away to both messages. This online community has been so supportive and it's important to give back to the people in it. Listening to the stories of others has made me think about retraining as a counsellor when Dad gets out. I want to do something that makes a difference to people's lives.

The two women at the next table drain their espressos. After paying the bill, they leave together, walking arm in arm along Rue Masséna. For the first time, I dare to imagine Dad and me having coffee here together. Is it really possible our struggle is almost over? Is life really about to begin again?

Dad will find the hearing difficult, I'm sure. Having to pretend to be reformed when he's done nothing wrong. If only we'd been granted the right to appeal after the trial. I still find it hard to believe the evidence Odette presented in court wasn't enough to prove his innocence. She got another barmaid from La Cave à Vin to testify that my father's alleged victim had not only flirted with him all night from behind the bar but had also boasted about going for a drink with a handsome sugar daddy at the end of her shift. We had statements from staff at the nightclub my father took her to. Everyone interviewed remembered seeing her dancing provocatively with him. Then there was the CCTV footage recovered from the InterContinental on the night of the attack, which showed Dad walking across the lobby with her; at no point did he touch her. As they waited for a lift to Dad's room, she was the one who kept touching him. A hand on his chest, her head on his shoulder. In the lift, the footage showed clearly that she took both his arms, wrapped them around her waist and pressed herself against him.

The defence team also tracked down one of her ex-boyfriends from university. A guy who stated she had a history of attention-seeking behaviour and had regularly engaged in BDSM sexual practices, with him and also with other men.

None of this proved enough to free my father. Before the trial began, Odette warned us the female judge was new to her post and determined to make an impression. The judge made it clear from the start that discrediting the victim was a tactic she would not look on favourably. Odette also believed Dad's trial was a convenient distraction from another taking place at the same time: two council officials from Marseilles charged with accepting bribes from a property developer. The corruption in the Riviera is no secret, but I never thought it would impact our lives so directly.

Having to listen to the evidence against Dad at the trial wasn't easy. Intimate details no daughter ever wants to hear about her father. I wished I could have stayed away, but I knew how important it was for me to be there. Even when I had to listen to lies about things Dad could never have done.

The alleged victim claims that during intercourse you held a cushion over her face and smothered her with it.

When I finally got the chance to speak, I told the court that when I was a teenager Dad had been full of warnings about boys' behaviour and what I would have to fend off. He'd also explained to me the power of the word 'no'. He'd said this small word would protect me if I used it well. He understood that no meant no because he'd told me so. I made it clear to the court that if any woman had refused Dad's advances, he would have listened.

Many factors led to the jury failing to class what happened as a clear case of rape. There was a lot of uncertainty about what my father's alleged victim consented to, but I like to think my statement helped. Without it, he might have been locked up much longer.

I close my eyes. I can see her, the plaintiff, standing in the witness box. Only a year older than me but my opposite in every way. Dark to my blonde. A small, heart-shaped face to my long, narrow one. Dark-brown eyes she kept fixed on me as she accused my father of violations I tried hard not to imagine. On one occasion, our eyes locked, and I sensed her contempt for me. Her disgust at my support for Dad.

I've looked her up often since then. How could I not? I've searched everywhere for her online but after taking my father away from me, she vanished. She will be thirty-one years old now, but I doubt she can look that different. At one point I thought about hiring a private investigator to track her down, but where to start? She could be anywhere in the world by now. I was also scared of getting found out and of getting Dad into even more trouble. I've often wondered if she changed her name and started a new life somewhere. Why do that? Why disappear if she didn't have anything to hide?

6

JANE

This morning, I wake first. It is still dark. April is too early in the year for sunrise to greet me, but the birds are louder than they were a few weeks ago. After a few moments, Michel stirs beside me. I turn and nestle my nose against his chest, inhaling his warm, musky scent. His hands roam across my bare back, waking my skin and making it tingle. Bringing me back to life.

When we kiss, I taste sleep on his tongue. He slips a hand between my legs, his practised fingers teasing me. When we first met, I often initiated sex. I haven't done that for a long time. I am not the same wild, uninhibited person I once was. Sometimes I worry Michel finds this disappointing, but he has often reassured me all couples with young kids experience changes to their sex life.

I'd like to believe that, but I know I've changed because of Sandy. What happened with him could have ruined my relationship with Michel, but, so far, I've been lucky.

I laugh when my husband pulls me on top of him.

'Morning,' he whispers.

'Morning.'

He is already hard when I reach for him. 'Wait,' he says, before I can ease him inside me.

'What is it?'

He takes my face in his hands. 'I have something to ask you.'

'What?' Anxiety flutters in my chest.

'Maman?'

Erratic footsteps on the landing. Seconds later, the bedroom door flies open. Michel laughs and pulls me down for a final kiss before I climb off him and put the bedside light on.

'Papa.'

Our son, his curly hair even more tangled than usual, clambers on to the bed and claims his rightful place at the centre of our attention. Michel speaks to him in French, asking him about his dreams. Theo chatters back. He was speaking at eighteen months, devouring words in French and English. Maybe the necessity to speak in both has accelerated his learning. Whatever the cause, we have a keen conversationalist on our hands.

My French is fluent now but there are still moments when I have to stop mid-sentence and think of the word I am looking for. I try to speak French whenever I need to hide something. Slowing down makes it harder for my secrets to slip out.

Michel is on breakfast duty this morning. Theo grumbles for a moment when his dad gets up and dresses, but he is soon snuggled into me, one hand touching my breast. I only breastfed him for six months, but he has never lost his fascination with that part of my body.

'*Je t'adore*,' Michel says when he opens the bedroom door.

'We love you,' Theo calls back.

'Michel,' I say, 'what did you want to ask me?'

He glances back at me. Hesitates. 'Later,' he says.

* * *

It is 6.30 a.m. Ten of the hotel's seventeen rooms are occupied and Michel will greet the guests as they come down to breakfast, wait on them and supervise

Darid, the chef. Later, Theo and I will go over to the hotel and have our breakfast there.

I doze while my son whispers and wriggles beside me. When I can't contain him any longer, we get up. I throw on baggy jeans and a black jumper and take Theo to the bathroom to get washed. Today, a Thursday, is only a half-day at his preschool but we need to be there by eight thirty. We talk about what he might do at school today as I wipe his sticky face with a flannel. When we're done, we pull faces at each other in the mirror. An essential part of our morning routine.

'*Regarde-moi*,' my son says as he twists his lips one way then another.

I look at his reflection, then at mine. My hair, dark and shoulder-length, is thick and straight. My eyes are brown, but Theo has inherited his dark-blue eyes from Michel. We have yet to see if he will have my average height and build or his dad's tall, skinny frame.

Theo squeals. 'Minette.'

Our black-and-white cat slinks into the bathroom and observes us both. Minette is only a year old but is very much the boss of our household.

'Minette. *Ici*.' Theo crouches down to stroke her.

'Gently, *bébé*,' I remind him.

'*Doucement*,' whispers Theo as his small hands caress her glossy coat.

'Good boy. She likes that.'

Minette submits to his attention with a loud purr, but after a minute she gets bored and wanders away.

'*Bisous*,' Theo calls after her and blows her a kiss.

After we've finished washing, Theo and I go to his bedroom. I bring out the khaki cargo pants his grandmother, his *mamie*, bought him for Christmas.

'*Trop cool, non?*' I say.

'*Pas vert.*'

'They are green. Khaki is a type of green.'

Theo looks dubious. My son goes through phases of being obsessed with a particular colour. His current favourite is green.

'I promise you, these trousers are green,' I say.

He shrugs his narrow shoulders. 'Okay.'

When he's dressed, I hurry him into the hallway. 'Time to go for breakfast.' I grab my keys from the hall table and unplug my phone from its charger. As I do so, a notification from Google Alerts flashes up on the screen.

'Breakfast, Maman,' Theo says.

Dread stirs in the pit of my stomach as I tap the notification and find a link waiting for me.

'Maman.' Theo tugs at my jeans.

I click on the link. 'Just a minute,' I say.

7

JANE

The sun is out when we finally walk across from our apartment to the hotel, but that doesn't stop me shivering. A warm breeze stirs the giant poppies that crowd the flowerbeds. Two red blooms dip their heads together, as if sharing gossip. As if they know what I have just discovered. The Hôtel des Arbres is a typical Provençal building. The grey shutters at every window are open, pressed flat against the building's faded yellow exterior. I want to slam every one of them shut. Bolt them tight against the outside world.

As soon as we enter the dining room, I compose myself. I am skilled at hiding what I need to, and I use these skills now, smiling at hotel guests as I seat Theo at a table at the back of the dining room. At the buffet table, while filling two glass bowls with fruit salad, I make small talk with Ingrid, an elderly guest from Munich.

'This is a beautiful dining room,' she says in clipped English.

'It is.' Large botanical paintings adorn the deep blue walls. My mother-in-law, Alazne, painted them. She also made the abstract wire sculptures that hang from the ceiling. Pierre, my father-in-law, bought the hotel not long after he and Alazne married. Michel grew up here, and when we first met, he said he had no intention of going into the family business. He didn't know then how circumstances could change. Neither of us did.

Ingrid shuffles back to her table with a plate full of cold meats. I take the bowls of fruit salad to my table and return to the buffet to grab a mini pain au chocolat for Theo. When I tell him the pastry will be his after he finishes his fruit, he gives a determined nod and picks up his spoon. We're lucky with him; he's not a fussy eater.

While my son digs into his fruit salad, I leave mine untouched. I normally eat a large breakfast, but what I saw on my phone this morning killed my appetite.

Sandy Gilligan might be getting an early release hearing. The link I clicked on earlier took me to a website for an organisation called Families for Justice and to the page Sandy's daughter has set up about him. According to her latest update, a successful hearing could take six months off his sentence. She didn't give a date for the hearing but said it would be soon.

A cold sweat erupts on my chest. I have always known an early release hearing was a possibility. After the trial it was explained to me how the prison system works here. When I was told the prison authorities don't inform the victim when the attacker is released, I couldn't believe it. I'd always assumed the victim would be the first to know.

Stay calm, I tell myself. From what I read, there is no guarantee Sandy will even get a hearing.

'Maman.' Theo points to his half-empty bowl.

'Well done. Eat it all up.'

'All up,' he says and manoeuvres a red grape on to his spoon.

The door to the kitchen swings open and Michel appears, oven gloves clamped around a silver buffet dish, which he places on the buffet table.

'Papa,' says Theo.

'Hello, *bébé*.' Michel smiles at us both before hurrying back to the kitchen.

The dread at the pit of my stomach stirs when I think what I have kept from my husband. The man I once promised to share everything with. Michel and I first met in Val d'Isère. He was a freelance graphic designer on a ski holiday, and I was doing marketing for a company that hired out luxury chalets. After graduating from university with a degree in French and English Literature, all I wanted to do was see the world. From the moment we met, Michel and I knew we wanted to spend our lives together. No one was as surprised as me. Coming from a family as large as mine, I'd longed to be a free spirit, no ties to anyone. Luckily, Michel loved travel as much as I did, and after we met, we spent eighteen months on the road together, living and working in Australia and then touring around South-East Asia. When we returned to France, we decided to live in Paris for a while. Michel got a job with a graphic design company, and I worked in bars and taught English to bring in extra money. Then Michel suggested we move back to Draguignan and start a family. I could imagine the life he wanted for us but felt it was too soon. I asked for time to think, but he said he couldn't be with someone who wanted different things from life. Finally, he broke up with me and came home to Draguignan alone. Lost and confused, I heard about the summer job at La Cave à Vin from a woman I'd worked with in Val d'Isère and decided to take it. I wanted to be by the sea, in a place full of bustle and life. A place I could forget about Michel. I told myself I wanted to get over him, but part of me hoped we would get back together. I'd only been working at the bar for a month when mutual friends informed me he was dating a girl from his university days. That's when I threw myself into my new existence in a reckless way, hoping to forget him with the aid of parties and one-night stands.

That's when I met Sandy Gilligan.

'Maman.' Theo points to his empty bowl.

'Well done.' I hand him the mini pain au chocolat from my side plate. He makes messy work of it, flakes of pastry sticking to his fingers, a smear of chocolate on his chin. Between mouthfuls, he shares his excitement about seeing his friends at school. To him, this is a normal day, and I must make sure it stays that way. Every choice I have made since that night with Sandy has brought me here, to the people I love, and I am determined to protect them from the past.

Six weeks after I met Sandy, Michel called and said he missed me. He claimed his recent relationship was a mistake and asked if we could get back together. As soon as I heard his voice, I knew I had to be with him. By that time, I had moved to Montpellier and found a job teaching English. When Michel turned up at my flat, I had every intention of telling him about Sandy.

Unwilling to spoil our first night back together, I resolved to tell him the next day. When the next day came, it felt too special, too fragile for my story, so I decided to wait another week. I was ashamed of what had happened with Sandy, and I was scared Michel would be ashamed of me too.

Hiding the aftermath of that night was not easy, but I have found myself to be a talented liar. One who has resisted numerous opportunities to tell the truth. I could have shown Michel the newspaper reports about Sandy's arrest and told him my story. When it was time for the trial, I told Michel I was going away for a week's holiday in Aix-en-Provence with a friend from university. He had no idea I was sitting in a court room with the man who had almost ruined my life. He had no idea I had rushed outside the Palais de Justice after the verdict and vomited in the street.

On the wall above the dining-room fireplace is a photograph from my wedding day. Michel and I married four months after Sandy went to prison. It felt to me like a safe time to make our relationship official. When we said our vows, I was already a month pregnant with Theo. I didn't want to put off my future any longer. Michel was surprised when I offered to take his surname. He didn't know how much I wanted a new identity. His surname, Durand, means to endure, and, after Sandy, enduring has become another talent of mine.

'*C'est Papi et Mamie*,' Theo says, pointing at the entrance to the dining room.

Michel's parents, Alazne and Pierre, live across the road from the hotel in a ground-floor apartment of a converted villa. They come for breakfast several times a week and help at the hotel when we're busy. This place is still home to them. Pierre is at his happiest behind the reception desk or chatting to guests in the courtyard.

When they reach our table, Alazne bends over to kiss her grandson. '*Bonjour mon petit.*'

Pierre lowers himself into a seat and rests his walking stick against the table. 'Hello, *bébé*,' he says to Theo.

Theo claps his hands. He loves his grandfather. His papi. He has only ever known him to walk slowly, with a cane, and to sleep in the afternoons and to speak with a slight slur when he gets tired. This is the way his papi has always been. Pierre had his stroke not long after Michel and I got back together. When we realised he would never regain full fitness, Michel made the choice to come back and take over most of the hotel management, as well as keeping his graphic design business going part-time. Audrey, his older sister, lives in Montreal with her husband and two daughters, so in the end it was up to us. I didn't mind. Keeping busy stopped me thinking about Sandy, and, in the end, the decision to come back to Draguignan made sense. We thought this would be a place we could start afresh and make a good life for ourselves.

Theo babbles away to his grandparents. Michel might complain about his bohemian, eccentric parents now and again, but he knows compared to my austere mother and father they are a dream. Pierre in his baggy jeans, his blue flat cap and the red scarf he knots around his neck in all seasons. Alazne with her olive skin, dark eyes and cropped grey hair. Her loose, flowing dresses and the long silver earrings she makes herself.

My devout Christian parents and I have never been close, but after Sandy, I drifted even further away from them. I could never tell them what happened. They have always been ashamed of me, and my story would make them even more so.

'You are okay, Jane?' Alazne asks. 'You look tired.'

'Bad night's sleep,' I say. Alazne often tells me I am like a daughter to her, and Pierre has described me more than once as a 'good girl'. A treasure. What would they say if they knew about Sandy?

As the early guests leave the dining room, Michel

joins us, bringing coffee and croissants for his parents. He sips on an espresso, his usual breakfast. Alazne and Pierre fuss over Theo while Michel and I drink our coffees and chat. He and I never run out of things to say to one another. Even when there are other people around to talk to, we'll often still find ourselves deep in conversation.

Ingrid from Munich, sitting alone at her table, glances over at us and smiles. I can imagine my life looks perfect to her at this moment. A dream.

A familiar sensation takes hold of me. A slipping away from the present. Our family eating breakfast together becomes a scene I watch as if excluded from it. As if I don't deserve to be here.

After we finish eating, Pierre and Alazne offer to take Theo to school, an offer my son accepts with a delighted squeal. I tell them where to find his school bag and coat and the three of them head to our apartment.

The dining room is empty, but four tables are still set for breakfast, meaning some guests have not come down yet.

'Shall I help you tidy up before the next lot arrive?' I ask Michel.

'In a moment.' He clears his throat. 'I was... I wanted to talk to you.'

'What about?' Why does he look so serious?

'I think it's time,' he says.

The dread stirs again. 'For what?'

His face breaks into a shy smile. 'Let's have another baby.'

'Oh.' I'm both relieved and disturbed this is what he wants to talk about. 'You want to start trying now?'

He shrugs. 'Why not?'

What's the rush? I am thirty-one years old, and Michel is thirty-four. We have plenty of time.

'Theo is at preschool,' he says, 'and we know what we are doing with the hotel now. Life is more chill.'

'I just... I wasn't expecting—'

'There's no pressure,' he says, 'but maybe we could think about it?'

My throat constricts.

'I know Theo wasn't easy at first,' he says, 'but we'll be prepared this time.'

I start coughing and find myself unable to stop.

'Are you okay?' Michel rushes to the buffet table and returns with a glass of water. He hands it to me, and I gulp the icy liquid back.

'Something stuck in my throat,' I say once the coughing has subsided.

The lies. All the lies I have told rise up in my throat from time to time. One day, I think they might choke me.

8

LYNNE

Today is the day of Sandy's early release hearing. I'm not a big fan of Mondays but today could turn out to be the best one I've ever had. If things go our way, the man I love will soon be out of prison and we can finally be together.

It's just coming up to eight in the morning and I'm at the hospital already, cracking on with some work. Hardly slept last night with all the nerves and excitement. When I spoke to Sandy a couple of days ago, he told me not to get my hopes up. Easier said than done. I've got a bottle of champagne chilling in the fridge at home. Aldi's finest.

Not even the weather can get to me today. April showers aplenty out there, the sky all grey and miserable. The office I share with Carol, the other estates department administrator, overlooks the dialysis unit, a squat, ugly building. Hardly a glamorous view but everything looks beautiful today. Maybe that's a good omen?

I peer at my computer screen. Best keep busy. Sandy's hearing isn't until this afternoon and the earliest I'll know anything is tonight. Luckily, I've got the invoices for the recent renovations to the maternity ward to sort out. Then there's the contract for the new gardening company to deal with. I do love my job. Keeps me on my toes. Never a dull moment, as my mother used to say. I've never been the Brain of Britain, but I tried hard at school, got some decent qualifications and I've been working my backside off since leaving education at sixteen.

After ten minutes of raising and filing invoices, my attention wanders. I open up my desk drawer and take out my Vision Book. I brought it with me from home this morning as a lucky charm. I started the Vision Book not long after I met Sandy. Got myself a large scrapbook and filled it with images I cut out from wedding magazines. I've got tons of pictures of wedding dresses for me – as a size fourteen woman with long red hair, I need something with a flattering shape and a colour that makes my hair pop. Also pasted into the book are loads of suits that would look good on Sandy. There are photographs of various types of venue too, as well as things like flowers and table decorations. Not that Sandy's proposed yet, but he will. He doesn't want to discuss what we'll do after his release in case he jinxes it. We know we want to spend the rest of our lives together, and that's all that matters. After two failed marriages, a lot of women would give up, but not me. I'll never give up on love.

I flick through the Vision Book, pausing to look at my favourite dress so far. A pale pink off-the-shoulder number. Simple and classy.

The phone on my desk rings. I pick up the receiver. 'Estates department, Lynne speaking.' George, the head porter, is on the other end, asking me to check if there's a van free for him this afternoon. A few clicks of my mouse and I'm through to the vehicle booking page. No vans available, but I promise George I'll shuffle the bookings around and get him what he needs.

'Thanks, Lynne,' he says. 'I don't know what we'd do without you.'

After hanging up, I realise George and all my other co-workers might have to do without me soon if Sandy's released. Who knows whether we'll end up living in France or the UK, but I'll go wherever he needs to be. I know his daughter will be his first priority when he gets out, but I don't mind. Not really. He'll need to spend time with her. I hope she doesn't think badly of me when he tells her about our relationship. I wanted to meet her after things got serious between us, but he said it wasn't the right time. I thought she might appreciate my support, but Sandy didn't want to cause her extra stress. He said he had to put her feelings first. She's lucky to have a dad like him. My old man never put anyone's feelings before his own.

Nearly eight thirty now. Carol will be in soon, and I can't wait to fill her in on the latest about my love life. She's just become a grandmother for the first time, and she's been in Leeds for the past fortnight, helping out her daughter with the new baby. Carol's the only person I've told about Sandy. Most people would judge him without knowing the truth. He was the wrong man in the wrong place with the wrong woman, but not everyone would understand that. I can imagine exactly the kind of young woman she was, one who would target a good-looking, worldly man like Sandy and expect him to pay for her and show her a good time in bed. I don't even know her name. I did ask Sandy once, but he said he had to respect her right to anonymity. How decent is that? Probably best I don't know; I'd have been tempted to track her down and put her straight about a few things.

Anyway, like I say, Carol's a decent sort. A good listener. She says a relationship only ever makes sense to the people in it. She's a great believer in each to his own.

She turns up a bit before nine, rain dripping from her beige mac. 'It's grim out there,' she says, dropping her brolly into the umbrella stand with a clatter. She trudges over to her desk and pulls out her swivel chair.

'Cuppa?' I ask.

'Please.'

I make us both a mug of Yorkshire Tea. Two sweetener tablets for Carol, who is always trying and failing to cut down on sugar. I should probably cut back on the sweet stuff too, although Sandy says he likes my curves. Having a bit of extra flesh at my age also means I don't have as many wrinkles as some skinny women.

Carol brings her chair over to my desk and, as I sip my tea, she bombards me with pictures of Max, her new grandson. She must have taken hundreds of snaps. He's a cute thing, though, and I show interest for her sake. I've never had much success with female friendships, but Carol's been good to me and, to be honest, she's got little else in her life. She's been unhappily married to the same man for thirty years and it shows. She's only fifty-four but with her lank grey hair and frumpy clothes she looks much older. I make an effort when I come to work. Put my face on, wear something smart.

'Here he is in the babygro I bought him,' Carol says, her mottled skin flushed with happiness. Sandy hasn't met his grandkids yet. He never says much about his son, but I know there's been a falling-out. Our wedding could fix that. Nothing like a wedding to bring people together. I picture Sandy and me on a dance floor, holding hands with his granddaughters as we groove on down to Abba.

After fifteen minutes of nothing but Max, I decide that's enough. Turn and turn about, Carol.

'Sandy might be getting out early,' I say.

'Oh.' She puts her phone on my desk, screen down, as if shielding baby Max from bad news. 'Why?'

Not quite the enthusiastic response I'd hoped for. 'He's got a special hearing. It's how things work over there. He could be out six months earlier than we thought.'

'Right.'

'I thought you'd be happy for me.'

Carol stares into her mug. 'I thought you might be over him in six months' time.'

'Over him?'

'I thought the novelty of it might have worn off.'

Novelty. This is the man I'm going to spend the rest of my life with.

'I'm sure the letters and the visits are all very romantic,' she says, 'but once he gets out, that's reality.'

She's not wrong about the romance. His letters are so beautiful they make me cry, and when I visit him in prison it's so intense. All that passion and desire we have to keep inside. All the pain I feel when it's time to say goodbye. Real, physical pain. Like my heart is being torn. Still, I'd trade all that in for the chance to wake up with him every morning. To drink tea together in bed. To go shopping together in a supermarket.

'What'll happen if he gets out?' Carol says. 'Will he come and live with you?'

'We've not sorted the logistics yet. He might want to stay in France.'

Carol frowns. 'You'd go and live in France with him?'

'Why not?'

'What about your flat? You love that place.'

'I'll do whatever it takes to make it work.' That goes without saying, but I feel a sharp pang of sadness when I think of my cosy one-bedroom flat in a new development not far from the hospital. The first home I've ever owned.

'You'd have to give up your job here,' Carol says.

'So? I'm a worker. I'll find something to do wherever I am.'

She sighs. 'Well, if he's as rich as you say at least he won't be after your money.'

'No, and I'm not after his.' I'll be making sure both his kids know his money's of no interest to me. As well as my flat, I've got a small amount of savings, including the money I've been putting away for the wedding. More importantly, I've got my pride.

'You'd be giving up an awful lot,' Carol says. 'Then again, you already have.'

'What do you mean?'

'Friday-night drinks for a start. You never come out any more.'

In the past, Carol and I would often have a few glasses of wine after work on Friday with the girls from the catering department. I stopped going in case I let something slip about Sandy once I'd had a few. Plus, I wanted to put any spare money I had into my wedding account or towards the bill for the calls Sandy makes to me from jail. Giving up a few nights out was a small sacrifice for a man who wasn't having any nights out at all.

'Thing is,' Carol says, leaning across the desk towards me, 'what do you really know about him? What if he isn't innocent?'

Anger prickles beneath my skin. 'Careful, Carol,' I say, 'or you and I will be falling out.'

'I'm just saying—'

'Don't. Just don't.' She's jealous, that's all. Her marriage has no passion or romance in it, and I'm pretty sure her husband's unfaithful to her. She's never said anything, but on a Friday night out, after a few drinks, I've often overheard her leaving anxious messages on his voicemail asking where he is and what he's up to. I know that every Friday night Sandy sits down in his cell and writes me one of his heartfelt letters. I never have to worry what he's up to.

'I just don't want you doing something you'll regret,' Carol says.

Her face blurs and shifts until I'm looking at my dead mother. My mother shakes her head at me, her expression one of gleeful spite. How I wish she was still alive so she could meet Sandy and see I've finally found my ideal man. Not like her. She was saddled with my father until he died. She put up with his drinking and his antics and she hated the thought of me ever being happy.

The phone on Carol's desk rings. She hurries over

to answer it. 'No problem, Sue,' she says, 'I'll be right down.'

'Sandy's the best thing that ever happened to me,' I say, 'and no one's going to keep us apart.'

'Well, then.' Carol gives me an uneasy smile. 'That's all that matters.'

As soon as she's gone, I open up my Vision Book. At the back is the *Daily Mail* article about Sandy and the photograph of him that changed my life. I gaze deep into his eyes. So much feeling in them. This is a man who raised two children, including a devoted daughter. A man who nursed his sick wife until the end.

I've never doubted his innocence, not once. I love him, and I could never love a man guilty of what that woman accused him of. No way. I'd have to be out of my mind.

9

JANE

Tuesday morning. I'm walking through the old town of Draguignan, heading to Boulevard Georges Clemenceau where I'll stop and have a coffee before picking Theo up from preschool. I'm far too early, but I had to get out of the house.

All day I have felt off-kilter. I woke at dawn still trapped in a dream of suffocation, face down in my pillow. I sat up gasping for air while Michel snored gently beside me. He didn't wake when I turned on the bedside lamp and whispered the names of familiar objects in the room, a ritual I use to remind myself where I am. Or rather, where I am not. I am not in a hotel room with Sandy Gilligan. The hours since dawn have retained an unnerving, dreamlike quality, and I have drifted through my routine – taking Theo to preschool, helping Darid the chef put in several food orders and catching up on emails for forthcoming bookings. All with a smile on my face.

The sky is still cloudy after this morning's thunderstorm, and a light wind stirs the washing hanging from the tenement windows above me. Concentrating on my surroundings as I walk helps me feel more grounded. I look at the buildings on the Rue des Dominicains. At the peeling ochre, pink and yellow paint. Unlike many other old towns in this region, the one in Draguignan is not full of expensive refurbished flats and holiday lets. It is, in parts, rundown and neglected. Many of the tenements house Draguignan's Maghreb and Turkish populations. As I pass a ground-floor window I peer in and see a group of women in headscarves chatting and drinking tea in a small sitting room.

I have come to love this town. I love that I know it so well it holds no surprises. I love that it is a good distance away from the superficial glitz of the coast, where everything went wrong for me. A good distance from the sea. The glitter of the Mediterranean always makes me flinch. It reminds me of leaving Sandy's hotel room at dawn and seeing the sea spread out in front of me. A blue and brilliant witness to my shame.

My phone buzzes in the pocket of my long denim skirt. A message from Michel asking me to pick up some extra ingredients for the stir-fry he's cooking tonight. I stop, type out an upbeat reply and sign it with a kiss. He has been in the small office next to our bedroom all day, working on a graphic design job for the University of Toulon. I told him I needed time to think about trying for another baby, and he assured me there is no rush. Despite his reassurances, I know he is keen to be a father again soon. I should be happy to take this next step and add another child to our family, but I can't help fearing the past is not done with me. Some days it takes all my willpower to keep Sandy at bay, and the thought of pregnancy, with all the physical and emotional vulnerability it can bring, fills me with dread.

I made Michel promise not to tell Alazne our potential plans. He agreed, reluctantly. At times I resent his closeness to his mother, the way he confides in her about everything, but I also know this close relationship has helped make him the man he is. A good one. I hope I can do the same with Theo.

Before putting my phone away, I check there are no new notifications from Google Alerts. If only I knew what day the hearing was. Last week, I checked my phone so often Michel asked jokingly if I had a lover.

We laughed about it, but I wanted to say yes, yes there is another man. One I have kept secret for years.

I slip my phone back into my pocket and continue along Rue des Dominicains and on to Rue Frédéric Mireur. The uncertainty about the hearing is the hardest part. Maybe knowing one way or another will relieve my anxiety. Sandy was always going to get out of prison at some point, and when that happens, I fear I will have to face the consequences of my choices. The guilty verdict and his jail sentence gave me some sense of safety. With him locked away, I could lock everything away too. When Theo began to grow inside me, I had even more reason to block out the past. To pretend to myself my ordeal was over.

At least I can be sure Colette will update the website once she knows the outcome of the hearing. She is still, it seems, her father's most loyal supporter. During the trial, there was a brief moment when her eyes met mine. I was shaking all over, but I held her gaze and I realised she had no idea what had happened between her father and me. No idea at all.

* * *

Theo is waiting for me when I reach the gates of the school on Boulevard Maréchal Joffre.

'Maman.' He waves but doesn't rush over to greet me. He is standing with an arm around his best friend, Lena. Her mother, Nathalie, smiles at me as I approach.

'*Salut,*' she says, and we kiss each other on both cheeks. '*Ca va?*'

'*Bien, bien.*'

Nathalie's husband, Bastien, is from Draguignan and went to school with Michel. They moved here from Paris to start a family and have a better quality of life. We see a lot of them, and Nathalie has been good to me since we moved here. Petite, with cropped black hair, she is dressed in her usual long black jersey dress and black cardigan. She looks far too young to have three-year-old Lena and six-month-old Nicole, who is strapped to her front in a sling, sleeping.

'Look at her.' I bend down to inspect Nicole's pale veiny eyelids, her dark lustrous lashes. 'So peaceful.'

Nathalie likes me to speak English when it is just us two. She says she needs the practice. Unlike other places in France, not everyone in Draguignan speaks English for the sake of the tourist industry. We do get British and European tourists here, but the town isn't a typical destination for foreign visitors. Another reason I love it.

'She is only peaceful in the day.' Nathalie's voice is

strained. 'We are up nearly all night with her. Every night.'

Theo and Lena dart away from us, chasing each other around the playground in circles. I inspect Nathalie's face. Hollow-eyed, a little gaunt, with a dazed, sleep-deprived expression.

'You'll hate me for reminding you of this,' I say, 'but it does get better.'

'I know. I know.' She shakes her head. 'You must think I am *pathétique*, sorry, pathetic for moaning to you?'

'Not at all.'

'I know it was not easy for you. With Theo.'

'No, but you forget the bad times.' This is not completely true. I remember well those foggy, heavy months after Theo's birth, when he refused to sleep so neither could I. Are these memories making me hesitant about getting pregnant again, or is Sandy the reason?

'You are right,' Nathalie says. 'I need patience.'

'I've got some of the sleeping pills the doctor prescribed me back then,' I say. 'They might still work if you want a few?'

'It's okay,' she says. 'Bastien can get stuff if I need it.'

'Having a nurse for a husband has its perks.'

Bastien works at the accident and emergency department of Draguignan's main hospital.

'He's driving me crazy,' she says. 'He is always working and then he is too tired to help me, you know? All the time we are arguing.'

'It's always tough in the first year,' I say.

Nathalie sighs. 'Last night I said to him I wish we were like Jane and Michel. They never argue.'

'Almost never,' I say to make her feel better. She's right, though. Michel and I have never really been a couple who argue or fight.

If he knew the truth about me, that might change.

'Theo,' I say, 'come on. We've got shopping to do.'

After retrieving our children, Nathalie and I walk together as far as the nearby Carrefour supermarket. We kiss each other goodbye and smile at each other as our children do the same.

'Too cute,' Nathalie says.

In the supermarket, I find a trolley with a child seat and squeeze Theo into it. He is almost too big for such captivity, but I don't have the energy today to chase him round the aisles.

'I'm hungry,' he says, a whiny edge to his voice. I search my handbag and find half a stale flapjack wrapped in a tissue. My son bites into it with enthusiasm when I hand it to him.

'Papa is cooking tonight,' I tell him as I steer us to the vegetable aisle to get the main ingredients for Michel's stir-fry. I get twice as many mushrooms as he put on his list. Michel is always bemused by my tendency to buy more than we need, but it comes from my childhood. As one of five children, meals were always unsatisfying in our house. There was never enough to go around, and we had to scrap to get our fair share. My dad was obsessed with keeping us free of all the deadly sins, especially greed. My siblings and I used to joke they were using hunger to bring forth a miracle, hoping we might multiply our meagre rations into larger ones.

We move from the vegetable aisle in search of coconut milk. When I reach the shelves of tinned goods, a strange sensation comes over me. A ripple of fear along my spine. I spin around, expecting to find Sandy standing behind me.

Theo tugs at my sleeve and points to the tinned fruit on the shelf in front of me.

'*Pêches*, Maman,' he says.

A loud pinging noise fills the air. With trembling hands, I take my phone from my pocket and find a notification from Google Alerts waiting for me. I click on the link, knowing exactly where it will take me.

Colette's update to her website page is short and simple.

We've done it! After a successful hearing, my father will soon be free.

'Maman.'

I look up to see my son staring at me with his wide blue eyes.

'Maman is sad?' he says.

I kiss the top of his head. 'No, *bébé*.'

No, Maman is not sad. Maman is scared.

PART II

10

COLETTE

I'm inside the passenger hall at Nice-Ville train station, waiting for Dad. He refused my offer to come and collect him from jail, insisting he needed to walk out of that place on his own and take his first step towards freedom and independence by getting the train home. Last week I left a wallet for him at the prison, filled with enough cash to get him to Nice and tide him over until we get to the bank and sort out a new bank card and access to all his finances.

His desire for independence is understandable, but I can't help fearing something will go wrong before he can get to me. I've been texting him on the pay-as-you-go phone I left at the prison with the wallet, and he keeps reassuring me he'll be here soon.

I just want him back home with me. Safe. Although he isn't ready to discuss long-term plans yet, he said he wants to spend the summer here in Nice, recovering from his ordeal. He wants to spend the summer with me; just the two of us.

The mid-May weather is perfect for his arrival. Clear blue sky, sunshine and temperatures in the mid-twenties. I didn't sleep much last night. Too nervous and excited. As a child I often went with Mum to meet Dad at a train station or airport when he was returning from one of his business trips. I feel like that child again.

His train should be pulling into the station now. I wait on one side of the ticket barriers. The station is busy, backpackers holding up the queues at the ticket machines and older tourists wheeling their suitcases into the locals pushing past them. The Cannes film festival starts soon, so everywhere along this stretch of coast is busier than usual.

The crowd behind the ticket barrier parts for a moment and there he is. Standing still in the middle of the throng, glancing about him, looking lost and uncertain. His black Antler duffle bag hangs by his side.

'Dad.'

He spots me when I wave, and his face breaks into a wide smile. He's on one side of the ticket barrier and

I'm on the other. As he slots his ticket into the barrier, I have the irrational fear it might refuse to let him through. I imagine an alarm sounding and a horde of policemen appearing and dragging him off. My hands are hot, my heart pounding.

'Dad.'

He keeps his eyes on mine as the barrier swallows his ticket and the gates part.

'Hey, kiddo,' he says as he strides towards me. Seconds later I am in his arms. I might be almost as tall as he is, but whenever he holds me, I feel small again. We've hugged in the prison visiting room many times, but now we don't have to say goodbye after an hour. We part with tears in our eyes.

'Christ's sake, look at us.' He wipes his eyes with the heel of his hand.

'We're a disaster,' I say, laughing through my tears.

We head out of the station building into the sunlight.

'Cab?' I say.

Dad slings his bag over his shoulder. 'Let's walk. I want as much fresh air as I can get.' He places a protective hand on my back as we cross the road. The gesture makes me want to start crying again. I'd forgotten what it felt like. That hand on my back, or my shoulder, guiding me. That unique sense of safety only a father can give. I wonder how many times in my life he's kept me from getting run over or saved me from some danger I would never have seen coming.

Something inside me softens. The part of me that has had to stay strong the whole time he's been in prison. The part of me that can afford to let go now.

On the other side of the road, we take Rue Gounod and head downhill towards the Promenade des Anglais.

'You look nice,' Dad says.

'Thanks.' I'm wearing a pale pink wraparound dress and black espadrille sandals. In my ears are the diamond studs Dad bought me for my eighteenth birthday. I wanted to wear the floral Prada dress he got for me not long before his arrest, but it's a size 6 and doesn't fit me just now. 'You've scrubbed up all right,' I say in a jokey voice.

He's wearing one of the outfits I took to the prison for him on my last visit – jeans, navy-blue T-shirt and his favourite Tommy Hilfiger sunglasses. No one would ever guess he'd just got out of jail.

We make swift progress down Rue Gounod. Dad has always been a fast walker and I have to speed up to stick with him. When I was growing up, Dad and I always enjoyed walking together. Mum never shared Dad's passion for the outdoors and Patch always ruined our rare family walks by sulking and complaining. In the end, the two of them left me and Dad to go off hiking together.

'God, I love this town,' Dad says, and for the first time in years, I remember I used to love it too. The belle époque buildings that line this street are beautiful. So vibrant with their yellow, blue and pink exteriors.

When we reach the promenade, Dad freezes amid the hordes of tourists and joggers. I remember all I've read about the disorientation he's likely to feel in these first weeks. How strange it will be for him to be among so many people again.

'Shall we sit down?' I say.

'Yes. Just for a minute.'

I lead us to a white wrought-iron bench overlooking the water. When we sit down, Dad puts an arm around my shoulder, and we gaze at the calm sheet of sea before us. I feel complete. Like I've got back a missing part of me. I forget all about the thieves and prostitutes on the promenade and the traffic chaos behind us on Route 98.

'The Bay of Angels,' he says. 'Wow.'

Suddenly the bay looks vast and open. An escape rather than a prison. My resentment of it vanishes, replaced by an urge to get in and swim.

Dad laughs when I say we should just run into the water now, fully clothed. Or strip down to our underwear.

'I'd love to, kiddo,' he says, 'but an arrest for indecent exposure won't look too good on my record.'

He smiles as he says it, but I feel wounded on his behalf. My father has a criminal record. One he didn't deserve, but it will be with him until he dies. If he didn't have money and still needed to work, every employer he approached would know about that record and turn him down.

'Come on,' he says, 'let's move on.'

We walk further along the promenade, passing a beggar who has taken over one of the benches. A guy around Dad's age, with straggly white hair and a lopsided smile. I glance away and keep walking, but Dad stops. When I look back, he's handing the guy a twenty-euro note. I've never seen him give money to beggars before. He was always unsympathetic about the destitute and homeless, insisting he'd made his money from sheer hard work and everyone else should do the same.

'Right,' he says, when he catches up with me, 'let's go home.'

* * *

I hear Kathy Cherish as soon as we reach the garden entrance to the apartment block. That terrible high-pitched laugh of hers. There are other voices too. Ronnie from number 1, which means Rose will be nearby and I'm sure I can make out David and Jean from number 5.

'We could use the front entrance?' I say to Dad. 'Or go in via the car park?'

He shakes his head. 'Might as well get it over with.'

The scene that greets us in the garden is worse than I thought. An impromptu picnic for the expat residents of our block. Platters of cheese and baskets of bread cover a small trestle table, along with two bottles of champagne in an ice bucket.

All I want to do is get Dad back to the apartment without any trouble.

Five blue-and-white-striped deckchairs are arranged in a semicircle in front of the table. Kathy sits in the centre clutching a flute of champagne, all dressed up in a cream linen skirt and lavender blouse. Holding court, everyone listening to her as she gossips away. To her right sit Ronnie and Rose. Ronnie, a seventy-two-year-old former bank manager, is a keen pétanque player who tried many times to recruit Dad for his matches against the French locals. White-haired and pot-bellied, he is dressed today in his usual salmon-pink trousers and white polo shirt. Rose looks nothing like her name. Her sixty-year-old skin is parched and wrinkled from too many years in the sun. Her dry, bleached hair is gathered in a high ponytail, and she wears a canary yellow vest top with her white Capri pants. To Kathy's left are David and Jean. David, who must be in his late sixties now, is bald and wiry and blandly dressed in a pair of beige chinos and a beige T-shirt. Jean is equally uninspiring in beige linen trousers and a cream T-shirt. Her steely grey hair clings to her scalp in tight curls.

I can't help recalling the day of Dad's arrest. Everyone here watching him being led away. His wary, haunted face suggests he's thinking of it too.

Kathy is the first to see us. Her sudden silence alerts the others to something amiss. One by one, heads turn. I can't help finding it amusing, how they all struggle to replace the shock on their faces with either neutrality or an uncomfortable smile.

'A welcome home party.' Dad turns on a big smile. 'Kathy, you shouldn't have.'

He puts his bag down and strides over to his neighbours. They press themselves back against the canvas of their deckchairs. A tiny movement, but I don't miss it and I bet Dad doesn't either. My pulse thrums as my amusement gives way to panic. What if one of them decides to call the police? Why would they? Dad hasn't done anything wrong. He's got just as much right to be here as they have.

'You look wonderful, Kathy,' Dad says. She's so stunned she sits there in silence. 'Good to see you again, Ronnie.' Dad holds out a hand and Ronnie, caught by surprise, shakes it.

When Dad walks over to the trestle table, the untouched residents deflate with relief. Kathy, Rose and Jean give Ronnie a dirty look. He shrugs. David looks down at his feet.

'Champagne, kiddo?' Dad picks up two flutes from the table.

'Why not?'

The ice in the bucket rattles as Dad lifts the champagne out. Now he's back, I realise how often I've given in to the subtle bullying of this crowd. I realise how tiring it's been, keeping my chin up in front of them. How much it has hurt to suffer their snide comments and cold stares.

Dad fills the two flutes to the brim and brings one over to me. 'Cheers everyone,' he says. No one raises their glasses. They're scared of him. He's an ex-convict, and they're frightened. It makes me want to laugh. As if Dad would ever dream of hurting them.

'I should really toast you all,' he says. 'When I was

in prison, worried about my daughter being here on her own, going through hell, at least I knew she had decent neighbours looking out for her.' He takes a sip of champagne. 'Mature adults who were able to put their misgivings about me aside and help out a young woman going through a tough time.'

Ronnie and David at least look shamefaced. The women exchange glances and shake their heads. Having Dad stick up for me like that, the way he always has done, makes me feel like the world is back on its axis again. I clink my glass against his and we both take a long glug of champagne.

'I'd love to stay and chat,' Dad says, picking up his bag, 'but I need to get myself settled in.' The smile he gives the group doesn't reach his eyes. 'Now I'm back for good, we'll all have plenty of time to catch up.'

With that, he turns and walks away, and I follow him.

11

COLETTE

We start laughing as soon as we are out of sight of the gardens and we keep laughing all the way up the stairs. As we reach our apartment, Dad's bravado vanishes. When I open the front door, he hovers for a while on the threshold, as if uncertain he is allowed in.

'Welcome home,' I say.

Once he reaches the open-plan living area, he drops his bag and stands still for a moment, clutching his glass of champagne as he takes in the home he has been kept from for nearly five years. I feel anxious as he looks around. As if I might not have been a good enough custodian.

'Christ.' He shakes his head. 'Please don't let this be a dream.'

I put an arm around his waist. 'It's real.'

Entwined, we go out on to the balcony. Down below, the deckchairs are empty, and the champagne is gone from the trestle table.

'Looks like we spoiled their party,' Dad says.

Bet they've retreated somewhere to discuss him. I try to shake off a feeling of unease. They can't do anything to him. Due to the reduced sentence ruling, he's out and free with no conditions. No probation, no requirement to report to the police. I suspect Kathy will be fuming when she finds that out.

Relax, I tell myself and take another sip of my champagne. It's crisp, cold and delicious. Now Dad's back, I feel safe to let go and enjoy a drink.

'Wait here,' I say and dash inside to get my phone. Back on the balcony I insist on taking a selfie of the two of us, the curve of the bay and the azure blue water in the background. Later, I'll do an update on the Families For Justice website and add this picture to it. It seems right to end Dad's story with him here, at home and free.

'You should send that picture to Patch,' Dad says.

I nod. Dad knows Patch doesn't want to speak to him, but he loves his son and wants to keep trying.

A buzzing noise. Dad pulls his mobile out of the pocket of his jeans. He glances at the screen and whatever he sees there makes him smile. Must be Uncle Jimmy, our only ally. He whooped for joy when I told him Dad was getting out early and promised to come and visit once Dad had settled in. A thought that makes me uneasy. Jimmy was one of the three men with Dad that weekend in Marseilles. Jimmy and the other two men flew back to London on the Sunday afternoon. Dad stayed on in Marseilles alone and on Sunday night visited La Cave à Vin. The night of the alleged attack.

My father jabs at the phone's keypad with his forefinger, clumsy and out of practice. I doubt anyone else will be getting in touch with him. Mum's brother, Brian, said he was glad the ordeal was over for my sake and advised me to return to England and leave Dad to it. Pete and Lesley, the couple who were my parents' best friends, didn't have much to say either. Pete at least sounded happy to hear Dad was getting out. When Lesley got on the phone, she made it clear that while they would always be there for me, Dad would never be welcome in their home.

When Dad's finished sending his message, we go back inside so I can show him the changes I've made to the apartment since he's been gone. Over the years I've added cushions to the white L-shaped sofa and covered the wooden floor with Moroccan rugs from a shop in the old town. And, of course, there are the bits I've brought from Riverbank Cottage. Ornaments, books and all our family photograph albums, which I keep in the vintage oak sideboard.

'You've done a great job with the place,' he says.

His approval makes me glow. 'I framed up some more photos this week.' I point to the collection of pictures on the sideboard. I looked through our family albums and chose some photographs I thought Dad would like.

He picks up the one of Riverbank Cottage. It was taken from the garden in summertime and reminds me of happy times there as a family. Dad stares at it and for a moment I worry it will upset him to remember everything we've lost. At least he didn't have to witness the graffiti I found spray painted in big red letters on our garage door the last time I was at the house. PEADO. I had to wash it off with our neighbours watching, past caring they could see me crying.

'These are great,' he says, putting the picture down among the others. He points at the TV, pushed back into the far corner of the living area. 'Same TV?'

'I didn't think there was any point upgrading. I don't watch it that often.' I much prefer reading in the evenings to watching TV.

Dad heads to the kitchen area and opens the

fridge. I've been stocking it with the food he likes for the past couple of days. Fruit and vegetables and a big selection of cheeses.

'Crikey,' he says, 'this could feed ten people.'

'Is it too much? Sorry.'

'No, it's great. All nice and healthy too. Well done.'

I've got rid of nearly all my treats now. The madeleines and dark chocolate Florentines and macaroons.

Dad shuts the fridge door and wanders out into the hallway. I follow him along it, like I used to when I was a kid and he came home from work. I would tell him about my day at school and he would tell me, or at least pretend to tell me, what he'd been up to at work that day. Mum used to joke he told me more than he told her.

When he gets to his bedroom, the first thing he does is throw himself on the bed. 'This mattress.' He groans. 'It's heaven.'

On his bedside table is a book I bought for him. *Living Free: How to Adjust to Life After Prison.* From my research, I know it will take him a while to adjust to his freedom. After four and a half years inside, he's bound to be institutionalised to some extent. Ex-prisoners can often feel overwhelmed when they come out. Disorientated by choice. Prone to mood swings and depression. I won't point the book out to him just now. He needs to enjoy the simple pleasures of being home first.

'I am going to sleep like the dead.' He lifts his head and smiles at me, a smile that fades within seconds. I follow his gaze to the back of the bedroom door where Mum's grey silk kimono hangs. After she died, Dad said he wanted to keep this reminder of her always, so I brought it over from Riverbank Cottage. It makes me think of those dark weeks following her death when Dad spent hours in the living room sobbing into the kimono, with 'Angie' by the Rolling Stones on repeat on his CD player.

'Pass us that over, love,' he says.

When I do so, he sits up and clasps the dressing gown to his chest. 'She'd be so ashamed of me,' he says.

'No, she wouldn't.' I sit on the bed beside him.

'I'm so sorry.'

'Dad.' I've lost count of how many times he's apologised. 'You don't have to say—'

'I let you down. Badly.'

'It wasn't your fault.'

'Yes, it was.'

I feel a beat of fear when he says that. I look at the

deep line between his eyebrows that didn't exist before he went to prison.

'I left myself open to accusations,' he says. 'I shouldn't have put myself in that position.'

The fear dissolves. 'It's over,' I say. 'You're out now.'

'And I'm never going back,' he says. 'I can promise you that. I'll make sure I never go back there again.'

12

JANE

Forget about Sandy Gilligan.

This has been my mantra for the past three weeks, ever since I read about his successful early release hearing. I have repeated it to myself over and over, but it hasn't erased him from my thoughts. Then, yesterday, thanks to another Google Alert, I found out the news I have dreaded most.

He is free.

'Jane,' Hugo, the hotel's handyman, says. '*Ici?*'

He is halfway up the ladder propped against the thick trunk of the ancient plane tree that dominates the centre of the courtyard. Cables radiate out from this tree to the others nearby. Last week I noticed some of the lights hanging from the cables needed replacing, and I also have some new lanterns I've asked Hugo to attach to the central tree. Now the weather is warming up, the hotel's restaurant serves lunch in the courtyard and guests like to have drinks outside in the evening. To my right are ten tables with wicker chairs and, at the other end of the courtyard, a number of garden sofas and lounge chairs cluster around a sunken fire pit.

'*Un peu à droite*,' I reply, and Hugo moves the yellow tasselled shade of the lantern to the right. '*Parfait*.'

Hugo takes a hammer from his tool belt and taps in a long nail to show where to fix the lantern in place. It is almost four in the afternoon, which means he will take his coffee break soon. As it is a Friday, he will no doubt leave shortly after that. When Pierre and Alazne bought the hotel, Hugo came with it. He's in his mid-sixties now, a short, stocky man with a quiff of greying hair and a thick, bristly moustache.

'Maman.' Theo looks up from where he is crouched on the gravel, a red plastic spade in his hand.

'Great job, *bébé*,' I say. He nods and returns to the task Hugo assigned him, his face screwed up in concentration as he uses his small spade to transfer potting soil from a large sack to a blue ceramic flowerpot.

'Lots of jobs,' he says with a sigh. He must have

heard me complaining about my to-do list earlier. The hotel has been busy, mostly with French visitors enjoying the numerous public holidays. Now we have a mixture of French, Dutch and German holidaymakers, as well as a few British guests. The busier we get, the longer my to-do list is. The hotel still needs a lot done to it in preparation for the summer season.

How strange it is, to be carrying on as normal. As if Sandy Gilligan is not a free man, walking the streets of Nice. Free to go wherever he wants.

While Hugo continues his hammering, I take my phone from the pocket of my jeans and look again at Colette's latest piece on the Families for Justice website. *I'm so happy to have Dad back home with me in Nice.* I scrutinise the photograph of Sandy and his daughter, taken on a balcony with the sky blue and clear behind them. Prison has aged him. His hair has thinned and turned silvery-grey. He has deep horizontal grooves across his forehead and a vertical one between his eyebrows. Women will still find him attractive, though. Women will call him a silver fox. They will gaze into those hypnotic hazel eyes as I once did and want to know him better.

In the article, Colette says she and her father will be spending the summer together in Nice. I had hoped his experiences with the French legal system would send him fleeing back to England as soon as he got out but no such luck. The thought of him being so close makes me shudder. He could drive here in just over an hour, depending on the traffic. Or he could take a train to Les Arcs and get a taxi to Draguignan. An easy journey.

I click out of the website and, as I have every day for the past three weeks, I do an Internet search for myself. Jane Durand brings up no results related to me. I have no social media presence, claiming to shun it for ethical reasons, but the truth is I want to be untraceable. Sandy knew my maiden name but he does not know my married one, and he has never known me as Jane. My parents named me after my maternal grandmother, whom I disliked from a young age. Before long, I insisted on being called Jane, my middle name. In the end, even my parents gave in, leaving only Grandma persisting with my original forename. The summer after my break-up with Michel, when I worked at La Cave à Vin, I decided I needed a fresh start. To distance myself from the person I'd been with him, I reverted to my original name. As the summer progressed, I got a kick out of behaving in ways my grandmother would have disapproved of. Before my wedding to Michel, I had my name changed officially to Jane, and erased my given Christian name forever.

'*Café?*' Hugo climbs down the ladder and wipes sweat from his forehead with a red handkerchief.

'*Non, merci.*'

He heads into the hotel to fetch his coffee. The red lantern he attached to the tree earlier is hanging at an odd angle. I climb the rungs of the ladder and stretch one arm out to reach the lantern. The narrow white cable connecting it to the thick black one is twisted. All I need to do is straighten it.

'Jane.'

I turn my head and see Michel walking towards us, hands in the pockets of his cargo pants, Minette slinking along at his side. When the cat sees Theo, she heads straight for him. He squeals with delight and drops his spade to stroke her.

'What are you doing up there?' Michel reaches the ladder and offers up a hand to help me down.

'I just need to fix this.'

'Come down, it's dangerous. Hugo will do it.'

Waving away his assistance, I descend the ladder. He is behaving as though I am already pregnant. As though I am a precious vessel he needs to protect. This morning he came into the bathroom just as I was taking my contraceptive pill out of the packet, and I caught the look of disappointment on his face as I swallowed it.

'Did you get the invoices done?' I ask once back on the ground. Michel has been dealing with our food suppliers all afternoon, chasing down missing invoices and getting our records in order for our accountant.

'It's all good.' He takes me in his arms and kisses me. A deep, urgent kiss that hints he will want more later when we are alone. We have had sex almost every day since he asked me about having another child. Even though I've yet to agree, there is a tenderness about him during our sex that makes me uneasy. He makes me feel we are in training for when it is time to conceive. He is so certain of our future happiness. So certain nothing could spoil it.

Minette, bored now of playing with my son, winds her way around my legs before darting beneath a nearby table and lying down in the shade.

'Guess who just called me?' Michel says.

'Who?'

'Giles. The guy I went to university with.'

'The guy who makes puppets?'

'Yes. Puppet man. He's just moved to Marseilles and he's invited us to lunch at his new place.'

'Marseilles?' That deep dread stirs again. 'When?'

'Next month sometime.'

'You should go on your own. Have a boys' reunion.'

'Let's all go. I want him to meet Theo.'

My pulse pounds at my temples. 'Why don't you take Theo? You know Marseilles isn't my favourite place.' Since we moved to Draguignan, my husband has only suggested going to Marseilles on a handful of occasions, and I've avoided most of them, claiming not to like the city. Too busy, too noisy. The one time we did go, when Theo was ten months old, the day was a disaster. Even with Sandy behind bars, I felt unsafe. I almost lost control of myself. I almost gave myself away.

'I know you're not a fan of Marseilles,' Michel says, 'but Giles wants to see us.'

In the silence that follows I hear the distant whine of the mopeds zipping up and down Boulevard de la Liberté, and the soft chatter of my son as he talks to himself while he plays.

'We haven't had a family day out for a while,' my husband says.

I remind myself Marseilles is probably the last place Sandy will want to be. After what happened there and his years in jail, I doubt he will want to see the city ever again.

Even if Sandy is not there, my memories of him will be.

'Maman. Papa.' Theo points at the ceramic pot, now half-full with dark, moist soil.

'Can I try?' Michel strolls over to our son and crouches beside him. Theo offers him the spade and he digs it deep into the soil. They look so sweet to-gether. My son's innocent face reminds me I have to stay strong. For his sake, I cannot let my past with Sandy ruin our lives. 'Tell Giles we'll come and visit,' I say.

Michel smiles. 'Thanks.'

I smile back but cannot help wondering if Sandy has thought about me. He must have; he has had four and a half years to do nothing else. Four and a half years to think about what really happened between us.

13

COLETTE

Monday. Dad wakes me at six thirty in the morning.

'Fancy a run?' He hovers in the doorway to my room, already kitted out in his black shorts, navy T-shirt and trainers.

'Sure.' I long to curl up and drift back to sleep, but he's only been home five days and I need to help him adjust in these early stages of release.

'We could run into town and get some breakfast there,' he says.

I suppress a yawn. 'Give me a few minutes.'

'Excellent.' He drums a busy rhythm on the doorframe.

'Did you get some sleep?'

'Some,' he says as he marches away down the hall.

That's an improvement, and at least he's sleeping in his own room now. The first night he was home, I woke at three in the morning to find him lying on the Moroccan rug beside my bed, his eyes wide open and Mum's dressing gown draped over him. A sliver of light from the full moon came in through the gap in my curtains and lit him up. When I asked if he was okay, he explained he wasn't used to being on his own.

All those years of yearning for privacy. Of being desperate to get home to his own bed and now he couldn't cope with having his own space.

I get up and pull on my Lycra leggings, sports bra, T-shirt and zip-up fleece. It's a while since I've done any regular running, but the exercise will do me good. When I turned fourteen and started gaining puppy fat, Dad got me motivated to exercise by taking me out jogging with him.

In the living area, I find him balanced on one leg, stretching out his quad muscles. He kept himself fit in prison but then he's always been a man of routine. Up early, out for a run, into a cold shower and then off to work. For the past four and a half years he's been tuned into a prison timetable, so it's important to help him re-establish his own patterns again.

My routine is all over the place, but that's okay. I've taken two weeks off work to help Dad settle in. He's my priority. When he first got out, he said I could pack in my job if I wanted to. Thanks to the help of his accountant back home, he finally has access to his banking and investments again, and he offered to support me for a few months so I could have a break. I said no. Dad's always been generous with me, but I do like to earn my own money.

The TV is on in the background. A French breakfast show. Male and female anchors with big smiles and false chemistry. The volume is up loud. In prison, Dad had to suffer the television being on in his cell almost twenty-four hours a day. He hated the noise and the fact he had no control over what his cellmates decided to watch. Is having the TV on an oddly comforting reminder of the hell he's left behind or is he enjoying controlling his own viewing for once?

A picture of Henri Breton, the French film star, fills the screen. A voiceover informs us he has just been arrested in Paris on suspicion of raping a hotel chambermaid. Henri Breton? He's known for being a family man. Married to the same woman for twenty-five years and a father to three daughters.

Dad picks up the remote and turns the TV off. I walk over to the kitchen sink and fill up my water bottle, the gushing stream from the tap pouring into the uncomfortable silence.

'Sorry about last night,' he says.

'That's okay.' The lid of my water bottle makes a popping sound as I push it down hard.

'I didn't mean to upset you.'

I turn and give him a bright smile. 'It's fine.'

Last night, after dinner, I showed him the Families for Justice website and the update I'd done on his page there. A dark expression came over his face and, when I asked what was wrong, he snapped at me. He said he didn't want anyone knowing anything more about him. Hadn't he already been exposed enough?

His anger made me feel I'd failed him. I apologised, desperate to smooth things over. After a couple of minutes, he calmed down and told me was just tired.

My research has warned me Dad might experience mood swings over these first few weeks. Completely natural when you think what he's been through. Only a psychopath could come out of prison unscathed.

'Okay,' I say, 'shall we go?'

'Let's do it.' Dad heads for the door.

'Aren't you forgetting something?'

'Sorry.' He rolls his eyes as he picks up his keys from the ceramic dish on the kitchen island. 'Still not used to them yet.'

I leave the flat first and let him lock the door behind us. Outside, we cross the gardens, and I'm relieved to find them empty. We walk down the steps, and I remind Dad of the code for the gate that leads us out into the street.

'We'll warm up first,' he says when we reach the pavement. That means he's about to burst into a power walk so fast I'll struggle to keep up. Instead of taking the winding boulevard downhill and joining up with the city streets, we take a shortcut down a flight of steps accessed from the other side of the road. At the foot of the steps, we join a path that winds past a pétanque pitch and several villas with gardens filled with cornflowers and roses and tall cypress trees.

'That's good, kiddo,' Dad says as he walks faster, 'let's get the blood moving.'

We pass the back entrance of numerous apartment blocks and, with the quick pace Dad is setting, we soon turn on to the first of a series of side streets. It isn't long before we reach the old port, coming out on to Quai Cassini.

'Beautiful,' Dad says.

The small port is lovely, with the grand Venetian-coloured buildings on all three sides and boats and yachts of all sizes bobbing in the marina.

'At least it's not too warm yet.' Dad glances up at the overcast sky. The clouds in the east are fringed with gold, suggesting the sun will break through soon. 'Right. Let's get going.'

We jog down Quai Lunel and turn out of the port on to Quai Rauba Capeu. As we jog along the promenade, we pass the steps that lead down to the area known as Rauba Capeu beach, although it doesn't feature in any tourist brochures about Nice and isn't really a beach at all. The steps lead down to a long strip of concrete with a huge pile of concrete tetrapods at one end. This area has become a popular sleeping spot for the homeless and, as we jog past, I see the outline of two figures sleeping under a heap of blankets. To the right of the steps, clusters of dark rocks meet the sea and extend into the aqua and jade shallows.

We jog on. Across the busy road, carved into the towering hillside, is a monument to the men from the area who died in the two world wars. Further on, we stop and take a selfie at the I LOVE NICE sculpture. Giant red and black letters. Beyond them is the Bay of Angels, still and serene.

We keep running. I get the feeling Dad could run for ever. Freedom can take some getting used to, I suppose. After a while, he surges ahead. I speed up but still can't catch him. I have the oddest feeling he's forgotten I'm even here. At various moments since his release, he's just like the dad I remember. At other times, he feels so distant from me. My research has warned me to expect emotional numbness from him. In prison, he had to keep his feelings to himself and hide any vulnerabilities. I've often worried his time in there could have changed him permanently. Hardened him.

On the Promenade des Anglais, by the entrance to the Beau Rivage beach restaurant, he stops so I can catch up.

'Sorry,' he says, 'couldn't help myself.'

'It's fine.' My words fight their way out between gasps.

'It's just incredible to be able to move.'

We set off again at a slower pace.

'You're doing well,' Dad says. 'We'll get you fit in no time.'

His comment suggests I'm unfit just now. A bit unfair, considering all I've had on my plate. He's right, though; I do need to get back into shape.

We're not the only ones out jogging. Long-limbed women in colourful leggings run past us with determined expressions on their faces. A tall, muscular runner in long black shorts and a black vest veers towards us as he attempts to avoid some dog muck. His elbow knocks against Dad's shoulder.

'Hey,' Dad says, his voice a low snarl, 'watch it.'

The man glances back, startled, before running on.

I suggest we go to my favourite bakery near the Beau Rivage Hôtel and get some takeaway food to eat on the beach. Dad nods, rubbing his shoulder.

The bakery is busy. We join the queue and inch past the display of croissants and brioche and patisseries as Nouvelle Vague's version of 'Tainted Love' plays in the background. When our turn comes to order, a young guy with a handlebar moustache asks Dad what he wants.

Dad hesitates.

'What would you like?' I ask him, knowing he's likely overwhelmed with choices he's not used to.

'I don't know.'

The vulnerability in his voice makes me sad. 'You can have anything you want.'

His eyes rove over the pastries. 'Sod it,' he says. 'I'll have a pain au chocolat.'

After he orders a double espresso to go with it, moustache man turns to me. Saliva coats my tongue at the thought of a warm chocolate croissant melting on my tongue.

'Fruit salad and a green tea,' I say.

* * *

Holding our breakfasts, we cross the busy road at the traffic lights and take the nearest set of steps down to the public beach. Hard pebbles dig into my flesh when we sit down. Out at sea, a paddleboarder makes calm progress through the water. A few people are swimming. Brave. The water is still chilly at this time of year.

A tall woman with long blonde hair walks past us, somehow managing not to slip and stumble on the pebbles. Her head turns toward Dad, and I see her coy smile. Women have looked this way at my father for as long as I can remember. When she nears the shore, she stops, drops her bag and peels off her leggings and zip-up top to reveal a red bikini. She saunters down to the shore and wades into the water. I glance at Dad, but he isn't watching her. He's looking at me. The smile on his face is for me alone.

'Tuck in, kiddo,' he says.

My fruit salad is bland and in no way filling. Dad devours his croissant with large, savage bites.

'So good.' He touches his flat stomach. 'I'll have to watch, or I'll end up like Uncle Jimmy.'

I laugh. Uncle Jimmy always jokes he's literally Dad's double. Identical in looks and double the size.

As I sip my tea, a plane lifts into the sky from the

airport out to the west. A fast, steep climb to escape gravity.

Dad pulls his phone from the pocket of his shorts. I often catch him looking at the screen and it makes me sad. Before all this happened, he was always on his phone. Always in demand. Now I doubt anyone other than Uncle Jimmy is going to call him. I expect he's hoping Patch will relent and get in touch, but I think that's unlikely. When Dad said he wanted to set up a trust fund for his granddaughters, I suggested he wait a while. I can imagine Patch accusing him of trying to buy forgiveness if he makes any kind of financial gesture.

'What are you planning to do for the rest of the day?' Dad says, slipping his phone back into his pocket.

'I thought we should go shopping. Don't you need some new clothes? You've hardly got anything at the apartment.'

'True, and I could do with a new laptop too. I need to get back into managing the finances and account-ing.' Dad wipes his hand on his T-shirt. 'Don't want to take up all your time, though. You must have things to do. Friends to catch up with.'

'There's nothing that can't wait.' Muriel, one of the women from my Pilates class texted me yesterday to see why I'd missed the class and to invite me out for coffee today. I lied and said I was busy with work. I'm not sure if I'll go back to the class again. Now Dad's home, it won't be as easy to hide the truth from her or the other women there. It strikes me that even when he has settled in, I don't have much of a 'normal' life to get back to.

Something must show on my face because Dad reaches out and rubs between my shoulder blades, a move he always used to comfort me when I was a kid.

'I'm so happy we've got this time together,' he says. 'We can get to know each other again outside of... that bloody awful place.' He glances west, along the coast-line and I wonder if part of him still feels like he's in prison.

'Yes,' I say, 'I'm happy too.'

'Can I ask you a favour?' he says.

'Of course.'

He clears his throat. 'That website you showed me last night.'

'Families for Justice.'

'Yes. Could you take down that stuff about me?'

'Your support page?'

'Please, love.'

'Why?'

'I'm done with strangers knowing my business. I

don't want anyone knowing where I'm living or what I'm doing.'

Guilt ripples through me as I remember the *Daily Mail* article I contributed to when Dad was in jail. I wanted to highlight the bad conditions in French prisons and the journalist I spoke to promised me the article would do exactly that. Instead, it turned into a piece about Dad and the trial, and he was furious when he found out what I'd done. He knew I'd only wanted to help, but it upset him to think of people back in England reading about what had happened.

The Families for Justice site is different, though. The community there supports us. 'I've already had emails from people saying your story has given them hope.'

'Which is great, but all that's behind us now.'

I feel hurt. I've put a lot of time and effort into keeping Dad's story alive. 'I've had so much support from the people I've met on there,' I say. 'I can't just turn my back on them because you're out of jail. That wouldn't be fair.'

He takes my hands in his. 'It's over now. Prison, lawyers, all of it.'

'But I—'

'It kills me knowing what I've put you through.

The fact you've had to rely on these folk makes me feel like the world's worst dad.'

'You're not. I've learned a lot from all of it.' His hands are rough and warm. Hands that held mine as he taught me to walk. Hands that have guided and protected me all my life. 'Being involved with Families for Justice has made me think about retraining as a counsellor.'

'A counsellor?' He looks at me with disbelief. 'No, Colette. You had a brilliant career going in London before I screwed everything up. This freelance stuff you've had to do is bad enough, but I'm not going to let you spend the rest of your life being worn down by other people's problems. You're not suited to that kind of work, and I want more than that for you.'

I look into the eyes that are a mirror of my own. Eyes full of love and concern. Hasn't Dad always known me better than anyone?

'I know how good those people have been to you,' he says, 'but I'm back now. You've got me to rely on.' He squeezes my hands. 'It's time for you to come out of prison and into the real world too.'

I'd never thought about it like that. 'Okay,' I say.

'You deserve a fun summer. I owe you that much at least.'

I smile. 'I'll take the piece off the website and re-move the page.'

'Thank you.' He lifts my hands to his lips and kisses them. 'No one understands me like you, kiddo. No one ever has.'

Everything I've been holding on to for the past four and a half years, that tight knot of anger and fear and shame, unravels. When I start to cry, Dad puts his arms around me and holds me close.

'We're both free now,' he says.

14

LYNNE

The third-floor apartment on Boulevard Jean Jaurès is smaller than it looked on the website, but I don't mind. Not really. The 'spacious' open-plan living area is just a living room with a basic galley kitchen along one wall. The furniture looks second-hand. A grey sofa all saggy in the middle, a coffee table in shiny fake pine and a small, round dining table with three mismatched chairs.

The windows are gorgeous, though. They look just like they did in the photographs. Two tall ones stretching all the way from the oak laminate floor to the high ceiling. I open the white shutters on each window wider, expecting the morning sunlight to flood in, but the room stays dim.

'Your website said this flat got the morning light,' I say to Sophia, the young woman from the rental agency who met me earlier outside the entrance to the four-storey building. From the way she keeps peeking at her phone, it seems I'm only one of many meet-and-greets she's got this morning. She's dressed in black yoga leggings and a matching hooded top and looks like she probably jogs between appointments.

She shrugs. 'At lunchtime you get a little light.' I don't let her get to me. I'm no stranger to French indifference, and, in comparison to some of the prison guards I've dealt with over here, she's a breeze.

I peer out of the window. The flat was advertised as an atmospheric property in the heart of Nice's old town, but this room overlooks a busy boulevard. Loads of traffic both ways and the tramline running along it too. Noisy rather than atmospheric. Across the street there are apartment blocks and grand municipal buildings painted yellow and pink and orange.

Who cares if the apartment isn't perfect? I'm here to be with Sandy. To make our relationship official. He did offer to pay the rent on this place, but I wouldn't let him. He also offered to refund me for the flights I took over here for prison visits and the phone calls I paid for while he was inside, but I refused.

'I will show you the rest of the apartment,' Sophia says.

The 'cosy' bedroom is a bit on the cramped side. Sophia points out the original fireplace from the belle époque era. Good job I won't be needing to light it; the end of the double bed is pushed right up against it. A shiver runs through me at the thought of Sandy and me in this bed together. The things we'll get up to. We won't care about the size of the room or the faded fleur-de-lys wallpaper. This'll be the room we have sex in for the first time. I sit on the edge of the bed and bounce up and down. At least the mattress is firm. I want to tell Sophia the bed is nice in French, but my early-morning flight has scrambled my brain. I've been practicing on my Duolingo app as much as possible, but languages were never my thing.

'*Très bien,*' is all I can muster.

The bathroom is next on our tour. Sophia opens the window behind the toilet and points outside.

'Here is the old town,' she says. 'Down here, Rue de la Boucherie. Lots of good shops.'

'Boucherie,' I say. 'I know that one. Butcher's Street. My first husband was a butcher.'

Sophia gives me a blank look. When she leaves the room, I glance out of the window but all I can see is a dirty-yellow building opposite. Almost close enough to touch.

This bathroom's a bit on the small side too. Sandy and I won't be getting up to anything in here. Hardly room for me to get in the shower, let alone the pair of us.

Back in the living room, Sophia nods at the large suitcase I left by the sofa.

'This is all you have?' she says.

'I travelled light. I won't be here that long.' I smile. 'My fiancé and I will probably move in together soon.'

I'm not quite Sandy's fiancé yet, but I will be. Now I'm here it won't be long until he pops the question.

Sophia hands me the keys. 'My number is in the folder on the table if you need something.'

After she leaves, I wheel my suitcase into the bedroom and start to unpack. I only got two hours' sleep last night before heading to Gatwick airport at an ungodly hour, but I'm all zingy with excitement. I sent Sandy a WhatsApp as soon as I landed.

I'm here!

He replied right away.

Fantastic. Can't wait to see you soon.

I can't wait either, but I'll have to. He's only been out of prison a week, and he needs to reconnect with his daughter before he introduces the two of us. He seemed surprised I was coming over so quickly, but, as I told him, what's the point of wasting any more time?

The tall, thin wardrobe beside the fireplace offers only a few wooden hangers. I should have brought some of my padded ones from home. As I hang up one of the long, linen dresses I bought for this trip, I think of my coat hangers packed away in storage with most of my other belongings. I still can't quite believe how quickly my life has changed. As soon as I knew Sandy was getting out, I handed in my notice at work. I could tell Carol had her doubts, but she was good enough to keep them to herself. Colchester is full of people wanting a decent rental and before long I found Lenny and Courtney, a nice young couple I felt I could trust with my home. I haven't told Sandy about quitting work or renting out the flat yet. Don't want to put any pressure on him while he gets used to life on the outside.

The thought of my cosy flat brings a lump to my throat. I look at myself in the mirror on the inside of the wardrobe door. 'This is the start of the rest of your life, Lynne Collins,' I tell my reflection.

I'm starting my new life looking like I've been

dragged through a hedge backwards. My hair, matted from the journey and from wearing my sun hat earlier, is sticking to my scalp. The freckles across my nose are darker already. I'll have to really slap on the sunscreen while I'm here. Can't be too careful with my colouring.

I send Sandy another message to let him know the apartment is fine and I'm getting settled in. Two ticks appear. He's reading it just now. I wait for a reply, but nothing comes. Never mind, he'll have his hands full with Colette.

As well as the wardrobe, the room has a chest of drawers wedged beneath the window. I give the drawers a wipe out with a tissue before putting the rest of my clothes away. On the bedside table I place the wooden box containing all of Sandy's letters. No way I was trusting those to storage. Last, but by no means least, I remove my Vision Book from the bottom of my suitcase and sit down on the bed with it open on my lap. I flick through the pages, admiring the images I've collected. Weddings take such a lot of planning and I want this one, my third, to be perfect. I got married to my first husband, Colin, when I was eighteen years old. He was four years older than me and lived in a rental flat above the butcher's shop where he worked. When he proposed, I said yes so I could leave home and get away from my dad. We had a registry office wedding at Huddersfield Town Hall. On the day, Colin turned up late with two of his mates in tow as witnesses. They'd been up all night drinking, but he managed to make it through the ceremony before falling asleep during our taxi ride back to his flat.

When I told my mother about Colin's proposal, she sneered. She said I'd never get away from my father, no matter how far I went. She said the same thing when I married Alan. I was twenty-five then and Alan was thirty-eight. He liked to be in charge, and I let him organise the wedding. We had the ceremony and reception in a budget hotel on the outskirts of Chelmsford. Alan even picked out my dress for me. I thought it was sweet of him, but I overheard my Auntie Janice in the toilets saying he was a control freak. She was, it turned out, a perceptive lady.

I leave the Vision Book on my bed and wander through to the living room and the tall windows that look out on to the boulevard. A tram glides past, its warning bell low and gloomy. My mother's face comes to me. That pinched, cruel look she had from so many years in a miserable marriage.

You'll never get away from your father. No matter how far you go.

'Piss off, Mother,' I say.

15

LYNNE

Not wanting to waste the morning, I change into navy cropped trousers, a white T-shirt and trainers. After slapping on some sun lotion, I grab my handbag and leave the apartment, hurrying down the three flights of stairs to the street. The building does have a lift but it's so small I came over all funny on the way up in it earlier.

The noise of the traffic hits me full on when I step out on to the street. How many mopeds? They're everywhere with their high-pitched, whiny engines. I turn right and pass a supermarket and a chemist. Handy. The next sharp right turn takes me on to Rue de la Boucherie.

This is more like it. I'm in the old town now. A narrow, curved street between tall buildings. They must be hundreds of years old. I join the people streaming along in both directions. So many different nationalities. I can hear Americans, Germans, French and plenty of Brits. Spaniards, too. I went to Malaga a few times with Alan, my second husband. Apart from that I've never been much of a traveller.

Like everyone else, I keep stopping to look at the souvenir and gift shops. A few sell cheese and charcuterie. I'll be popping down here for something to go with my wine, that's for sure. I pass a nougat shop full of big hunks of the stuff in all different colours and flavours. Further on I stop to admire a display of tea towels and soap. Once I'm settled in, I might send a tea towel to Carol. She could do with one for the staff kitchen. We might not be as close as we were, but she's the only person who knows about Sandy and, in her own way, she's been a good friend to me.

There's some gorgeous clothes shops here too, but I'm desperate to see the Promenade des Anglais and the bay. Sandy's told me so many times how beautiful the view is. With the help of the map on my phone, it isn't long before I cross the square in front of the Palais de Justice. From here it's only a few minutes to reach Route 98, the main road through the city. It takes me a while to cross it. Tons of traffic, a bike lane to contend with and zebra crossings no one seems to want to stop at. It's gone noon now and the sun is already making my bare arms tingle. This is only the end of May. Lord knows how I'll cope when it gets hotter.

By the time I reach the promenade, I'm breathless and sweaty. Worth it, though. Look at the bay. So bloody blue. I don't have the words to describe it, but even as someone who knows nothing about art, I can understand why so many artists came here and painted it.

I stay on the promenade for a while, watching the people walking and jogging and zipping past on electric scooters. The women are so stylish here. The Italian sunglasses I got in the sale at TK Maxx are perfect for Nice. Sandy said he'd take me shopping once I got settled, but I don't expect him to buy me things.

How weird to be in the same city as him. I look east along the bay. That's where he lives, somewhere up on those hills behind the port. I don't know his exact address yet. All in good time. Maybe I'll move in there once my rental agreement is up. Or maybe we'll look for somewhere new together, either here or back home.

I've no idea how I'll sleep tonight. Knowing he's so close and yet so far.

I find a set of steps down to the beach. What a sight

I must be, hobbling across the pebbles. This strip of public beach is quiet. A group of teenagers sits near the water, talking and smoking. A lone swimmer out at sea does front crawl back and forth. A few speedboats zip about and two figures in kayaks are paddling away from the shore. After plonking myself down on the warm pebbles, I take my phone out of my bag and snap a few pictures of the sea. I WhatsApp them to Carol with a short message.

I feel like I'm in a dream.

I do. Look at this place.

I check my phone again. Still no word from Sandy, but that's okay. He's with his daughter. No need for me to get suspicious. My ex-husbands, both of them unfaithful, were good at bringing that out in me.

Out in the bay, the lone swimmer dives beneath the water and, seconds later, surfaces with a whoop. I'm dying to get in for a dip, but I'll wait until Sandy's with me. I picture him leading me by the hand into the water, pulling me close for a kiss in the shallows before we swim out. People will see us and think we should get a room.

Unable to resist a paddle, I make my way closer to the sea and slip off my socks and sandals. When I wade in, the water is colder than I expected, and I let out a little scream. The teenagers behind me snigger, but I don't mind. Not really. I'm here,, in France, to be with the man I've been waiting for all my life. A dream come true, and nothing can spoil it.

A little way out, a speedboat roars past, close enough to the shore to trigger a series of large waves. As they rush towards me, I step backwards to avoid getting soaked but instead stumble over a pile of pebbles and fall flat on my backside.

Laughter erupts from the watching teenagers as I flounder in the crashing waves, lifting my handbag over my head to protect it from the water. When I turn over on to my knees, I see one boy has his phone pointed at me, videoing my humiliation.

'Pack that in,' I say, wishing I'd learned some French swear words. The kids don't care. They keep laughing as I get to my feet and crunch my way back across the pebbles, the burning in my cheeks as warm as the sun on my wet and trembling back.

16

COLETTE

We have a perfect morning for a drive. Cloudless, blue sky and the sun already hotting up. The sea breeze is perfect. Enough to keep us cool but not strong enough to make our journey in this MG convertible uncomfortable.

Dad rented the racing-green vintage model yesterday. I did offer to put him on the insurance for my car, but he wanted to treat himself to something special for his first driving experience in years. Now we've got the roof down and we're heading past Nice airport on our way to Cannes for morning coffee and a walk. A great way to spend a Friday. The journey should only take forty-five minutes if the traffic's okay. Dad found a radio station playing music from the sixties, and we sing along to 'All You Need Is Love' by the Beatles as he steers us on to the coastal road that will take us past Antibes and Juan-les-Pins. Much more fun than taking the highway.

'You look very Grace Kelly,' he says.

'Why, thank you.' I adjust the sunglasses he presented me with when I got into the car this morning. An unexpected gift. 'You can't beat Chanel.' I've been coveting this classic oval bow style for a while. Trust Dad to buy me exactly what I wanted. He's always had great taste.

'Good to get out of town,' Dad says as Nice and its suburbs disappear behind us. With him at the wheel, good music on the radio, it feels as if no time has passed since we were together. As if the years in prison were a nightmare now forgotten.

Four days have gone by since Dad asked me to take his story down from the FFJ website. I did so reluctantly, after first sending goodbye emails to the people who've been so kind to me. At first, I struggled with guilt about abandoning my online friends, but, after a day or so, I began to think Dad was right. I feel lighter somehow, less connected to the stress and trauma of the past five years.

Dad was so grateful to me for doing it. He seems happier too. This morning I got up to find him looking through our family photo albums. He'd found some pictures of us on holiday in Cannes, a few months after my wedding to Liam. He showed me one of Liam and me with him and Mum, standing in front of our five-star hotel, Le Majestic. That's when he suggested we take a drive to Cannes for old times' sake and relive some happy family memories.

I'm in no mood for dredging up memories of Liam, but I can tell this trip means a lot to Dad and it's great to see him happy.

'This is the best,' Dad says, slipping an arm around my shoulder and steering with one hand. 'Isn't it?'

'The best.' His arm is warm and solid. The sea glitters on our left. Luxurious villas cling to the coastline. It all seems unreal, like a scene from a film. In my new sunglasses, I feel for a moment like a character in this film, one who has endured terrible things but now has her happy ending and is driving off into it.

It takes us just under an hour to get to Cannes. We find a free parking space on a street behind the train station. The film festival is over now, leaving the town relatively quiet, but as we walk from the station, I spot film posters on every bus stop.

We meander along Rue Meynadier, into the heart of the old town and then cut down a side street to the old port and stroll along the Promenade de la Pantiero, stopping occasionally to admire the yachts of the super-wealthy. My new sunglasses are an ideal prop for these surroundings. Dad looks smart too, in the navy polo shirt and dark-blue jeans I picked out for him in Galeries Lafayette when we went shopping. Aviator sunglasses hide his eyes. Soon we hit La Croisette, the city's famous promenade, and before long we reach the Palais des Festivals where film stars pose on the red carpet before their premieres. Further on we hit the kids' park area and inhale the scent of warm doughnuts and chips from the outdoor food court.

Memories of Liam flood into my mind. We spent a morning here, playing with the remote-control boats in the pond, and afterwards we went on the carousel Dad and I are walking past now. It is still golden and glitzy, the horses inside it doing a lazy circuit in time to tinny accordion music.

'There it is.' Dad is looking across the road at an imposing white building. Le Majestic. A shadow passes over his face.

'We don't have to go in,' I say.

'I'm fine.'

'You're thinking about Mum.' His grief for her is still palpable at times.

He lets out a deep sigh. 'So many memories.'

'We could walk into the town and get a coffee there?'

'It's all good, kiddo.' He slips his arm through mine. 'Come on, let's go in.'

* * *

Le Majestic is as opulent as I remember. Two silver Rolls-Royces parked outside the main entrance. Manicured flowerbeds bursting with bird of paradise flowers, miniature palm trees and flowering cacti. A vast chandelier dominates the lobby – diamond-shaped fragments of glass suspended from long, thin wires. Huge tapestries hang behind the long wooden reception desk, and the air is heavy with a synthetic floral perfume. All around the lobby, luxury items are displayed in glass cabinets. A Gucci handbag, a Rolex watch, a single Nike trainer.

'Honestly,' Dad says, 'a bloody shoe? Some people have more money than sense.' He looks relaxed, hands in his pockets as he surveys his surroundings. A hint of his old confidence. He always said we were as good as anyone else in these places and that we'd earned our right to be here.

The concierge directs us to the bar for coffee. On the way there, we stop to admire the black-and-white portraits of film stars that occupy every available wall space. In the bar, we sink into deep velvet-covered seats and order two cappuccinos. I try not to stare at the American woman at the next table whose face is taut and lopsided after too much plastic surgery.

'Good people-watching,' I say. Dad nods but says nothing. All of a sudden, he has closed himself off. Retreated to a place I cannot reach. When our coffees arrive, he sips his in silence, brooding.

I slip away into thoughts of Liam and our time here. When Dad invited us to join him and Mum in Cannes, Liam and I had only just moved into our flat in Denmark Hill. Liam wanted us to stay at home and get some decorating done, but Dad was so keen for us to come and, as I did point out to Liam, Dad had given us the deposit for the flat. Not that I felt I owed him, but it did seem bad manners to say no. Especially when he'd paid for our two-week honeymoon in the Seychelles as well. Liam cheered up once we arrived and saw how beautiful our hotel room was. Our first

night here we took a long bath together and decided
we would have three children. We couldn't agree on all
the names, but we knew our first child would be Alfie
for a boy or Ava for a girl.

'Hey,' Dad says. 'He was never good enough for
you.'

My father has always been able to guess what I'm
thinking.

'You deserved better than him,' Dad says. He was
never keen on Liam; he didn't think him dynamic
enough. Liam had a good job with HSBC Bank, but, on
more than one occasion, I overheard Dad referring to
him as a 'nothing guy'.

'Sorry,' I say. 'I'll stop thinking about him.'

'Sometimes it's good to relive memories.' That
deep groove appears between Dad's eyebrows. 'Remind yourself how things really were.'

'Maybe.'

'When you're in prison, things get distorted. You
wonder what was real and what wasn't.'

He gets up and excuses himself to go to the toilet. I
finish my coffee, along with both the complimentary
madeleines the waiter left on our table. Dad won't
want his.

Ten minutes pass. Where is he?

Another five minutes. I'm beginning to get concerned.

'Sorry.' Dad strides over to me from the direction of the lobby.

'Are you okay?' He looks pale, shaken. 'What's wrong?'

He rubs his jaw. 'It was silly. I was coming out of the gents, and I passed the lift. Some people were getting in so I joined them and pressed the button for the fifth floor.'

'Didn't you and Mum stay on the fifth floor the last time you were here?'

'Room 501. I went back there and stood outside it.'

'Dad, you—'

'I know, I know. It's silly. It's not like she would still be there.'

'I understand. Really, I—'

'Stupid. Really stupid. I don't know what I thought I'd find.' He shakes his head. 'Evidence we were there, maybe? Listen to me, I sound nuts.'

I put my hand on his. 'It's okay. You've just come out of... you've just come out and it's going to take you a while to feel normal.'

'Normal. Christ.' The muscles in the side of his face clench.

'Sorry, I didn't mean—'

He takes out his wallet and tosses thirty euros on the table. 'Let's go home.'

* * *

We drive back to Nice on the A8 highway with the roof of the MG up and no radio to fill the silence between us. A dark mood has settled on my father, one my attempts at small talk cannot shift.

I think back to our journey to Cannes this morning. Dad's arm around my shoulder. The sense we were driving, finally, into the future. We should never have gone back to the Majestic Hôtel. We should not have gone back to the past.

When we get to Mont Boron, I expect Dad to stop at our block and put the MG in the underground garage but when we reach home he keeps on driving.

'Where are you going?' I ask.

'Monaco,' he says, manoeuvring the MG round a tight bend.

'Monaco?'

'Why not? We've got all day and I feel like driving.'

I'm getting hungry and could do with the toilet, but Dad seems determined to keep going.

'We'll take the Grand Corniche,' he says. 'Be in Monaco for a late lunch.'

The Grand Corniche. One of the three routes connecting Nice to Menton on the Italian border. The Grand is the highest of the three roads and the hardest to drive. It goes up into the Pre-Alps and is known for its sharp bends, steep drops and spectacular clifftop views.

Dad pulls over and takes the roof of the car down. 'Buckle up, kiddo.'

We follow the road out of Nice towards Villefranche-sur-Mer and begin our climb into the Pre-Alps, the wheels of the car hugging the road famous for appearing in a Hitchcock film. Grace Kelly driving Cary Grant in a stylish convertible, her white gloves on the steering wheel.

The sun beats down on us, but the air feels cooler the higher we climb. I want to put the radio on, but Dad's stern expression stops me. He's so focused on guiding the MG around the challenging bends that he seems to have forgotten I'm here.

The views are, to use one of my tired copywriting phrases, breathtaking. No other word for them. The startling blue of the Mediterranean, the dramatic limestone mountains. Soon the medieval hilltop village of Èze is below us.

'We should stop and take some pictures,' I say as

we approach a viewpoint where several other cars have stopped.

'In a bit.'

He drives as if he has some personal record to break. The car's engine strains as he floors the uphill sections. Nerves and nausea niggle in my stomach. What the hell is he playing at? I open my mouth to tell him to slow down but nothing comes out. At times, my father has a way of muting me.

On one downhill section, with no cars in front of us, Dad lets the car pick up speed until I'm not sure if he's even in control any more.

Fear unmutes me. 'Dad.'

On our right, a drop into a deep gorge. The wheels of the car flirt with the edge of the tarmac.

'Dad. Slow down.'

When he turns to look at me, my expression seems to startle him. He slows down and, after the next up-hill stretch, pulls into a viewing point.

We sit there for a moment, the car engine idling as if exhausted, sounding as grateful as I feel.

'Sorry, love,' he says. 'I shouldn't have scared you like that.'

'It's okay.' My pale face in the passenger mirror contradicts me.

'No. It's not.' He slams his hands on the steering wheel. 'Fuck.'

'Is it me? Have I done something wrong?' My voice sounds childish and feeble. I don't often make my father angry, but, when I do, I feel like I've failed him.

'It's not you.' He lets out a weary sigh. 'I was thinking about her.'

'Mum?' Is that why he's angry? There are times I'm furious with her too. If she hadn't died and left us, none of this would have happened.

'No,' he says, 'not your mum.'

He's thinking about Ella Watson. I usually avoid thinking of her name as it brings up all sorts of dark feelings in me, but at this moment I can't ignore her. She is here, and he is thinking of her. Today has reminded him of everything he lost and of who took it from him.

'I get angry sometimes,' he says. 'I can't help it.'

Thoughts of her made him furious. She made him drive like that, reckless and oblivious to everything.

'She's in the past,' I say, 'we need to forget about her.'

'I know. I should.'

Some of his fury flashes through me. She is still here, coming between us.

'I can't help wondering what she's up to,' he says.

'You need to focus on what you're up to.'

'She's had years to rebuild her life.' He gestures at the family getting out of the jeep next to us. Mum, dad and two young boys. 'She might have got married or started a family.'

'It doesn't matter.'

'I know. I know you're right.' He rubs his lower lip with the tip of his thumb. 'Still, I'd love to know what she's up to now.'

17

JANE

'Maman,' Theo says from his vantage point high on Michel's shoulders. '*Le dragon.*' He points to the sign for the Place du Dragon, the street we are walking down on our way to the market square at the centre of the old town. Draguignan gets its name from the Latin word for dragon. Theo is fascinated by the old legend Michel told him recently. The one about how pilgrims on their way to a nearby monastery were often terrorised by a dragon who lived in the misty marshes that surrounded our town.

'Maman.' Theo shields his eyes with one hand. He is on the lookout.

'*Oui, le dragon.*' I am walking a little way behind my husband and son, my wicker shopping basket swinging at my side, as if this is a normal Saturday-morning trip to the markets. As if Sandy Gilligan does not exist.

Michel slows down as he and Theo pretend to be wary of the town's mythical predator. They mime fear and terror as they approach the medieval city gate.

My breath is shallow. My temples fizz with the start of a headache.

Sandy Gilligan is not a myth. He is real, and he is out of jail.

Michel and Theo cheer when they pass through the arched gateway. In this game of theirs, they are safe now. The dragon cannot get them.

Passing through the gate gives me no such feeling of safety.

Michel waits for me on the other side. 'You made it,' he says, a broad smile on his face.

Theo clamours to walk. Michel lowers him to the ground, and we stroll down Grand'Rue Lily Pons, swinging our son between us until he wriggles free and ambles along at his own pace, one hand trailing along the side of the buildings. The street is quiet. Pressure builds in my chest, and the air around me seems to quiver with tension, as if a thunderstorm is coming. I glance up at the sky but find it clear and blue.

'We're meeting Bastien and Nathalie at Café de Flore,' Michel says. 'They have a table.'

'Great.'

Every Saturday we follow the same routine. A trip to Draguignan's weekend market, where we stock up on treats and have coffee with Nathalie and Bastien and, when they aren't away for the weekend, Jacques and Elyna. This is the simple life we wanted for ourselves when we moved here. I will do everything I can to make sure it stays that way.

The noise hits me as soon as we enter Place du Marché. Only ten thirty and already so many people. It always seems as if the whole town is here on a Saturday, and this last market day of May is especially busy. Usually I love the buzz, but today the volume of chatter and the music coming from Bar du Marché further down the square puts me on edge. I tell myself to stay calm. This town is not a popular tourist destination for people from more glamorous parts of the region. Sandy is unlikely to come here on a day trip.

Theo protests when Michel scoops him up.

'We're going for hot chocolate,' Michel says to placate him. 'Look who is waiting for us.'

On the opposite side of the square, outside Café de Flore, sit Nathalie and Bastien. Nathalie has the baby with her.

'Where is Lena?' Theo asks.

'I don't know, *bébé*,' I say. Nathalie spots us and waves. 'You go on,' I tell Michel, 'I want to get some bread before they sell out.'

Without waiting for his reply, I dart off into the square. Stalls with red canopies line two sides of it. Some, like my favourite cheese stall are besieged by long queues. I move through the crowd towards the boulangerie stall. Each time someone pushes past me, I flinch at what feels like unbearable contact. Everything is heightened. The vivid greens of the olives on one of the stalls I pass. The fleshy red of the peaches on the fruit stall. The features on the faces looming out at me.

At the boulangerie stall, I join the queue. While waiting, I take out my phone and check the Families for Justice website. Two days ago, I clicked on the link for Colette's latest article only to find it had disappeared. The whole page dedicated to her father has gone.

Luckily, I had already spent enough time scrutinising the photograph of Sandy and Colette to get what I needed. Judging from the view behind them, and the plane taking off from the west, I guessed they must live in the east of the city. I pored over a map of Nice and decided the most likely place was the residential area of Mont Boron.

The queue moves forward. When my turn comes, I put my phone away and stare at the array of bread on offer, forgetting what I came for.

'*Un pain de seigle au levain,*' says Samia, the cheery woman who serves me every week.

'*Oui,*' I say, relieved she has remembered my usual order. '*Merci.*'

Walking away from the boulangerie, I am greeted by Reine Garnier, one of Theo's teachers at preschool. Young, enthusiastic, her blonde hair always tied up into a bouncy ponytail. After we exchange quick hellos, I hurry to the cheese stall and find myself queuing next to one of the hotel's part-time chambermaids. I have always liked how knowable this town and its people are, but today this lack of anonymity makes me feel my secrets are under threat.

After a few more purchases, I make my way through the throng of shoppers towards Café de Flore. Towards my family and friends. People who think they know me but really have no idea.

If only I did not have to think about Sandy Gilligan. If only he did not exist.

After failing to find his photograph again, I did a general online search to see if I could find him elsewhere. I found no trace, but I did discover a recent article about a fatal knife attack in Baumettes prison. The anger I have kept hidden in recent years surged through me. If only Sandy had died in that attack. An uncharitable thought, but I couldn't stop thinking it. The night after reading that story, dark fantasies kept me awake. I imagined Sandy lying in a pool of blood in a prison exercise yard. I imagined myself having paid another prisoner to kill him.

I even imagined doing it myself.

* * *

'*Santé*,' Michel says, raising his bottle of beer. I touch my espresso cup to it.

'*Santé*,' my friends chorus, and a noisy clinking of cups and glasses follows.

'*Santé*,' Theo says, lifting his plastic beaker, now full of the hot chocolate I poured into it.

'So cute,' Nathalie says in French. We usually speak French when together in a group. That suits me today. With everything that's on my mind, I need the tiny hesitation my brain takes before each word of my second language.

Theo soaks up the attention from our friends. I grip my coffee cup tight and try to stay focused on where I am and who I am with. Nathalie has baby Nicole in her arms, trying to lull her to sleep. Bastien, bulky beside his tiny wife, is scratching his dark, bushy beard. He has been on night shifts for a week and looks exhausted. His mother is looking after Lena today, much to Theo's disappointment. Disappointment he is expressing by ignoring Nicole.

'When do Jacques and Elyna come back from Paris?' I ask Nathalie.

'Tuesday,' she says.

Our friends Elyna and Jacques have taken their eight-year-old twin boys to Disneyland Paris for a long weekend.

'You should see the hotel they're staying in,' Bastien says. 'Five-star luxury.'

Jacques is a lawyer specialising in wills and estates, and Elyna is head of finance at the University of Toulon. We often joke they are our rich, grown-up friends.

The café is packed. Women in patterned Provençal dresses chat about their market purchases, comparing the leafy greens poking out of their shopping bags. Middle-class men in navy blazers and striped shirts sit with their ruddy faces turned up to the sun. At the table next to us, an elderly lady feeds a croissant to the French bulldog on her lap.

Drinking starts early on market day, and many of the people around us are enjoying a beer or a glass of rosé. Nathalie is avoiding alcohol while she breast-feeds, but I stopped drinking after that night with Sandy. I think of him leaning across the bar at La Cave á Vin, asking if he could get me a drink. Shame pulses through me when I recall my coy reply.

No, but you can take me for a drink after my shift.

'It's awful, isn't it, Jane?'

I snap out of the past to find Nathalie looking at me. 'What is?'

'Henri Breton,' says Bastien. 'You haven't heard?'

'Heard what?' Michel asks.

'He's been charged with attacking a hotel chambermaid.' Nathalie shakes her head. 'I had posters of him on my wall when I was a teenager.'

Theo asks me for his colouring book. With trembling hands, I take his book and pencils out of my handbag and pass them to him. 'Good boy.' I kiss the top of his head. I have always liked Henri Breton too. Why am I always so surprised when these stories appear in the news?

Nicole starts grizzling.

'She can't be hungry,' Nathalie says, 'she's not due a feed for an hour.'

'Here.' Bastien takes the baby in his solid arms. 'Hello, beautiful girl.'

This father–daughter moment should be heart-warming, but I can't help thinking of Sandy and Colette. What would Nicole do if one day someone accused Bastien of something terrible? Would she stick by him no matter what? Seeing Colette and Sandy in that photograph together shook me up. I had forgotten how much she looked like him. I think of her at the trial, sitting there in court every day, her mere presence a vital part of his defence. The newspapers made much of the 'loyal, loving daughter' who believed in her father's innocence. When she testified on his behalf and told the court what a wonderful father he was, what a kind and honest man, I feared everyone listening would doubt my story.

'Okay, time for Uncle Michel,' Bastien says as Nicole starts to wail.

Michel holds out his arms and Bastien hands over his daughter. As soon as Michel brings her close to his chest, the wailing stops.

'See,' Bastien says, 'I hate this guy.'

'Can you move in with us?' Nathalie says.

Michel is too wrapped up in the baby to answer. I remember how good he was with Theo during that difficult first year.

'Good baby.' Theo, keen to wrestle back some of his father's attention, leans over and pats Nicole's head.

'Softly,' Michel says, 'you have to be very gentle.'

Looking at Michel with the baby, I see an image of what my future could be. A future Sandy could jeopardise.

'I think someone's broody,' Nathalie says to my husband.

Michel flashes me a loving smile. To avoid looking at him, I focus on the crowd of people still browsing the market stalls. Among the shoppers, I see a man with silvery-grey hair. I sit up straight. A man with Sandy's height and build.

Pulse jumping, I push back my chair and stand up.

'Where are you going?' Michel asks.

'Won't be a minute.'

I head away from the café and into the heart of the market. Where is he? I scan the crowd until I see the head of silver hair. The man is standing in front of a baklava stall, handing over a ten-euro note in exchange for a white paper bag shiny with grease.

Is it Sandy? I cannot see his face.

He turns away. The crowd swallows him. Muttering apologies, I push people aside until I glimpse him again near a tagine stall. If only I could see his face.

'Jane.' Reine Garnier, Theo's teacher, steps in front of me. 'Sorry, I meant to ask you something earlier.'

'Sorry. I need to—'

'It won't take a minute.' Her ponytail bobs up and down as she announces there will be a school open day next month. 'We're looking for parent volunteers to help out,' she says.

The man walks away from the tagine stall. A pigeon flapping overhead catches his attention, and he turns his eyes skyward. I will him to turn around.

'What do you think?' asks Reine.

The man sets off again, into the noisy mob of shoppers.

'It would be amazing if you'd help out,' she says.

'Of course.' I only take my eyes off the man long enough to give my son's teacher a friendly smile, but when I look back again, he is gone.

18

LYNNE

Tonight's the night. Tonight, I'm going to see Sandy in the outside world for the first time. Tonight, we can finally have sex.

Five days since I got here. Feels like an eternity. I don't mind. Not really. He's been busy with his daughter, and in one of his texts he said he wanted to get prison out of his system before he saw me. He wants us to start again, as if we're two people meeting for the first time. As if prison never happened.

I'm sitting on the saggy grey sofa, my phone in my lap, staring at the message he sent this morning.

Be with you 6 pm tonight. Booked us nice restaurant.
S xx

All day I've been checking his words, just to make sure I've not imagined them.

In an hour and fifteen minutes he'll be here.

Time to get my pre-Sandy routine started.

Into the cramped shower cubicle I go. The water never gets past lukewarm, but it's hot enough for a thorough wash and to do my hair. I did most of my beauty duty before leaving Colchester – leg and bikini line waxed; eyebrows, chin and upper lip threaded – but in the shower I pass a razor over my legs to make sure they're silky smooth. The rose musk soap I'm using is from one of the shops on Rue de la Boucherie. I've explored the old town a bit since I've been here, and walked along the promenade a few times, but I want to wait until I'm with Sandy to see more of the city.

After drying myself off, I inspect myself in the bathroom mirror. Thank Christ my lips are okay. I've always been a right one for cold sores when stressed or excited.

Getting ready like this reminds me of seeing Sandy in prison. Before each visit, I spent the night in a budget hotel in the centre of Marseilles, too excited to sleep. Then it was up early to get dressed and put my face on before the bus ride to the prison. I only went four times. Sandy said prison was no place for a

woman like me, but in the end, we couldn't live
without seeing each other.

I give my teeth a good clean and gargle with
mouthwash. Then into the bedroom to blow-dry my
hair. Once that's done, I apply a thick coating of deodorant to my armpits, cover my skin with cocoa body
cream and spray myself with the Chanel No. 5 I treated
myself to at the airport. Even though I know it's a bad
idea, I inspect my naked body in the wardrobe mirror.
It won't be long before Sandy gets to see me without
my clothes on. The real me. Stretch marks, slapping
on my HRT gel in the mornings, no make-up. That
scares me a bit. What if he doesn't like the real me?

'Give over, Lynne Collins,' I say aloud. 'That man
can't wait to get his hands on you.'

Into my new set of underwear. I splashed out on a
black lacy set from Marks and Spencer. Sandy deserves something classy. I always wore nice underwear
when I visited him in prison, not that he got to see it.
He could have, though. In French prisons, visitors get
to be on their own with the prisoner in a private cubicle. The guards are supposed to monitor what goes on
in there, but they turn a blind eye. One time when I
was visiting, we heard a couple in the next cubicle
having sex. I was sitting on Sandy's lap at the time. The
thought of doing it with him in there was a right turn

on. It would have been easy for me to slip my knickers off and for us to get into it. When I kissed his neck, he moaned but moved my head away.

'Not like this,' he said. 'Not here.'

I told him I didn't mind, but he refused to go any further.

'No, Lynne,' he said, 'we're not animals.'

That's Sandy all over. A proper gentleman.

* * *

Soon I am ready and waiting. I make sure the bedroom is tidy. Earlier I changed the bed linen and hid my Vision Book in my suitcase under the bed. No need for him to see it until the time's right.

In the living area, I plump up the sofa cushions and give the kitchen worktops a final wipe-down. What if Sandy finds the place shabby and off-putting? Give over, Lynne. After prison, he should find anywhere palatial, and he'll be too busy thinking about sex to care what the apartment looks like. It's polite of him to pretend he's made an early booking at a restaurant, but everyone knows the French eat late. He's getting here early for one reason and one reason only.

I wonder where we'll do it first? I doubt we'll get as far as the bedroom. The Moroccan rug in front of the sofa looks a bit grubby. Don't fancy that. The sofa's a possibility. I fantasise about Sandy picking me up and shagging me against the wall next to the window, our moans and cries drifting down to the street below.

Fifteen minutes later, the tension is unbearable. Two years of waiting but this last fifteen minutes is the worst. I want to cry. I've started to sweat so I whip off my low-cut, black dress, wash my armpits over the bathroom sink and put some fresh deodorant on.

Six o'clock. I told Sandy to buzz from outside when he gets here, and I'll let him in with the entryphone.

Five minutes later, there's still no sign of him. I check my phone in case he's messaged to say he's running late. I look out of one of the tall windows to the boulevard below but see no sign of him.

A tram glides past, its warning bell deep and mournful. Bring out your dead, it seems to say. Bring out your dead.

Ten minutes past six. Eleven minutes past. Twelve—

My mobile pings. A message from Sandy.

Main door was open. On my way up.

I wait behind the front door, heart bouncing

around my ribcage, legs shaking. I hear the loud whirring sound as the poky lift approaches my floor. The metallic rattle as he pulls the lift door across.

I open the door before he has time to knock. There he is at last, Sandy Gilligan, a free man. In his hand, a bouquet of red roses.

'Hello, love,' he says.

19

LYNNE

We look at one another, the air electric between us.

'It's you,' I say. 'It's really bloody you.'

He looks smaller than he did in prison. Sexy as ever, though, and with some colour in his face for once. Well dressed, too. Smart blue jeans, black linen shirt and a pair of navy plimsolls.

'Well,' he says, 'don't I get a kiss?'

I smile. 'Come here, you.'

He steps into the hallway and pulls me to him. The cellophane wrapping around the roses makes a crackling sound as they press against my back.

'It's so good to see you,' he says.

He smells different than he did in prison. He's washed himself with a different soap and he's got aftershave on too. That's a first. When I close my eyes, I'm not even sure it's him. I wouldn't have picked him out in a blind testing.

He tilts my head up to his and we share a long, hot kiss. We've kissed before, plenty of times in prison, but this feels different. This kiss is leading to something. Before long, my hand reaches for the waistband of his jeans. He moans but puts a hand over mine to stop me going further.

'I need to take this slowly,' he says.

'We can have a cup of tea first if you like?'

He laughs. 'Oh, Lynne.' He kisses the top of my head. 'I don't want our first time to be rushed. It means too much to me.'

'No. I mean yes. No, we shouldn't rush.'

'I'm a man who likes to treat a woman right. Let's at least go for dinner.'

So, he has booked an early table somewhere. I don't know whether to feel disappointed or pleased he's treating me with such respect.

'I want this to be a proper first date,' he says, looking so nervous I can't help feeling touched.

'Well then,' I say, 'let me freshen up my lippy and we'll be off.'

* * *

The Italian restaurant he's chosen for tonight is in a residential part of town I haven't been to yet. To get here we had to cross Boulevard Jean Jaurès and walk for fifteen minutes through streets lined with apartment blocks. Palazzo Petrucci is sandwiched between a laundrette and a tobacco shop and looks a bit shabby from the outside. Why here? Surely, we want somewhere special for our first night together?

'I'm looking forward to this,' Sandy says. I suppose anything will taste good to him after all those years of prison food.

As soon as we step inside, I see I've been too quick to judge. The place is cosy and inviting and full of incredible smells – onions and garlic frying and freshly baked bread. A plump middle-aged waiter with thinning black hair appears. After introducing himself as Manlio, he leads us to a table at the centre of the small, square room. It has a white tablecloth, gleaming silver cutlery and, at its centre, a tea light flickers in a glass holder.

'*Non*,' Sandy says to the waiter. '*Désolé. Non.*'

'What is wrong?' Manlio asks in English.

The table looks perfect to me, but Sandy points to another one by the rear wall of the restaurant. Manlio nods and, with an obliging smile, shows us to Sandy's choice.

'*Merci*,' Sandy says, claiming the chair with the wall behind it.

We were lucky to be able to switch. Every other table is full. Couples, mostly.

Manlio fusses around us, filling up our glasses with water and handing out menus. I notice beads of sweat on Sandy's forehead. He keeps fiddling with the collar of his shirt. After a few minutes of looking at the menu, he lets out a sigh.

'Sorry,' he says, 'I couldn't sit in the middle of the restaurant like that.'

'Why?'

'Back to the wall.'

'What?'

'In the exercise yard, I always had to keep my back to the wall in case someone attacked me from behind.'

Poor Sandy. What's the word people use nowadays? Triggered. The thought of sitting exposed like that must have triggered him.

I reach across the table and take his hand. 'Thanks for bringing me here,' I say. When we first left the apartment, it seemed silly to be in the outside world, surrounded by people, when we could have been indoors, finally on our own for the first time ever. The longer we walked, I realised it felt good to be outdoors together. Breathing in fresh air, instead of the muggy, sweaty fug of the prison.

'I still can't believe we're sitting here,' he says. 'I keep waiting for the bell to go at the end of visiting time.'

'I hated that bell.'

'Me too.' He lowers his eyes to the menu again. 'These are all dishes from Naples. Some of the best Italian food is from there.'

I let go of his hand. Did he come here with Angie when she was alive? Not that I'd ask that question. I've resolved not to give in to petty jealousy where his dead wife's concerned. I'm not that kind of woman any more.

'I looked it up on Tripadvisor,' he adds. 'It gets brilliant reviews.'

He's chosen this place for me. For us. Bless him.

He's so excited about the menu I let him order for both of us. He insists we have a proper four-course dinner that includes rack of lamb for the meat dish.

'Fine by me,' I say, determined to leave a bit of each course so I'm not too full for sex. I leave the drinks order to Sandy as well. After a long conversation with Manlio about the wine list, he orders the most expensive bottle of red available.

'You're welcome to a cocktail if you want one before the wine,' Sandy says when the waiter marches away with our order.

'Are you having one?'

He shakes his head. 'I'm out of practice. I need to pace myself.'

'None of us can drink as much as we used to.'

'I don't want to.' He rubs his thumb along his lower lip. 'There's a lot about myself I want to change, Lynne. I've had a lot of time to think about how I can do things differently.'

I look into his soft, kind eyes. 'I think you're a good enough man already.'

'I'm going to make sure my kids never go through anything like that again.'

His kids don't have to worry about him any more. Not now I'm here. I ask how he's getting on with Colette and try not to look disappointed when he says he hasn't told her about me yet. He needs to get it right; I understand that. She sounds like a lovely girl, and I'm sure she'll want what's best for him.

If I had kids, I'd want them to be accepting of Sandy. I always hoped to be a mum, but it never happened for me. I was wise enough to keep taking the pill when I was with my waste-of-space first husband, and my second husband said he didn't want a kid coming between the two of us. I thought that was romantic at first, but his constant monitoring of my contraception got me down after a while.

Manlio appears with our wine and pours a small amount for Sandy to try.

'Oh no,' I say when Sandy pushes the glass over to me. 'I've not got the palate for it.'

'Wine is easy,' he says, 'you either like it or you don't.'

Heat floods into my cheeks as I take a sip. 'I like it,' I say, hoping he won't ask me to elaborate on notes and hints and all the other things wine people talk about.

'That's good enough for me,' says Sandy.

Manlio pours for us. Before he turns away, I hold out my phone and ask him to take a picture of us.

'Of course,' he says.

Sandy and I clink our glasses together while Manlio takes several snaps.

'This lady is *bellissima*, no?' he says to Sandy.

'Yes,' Sandy says, 'she's very beautiful.'

My heart swells. What did I do to deserve a man like this?

'Just nipping to the bathroom,' Sandy says when Manlio hands my phone back.

Once he's gone, I inspect the photographs. The first shot is perfect. Both of us beaming with happiness. I send it to Carol. The first time I showed her a photo of Sandy, she said when a man was that hand-some a woman needed to look out.

When Sandy returns, he lifts his wine glass again. 'To us,' he says.

'To the future.' My pulse flutters at the first of many toasts we will share.

Our starter of buffalo mozzarella and cold-cut meats arrives. It doesn't take us long to demolish that and then comes the pasta course. Spaghetti with a simple tomato sauce. When I leave half of mine, Sandy polishes it off.

'Good lord,' I say when the rack of lamb appears. 'It's huge.'

'Should I ask them to cut it up for you?' Sandy says.

'No need.' I pick up my meat knife, slide it between two rib bones and cut myself off a rare, bloody chop. 'My first husband came in handy for something.'

Colin was a whizz with his knives and taught me a thing or two. Sometimes I'd help in the shop when he was busy. He thought the carcasses hanging in the back would make me queasy, but I had the stomach for it.

'That's right, I forgot he was a butcher,' Sandy says.

I've told Sandy everything about myself. Almost everything. Ours is not a relationship based on lies.

The meat is delicious, and I can't resist eating all of it. When Manlio clears our plates away, we tell him we'll share one dessert between us. When our plate of *sfogliatella* arrives, I eat one of the cream-filled pastries and let Sandy have the rest.

'That was heaven,' he says after swallowing the last mouthful. A waitress walks past holding two large pizzas on wooden boards. 'Next time, we'll try some of those.'

Next time. Happy tears hot in my throat. Here we are, the two of us, making memories on the outside. Discussing future experiences we'll enjoy together. I'm so overwhelmed with emotion that if Sandy were to drop to his knees and propose right now, I don't think I'd be able to get my words out.

* * *

After leaving the restaurant, we walk to the Promenade des Anglais. Part of me wants us to get straight back to the apartment and into bed, but I'm also glad of a walk to let some of this food go down. Sandy's arm around my waist is a welcome support. My wedge-heeled sandals are a bit lethal after half a bottle of wine.

It's getting dark when we arrive. The street lamps

are on all along the promenade, and the lights of all the buildings that line the bay and cluster in the hills make the view each way sparkle. I can still see traces of sunset. Behind the hills to the west, near the airport, the sky is pale blue with streaks of dusky pink. Patches of smoky cloud drift over the bay.

'It's gorgeous,' I say. I've only been on the promenade in the daytime so far and it has a more romantic feel to it now. Sandy and I aren't the only couple with our arms wrapped around one another.

'I do appreciate you being here,' he says. 'You taking a few months off work to be with me means the world.'

'Where else would I be?' I will tell him I've quit my job. When the time's right.

'My friends certainly aren't rushing to get in touch.' He sighs. 'I thought they might call once I got out.'

'Give them time.'

He shakes his head. 'They're not like you, Lynne. They don't believe in me like you do.'

'More fool them.'

'How can they think I was guilty?' His voice is low with anger. 'I was happily married for years, and now I'm in a relationship with a woman my own age. Hardly like I'm chasing young bits of skirt around.'

We're in a relationship. Hearing him say it makes me so happy.

He spins me round and holds me so tight I can barely breathe. 'If it wasn't for you, I might end up believing I'm as bad as they think.' He dips his head and kisses me. A group of teenagers walking past rewards us with applause and wolf whistles.

'Give over,' I say, when he lets me go, but I'm so happy I could cry. Now I understand we were right to come out together, in public, where everyone can see us. We've nothing to hide from. Nothing to be ashamed of.

'Hang on.' Sandy takes his phone out of his pocket. 'I want a picture of you.'

'Daft sod,' I say, but he is already jogging backwards. When he stops and raises his phone, I twist to one side and lift the back of my right foot, like celebrities do on the red carpet. After the flash on his camera goes off several times, he gives me the thumbs-up to signal he's done.

The strap of my right sandal has come undone. I bend over to fasten it again, and when I straighten up, I see Sandy talking to a young woman. Or rather she's talking to him. She's standing in the shadow between two street lamps, but I can see she's slim with wavy dark hair just skimming her shoulders. She's wearing insanely high stilettos and a backless mini-dress so short I catch a glimpse of her red lacy knickers.

She's not talking *to* Sandy, she's talking *at* him. In French. Her voice is raised and her arms flap wildly about her. She seems angry. When he walks away from her, she grabs hold of his shirt. He shakes her off and holds up his hands to her as if to warn her to back off. When she carries on yelling at him, he takes his wallet from his jeans pocket and hands her a wad of cash.

'What's going on?' I say when he reaches me.

'Nothing.' His hand presses into the small of my back as he guides me along the promenade, away from the woman.

'Who was that?'

'No one.'

'She looked like she knew you.'

Sandy glances over his shoulder. I do the same. The woman has gone.

The fears and insecurities that come from two marriages to unfaithful men rise up in me. I know I should press my lips together and seal my fears inside, but I can't help myself.

'Sandy,' I say, 'who was she?'

20

COLETTE

On the first day of June, a Friday, I wake just after 7 a.m. to find Dad has gone jogging without me. Again. His bedroom is empty, his bedcovers knotted together at the centre of his mattress. Yesterday, when he returned from his solo run, he apologised and said he hadn't slept much and needed to get out in the fresh air. Did he sleep badly again last night too?

The dark mood that made him drive our car so close to the cliff edge on the Grand Corniche hasn't lifted. He keeps retreating into himself, his face taken over by dark shadows. When he catches me watching him, he snaps out of it and puts on a show of cheerfulness, but I can tell our trip and his thoughts of the past have unsettled him.

They have unsettled me, too. A week has passed since our trip to Cannes, but I can still sense Ella Watson here in our home, coming between us. The day after Cannes, a Saturday, Dad went for a drive on his own. He was gone from early morning until late afternoon and gave only vague answers to my enquiries about where he'd been. He claimed he'd spent the day driving up and down the coast, enjoying his freedom. I wanted to press him for details but after all his time in prison, I don't want him thinking of me as another jailer. I trust him, of course I do, but I still like to know where he is.

In the hallway outside his room, I trip over his plimsolls. With a sigh I pick them up and return them to the shoe rack by the front door. I've asked him several times to put his shoes away properly but leaving them lying around has always been a bad habit of his. It used to drive Mum crazy. In prison he had to keep his cramped cell immaculate, but now he's out he seems to want to spread his belongings all over the place. While he was inside, I cleaned the flat myself, but now we're both here I should ask the cleaners who work for this block to come every few weeks. Dad's grown so used to me doing his laundry he now leaves his dirty clothes in the drum of the washing machine for me to deal with. When he was in business, he always had a secretary or a personal assistant sorting his life out for him. Smart, efficient, middle-aged women, all of them vetted by Mum.

In the living room, I open the balcony doors. Soon it will be time to start using the air con but for now it's good to let the cooler morning air in. Outside, a beautiful morning beckons. At least this year I can enjoy the bright blue slide into summer without worrying about Dad being too hot in prison. At times I couldn't enjoy the sunshine, thinking about him sweating it out in his cell without air conditioning.

I make myself a cup of green tea and think about the day ahead. I have a new piece to start for work. Copy for the website of a luxury safari lodge in South Africa's Kruger National Park. If Dad's here, I'll have to go out to a café or to the nearby public library to work. He seems unable to be in the flat without the TV on loud in the background. The noise makes it impossible for me to concentrate, even in my bedroom. Still, I'd much rather he was here, annoying me with his habits, than back in prison.

He does try to be considerate. A few nights ago, when I was wrestling with a work deadline, he insisted on going out so I could have the place to myself. I was surprised to see him all dressed up in his new jeans and a black linen shirt, but he said it was time he got out and about. He said he was going for a few beers in the old town, followed by dinner out. I did offer to join him later for the meal, but he said I should concentrate on my work and enjoy having the flat to myself. He was gone for a long time, and I found it hard to relax. I couldn't help fearing he might not return and that I'd get a phone call from the police telling me he'd been arrested.

When I fill up the kettle to make a fresh cup of tea, I notice an empty Shiraz bottle next to the sink. The new one I bought yesterday and hadn't opened. Next to it a wine glass, stained red. Dad must have stayed up after I'd gone to bed and drunk the whole bottle.

I glance around the apartment. The hollow ache in my stomach feels like a warning something unpleasant is waiting for me. That's when I notice my blue box file on the sofa. The file where I keep all the newspaper articles related to Dad's arrest and the trial. It also contains the legal paperwork I've collected over the years. Dad must have found it in the sideboard when he was looking for something else.

I hurry over to the sofa. The contents of the file are strewn all over the cushions. Lifting a pile of papers, I find his MacBook Air underneath. I picture him sitting up alone, drinking, reading through all the lies journalists have written about him and surfing the Internet for more stories about himself. As I gather up the various papers, I come across one of the *Nice-Matin* articles.

La femme travaillait à La Cave à Vin le soir où
Sandy Gilligan…

Dad must have been thinking about Ella last night as he read through the contents of this box. How can he move on from the past with memories like this surrounding him? He's already paid a heavy price for a crime he didn't commit. If he's not careful, his thoughts of her might become a prison. I think of him sitting in the car after I made him stop at the viewpoint. That haunted look on his face.

I'd love to know what she's up to now.

If he was searching for her online last night, he would have hit a dead end like I did. Surely, he wouldn't try to track her down? Then again, she has cost him so much, and Dad has never been one to let a grudge go. I remember arriving home from school one afternoon, aged fourteen, to find my parents drinking a bottle of Möet & Chandon. When I asked what they were celebrating, Dad said he'd put a rival out of business by taking a major hospital laundry contract from him. I must have looked a bit shocked because Mum then explained this rival had pulled a similar stunt ten years ago. A stunt that had nearly cost Dad everything. Dad refilled his glass and toasted his own patience. *I always knew I'd get him in the end.*

* * *

I dress in a hurry – shorts, T-shirt and flip-flops – and take the file and a box of matches downstairs to the gardens. No one in sight. The air is filled with the citrusy scent coming from the orange trees and a light breeze stirs the branches of the stone pines.

On a paved area by the garden wall sits the communal barbecue. A black, shiny monster, meant for cooking up steaks and burgers for large numbers of people. I contributed to its purchase last year, even though I've never used it, nor been invited to any of the meals cooked on it.

The lid lifts without a noise, the hinges well-greased, probably by Ronnie, who usually volunteers for such jobs. He's the secretary of the block's committee. Kathy, of course, is the chairwoman.

I scatter the contents of the box file inside, light a match and hold it to the closest sheet of paper. When the corner flares and curls, I wonder if I'm doing the right thing. During the trial, I spent so long keeping track of anything that appeared in the press, as well as all the paperwork from Dad's lawyer, just in case the verdict didn't go our way. Even after we failed to get an appeal, I kept hold of everything, both in digital and print form, as if being informed and prepared could lessen what Dad was going through. The idea of letting go makes me feel vulnerable. Still, it must be done. We have to move on. The less Dad thinks about the past and about her, the better.

I pick up the tongs attached to the side of the barbecue and prod the burgeoning flames. A burst of breeze comes to my aid, making the flames leap and surge.

'Morning.'

I turn to find Kathy behind me, her tanned, skinny legs encased in black Lycra shorts, Ramona squirming in her arms.

'Hello, Kathy.'

Another burst of breeze, this one large enough to lift a sheet of paper not yet consumed by the flames and blow it to the ground. Ramona wriggles and yaps until Kathy puts her down. The scrawny dog pounces on the piece of newspaper.

'Ramona, my sweet. Leave that alone.'

Ramona is standing on the *Nice-Matin* article I looked at earlier, her tiny paws padding back and forth across it. Kathy bends down and picks up the paper, holding it between her thumb and forefinger as if it might infect her.

'Probably a good idea to get rid of all that,' she says, waving the article in front of her. 'I don't suppose you want to be reminded of what he did.'

I snatch it back, suppressing the urge to tell Kathy to go fuck herself.

'I suppose anyone can still read about it online if they want to,' she adds.

The paper in the barbecue has burned itself into black roses with glowing hearts.

'Remember to empty the ashes when you're done,' Kathy said, nodding at the laminated set of instructions attached to the side of the barbecue.

'Yes, Kathy.' I wag the hot tongs in her direction. 'I'll be sure to follow the rules.'

I don't know what she sees in my expression, but she bends down, gathers Ramona up in her arms and stalks off.

I return the article to the flames and watch it catch light. As the blackened edges move towards the centre of the paper, I see the same fragment I read before.

The woman was working at La Cave à Vin the night that Sandy Gilligan…

The words vanish, devoured by the flames. It gives me some satisfaction to see Ella Watson gone. As if the ritual of burning might finally cleanse her from our lives. I'll never forget the smile that flashed across her face when the guilty verdict came. At that moment, I hated her. Can I really blame Dad for hating her too?

21

COLETTE

When I return to the apartment, Dad is already back from his run. He must have come in through the front entrance to the block. He's sitting at the kitchen island with a bowl of muesli in front of him, his grey T-shirt stained with sweat.

'You were out early,' I say.

He swallows a mouthful of cereal. 'Couldn't sleep.'

He has a copy of the *Independent* spread out in front of him. Every day for the past week he's bought a copy of a British newspaper. He keeps reading out random snippets about British politics to me or stories from the sports pages. It makes me feel like we're exiles, nostalgic for the country we can't return to. All the anger I thought I just burned away comes rushing back.

Dad spots the matches in my hand and the empty box file. 'Where have you been?'

'In the gardens.'

He points his spoon at the box file. 'I was wondering where that had gone. Did you tidy all that stuff away?'

I hesitate. A childish dread of being told off comes over me. 'I burned it all.'

'Christ, Colette,' he snaps. 'Why?'

The anger in his voice makes me recoil. 'What's the point of going over it all?'

'I needed to remind myself what people said about me.'

During the trial, Odette, Dad's lawyer, had advised him not to read anything the press had written. Their stories played down his dual national status to create a narrative about a foreigner picking on a vulnerable Englishwoman. One he thought would be too afraid to report the crime to a foreign police force and pursue it in a foreign court. As though Dad had planned that night and selected his 'victim'. The coverage made much of the number of assaults that go unreported each year by tourists and visitors. Journalists revelled in what they perceived as Dad picking the wrong woman to mess with. A young woman unafraid. A shining example to everyone.

'I burned everything because you were angry the other day,' I say. 'About her.'

Dad pushes his cereal bowl away. 'Come on, love. This is silly.'

'You were angry about Ella. You said so.'

'I was angry. Yes.'

'You can't ever speak to her again,' I said. 'You do know that?'

'Colette, I'm not—'

'Your lawyer said so. You can't make any attempt to find her or contact her.'

'Is that what this is about?'

'You said you'd love to know what she was up to now.' I want him to understand I'm worried about him. I want him free of the past for good.

'I was just sounding off. I don't care about Ella. Trust me.'

'I know, I just—'

'Trust me, I'm not interested in her.' Dad comes over to me and puts his hands on my shoulders. 'I'm not interested in her at all.'

I search his eyes and find only truth there. Truth and a hint of a smile.

'Maybe burning it all was a bit dramatic?' he says.

'Don't tease me.'

'Did you cast a spell while you were doing it?'

'Shut up.' I can't help smiling. 'Kathy wasn't too chuffed when she saw me.'

'I bet. She won't fancy cooking a steak over my remains.'

'I'll clear the barbecue out later.'

'Good idea. Keep the neighbours happy.' Dad kisses the top of my head before returning to his seat at the breakfast bar. 'What are your plans today?'

'Work.' I have a new piece to start about a honeymoon resort just opened in the Maldives. The thought of enthusing about romance and marriage doesn't fill me with joy, but I couldn't refuse the work. 'I think I'll go to the library for a few hours. If you'll be okay here?'

'Course I will. Do you want breakfast before you go?'

'I'll get something on the way.' The café next to the library does a great pain au chocolat. Although maybe I shouldn't indulge. I have lost a few pounds since Dad's been back.

By the time I'm ready to leave, Dad is on the sofa with the newspaper on his lap and the TV news on.

'Have fun,' he says as I haul my backpack on to my shoulders.

'Love you,' I say as I head for the front door.

* * *

Five minutes into my walk to the library, I realise I've forgotten my laptop charger. I can see it plugged into my bedroom wall. I meant to charge my computer last night and forgot, which means it won't last even an hour this morning.

Annoyed at my forgetfulness, I turn and head for home. When I reach our block, I enter through the front entrance and take the stairs two at a time.

I hear Dad's voice as soon as I let myself into the apartment. Something in his voice, a hard edge to it, makes me stop, just inside the door.

'Miguel told me to contact you,' he says. He is on the phone, in his bedroom, his voice drifting down the hall. 'That's right. We shared a cell for a while.'

Who is he talking to?

'He told me you're the best,' Dad says. 'Is that true?'

My stomach knots.

'I know it'll cost me. I can pay.'

I should leave now. Before I hear any more.

'Good,' Dad says. 'I need you to find someone for me. A woman.'

22

LYNNE

I open the living-room windows and look out on to another glorious Côte d'Azur morning. Only seven o'clock and the sun is already giving off heat. The sky is the kind of blue that makes me feel hopeful. Not even the miserable toll of the tram bell as it glides along Boulevard Jean Jaurès can get to me. It's going to be a glorious Saturday.

The street below is slowly coming to life. Lots of folk out walking their dogs. I spot Amira, the teenage girl who works at the Carrefour a few doors along from here. She's loitering near the shop entrance, smoking a cigarette. She must be about to start her shift. She's been ever so patient when I've practiced my terrible French on her at the checkout.

'*Bonjour*, Amira.'

She hears me calling out and looks up, a puzzled expression on her face. When I wave, she gives me a hesitant wave back. She still looks half-asleep, bless her.

I'm about to ask how she is today – *comment ça va?* – when I see Sandy jogging down the street in his black shorts and grey T-shirt. Bang on time as usual. When he gets closer, he looks up at my window and waves. I blow him a kiss in return. I imagine him dropping to one knee in front of Amira and all the passers-by and shouting a proposal of marriage up to me. Everyone will stop and look up, all eyes on me, waiting for my reply. When I accept, they'll burst into applause and everyone in the stores along the street will come out to see what all the fuss is about and the people in the flats opposite me will come to their windows and Sandy and I will ignore them all, eyes only for each other.

* * *

When I let him into the flat, he is all breathless and sweaty. We kiss in the hallway. He smells of plain soap, stale aftershave and sweat. So sexy.

I'm wearing the black silk robe I bought with

Sandy in mind. He's seen me in it before, but he's still not untied it and ripped it off me like I want him to.

My hands caress the front of his shorts. He moans.

'You, Lynne Collins, are a very naughty girl,' he says.

'I could be.' I wrap my arms around him. 'Take me to bed and you'll find out.'

'Don't tempt me.'

'I want to tempt you.'

'So naughty.' He removes my arms, brings my hands to his lips and kisses them. 'Like I said the other night, I can wait.'

'We don't have to.'

'I don't want our first time to be rushed.' He kisses my hands again. 'You deserve more than a quickie against the wall.'

'You're right,' I say, although I'd settle for a quickie anywhere right now.

'I have brought you breakfast.' He holds up a greasy brown paper bag.

'Well, that'll do me for now.' A lie, but I don't want to pressure him.

We move through to the living area. While Sandy goes to the bathroom for a quick wash, I make us a cafetière of coffee. Be patient, I tell myself, you're lucky he's still here after the way you behaved the other night.

Makes me cringe, recalling how I spoke to Sandy on the promenade. Turned out the woman who had a go at him was a prostitute. She'd approached Sandy, touting her wares, and when he said he wasn't interested she got all aggressive. When I asked why he'd given her money, he said he wanted to get her off the streets for a night. He said the poor girl was someone's daughter after all. According to him, the promenade is a popular haunt for hookers. I've researched it online since then, and he's not lying.

After he explained everything, we left the promenade and walked back here. I was hoping he'd stay so we could finally be together, but at the front door he excused himself and said he should get home. He assured me I'd done nothing wrong. He needed time to adjust, he said, he'd not been with a woman for nearly five years. I remembered then that his last sexual encounter had landed him in jail. No wonder he needs to go slow with me. What's the rush, anyway? As he's told me countless times, we'll be spending the rest of our lives together.

'I can't stay that long,' Sandy says when he emerges from the bathroom. 'Colette will be waiting for me.'

He's been sneaking out of his apartment the past few mornings. It's nice he wants to see me so badly, but him lying about our relationship reminds me of Brian Williams. After my second marriage ended, I started working in the council tax department of Chelmsford County Council and that's where I met Brian. He'd been married for eight years and had three children under six years old. Our affair lasted two years. At first, I didn't mind being his mistress, but the constant waiting around and fitting into his schedule did become upsetting.

I pour out two mugs of coffee, add milk, and bring them over to the sofa where Sandy has settled himself.

'Thanks, love,' he says, taking both mugs from me and putting them on the coffee table. 'How about a plate for this breakfast of yours?'

I fetch the plate and sit down next to Sandy. He opens the greasy paper bag, puts a pain au chocolat on the plate and hands it to me. There is wonder, even in the small things with Sandy. The fact he's sitting next to me, a free man, handing me breakfast. I should be grateful for such miracles.

'This is so good,' I say, after my first bite of the warm, soft pastry. 'Too good.' I break a piece off and hand it to Sandy who wolfs it down.

'I need all this running just to keep myself trim,' he says.

'Give over, there's nothing of you.' I tear off another buttery chunk of pastry for myself. 'I'll be needing a diet soon.'

'You, lady, are perfect just as you are.'

We share a chocolatey kiss.

'Thanks for being so patient with me,' he says when we part. 'I do appreciate it.'

I don't feel patient. I want to drag him into the bedroom and do everything I've fantasised about for the past two years. Then again, I should be glad Sandy's a man with some self-restraint. Brian was all about the sex. Any chance he could get, even in the ladies' toilets of the council building on our tea break. Sandy's not like Brian. Not at all. I've always known he didn't attack that girl, but his behaviour towards me is even further proof. He's hardly a man unable to contain himself.

'It's lovely just to be here with you,' he says. 'I've never been into that mindfulness stuff, but when I'm with you, I get it. Being in the moment is enough.'

I clink my coffee mug against his. 'To being here in this moment,' I say, even though there's a ton of not-in-the-moment stuff we need to discuss at some point. A proposal, for starters. An engagement party, if we even want one at our age? And the wedding of course. So much to sort out.

Steady, Lynne, I think. Let the poor guy catch his breath.

'You know what I love about being with you?' he says, just as I put a huge chunk of pastry in my mouth.

I shake my head and keep chewing.

'I don't think about the past when we're together.' He tucks a stray strand of hair behind my ear. 'You don't know what a relief that is.'

I swallow my half-chewed mouthful and smile. More chance of him thinking about our future if he isn't fixated on his past. His lack of bitterness about it all is admirable. He could complain non-stop about the lies that girl told that put him in prison. He could have done more in court to show her up for the liar she is, but, as he told me, he didn't feel comfortable humiliating her. Not when she was, after all, another man's daughter and nearly the same age as his own.

'I wish Colette didn't worry about it all so much,' he says. 'She's a great kid and she's done so much for me, but she needs to let the past go. For both our sakes.'

A buzzing sound. Sandy pulls his phone from the pocket of his shorts.

'Colette?' I say.

'Sorry, I need to take this.' He gets up from the sofa. 'Hello.' He hurries out of the room, the phone pressed to his ear. I hear his footsteps as he makes his way to the bathroom. The bathroom door opens and shuts.

I pick up my empty plate, but instead of going over to the sink I leave the room and hover in the hallway outside the bathroom.

'Yes, I'm happy with those terms,' Sandy says, his tone curt and businesslike. 'Yes, she's my priority. She's the one I need.' Silence as he listens to the person on the other end of the phone. 'Can't talk now. I'll have to call you back.'

I tiptoe to the kitchen and clatter my plate into the sink, humming as I wash it beneath the running tap. Who's this 'she'? Why is 'she' his priority? He certainly wasn't talking to Colette. He sounded abrupt. Cold. Maybe that's his business voice. They do say you need a killer instinct to make a lot of money in this life. Maybe 'she' has got something to do with a business deal of his.

When he returns to the room, he sidles up behind me. 'Right, better get going.' His lips nuzzle into my neck. 'God, you're beautiful.'

'You old charmer.' I consider asking again if he was

speaking to Colette but stop myself. What if he says yes? If he does, I'll know he's lying.

Don't go down that road, Lynne. Don't give in to suspicion. That's when all the trouble starts.

23

JANE

Half an hour into our drive to Marseilles, Michel takes one hand off the steering wheel of our Citröen C3 and gives my shoulder a rub.

'You okay?' he says.

'I'm good.' My voice is a little too high. A little too bright.

'You look tired.'

'I didn't sleep that well.' I didn't sleep at all, but I feel wide awake. All my senses on high alert.

He puts his hand back on the steering wheel to overtake the white transit van ahead of us in the slow lane. It is almost 10 a.m. but the A8 is already busy with Saturday traffic. The forecast is for a hot June day, with temperatures up to 29 degrees in Marseilles by lunchtime.

Perfect weather for lunch with an old friend.

'Maman, Maman.' Theo, already bored of being strapped into his child seat behind us, digs the toes of his red Kickers boots into the back of my seat.

'Stop it, *bébé*,' I say.

Perfect weather for a nice family day out.

A smacking sound behind me as Theo bounces his heels off the back seat.

'That's enough.' I turn and give him a warning glare. He glares back. His challenging mood started when I was getting him washed and dressed this morning.

'*J'ai faim*,' he says.

When I tell him he should have eaten his breakfast like I asked him to, his heels start a drum roll of fury against the seat.

'Give him a snack bar.' Michel glances into his rear-view mirror and tuts as a motorbike zooms past us.

'He should have eaten his breakfast.' I search in my handbag, find a sugar-free snack bar and unwrap it. 'What do you say?' I ask my son as I pass it back to him.

'*Merci, merci, merci*,' he shouts.

'Come on, Theo,' Michel says, 'that's not cool.'

'Sorry, Papa.'

My forehead throbs. I take my sunglasses out of my bag and put them on. 'I hope he's not going to be like this all day.'

'He'll settle down,' Michel says.

'Maybe he remembers what happened last time we went to Marseilles,' I say.

'How could he? He was ten months old.'

'So?' I lower my voice. 'What if it's stored in his subconscious somewhere?'

'Hey,' Michel says, eyes fixed on the road, 'I thought we were over all that?'

'I'm just saying he—'

'You weren't well back then. Things are different now.'

'You're right,' I say, wanting out of the conversation. 'Ignore me.'

I sink back into my seat. A week has passed since I thought I saw Sandy in the market square. Maybe it wasn't him. Maybe he is trying to get on with his life and wants to forget about the past as much as I do. Maybe my fears only exist in my imagination.

But what if I am wrong?

I am afraid he will come for me. I am afraid he

filled those dark, lonely hours in prison with thoughts of what he might do to me.

'Music, Papa,' Theo says. 'Please.'

Michel turns on the radio. Donna Summer's 'I Feel Love' fills the car.

'*C'est un classique, mon fils*,' Michel says to Theo. '*C'est un classique.*'

Theo wriggles in his seat. '*C'est disco.*'

'*Oui, c'est disco.*' Michel turns to me and smiles. Ignoring the throbbing in my forehead, I smile back. How is he to know this song reminds me of Sandy?

That night, after I finished my shift, Sandy and I went to a nearby nightclub and drank vodka shots before hitting the dance floor. The music was 1970s disco. Sandy shouted in my ear that he liked the music. It was his era. I danced close to him, moving my body against his. I liked the sense of power my youth gave me. I could see the desire in his eyes, his hunger for me.

'Maman,' Theo wails when I switch the radio off.

'My head's killing me,' I say.

Michel gives me a concerned look. 'Maman has a headache,' he tells Theo.

A motorway marker warns me we are only thirty kilometres from Marseilles. Anxiety cramps my stomach. This city holds nothing but dark memories for me.

'Hey.' Michel's hand on my thigh. 'You okay?'

I nod but keep my eyes closed.

'It's all good,' he says. 'The past is behind us now.'

Poor Michel. He thinks he knows why I am anxious. He thinks he knows why today might be difficult for me. He does not have a clue.

* * *

By the time we reach the outskirts of the city, my headache is intense. Mostly due to my son crying for the rest of the journey. Michel parks as close to the old port as he can, on a steep street of tall tenement buildings. Yellow facades and white wrought-iron balconies. Washing hangs from some of them and flaps in the sea breeze.

I get out of the car and inhale my first lungful of Marseilles air. I am here. My heart is pounding, my stomach churning with fear.

Theo, who has swapped crying for intermittent grizzling, makes a fuss about going in his buggy. Michel explains we have a lot of distance to cover, but Theo pulls the old trick of keeping his body too stiff and straight to go into the buggy. I long to slap him on

the back of his legs, even though one of the non-nego-
tiable parenting rules Michel and I have is never to
smack our son. Michel's parents never smacked him,
and he would never dream of hitting Theo. My parents
often kept us in line with 'good hidings', a family tradition I have no intention of carrying on.

'No buggy,' Theo says, his small voice anguished.
What if he is picking up on my fear and misbehaving
because of it? The thought fills me with guilt.

'Fine.' Michel takes Theo's hand and gives me the
empty buggy to push. By the time we reach the end of
the street, Theo's hands are up in the air. With a sigh,
Michel scoops him up and carries him. 'Only until we
get to the port. Then it's buggy. Okay?'

'Okay, Papa.' Theo kisses Michel's head, a gesture
that makes my heart soften.

'We're going to have fun today,' I tell my son. We
are. For Theo's sake, I am going to show Sandy
Gilligan I am not afraid to be here. I am going to prove
to myself that the past does not control me.

We walk down towards the old port. The sights
and sounds of Marseilles assault us. Theo insists we
stop and watch a group of men break-dancing outside
a metro station. So much colour everywhere. The sun
highlights the bright buildings and the copious graffiti.

Michel takes us down to the Quai de Rive Neuve.

We walk along it, holding Theo's hands, showing him the yachts and motorboats. I look across to the other side of the port. I can't help thinking of Sandy and me walking late at night next to the sea.

Theo starts crying. As if he is acting out my hidden feelings.

'Hey.' I pick him up and ask if he wants a hot chocolate.

'*Oui*,' he says, through his tears. I hate Sandy. I can't help thinking my son's distress is his fault. Everything I've done, both before and after the trial, has been to protect the people I love. What if it has all been for nothing?

We traipse several streets back from the waterfront and sit on the terrace of a trendy vegan café. A black girl with waves tattooed on her slender arms comes to take our order. She coaxes a smile out of Theo when she returns with his hot chocolate, but he soon starts whining again. The family at the next table have twin girls in a double buggy. Blonde angels sucking quietly on the spouts of their drinking beakers. Their mother shoots me a condescending look when Theo refuses to sit still on my lap. Fatigue and irritation swamp my determination to make a success of the day.

'He's doing my head in,' I say, passing him to Michel.

'He's just over-excited.' Michel places Theo on his lap while I pour the hot chocolate into his beaker.

Michel's phone pings. He picks it up from the table and checks the screen. 'Giles is confirming one o'clock for lunch.'

'If Theo even lasts until then.' I push my chair back from the table and stand up.

'Where are you going?' Michel says.

'For a walk.'

'Sit down. We'll go together when we're finished.'

'I need to clear my head.'

'Maman,' Theo says.

'You can't just go off.' Panic flits across my husband's face.

'I won't be long.'

I leave them sitting there and hurry back to the old port. I know where I have to go. Heart racing, I walk past the opera house to the other side of the water, the Quai de Port. The route to the InterContinental is fresh in my mind. I looked the hotel up online when I couldn't sleep last night. A bad idea, but I couldn't stop myself.

As soon as I hit the Quai de Port, I veer right up a narrow street that leads me to the Grand Rue and into the heart of the Panier district. There, on Place Daviel is the InterContinental, an imposing, nineteenth-century building opened by Napoleon III and built on the site of what had been a hospital for eight hundred years.

I know all about the InterContinental Hôtel.

A pleasant numbness washes over me as I climb the wide stone steps to the hotel's entrance. Inside, the reception area is spacious and cool, the decor sleek and modern. The staff behind the desk smile as I walk past, and I smile back, as if I belong here. A smile I maintain while following the signs to the lifts.

I don't take the first lift available. I wait until a tall, elderly man steps into one, his room key ready to enable it.

'What floor?' he asks in a clipped Nordic accent when I join him.

'Three. Thank you.'

He passes his card key over the control panel. The lift sets off, smooth and quiet. Standing beside the stranger, I think of Sandy and me side by side in a lift, heading up to his room, still buzzing with energy from the nightclub. Me still radiant with my false sense of power.

At floor three the doors slide open. I hesitate, my legs weak beneath me.

'This is you,' the man says.

I step out into the corridor. Dark carpet underfoot. Subtle uplights on the wall.

Room 303. They put the room number in one of the news articles. *The alleged attack took place in room 303 of the InterContinental in Marseilles.* When I reach it, I half-expect to see crime-scene tape across the door. Instead, the door is open, and a housekeeping trolley stacked with towels and toiletries sits outside it.

I should turn and walk away. I should go back to my husband and my son.

A crackling noise. A chambermaid comes out of the room, leaving the door wide open. She has a walkie-talkie in her hand. '*Oui,*' she says into it. '*Pas de problème.*'

As soon as she disappears, I slip into the room. It is a large space decorated in cream and numerous shades of brown. A vast king-size bed at the centre, busy with plumped-up cushions. Lampshades hang from the ceiling at varying heights. Glass doors open on to a small balcony, which has a view of the Basilique Notre-Dame.

This was where it happened.

I sit on the edge of the bed, my pulse jumping, my mouth dry.

Here, in this room, on this bed.

Here, in this room, Sandy Gilligan raped another

victim. Another barmaid. La Cave à Vin is a small chain of wine bars, and this barmaid, Ella Watson, worked at the one in Marseilles. It has almost identical decor to the one I worked at in Cannes. Sandy picked her up at the end of her shift, took her to a nightclub and then brought her back here to this room, where he raped her, just as he'd raped me in the Majestic Hôtel in Cannes two years previously.

I lie on the bed and look up at the ceiling. Did his victim look at the very same spot during her ordeal? I pick up a thick velvet cushion, place it over my face and press down on it. The soft, deadly pressure makes me want to scream. A violent rush of panic makes me throw the cushion to the floor.

'*Madame?*'

The housekeeping girl has returned. She stands at the end of the bed, looking down at me, her dark eyes wide with concern. '*Madame? Puis-je vous aider?*'

PART III

24

COLETTE

I'm worried about him. Five days have passed since I overheard him on the phone, but I've said nothing. I've no idea who he was speaking to, but I'm sure he's trying to find Ella Watson.

I have, however, been keeping an eye on him. Today, my alarm goes off early and I'm up and into my running gear before he can leave the apartment.

'Ready when you are,' I say, knocking on his bedroom door. For the past few days, I've stuck to this routine so he can't sneak off in the mornings without me.

'Give me a few minutes,' he says, his voice groggy with sleep.

When he comes into the living room, I'm already stretching out my sore calves.

'Are you sure you want to come?' he says. 'You really struggled yesterday.'

'It's good for me,' I say, my leg muscles telling me otherwise. 'I think I'm having a fitness breakthrough.'

He shrugs. 'Up to you, kiddo.'

By the time we reach the port and turn on to Quai Rauba Capeu, I have a stitch in my side and sweat running down my back. The sky is predictably blue and the sun shining down on us will take the temperatures into the high twenties by noon.

'Need a quick breather,' I say.

We stop for a moment by the sea wall and look down on to Rauba Capeu beach. A homeless man and woman lie side by side on a tattered blanket, both wearing eye masks to block out the morning light.

'Isn't it a gorgeous day?' Dad says. The dark mood that plagued him after our trip to Cannes has lifted. I wish I felt as cheerful. After overhearing him on the phone, I didn't know what to do. I crept out of the flat and closed the front door as quietly as I could. I went to the library as planned and stared at my laptop screen without writing a word until the battery ran out. When I returned home, I found him with a big smile on his face and a biscuit tin in his hands. The one where I used to store my treats. Inside were the ashes from the barbecue. Dad had scooped them out and kept them. He said my weird ritual had worked; he felt happier already. He suggested we scatter the ashes somewhere. Make a symbolic burial of the past.

We brought the ashes here, to this beach that isn't really a beach, and we threw them into the bay.

'Okay,' Dad says, 'ready to rock and roll?'

I nod, and we set off again. His recent positivity makes me doubt what I overheard that day. After we gave the ashes to the sea, Dad put an arm around me and pulled me close. He told me we were done with the past. Time to embrace our future.

Surely, he wouldn't do anything to ruin that? I could confess to overhearing the phone call and ask him to put my mind at rest, but I don't want to spoil his good mood. I don't want to bring the darkness back.

By the time we reach the Promenade, my lungs are burning, and my thighs are rubbery and unresponsive. Dad stops and shakes his head.

'Look at the state of you,' he said. 'Let's call it quits.'

'Sorry.' I bend over and take a few deep breaths. 'You go on if you want.'

He glances towards the old town. 'No, it's fine. Let's head home and eat.'

Back at the apartment, we eat a breakfast of fruit salad and rye bread toast on the balcony, Dad leafing through a copy of the *Daily Express*. The French actor,

Henri Breton, has made it into the British papers now. There is a photograph of him on page six. Dad ignores the story and turns to the sports pages at the back.

'Man City are doing well,' he says. If we weren't living here, he would watch his beloved team play regularly, like he used to when he had his VIP season ticket. Every now and then he breaks away from the newspaper to check his phone or to text. Is he waiting to hear back from whoever he spoke to a few days ago?

I need you to find someone for me. A woman.

Maybe I'm wrong to assume the woman he's looking for is Ella, but who else can it be? In the week before Dad's release, I had a final phone call with his lawyer. Odette stressed that under no circumstances should Dad contact Ella. She said sometimes offenders felt an urge to contact their victims to apologise or seek closure. I reminded her Dad was not an offender, and Ella was not his victim. She didn't respond to that. I suppose she no longer needs to care about Dad's reputation. She's made her money and now she never has to deal with him again.

'Are you okay, love?' Dad folds his newspaper in half.

'Fine.'

After breakfast, he goes to the gardens and sits in a deckchair to soak up the sun and finish reading his newspaper. I set up my laptop on the kitchen island and start work on a piece about wild swimming spots in Helsinki. I write about the clear bracing waters off Hietaranta beach as the temperature rises outside. When I break for coffee, I go out on to the balcony and look down into the gardens. Dad is sitting on a stripy deckchair under the full glare of the sun. Jean and David emerge from the entrance of the block, Kathy tagging along with them. They stop when they see Dad and, after a short, whispered conversation, they turn and disappear back inside.

Dad's phone rings. One of the shrill, standard ring-tones used only by old people or characters in TV dramas.

He answers it right away. The breeze fails to carry his words to me. I slip back inside, not wanting him to know I'm watching. Back at my laptop, my cursor blinks on the screen. *Here in the icy, restorative waters of...*

As I sip my coffee, I think again of Dad putting his business rival out of action. *I always knew I'd get him in the end.* Ella isn't business. Ella couldn't be more personal.

Maybe he's just curious. He said he'd love to know what she's up to now. To be honest, so would I. It's im-possible not to picture her in some new, perfect life with the past behind her, whereas we seem to be stuck with it.

'I'm back.' The apartment door slams as Dad bursts in. 'Don't worry, I won't disturb you.'

'It's okay if—'

'I'm heading out for a few hours.' His plimsolls echo against the tiles as he hurries down the hall to his bedroom.

Unease creeps through me. 'Where are you going?' I ask when he emerges ten minutes later in jeans and a fresh T-shirt, the scent of aftershave clinging to him.

'Out. Might walk up to the Matisse museum. Go for a coffee, maybe.'

Unease becomes anxiety. 'Dad, where are you going?'

'Makes sense for me to get out while you're working.'

'Please, don't lie to me.'

Anger flashes in his eyes, but after a few seconds, his gaze softens. 'Look,' he says, 'I didn't want to involve you, but—'

'What?'

'It's nothing.' He pulls out a stool at the kitchen island and sits opposite me. 'I've got to do a favour for someone.'

'Who?'

'A guy I was in prison with.'

My stomach lurches. 'What kind of favour?'

'Nothing bad. He was one of the good guys.' Dad runs a hand through his thinning hair. 'He asked me to find his daughter and make sure she's okay.'

'I see.' I sag in my seat, relieved my worries were unfounded. Still, there's no way I want Dad in touch with anyone from prison.

'Turns out she lives here in Nice,' Dad says. 'I thought I'd go and see her. She's in a tough situation just now, and this guy, her father, he had my back a few times in there. I thought I'd give her some money. Help her out a bit.'

Typical of Dad to want to help someone, and I know he'd hate to think of me in a similar situation. 'Sorry, but you can't help her,' I say, 'you do realise that?'

'Why?'

'I don't want you connected to anyone in that place.'

'It's only a favour for a friend.'

'No, Dad. You said prison was behind us now.'

'It is.'

'Then don't do this.' My eyes meet his. 'What if you get mixed up with dodgy people? What would the police think?'

'I just need to—'

'Please,' I say. 'For me.'

'Fine.' He sighs. 'Okay.'

'Thank you.' I give him a grateful smile. 'I knew something was troubling you. I've been worried.'

Dad glances down at the granite worktop. 'There is something else I need to tell you. Something I should have told you before.'

'What?' An icy shaft of fear down my spine. 'What is it?'

25

COLETTE

I sit at the kitchen island, my heart thumping against my ribs, trying to take in what Dad has just told me. He has a girlfriend. Lynne. Two years they were writing to each other when he was in prison. Two years, and I had no idea. How am I supposed to get my head round that?

'Did she come and visit you?' I ask.

He glances away from me. 'Only a few times.'

I thought he and I shared everything. So many nights I sat in this apartment worrying about him. Thinking he had no one else apart from me.

'I can't believe you lied to me,' I say.

'No... no. I didn't lie. I was just waiting for the right

time to tell you.' His hand reaches for mine across the kitchen island.

'Don't.' When I pull my hand away, it knocks over my mug of lukewarm coffee. 'Shit.' I grab my laptop and lift it clear of the dark liquid pooling on the granite surface.

'It's okay.' Dad leaps up and grabs a tea towel from the kitchen worktop behind him. 'Let me clear that up.'

'No,' I say, closing my laptop and putting it out of harm's way. 'I'll do it.'

With a reluctant sigh, Dad hands me the tea towel and sits down opposite me.

'I assume she's some kind of weirdo?' I say as I mop up the spilt coffee. 'Isn't that always the case with women who write to men in prison?' There must be something wrong with her. Why else would she write to him for over two years and be content with only a few visits?

'Lynne's totally normal,' Dad says. 'A good sort.'

I toss the sodden tea towel to one side. 'How old is she?'

A hurt expression flashes across Dad's face. 'Fifty.'

'Oh.' Earlier, I suspected he was about to admit to searching for Ella Watson. I should be grateful this is all he has to tell me, but instead I'm furious. 'Why you?' I ask. 'Why did she write to you?'

'We met through a prison pen pal service. We enjoyed writing to each other, and it took off from there.'

I must look unconvinced because Dad goes on to tell me Lynne has a good job, owns her own home and has been married before. When I ask if she has kids, Dad shakes his head.

'At least I won't have step-siblings to contend with,' I say.

'Steady,' Dad says. 'I've no intention of marrying her.'

'It's not serious, then?'

'Your mum was the only wife I'll ever have.' His eyes shine with tears. 'I could never replace her.'

My fury loses some of its heat. 'Lynne must be important to you. Otherwise, you wouldn't have told me about her.'

'She's been good to me, and I'm fond of her. I thought she deserved for us to get to know one another better.' He clears his throat. 'She was happy to take some time off work, and she's never been to the South of France, so we thought—'

'She's coming here?'

Dad has the guilty look of a child caught in the act. 'Actually, love, she's—'

'She's already here,' I say, 'isn't she?'

'Yes. She's been here nearly three weeks.'

Fresh fuel for my anger. 'So that's where you've been sneaking off to every morning?'

'Not all the time.'

'You've been sneaking off to have sex with your girlfriend? Jesus, Dad.'

'No.' Dad slams his hands against the granite. 'No. Lynne and I haven't... we haven't consummated our relationship.'

My stomach dips. 'I really don't want to know.'

'It's important you do know.' His eyes meet mine. 'Nothing like that's happened yet. We're taking our time. Getting to know one another.'

I know when my father is telling the truth, and he is telling it now. Not that anyone would blame him for wanting his needs met. He was in prison for nearly five years. 'Why didn't you tell me about her as soon as she came to Nice?'

'I wanted to spend time with her outside of prison so I could be sure she was worthy of meeting you.' He reaches for my hand again and this time I let him take it. 'You're my main priority. You always will be.'

I free my hand from his. 'She can't be that decent if she's been happy for you to lie to me.'

'That's on me,' he says. 'When I was in prison, Lynne asked if I'd introduce the two of you. She thought you might have liked her support.'

'Why didn't you? You knew how isolated I was.'

'I thought bringing Lynne into your life might cause you extra stress. You already had so much to deal with.' He shakes his head. 'I got it wrong. I'm sorry.'

He looks so desolate I almost get up and hug him. I hold back, still hurt by his actions. His lack of thought.

'In an odd way, she has helped you,' he says.

'What do you mean?'

'I had some low moments in jail. Really low. There were times I thought I'd never get through it.'

'Why didn't you tell me?' I knew Dad put on a cheery act whenever I visited, but I never thought prison had him beaten.

'There are some thoughts no father should ever burden a daughter with. Thanks to Lynne, I could spare you that burden.'

'Who says I needed to be spared?'

'I needed to feel I was protecting you. I'm your father.' He shakes his head. 'What a mess I've made of this. I wanted to do the right thing by everyone and instead I've upset you.'

'You should have told me earlier.'

'I know. It's been one mistake after another. My first mistake was asking Ella out for a drink. Since then I've—'

'Ella was not your fault.' I thought we'd started to put her behind us. I don't want him dwelling on her again.

'At this point in time, you and Lynne are the only women I know who believe that.' He lets out a short, cynical laugh. 'Let's face it, I'm not exactly the most eligible bachelor in town.'

'Dad. Don't be—'

'It's true. How many women will want me when they find out about my criminal record? How many women will believe I'm innocent? When I think about the reality of my situation, meeting Lynne seems like a bloody miracle.'

He isn't wrong. Women who have known him over thirty years have turned their backs on him. Anger and sadness swirl inside me. Sadness for my father and anger for Ella and all the future opportunities she's taken from him.

This time it is my hand that reaches for his. We sit in silence for a moment, the tip of his thumb digging into the centre of my palm.

'I know I've messed up,' Dad says eventually, 'and I know I've hurt you, but I really didn't mean to.' He looks at me with pleading eyes. 'Can you ever forgive me?'

26

JANE

I have never told anyone what Sandy Gilligan did to me. For seven years I have kept that night to myself. A shameful secret I have tried and failed to forget.

I took the job at La Cave à Vin in Cannes to try to get over my break-up with Michel. I wanted to lose myself in the superficial glamour of the city. Everyone knew me as Louise, my first name. The bar work was entertaining, and I made good money in tips. I shared a cheap apartment with Billie, a girl from Hackney who worked as a blackjack croupier at the casino. I partied in the city's nightclubs after my shifts at the bar and brought men back to my apartment for one-night stands. I spent most days nursing a hangover on the beach before heading to the bar to begin another night of debauchery.

Six weeks after Sandy raped me, when I was living in Montpellier, I got the phone call from Michel. The one where he apologised, told me he missed me and said he wanted us to be together. As soon as I heard his voice, the terror and confusion of the recent past receded. I knew I was getting a second chance at the future I'd turned down before, and I didn't want to mess it up. All I had to do was forget about Sandy and get on with my life. When Michel came to Montpellier to see me, we both knew we had to be together. We moved back to Paris, but it wasn't long before Pierre's stroke brought us back to Draguignan. By then I was ready to hide away here. By then I had buried Sandy so deep he could only make the occasional appearance. When I was changing the sheets in one of the hotel bedrooms, or helping out behind the bar on a busy evening.

I became an expert at forgetting.

Then, one August morning, just over two years after Sandy attacked me, I saw a picture of him on the front of *Draguignan-Matin*. A hotel guest had left the paper at her breakfast table and, when I picked it up to clear it away, I saw Sandy staring out at me. Same warm smile, same hypnotic hazel eyes. He did not look like a criminal. He looked like a handsome middle-aged man. The article said he had been arrested in Nice. It sickened me to think he had been so close, and I had not suspected.

The name of his victim did not appear in that article or in any of those that followed. I called her Girl X but longed to know her name and to know if she and I looked alike. Did Sandy Gilligan have a type? Most of all, I longed to apologise to her. What if my silence was the reason she ended up in room 303 of the InterContinental?

For the sake of Girl X, I decided to go to the trial. I promised myself I would speak up if the verdict did not go her way. When I told Michel I was going away for a week's holiday to Aix-en-Provence with a university friend, he had no reason to disbelieve me. I stayed in a budget hotel on the outskirts of Marseilles and prepared myself for the first day in court. Blonde wig with a long fringe. Non-prescription glasses with thick black frames.

On the first day of proceedings, I almost bottled out of going, but I forced myself to enter the public gallery at the last moment and took a seat on the back row by the door, so I could make a quick exit if necessary. Luckily, the layout of the court meant Sandy was tucked beneath the public gallery, unable to look up and see me. On that first day, his voice was enough to make me flee the courtroom, but not before I learned the name of the girl from room 303. Not before I laid eyes on Ella Watson.

* * *

'Jane?'

Startled, I look up from the stack of bill printouts on the reception desk. Alazne stands on the other side of the counter, long silver spirals swaying from her ears.

'Sorry,' she says, 'did I scare you?'

'No.' No, she did not scare me, but my recent visit to Marseilles has left me feeling unsafe. The fear that gripped me in the weeks after Sandy attacked me is back. An ever-present hum of terror.

'Can you help with breakfast?' she says. 'It is suddenly so busy.'

'Of course.' I push the bills to one side and stand up.

'How are you this morning?' she asks as we walk to the dining room together, her arm around my waist. 'Better?'

Shame floods through me at her concerned tone. 'Yes,' I say, 'much better.'

Tomorrow it will be a week since the disastrous trip to Marseilles, and Alazne has asked me the same question every morning. All I want is to forget that day ever happened. At least she knows nothing of Michel's yearning for another child. I don't want her to be concerned about that as well.

In the dining room, she points out three tables yet to order hot drinks.

'I'm going to help Michel in the kitchen,' she says. Darid, our chef, is off sick today, so Michel has taken over the food preparation. This morning I woke alone. When I went to Theo's room, I found Michel sleeping next to our son, his long legs dangling over the edge of the bed. He said he heard Theo crying in the night, but I think he wanted some space from me.

I move from one table to the next with a false smile on my face, taking orders, answering questions, making small talk. Relieved the hotel guests know nothing about me or what happened in Marseilles. They don't know about my flustered exit from room 303 of the InterContinental Hôtel, apologising to the bewildered chambermaid as I fled. They don't know about the hour I spent wandering the streets of the Panier district, my phone on silent, ignoring the string of calls from my husband. They don't know that, thanks to me, we had to cancel our visit to Giles and come home.

Theo, seated with Pierre at the table by the patio doors, waves at me as I pass and announces he has eaten a whole boiled egg.

'That's good, *bébé*,' I say.

After preparing pots of tea and cafetières of coffee behind the bar, I take them to the tables and then check the breakfast buffet. The large glass bowls of fruit salad and muesli need refilling. I carry them to the kitchen and push the door open with my foot. Michel and Alazne are deep in conversation but stop talking as soon as I come in.

'Thank you, darling.' Alazne takes the bowls from me. 'I will see to these.'

Michel is carving a watermelon, the long knife deep in its red, pulpy heart. He turns and gives me a brief smile before returning to his task. Since Marseilles, he has been distant and preoccupied. I want to wrap my arms around him and beg him to let that day go. To not dig into the cause of my behaviour. For all our sakes.

'Anything else I can do?' I say. 'If not, I'll get back to reception.'

'No, no, you go,' Alazne says. 'It's all good.'

All good? I suppress the urge to laugh. She could not be more wrong.

* * *

Back at reception, an Englishwoman in her early twenties travelling alone is waiting to check out.

'I've had such a brilliant time,' she says. 'This hotel is super cute. I'll totally give you five stars on Tripadvisor.'

'Thanks, we'd really appreciate that.' I show her a printout of the bill and she hands over her credit card.

'How long have you lived here?' she asks.

'Almost seven years.' I slot her Mastercard into the card machine.

'I can't believe you get to live here, like, all the time.' I hand her the machine and she punches in her pin code. 'You've got the perfect life.'

'Well, I—'

'I'm heading to the sea next,' she says. 'The Côte d'Azur is so beautiful.'

'It has its dark side,' I say.

'Sure, but—'

'Bad things happen here too, trust me. Just like anywhere else in the world.'

I hand back her credit card and her receipt. She

looks deflated as she wheels her suitcase out of the door, her dreams punctured. There goes the five-star review.

I settle behind the computer and bring up the reservations email account. Instead of dealing with the unanswered queries and booking requests in the inbox, I think about Marseilles.

Two and a half years ago, when Theo was almost ten months old, Michel suggested a day trip to Marseilles. Even with Sandy behind bars, I had no desire to visit the city that held him, but I couldn't refuse without inviting questions. I told myself I could cope. What harm could one day do? After Sandy was sentenced and after I had become pregnant with Theo, I had returned to my trusted methods of repression, putting Sandy and Ella out of my mind.

But, since his birth, my son had slowly eroded my self-control. After we brought him home from the hospital, he refused to settle into any kind of sleeping pattern. We'd expected that. All newborns bring sleep deprivation. While the babies of my mothering peers began to sleep for longer at night, Theo kept us, mostly me, awake for hours, only for him to fall asleep during the day when I had little time to rest. I became exhausted and spaced out, existing in a numb haze. That day in Marseilles, Michel left me with Theo at a café while he visited a nearby record store. With Theo strapped into his buggy beside my chair, I downed my third espresso of the day. The caffeine didn't touch the sides of my crushing fatigue. As I sat and stared out at the old port, Ella came for me. I felt sick with shame. As if I should be the one behind bars.

I looked down at the buggy to see Theo smiling up at me. I didn't deserve this life, this happiness, this beautiful boy. I stood up and walked away from the café, losing myself in the labyrinthine streets. The further I walked, the further Michel and Theo receded. I thought only of Ella. How I was a coward, and she was not. I kept walking, stopping once for a double brandy in a bar full of working men. The police found me several hours later, asleep on a park bench in the Jardin des Vestiges.

Fortunately, the staff at the café where I'd abandoned my son had kept an eye on him until Michel appeared. When the police reunited me with my husband, he showed me nothing but love and concern. That was the worst part. Michel, Pierre, Alazne and all of our friends were so understanding. Michel apologised for not realising how badly I had needed help. Everyone rallied around to give me time to rest and heal, and Alazne arranged for me to have therapy with Julia Martin, a clinical psychologist based here in Draguignan. A good therapist, who did her best to solve the surface issues I presented her with. She talked a lot about the trauma of motherhood, unaware I was failing to process another trauma. In time, with the help of medication and what felt like a miraculous improvement in Theo's sleeping patterns, our little family got itself back on track. I banished all thoughts of Sandy and Ella to a place outside my borders. A wilderness I tried not to stray into.

Now, since our recent revisit to Marseilles, everyone is looking at me with concern. *Poor Jane, reliving that awful day. You remember? The one where she went missing.* Once again, their kindness makes me feel ashamed. I don't deserve it.

When we got back from Marseilles last week, Michel held me in his arms and asked if I was unhappy. How to answer that? I considered telling him the truth, but I was too scared. Scared the truth could not justify my years of lying to him. Scared of what he would think of me. Scared my marriage might not survive.

I lied again and told him the idea of trying for another child had brought difficult memories back. He held me tighter still and said we didn't need to have another child if the idea made me so unhappy. I insisted I would be fine and just needed time to adjust to the idea.

'Maman.' Theo appears, leading his Papi by the hand. Pierre is dropping him at preschool this morning. 'I am ready.'

When I come out from behind the reception desk, my son wraps his arms around me and buries his face in my legs. He has been more clingy than usual since we went to Marseilles. I crouch down and kiss him and promise to pick him up later. Satisfied, he returns to Pierre, and I wave them both goodbye as they head out into the courtyard.

I must hold myself together for Theo's sake. To think I once walked away and abandoned him like that. Yes, he was only ten months old, but what if he sensed what was happening? What if a memory formed somewhere in his impressionable core? Some nagging sense of me not loving him enough. Isn't that one of the reasons why men like Sandy do what they do? Some sort of rejection or abandonment by a woman at some point in their lives. Or did Sandy's mother love him too much? Did she make him feel so special he thought he could get away with anything?

* * *

I check the dining room. Only one table is still occupied by guests. Alazne is having coffee with Denis, the delivery man from the wine company we use. I refuse her offer of an espresso and begin clearing the table nearest to me.

When I enter the kitchen with a tray full of glass cereal bowls, I find Michel with his back to me, his hands in the sink. He is doing the washing-up by hand, a stack of bowls and plates on the worktop beside him. The kitchen has an industrial dishwasher he could use, but his arm moves in a circular motion as he scours a plate with a washing-up brush.

My husband does the washing-up when he is worried or unhappy. It's his thing. He says he finds it soothing. Watching him place the clean plate on the draining board and lift another dirty one from the worktop fills me with apprehension.

'Need a hand?' I say.

'If you like.' His back stays turned.

I grab a dishtowel and pick up the plate he's just laid down. Suds soak into the towel as I rub at them.

Elbow-deep in soapy water, he turns to me.

'Jane,' he says, 'we need to talk.'

27

COLETTE

She's not what I expected. When Dad told me about her, I imagined someone sad and rough and desperate-looking, like many of the women I saw when visiting the prison.

She's out on the balcony with him now, her flouncy white skirt billowing in the breeze. God knows where she got that straw sun hat from. The brim is so wide it almost smacked me in the face when I shook hands with her. To be fair, she seems quite normal, although she's not the type I thought Dad would find attractive. Her wide brown eyes give her an innocent look, which is odd for a divorced woman in her fifties.

Dad suggested we go to a restaurant for this first meeting, but I insisted on Sunday lunch here in the apartment. My territory. After the way he's deceived me recently, I think it's only fair we do this on my terms.

Since he told me about Lynne, I've thought of little else. At the end of our argument, when he asked if I could forgive him, he looked so sad and lost I had to say yes. I have forgiven him – he's my father – but I'm still not happy he kept this relationship from me. He may have been trying to do the right thing, but over the past few days I've made it clear how much he's hurt me.

At one point I asked him if he loved Lynne. He said it isn't love but he does care about her. He also said he was one of those men who was no good on his own. When I pointed out he had me, he insisted I'll have to get on with my own life at some point. He said I might meet someone and want to marry again. Is he only going out with Lynne to make my life easier? He's always been like that. Thinking of others before himself.

'You just can't get sick of that view, can you?' Lynne says when I join them on the balcony. She gestures at the sea, a calm, glittering mirror of the cloudless sky.

'Never,' Dad says.

Lynne sighs. 'I don't think I've ever seen colours so beautiful.'

She strikes me as someone who'd fall for the nonsense I write for holiday websites. *The Cote d'Azur, jewel of the French South.* 'It is stunning,' I say.

Dad gives me a grateful smile. He needn't worry. I know how to be a good hostess. When I was growing up, he and Mum often held dinner parties at the house for important business contacts. I learned how to be polite and entertaining. How to be an asset.

'I can't believe I'll be here all summer,' Lynne says.

Neither can I. What about the fun summer Dad and I were going to spend together? Didn't he say he owed me that?

'Ready for lunch?' I say. 'I hope you like cheese, Lynne? I got us a great selection from our favourite place in the old town.'

'Oh, I'm mad for cheese,' she says. 'Bring it on.'

'Why don't we eat in the gardens?' Dad says. 'Make a picnic of it.'

'In the gardens?' I say. Really? Where our neighbours can see us?

He shrugs. 'Why not? We've as much right to be there as anyone else.'

* * *

Lynne insists on helping me pack the lunch into my wicker shopping basket and on carrying it down to the gardens when we're done. Dad trails behind us, clutching a bottle of Chablis and three glasses. Lynne is deep into a monologue about the trials and tribulations of her old job at Colchester General Hospital. If she carries on like this, I'll have to abandon my moderate approach to alcohol and get Dad to bring down another bottle.

In the gardens, we claim the shady spot beneath the stone pines. Dad brings over three of the stripy deckchairs, while I lay out the blue-and-white gingham picnic blanket.

'That's pretty,' Lynne says.

'Yes.' I smooth the blanket out. 'Mum bought it the first year we stayed here.'

'She obviously had great taste,' Lynne says, apparently unruffled by my mention of Mum.

'She did,' Dad says.

Before she died, Mum gathered us all together and told us she didn't want Dad to be on his own for the rest of his life. Not that he would be, she joked, he couldn't cope five minutes without a woman. Dad told her he couldn't imagine being with anyone else, but she made him promise to find someone new and be happy.

I can't imagine she had someone like Lynne in mind when she said it.

Dad pours out the wine and we all clink glasses.

'*Santé*,' Lynne says, mispronouncing the e at the end so the word sounds like santy. When Dad corrects her, I sip my wine to hide my smile.

'Languages were never my thing.' Lynne places a hand on Dad's knee. 'If I end up staying here, I'll have to get French lessons. Can't rely on Duolingo for ever.'

Dad winks at me as he pats Lynne's hand. The wink is to reassure me I've nothing to worry about. To confirm I'm still the most important person in his world.

I look away, unwilling to let him think he is fully back in favour.

'I'm so glad you two are finally getting to meet,' he says.

'Me too.' Lynne nestles back in her deckchair. 'You're even more beautiful in real life than in your pictures, Colette.'

'Oh. Thanks.' I suppose it's sweet he showed her photographs of me.

I unpack the picnic basket and lay everything out – two fresh baguettes, a selection of cheese, ripe tomatoes and some sliced apple. Dad asks Lynne what she thinks of the wine.

'It's doing the trick,' she says. 'Can't ask for more than that.'

I unwrap the cheese portions from the white, waxy paper and arrange them on the wooden board I brought down with me. Brie, Roquefort and a local goat's cheese. I add shiny red grapes to the board and several cheese knives.

'That looks amazing,' Lynne says. Maybe Dad likes having someone so positive around. If she was this cheery while he was in prison, I suppose I can see the attraction.

I pass around plates and cutlery. Dad breaks off some of the baguette for Lynne, as well as a smaller portion for himself.

'Dig in,' I say to Lynne as I hand her the cheese board.

'Don't be shy,' Dad says, but he needn't have bothered as Lynne picks up a knife and goes straight for the Brie, cutting off the nose as she takes a hefty chunk. Dad doesn't look at me, but he'll be thinking of Mum too. *Don't cut the nose off the cheese. It's bad manners.* She was particular about things like that. Etiquette she'd read about in the process of transforming herself from a working-class girl from Manchester to a millionaire's wife.

When it's his turn, Dad takes a thin slither from the side of each wedge, just like Mum would have done. I do the same.

'Chutney,' Dad says. 'We forgot it.'

'I'll go and get some,' I say.

'No.' Dad is up and out of his chair in seconds. 'I'll do it.'

'Thanks, love.' Lynne lifts her face towards him as if expecting a kiss. He bends down and gives her a tame peck on the cheek, risking entanglement with her ridiculous hat as he backs off. His awkward body language makes me believe he hasn't slept with her yet. She wants him, though. It's clear from the longing in her eyes as she watches him stride away.

'Bless him,' she says and bites into a cheese-loaded hunk of baguette.

I'm sure he's left me and Lynne alone on purpose, for some 'girl' time. This needs wine. Lynne thanks me when I add a splash to hers. Mine I fill to the brim. An awkward moment of silence passes, broken only by the sound of Lynne chewing, the shrill calls of seabirds and the hum of distant traffic.

'What made you write to my dad?' I say.

A slurping sound as Lynne washes down her baguette with Chablis. 'His eyes.' She flashes a girlish smile. 'Sounds daft I know, but when I saw his picture in the paper, I looked right into his eyes and knew he was a good man.'

I frown. 'What paper?'

'That *Daily Mail* article.'

'I thought you met through a prison pen pal service?' Isn't that what Dad said?

'After I saw the article, I wrote to him at the prison, yes.'

Dad either forgot to tell me Lynne saw him in the article or he feels embarrassed by the story of how they met. Maybe he thought I'd label Lynne crazy.

'Trust me,' she says, 'after two failed marriages, I can tell the difference between a good man and a wrong 'un.'

Two ex-husbands? I keep my face neutral, my surprise hidden. Dad didn't tell me she'd been married twice. Then again, he didn't say she'd been married once either. As I recall, he said only that she'd been married before.

'Your dad's one of the good guys,' she says.

I'm not sure Lynne, with her two failed marriages, can be considered a good judge of character when it comes to men. Still, I can't help feeling pleased she sees in him what I've always known.

'I wish I could have helped you when Sandy was in prison,' she says.

'That's okay, you—'

'Sandy, I said, that girl's been through hell. She could do with a helping hand.'

An unexpected tightness in my throat. 'It was hard at times, but I managed.'

'As they say in Yorkshire, you did well for a lass of your age.'

'Thanks.' Maybe I shouldn't judge Lynne too quickly. I can't recall anyone else complimenting me during the past five years. No one has ever appreciated the hours I put in with the lawyer, or how tough those days were in court or how it felt to lose my marriage, my job, my friends.

'Worth doing for a dad like Sandy, though.' Lynne drains her glass and holds it out when I offer her a re-fill. 'I wouldn't have done the same for mine. Truth be told, I'd have been delighted if he'd gone to prison.'

'Dad and I always had each other's backs,' I say. Maybe it's just the wine, but there's a warmth about Lynne that makes me want to relax and open up. I tell her about the time I went to a birthday party, aged five, and was accused of stealing a valuable ring from the mother of Gemma, the birthday girl. Gemma claimed to have seen me in her mother's bedroom, searching through her jewellery box. This accusation stuck, despite me not having the ring either on me or among my possessions. The kids in my class stopped talking to me. Even Mum doubted my version of events and thought I must have taken the ring and hidden it somewhere. Only Dad believed me and stuck by me. He promised me the truth would come out eventually and it did. Gemma admitted to taking the ring to school with her one day and losing it. Her mother was shamefaced and apologetic when she turned up at our house to share the news.

'Here we are.' Dad reappears brandishing two jars of chutney. 'One tomato, one fig.' He sits down and fumbles with the jars as he opens them. 'Dig in, ladies.'

His smile is an anxious one. It's obvious he's trying to make this a nice occasion. I remember how loyal he's always been to me and tell myself to cut him some slack.

We settle back down to our picnic and make small talk about Nice. Lynne, it appears, is in love with the city. Of course she is. Even her trips to the prison don't appear to have put her off the Côte d'Azur.

'I can't get enough of the old town,' she says. 'My flat's right next door to it. I love all the old buildings.'

I spot Kathy Cherish coming out of the block, Ramona skittish on her lead. A little way behind is Jean, a bland vision in a beige T-shirt and beige Capri pants. When they see the three of us sitting here, they stop and stare. Uncertain as I am about Lynne's intrusion into my life, I can't help enjoying the look of shock on

Kathy's face when Lynne rests her head on Dad's shoulder for a moment. An intimate gesture Kathy looks like she can't quite process.

Kathy and Jean confer in whispers and, to my surprise, come marching over to us. Jean lags behind a little, like a soldier reluctantly following orders.

'Have you heard about the break-in?' Kathy says.

'Attempted break-in,' Jean adds, her face flushed.

'Afternoon, Kathy,' I say. 'Lovely day, isn't it?'

'What break-in?' Dad's voice is strained. 'What happened?'

'Ronnie and Rose woke in the night and heard someone prowling around on their balcony,' Kathy says. 'Whoever it was tried to get in the balcony doors.'

'Are they okay?' Dad asks.

'They're fine,' Jean says, 'really.'

'We've never had an incident like this,' Kathy says. 'Not in all the time I've been living here.'

Lynne sits up straight. 'What are you implying?'

'Sorry?' Kathy says. 'Who are you?'

'I'm Lynne, Sandy's girlfriend.'

The word girlfriend makes me cringe, but the look on Kathy's face is priceless.

'It's all right, Lynne,' Dad says.

'No, it's not.' Lynne glares at Kathy. 'What exactly are you saying? Come on. Spit it out.'

Ramona lets out a volley of short, sharp barks.

'Funny this happens right after you come out of prison,' Kathy says to Dad. 'Can't be a coincidence.'

He looks wounded.

'That's enough, Kathy,' I say. 'You can't make accusations like that.'

'There's a policeman with Ronnie and Rose at the moment,' Jean says, 'taking a statement.'

'I've already made the officer aware of you,' Kathy says to Dad. 'You can rest assured he'll be wanting a word.'

'You've got a cheek, lady.' Lynne bristles with anger. She's behind Dad one hundred per cent. No doubt about that.

At that moment a policeman in a dark-blue uniform and cap emerges from the building. He is tall, broad-shouldered and unsmiling. As he walks across the grass, I remember the morning of Dad's arrest. The two officers leading him across the gardens with everyone watching.

'Here, officer,' Kathy says. 'This is the man you need to speak to.'

28

JANE

'It has been a long time.' Julia Martin adjusts her black-framed rectangular glasses and jots down words I cannot see on the notepad in front of her.

'Which is a good thing.' I smile, keen to demonstrate I am a different woman from the one she treated before. I am balanced. In control. A happily married woman and a doting mother who cannot wait to get pregnant again.

If that were true, I would not be here.

Michel suggested I see Julia. *Jane, we need to talk.* When he first confronted me in the kitchen, I thought he had somehow discovered the truth about Sandy. When he said I should try therapy again, I felt relieved, but anxiety soon followed. He thinks therapy will be good both for me and for our marriage, but if I truly open up and tell Julia what is on my mind, we might not have a marriage left.

All I need to do is get through this hour without giving myself away.

Julia looks no different than she did last time I was here. In her mid-fifties, with a wavy mane of bleached hair and thick, arched eyebrows, she dresses in a way that's both youthful and stylish. Khaki silk blouse, black cargo pants and flat silver sandals. A black leather jacket hangs on the back of the consulting-room door, along with her red moped helmet.

'One moment.' She gets up and closes the tall windows that open on to the tree-lined courtyard at the back of the villa, shutting out the warm afternoon air. Her consulting room is in a converted villa just off Boulevard Marx Bormoy. A building she shares with two physiotherapists, a psychiatrist and an orthodontist. A vase of white lilies in the corner of the room fills it with a sweet, pungent scent.

'Okay.' She settles into the wing-backed armchair opposite mine. 'Tell me how things are with you. What made you come now?'

We are speaking English. For now. I can always switch to French if I need to.

'Michel and I want to try for another child,' I say.

She nods. 'Yes. Okay.'

To give her something to work with, I tell her what happened in Marseilles last week.

'This is not so surprising,' she says. 'There were bad memories there for you and it is totally natural, no, that now you are thinking about becoming pregnant, these traumas are coming to the surface.'

'Yes.'

'You are worried about pregnancy affecting your mental health like before?'

'Maybe.'

'Do you feel ready for another child?'

'I should be.'

'But you are not?'

My heart thumps against my ribs. 'I'm scared.'

This, at least, is not a lie.

'Scared of what?' Julia asks.

How would it feel to tell her everything? To say it aloud.

'Jane?'

'I don't... I don't want to lose myself like last time.'

'Like with Theo?'

I nod, hating myself for this lie most of all. For hiding behind my son.

'After Theo's birth you had exhaustion and postnatal depression,' Julia says. 'It is natural, no, that you are feeling anxious about having another child?'

Perhaps I did have exhaustion and postnatal depression, but I abandoned my son in Marseilles that day because of Sandy.

Julia rests her hands on her notepad. 'Before, when you came to me, you said you believed you deserved your depression.'

'Yes.' I did say that, but I did not share the real reason for that belief. Instead, I told Julia about the abortion I had at sixteen. The one that, according to my father, brought disgrace upon my family in the eyes of the church and the community. He told me many times I would pay for my sins in later years. I told Julia my father would see my postnatal depression as a down payment on those sins.

That particular shame I shared, but I said nothing about my cowardice and what it had cost Ella Watson. By staying silent, I had allowed Sandy to attack again. The depression I felt after Theo's birth felt fitting. Why should I enjoy motherhood when another woman had suffered because of me?

'Are you worried about being punished again?' Julia asks.

I should be. Not for what I have done, but for what I have not.

'How is everything with you and Michel?' she says.

'We're okay.' I switch to French. I need to think before speaking in case I give anything away.

'Only okay?'

'I'm not sure it's the right time for us to try again.'

'You think what happened in Marseilles means you're not ready?'

'Maybe.'

To Michel and everyone else, the timing must seem perfect. I have a healthy son who is now at preschool. I have a great support network of friends and family. No reason not to have a baby. No reason anyone knows about.

'Do you want to wait until Theo is a little older?' Julia says.

'No. I don't know.'

'It sounds like there is something stopping you?'

Not something. Someone. Sandy Gilligan.

* * *

After the session, I wander along Boulevard Marx Bormoy. Michel is picking Theo up from preschool today, so I don't need to rush back. He did offer to come and meet me, but I said the walk home would help to clear my head.

The wide, tree-lined street is peaceful, the gated villas keeping themselves to themselves. A tranquil setting, but anxiety has a tight grip on my chest. I survived the hour with Julia with my secret intact, but before I left, she urged me to reach out to the people who love me and let them help.

The people who love me don't know the real me. They think I am good. Jane the good girl. Telling them the truth will shatter that. I chose not to tell Michel or anyone else about Sandy because I did not want that one terrible event to define me. I still don't. My secret is a hard one to keep, but I fear the consequences of telling the truth would be greater than the effort of staying silent.

Ella Watson was not a good girl. During the trial, I watched and listened as Sandy's lawyer shared intimate details of Ella's past sex life and insisted she had consented not only to drinks and dancing with Sandy but to everything that followed. Ella, she implied, was an unreliable narrator of her own experience. I longed to stand up and tell that lawyer there was a huge difference between what Sandy did *with* Ella and what he did *to* her. A difference I understood only too well.

During the trial, I had a clear view of Ella. Her dark hair and dark eyes, her build identical to mine. It was easy to imagine myself sitting in her place, listening to a relentless assassination of my character. Would I be seen as unreliable too, I wondered? Would my memories of that night withstand interrogation? I could not, for example, recall what clothes I had on. I could, however, remember other details. Ones I would rather forget. As the trial progressed, I became desperate for the jury to find Sandy guilty. Not only because he deserved to go to jail, but also because I could then avoid sharing my story. As soon as I heard the verdict, I fled the courtroom. Outside the main entrance of the Palais de Justice, I bent double between two grand neoclassical columns and vomited with relief. In an attempt to feel less ashamed of my cowardice, I reasoned Sandy could have assaulted other women before me. Women who, like me, stayed silent, allowing him to carry on. Why should I be the one to go public?

I check my watch. Almost 3 p.m. I slow down, keen to delay my return home. Before the end of the boulevard, I turn left on to a narrow street that leads past a complex of two-storey apartments. Glancing up, I see thick white clouds massing overhead. There will be rain before nightfall.

Fear ripples across my back. I stop and look behind me, but the street is empty. I carry on, picking up speed. My skin crawls. I stop again and look around but find myself alone.

My pulse thuds and swooshes in my ears as I walk on. I tell myself to stay calm. My fears could be fiction, not fact. Why would Sandy come looking for me? I have never told anyone what happened. Never accused him of anything. Did he see something in me when we first met that made him sure I would keep quiet? Some meekness? Some cowardice?

Ella did not keep quiet. The photographs of Sandy's back and chest exhibited at the trial showed she also fought back. She scratched and punched and clawed.

I did not fight. When I cried, he took it as a sign of emotional overwhelm. *It's okay. You can let it out.* When I begged him to stop, he told me to relax and go with it. He told me it was often hard to tell the difference between pleasure and pain. After he'd finished assaulting me, he turned over and went to sleep, apparently unaware of what he had done. So much so I questioned what had happened. Did he really force me to have sex with him? When I left the hotel at dawn, blood seeping into my knickers, I even smiled at the concierge as I crossed reception. The same man who had seen me enter the hotel with Sandy earlier and given me a disapproving look. Once outside, the sea was waiting, calm and unforgiving. I crossed the road and stood next to the still, silent carousel. I was hungover and unsure exactly what had just happened, but I knew I would not talk of it. As I looked at the painted horses with their golden manes, I felt keenly the loss of an innocence I did not know I had possessed.

No, I have given Sandy no cause for concern.

At the trial he pleaded not guilty, and he sounded convinced of his innocence. If he still believes he was innocent of that crime, why would he think he was guilty of doing anything wrong to me?

He might not have thought of me before Ella had him arrested, but what if, during his years in jail, he either realised, or admitted to himself, that he raped me too? Another crime with consequences for him, should I decide to report it.

Does he now think he has something to worry about?

29

LYNNE

Thursday morning, four days after my visit to Sandy's place and I'm sitting in bed with a cup of Yorkshire Tea. Thank God I brought my own tea bags with me. You can't get a decent cup of tea in Nice for love nor money. I can't get cool either. The air-conditioning unit in my bedroom is broken and the nights are getting hotter. I've got a white plastic fan whirring round in the corner of the room. Makes a right racket.

I pick up my Nice guidebook and flick through it in search of something to do today. Sandy's taking Colette out for a drive somewhere. Not that I mind. Not really. After all the drama with the police the other day, the two of them need a bit of R and R.

What a thing to happen during my first meeting

with Colette. I'd been so nervous about seeing her, but the day was going smashing up until that point. Still, even though the police spoiled the mood a bit, I'm relieved she finally knows about me. I thought Sandy might give me some idea what she thought of me, but when I asked him about it the next day, he kissed my forehead and told me Colette thought I was great. Keen as I was for more details, I didn't want to look desperate. Men, honestly. Even the best of them don't understand what we need sometimes.

She looks like her dad. Same eyes, same big smile, same confident walk. She's a bit on the thin side, though. Nibbled at her lunch, the way women do when they're watching their figures. Sandy dotes on her. You can tell from the way he looks at her. He's so proud of how she's coped with everything that's happened. She might come across as a pretty, posh girl but she's got a tough side to her. Sandy says she can be bossy sometimes, but I'd say she's got backbone. I wish I'd been more like that at her age.

The best bit for me was meeting someone else who sees Sandy the way I do. Someone I don't have to lie to about the man I love.

Maybe I was a bit gobby when Kathy turned up, but hopefully Colette could see I was sticking up for her dad. The cheek of that woman. People can be so

narrow-minded. She more or less said Sandy was at-
tracting criminals to the area.

As soon as the policeman appeared, all the colour
drained from Colette's face. Must have brought back
bad memories for her, the poor thing. Sandy introduced himself to the officer, calm as you like and suggested we all go up to the apartment to talk. Kathy
looked put out at that. Bet she was hoping for a ring-
side seat.

Once we got inside, Sandy and Colette started
talking to the policeman in French. I didn't have a clue
what was going on, but I did manage to ask the officer
if he wanted a coffee. Thanks, Duolingo. It didn't take
me long to find my way around the kitchen and by the
time I'd put the lunch stuff back in the fridge and
made the policeman his coffee I felt quite at home. Colette seemed glad of the support. I wanted her to see
I'm here for the hard times as well as the good. Yes, I'm
a romantic at heart, but I can deal with reality too.
Sandy will have that criminal record for life, but our
love is greater than any barrier we might come up
against.

After the officer left, Sandy explained he'd only
asked routine questions. Had they heard anything unusual last night or seen anyone loitering around the
area?

'Well then,' I said, 'nothing for you to worry about.'

He did worry, though. He spent the next hour on-line, looking up reports of robberies in Nice and researching the city's alarmingly high crime statistics.

'See,' he said, after reading out an article about a burglary in Mont Boron, 'things like that do happen around here.'

'Exactly,' Colette said. 'Kathy just wants to stir up trouble.'

Sandy nodded. 'It was just a random break-in. Nothing more.'

* * *

Mid-morning, I decide to head out and visit the Gallery of Modern Art. I've never been big on galleries, but I've got to do something constructive with my day. This life is a dream, I know, but I've always been a worker. I'm not used to having all this time on my hands.

On Boulevard Jean Jaurès I pass Amira on her fag break outside the Carrefour with one of her colleagues, a tall, gangly lad with a fluffy moustache.

'*Bonjour*,' I say. She gives me a bemused nod in return.

All of a sudden, I picture myself back in the estates

office, sorting out some kind of crisis as usual. On the phone with the porters or wading through an inbox full of invoices. *Lynne, can you just... Lynne, if anyone can sort this you can...*

Daft of me, to want to be back there. A bit of homesickness, I expect. Totally natural. Unlike this heat, which is getting to me already. No breeze today and the sun is stinging my arms and chest.

I carry on down the street. According to the map on my phone, I need to get to the end of Jean Jaurès, cross over and head up into the other side of town.

What I love about this street is all the entrances that lead off it into the old town. I pass the Descente du Marché and peer into the narrow passageway with its colourful buildings and green shutters. What would it be like living smack bang in the old town? I could see myself in one of those old buildings. Don't get me wrong, I love Sandy's apartment, but do we really want to stay there after we're married? With neighbours like that? I'm sure Sandy will want to make a fresh start, and I like the idea of us getting somewhere with character we can make our own. I've never done a big renovation project, but I've watched enough episodes of *Escape to the Chateau* to give it a go.

I wonder what he's up to today? He didn't say where he and Colette might go on their drive. Takes a bit of getting used to, him roaming around a free man. When he was in prison I always knew exactly where he was.

The next entrance into the old town is a fancy one. The steps leading down from Jean Jaurès have marble walls on either side and an arched roof overhead painted gold. Like something out of a church or a mosque.

I stop to take a picture, but before I can lift up my phone, a familiar figure strides past the pizzeria at the foot of the steps.

Sandy?

He disappears down the street at the side of the restaurant. Give over, Lynne. Sandy's out with Colette. You're imagining things.

I hurry down the steps and head for the street next to the pizzeria. There, in front of me, is the man I thought was Sandy. At the end of the street is a sunny square. I hold back and let the man go first.

It is Sandy. No doubt about it. He's crossing the square, sunglasses on, head down. I almost call out, but the purposeful way he's walking stops me. When he reaches the other side of the square, he disappears down another narrow street. I rush across the square to follow him. Daft, really. I should just call out. I'm sure he'd turn around and smile and say,

'Lynne, how wonderful. I was just on my way to see you.'

He's walking in the opposite direction to my place.

I've got him in my sights now. The cramped street is busy, the shops displaying their goods outside. Fruit and vegetables on trestle tables, rails of clothing and carpets. Cafés and bars provide further obstruction with outside tables. Plenty of people about, which makes it easier to keep Sandy in sight without him spotting me.

I should stop. Really, I should. At one point during my affair with Brian, I was convinced I wasn't his only bit on the side. I started following him when he left the office at the end of the day. One time, I caught him in a pub with a woman. He swore she was just an old friend, but I didn't believe him. He also said if I ever followed him again or made another scene in public, he'd report me to the police for harassment. I had to do what he said. He was clever, Brian. No phone calls between us. No texts or emails. When he ended our affair shortly after that episode, it was like I'd never existed.

The street opens out on to another, smaller square with a grotty fountain at its centre. I've not been to this area before. It's quiet and the buildings are more run-down than other parts of the old town.

I stay out of sight at the end of the street, pressed against the side of a building. Sandy stops outside a shabby-looking café with a few plastic chairs and tables outside and a large sign over the front door. Café Corsica. At one table a group of men sit in silence, smoking. Sandy sits at the table next to them, facing the door of the café.

A woman comes out of the door. I don't have the best view of her from here, but she looks young. Early twenties, maybe. Dark hair in a short ponytail at the back of her head. Tight, stonewashed jeans and a black apron over her white T-shirt. She saunters towards Sandy's table. He leans towards her and starts talking, as if he already knows her. Whatever he says makes her put her hands on her hips, all defensive. Within seconds, she is shouting at him, words I cannot translate drifting across the square.

The men at the next table stir and seem to be offering the woman assistance. When she waves away their help, they settle back into their chairs. Sandy reaches into the back pocket of his shorts, pulls out a white envelope and offers it to her. She opens it and pulls out a handful of what look like euros.

Money? Why is he giving her money?

The woman tucks the euros into her apron pocket. After saying something in a quiet voice to Sandy, she marches inside the café. I ready myself to run, thinking Sandy will come this way towards me, but instead he walks straight ahead and takes the next street on the left, out of my sight.

My pulse hammers in my ears. Tears prick my eyes. Sandy Gilligan, what on earth are you up to?

30

COLETTE

'*Est-ce que je nettoie le four?*' Marcie, the cleaner, points inside the oven, a scourer in her slender hands.

'*Oui, merci.*' I ask again if she wants a coffee, but she shakes her head. Marcie is the niece of the woman who usually cleans the apartments in our block, and this is the first time we've met. She's in her twenties, thick black hair pinned on top of her head and startling blue eyes that make me uncomfortable whenever she turns them on me. She has a challenging air about her I don't like, but she's here now and the apartment needs a proper clean.

As soon as she arrived earlier, I regretted having booked her. Dad was here and from the disdainful way she looked at him, I knew she'd heard the gossip about him from her aunt. She even hesitated when he said hello and offered her his hand to shake. Dad pretended not to care, but his subdued manner when he left to go and see Lynne told me otherwise.

I leave her to it and take a coffee and my laptop out on to the shady balcony to get on with some work. It's a beautiful morning. Cloudless sky and the temperature is predicted to hit the early thirties by lunchtime. I can't believe we're halfway through June already. Time seems to have sped up since Dad got released.

After downing my coffee, I open my laptop and get to work creating website content for a luxury hotel in Bangkok. *The Lotus House is an oasis of calm and tranquillity in one of the world's most vibrant and exciting cities.* Being positive about every aspect of a destination gets wearing after a while. I'm not sure how much longer I can stick this job now Dad's out. What else will I do? Go back to London and try to resurrect my advertising career? My old firm won't want me back and I've been out of that environment for almost five years.

Now and then I revisit my idea of becoming a counsellor. Is Dad right about me not being suited for it? He does know me better than anyone. I can't help thinking I need a plan. I've no friends in London any more. Nothing to go back for. Now that my French is so much better, I could apply for work in Paris. With Dad away seeing Lynne again, it strikes me he has more of a life than I do. What if their relationship does last long-term? Where does that leave me? From what I've observed, I'm sure they haven't slept together yet, but I suppose it's only a matter of time.

An uncomfortable memory comes to me. Dad and Uncle Jimmy here in the apartment the day before they left for the boys' weekend in Marseilles. I overheard Jimmy telling Dad he had to get laid. *Angie's gone. Time to get back in the saddle.* Dad told him he didn't want to get back in any saddle. He said he couldn't dream of sleeping with someone who wasn't his wife. At the time, difficult as it was to think of Dad having sex with another woman, part of me hoped he might do so during the weekend. He needed something, or someone, to puncture his terrible grief.

From indoors comes a burst of techno music, followed by Marcie's voice, low and conspiratorial. I peer inside and see she is on her phone. I can't hear what she's saying but her tone makes me suspect she's discussing Dad.

I step inside. 'Marcie?' She turns to face me, her phone in one hand, a smirk hovering on her lips. In French I tell her that when she's finished in the kitchen, I only want her to do the bathroom. 'Not the bedrooms,' I say. I don't want her nosing around in our private space.

She shrugs before saying goodbye to whoever is on the phone and turning back to the oven. Her disrespect of me is obvious. She knows about Dad, and she's judging me for standing by him. I should be immune to such judgement by now, but it still gets to me.

Back out on the balcony, I'm greeted by Ramona's grating bark from below. Kathy is in the gardens talking to Ronnie and Rose. I shrink back in my chair, not wanting them to see me.

I imagine Marcie has heard all about the incident with the police too. When I saw that officer walking across the gardens towards us and imagined Dad being taken from me again, I could hardly breathe.

We handled it as well as we could. I'm not sure what the officer had heard about Dad from Kathy, but when he came up to us in the gardens, he looked a bit confused to find a polite, well-dressed man enjoying a picnic with his daughter and girlfriend.

Girlfriend. I still hesitate to use that phrase about Lynne, but there's no doubt her presence made a difference to the policeman. When we came up to the apartment, I was still distressed by having an officer there, but Lynne made him feel welcome right away by offering him coffee. Afterwards, she sat beside Dad on the sofa with her hand in his, and I could see that her and me being there made the policeman's attitude and body language soften. It felt good to have an ally for once. Lynne was brilliant with Kathy too, although at one point I worried she might get up and punch her.

Dad handled the situation with the policeman well. He stayed relaxed and co-operative throughout, but as soon as the officer left, he looked washed out and weary. As if he realised the past could always come back to get him, no matter what he does to move on. It made me sad to see him like that. He's no criminal, whatever his official record says.

* * *

When I go back inside to make another coffee, Marcie is nowhere to be seen. She should be in the bathroom, but when I peer down the hallway, the bathroom door is open, and the light is off.

I creep down the hallway and stand outside Dad's room. Marcie is on her phone again, talking to someone in a low voice in French.

'I'm in his room,' she says, 'how creepy is that? No, it looks totally normal.'

She jumps when I open the door and step into the room.

'Get out,' I say. She looks at me with a mixture of disgust and panic. As if I'm a criminal. As if I'm someone to fear.

'Get out,' I say, 'and don't expect to be paid for today.'

She mutters something as she pushes past me, clutching her phone.

'Excuse me?' I say.

She sneers at me from the doorway. 'You should be ashamed of yourself.'

When the front door slams, I sink on to Dad's bed and wait for my heart to stop thumping. I've dealt with worse. I know the truth and that's all that matters. Dad is free now and the past is behind us. Even Lynne, although she won't be around for long, is a sign he wants to move on.

The fresh laundry sits in a pile on the bed beside me, waiting for Dad to put it away. To calm myself, I begin folding it. T-shirts first – sleeves to the midpoint then fold the whole thing in half. Mindless, soothing activity and, as I work my way through the T-shirts and move on to the trousers, I start to feel calmer. After the trousers, his boxer shorts. I fold all six pairs up and start putting everything away. Despite the mess he can leave in other parts of the house, Dad's drawers are neat and orderly. When I put the boxer shorts away, I have to move some of the pairs of white sports socks to make room for them. A balled pair of socks falls to the wooden floor with a surprisingly heavy thud.

When I bend down and pick up the socks, I feel a hard object inside the towelling fabric. Pulse thrumming, I reach in and pull out what looks like a black knife handle. It's made of leather and has a silver cap at either end.

Then I see a curved ridge of steel tucked within the handle. I pull it out. The sharp blade glints as I turn it this way and that, catching the sunlight pouring through the bedroom windows.

A switchblade knife.

I shiver.

A switchblade knife.

Where did he get it? What does he want it for?

31

JANE

La Pierre de la Fée, or the giant's table as it is known locally, is an ancient megalithic tomb a short walk from the hotel. It is one of the few things Draguignan is famous for and my son loves it.

It is early afternoon, and we are walking down Avenue de Montferrat with Theo in the buggy, past the sprawling villas that dominate this quiet residential area. Past gardens populated by olive trees and rose bushes. My pleasant surroundings are a reminder of all I have to be grateful for. A reminder of all I have to lose.

Theo sings to himself as Michel pushes him along. My son had me up most of the night, complaining of a sore stomach. This morning I kept him off school, just in case, but by mid-morning he had, unsurprisingly, made a miraculous recovery.

Michel and I walk in silence, the atmosphere strained between us. What if we become one of those couples who stop speaking to one another? When I returned from seeing Julia Martin, I told Michel the session was useful and promised to book another one. I also asked for time and space to process what Julia and I had discussed.

I didn't tell him I thought someone had followed me that day. Since then, I have had similar experiences while walking around town. That crawling sensation beneath my skin. My spine tingling with panic. Each time, I remind myself my fears may exist only in my imagination. If that is true, I have no need to tell anyone my secret.

If only I could erase Sandy from my mind. If only he did not exist.

Michel breaks the silence first, telling me Bastien called this morning to invite us for dinner next weekend, along with Elyna and Jacques. We discuss whether I should make a clafoutis to take for dessert. Safe territory. Unlike the subject of when we will have another child.

Fifteen minutes later, we turn off the road on to a small path and follow the sign for La Pierre de la Fée.

The properties in this area are more rural and have views out to the craggy limestone hills that surround Draguignan. Views of the sloping vineyards and pine forests.

'The table,' Theo says when La Pierre de la Fée comes into view. When I first heard about the tomb, I expected to find it located in a large field in isolated splendour. Instead, it stands next to the front garden of a large farmhouse.

Once free from the buggy, Theo runs up the driveway ahead of us. I catch him just before he reaches the tomb and pick him up. He squeals as I run the last part, depositing him in front of a monument almost five thousand years old. Three tall standing stones supporting a huge slab of limestone. He can only see it the way it is described in local folklore, as the table of a giant who lives in the hills outside Draguignan. He has loved that story ever since his father told it to him.

When Michel catches us up, we all enter the tomb. The air is cool inside. We sit in a circle on the scrubby ground and, as always, Theo makes Michel repeat the story about the giant who comes down at night from the nearby hill to lay a picnic out on the slab above us.

'Lena is scared of the giant,' Theo says.

'Is she?' Michel asks. 'Why?'

'She's a girl,' says Theo.

Michel smiles. 'I'm sure that's not the reason.'

I'm sure it is. I bet Nathalie's daughter knows instinctively that as a woman she will always have something or someone to fear. With age, it will not be giants that scare her. It will be men. Men like Sandy Gilligan.

Overcome with a surge of energy, Theo scrambles to his feet and dashes out of the tomb. I watch him as he runs in circles on the grass. What kind of man will he grow into? How can I make sure he becomes a good one? The responsibility of it makes me suddenly weary and resentful. What if I get pregnant with another boy? Then I will have two of them to mould into adults incapable of doing harm.

Theo picks up a stick from the grass and smacks it against one of the giant stones. When I ask him to stop, he ignores me and carries on.

'Theo,' I say, 'stop that right now.'

My son lowers the stick and eyes me warily. My son with his dark curls and his big blue eyes. Adorable now, but who knows what he might grow into? He could be a time bomb, waiting to go off.

'He's only playing,' Michel says. He leaves the tomb and sits on the grass with Theo. He finds another stick and soon has Theo drumming out a rhythm with them on the grass. As I watch them play together, I wonder how Michel would react if I told him about

Sandy. Maybe the issue is not what he might think of me but what I might think of him. What if he responds in a way I find unacceptable? What if he says the wrong thing? Could I stay with him if that happened?

Michel lifts Theo on to his lap for a cuddle. If I told my husband about Sandy, would he be angry on my behalf? Would he get in our car and drive to Nice and make Sandy pay for what he did to me? He would be physically capable of harming Sandy, but I married him because he's the kind of man who would never do something like that.

Michel returns to the tomb and sits beside me. The needy warmth of his body makes me want to pull away, but I let him lean in and kiss my neck. I let his hand roam across my thighs.

Towards the end of my session with Julia, she asked me to think back to when Michel and I split up and I went to work in Cannes. She was making a link between us splitting up because Michel wanted to start a family and his recent request for us to have another child. She asked if I felt pressured to get pregnant to keep my relationship. I said no, not at all, but sitting here now, with my husband's hand reaching beneath my skirt, I feel rage blaze through me. If Michel had only been patient all those years ago, if he had waited like I had asked him to, I would never have gone to Cannes. I would never have met Sandy.

'You know,' Michel says, 'my mother told me that when she was a kid, women here believed these stones had magic powers.'

'Really?' I want to pull my legs tight into my body, away from his touch.

'They're supposed to make you more fertile.'

I sit up and push his hand away.

'What?' he said.

'You've told her, haven't you?'

'About what?'

'You told your mother about us trying for another baby.'

'Except we're not. Not yet.'

'You promised you wouldn't tell her.'

'Jesus.' Hurt flashes across his face. 'She wanted to know what was wrong. She wanted to make sure I hadn't done anything to upset you.'

'Fuck you.' I scramble to my feet and storm out of the tomb, into the sun's probing glare.

* * *

I ignore Michel during the walk back to the hotel, despite knowing I am wrong to punish him. He is a good man because of the way his mother raised him and because of the close bond they have. A bond I would like to have with Theo. One that enables him to tell me anything without feeling shame. Maybe that is why I am so angry. How will I ever have a relationship like that with my son if I cannot be honest about who I am and everything that has happened to me?

We arrive to find Pierre on reception, checking in an elderly German couple. When he waves me over to ask for a hand with the computer, Michel says he will take Theo back to our apartment.

After helping Pierre with the check-in, I leave the hotel and head across the courtyard, where Lili is sweeping up the leaves around the lunch tables. Lili, nineteen, is the daughter of Pierre's cousin, Martha. She works as a part-time waitress for us, fitting us in between two other jobs. During the summer season, she often helps out on reception too.

'Hey,' she says, as I walk past her, 'someone was asking for you earlier.'

'Who?' A cold knot in my gut. 'Someone I know?'

'He came in for coffee. He said he stayed here five years ago.'

'What was his name?'

My sharp tone makes Lili stop sweeping. She examines my face. No doubt news of my recent escapade in Marseilles has been discussed among the staff.

'Monsieur James,' she says.

I tell myself not to panic. It is not unusual for a former guest to come back to the hotel and say hello. We are a family business. We pride ourselves on making friends with the guests.

'James.' I try to put a face to the name but fail. How can I remember every guest I've met over the years? 'Was he French or English?'

When she tells me he was French, my shoulder muscles uncoil a little. Then I remember Sandy is a dual national and probably speaks both languages. 'What did he look like?' I ask.

She shrugs. 'Just a guy, you know?'

'How old?'

'I don't know... middle-aged.'

'Was he good-looking? A bit rugged?'

Lili stares at me. My throat is tight, my heart beating far too fast.

'No.' She giggles. 'This guy was not handsome.' She describes a short, overweight man with pasty skin and round, steel-rimmed glasses. No way it could have been Sandy.

I should feel relieved, but my prey's instinct, now

aroused, will not let me relax. 'I really don't remember a Monsieur James.'

'I think he maybe had a crush on you.'

'Why?'

'He asked so many questions about you.'

'What sort of questions?'

'What days of the week do you work? Do you live here at the hotel? That sort of thing.'

'What did you tell him?'

'I said I didn't know your exact work hours, but I said you were usually around.'

Are these normal questions for a former guest to ask or is something more sinister going on?

'He was really happy to hear about Theo,' Lili says.

'You told him I have a son?'

Lili looks confused. 'Of course. Why not?'

'Sorry. Yes.' I smile, not wanting her to think I am behaving oddly.

Lili returns to her sweeping, the leaves making a crispy swish as the broom herds them. 'He said he remembers you as an excellent barmaid.'

My breath catches in my chest. Did this stranger mean I had served him drinks here at the hotel, or was he dropping a hint about my time at La Cave à Vin?

'He did ask me to give you a message.' Lili bends

down to free a tangle of leaves from the head of the broom.

'What message? What did he say?'

'Hang on.' She pauses for a moment, as if trying to remember. 'He said, tell Jane I hope to catch her soon.'

32

COLETTE

By the time the MG reaches the Promenade des Anglais, the street lights are on. The night air is warm, only a hint of a breeze. We have the top of the car down and the radio blaring out seventies disco hits.

'Christ, look at the traffic,' Dad says when we pull up at the lights outside the Hôtel Negresco. A long line of cars and vans snakes ahead of us.

'We've been lucky all day,' I say.

Dad smiles at me. 'Sun shines on the righteous.'

I give him an uneasy smile back. I still can't get that knife out of my mind.

Since discovering it, I've said nothing. I put it back where I found it, not wanting him to suspect me of snooping. Once or twice, when he's been running in the morning or out with Lynne, I've gone back in to check it's there. Each time I've found it still hidden inside his socks. I keep telling myself he may have needed a knife in prison for protection. That's common, isn't it? Maybe now, on the outside, he still feels the need for this protection. Nice does have a violent underbelly. Stabbings are not uncommon here. More in the housing projects than the nicer residential areas, but it still happens.

'That was a great day, kiddo,' he says, fingers tapping along to Chic's 'Le Freak' on the steering wheel.

'It was.'

We've been in Saint-Tropez all day. We left first thing this morning and drove the scenic route along the coast. For lunch we shared a seafood platter in a restaurant in the old harbour. We reminisced about past family holidays, and I even managed to forget about the knife for a while. Then we walked through the old town and browsed in the shops and art galleries.

The music stops for a round-up of the day's news. The first item is about a forest fire near Avignon, the second is about disgraced actor Henri Breton. The newsreader is just about to announce the date of his upcoming trial when Dad turns the radio off.

The lights change. We creep forward.

'Are you hungry?' Dad asks.

'I could eat something, I guess.' I've been eating a lot the past few days. Taking my laptop along to Brasserie Le Magenta and indulging myself with cake while I work.

'Shall we treat ourselves to chips?' he says.

'Fat Mermaid?'

'Where else?'

The Fat Mermaid is the best fish and chip shop in Nice. Dad says nothing beats Manchester fish and chips, but the Fat Mermaid comes close.

We crawl along Route 98. At the outskirts of the old town, Dad turns left and parks on a double yellow near the market square.

'I don't think you can park here,' I say.

'It'll be fine.'

This minor crime worries me. I don't want him getting into any kind of trouble. I think again about the knife and what would have happened if the policeman had searched the apartment the other day and found it there.

'I'll get the grub,' he says when I reach for the passenger door. 'You keep your eye out for traffic wardens.'

He disappears down a street on the left. I wonder if his craving for chips is connected to his recent nostalgia about Nana Gilligan. Yesterday would have been her eighty-fourth birthday. I came back from work in the afternoon to find him sitting on the couch clutching her photograph. His eyes had a haunted look.

'I should have been there when she died,' he said. 'I let her down.'

'It wasn't your fault.'

'Ella took that moment from me,' he said. 'Am I supposed to just forget that?'

The bitterness in his voice unnerved me. My latent rage for Ella Watson flared up. Thanks to her, my father was a changed man. Damaged by her false claims and the years in prison that resulted from them.

'All that stuff she said in court about trauma.' Dad shook his head. 'She made bloody sure I feel as bad as she claimed she did.'

I agreed with him but stayed silent, not wanting to fuel his anger.

'I promise you this,' he said, 'no one will ever make me miss a big life moment like that again. Ever.'

* * *

Dad soon reappears clutching two cardboard cartons. 'I got the small portion for you,' he says, handing both cartons over.

I could easily eat the large and then some, but I thank him anyway.

When we arrive home, it is almost half past ten. The sedate, residential streets are quiet. Dad swings the MG into the underground car park and pulls up next to my Renault Clio. We are on the first set of stairs up to the apartment when I realise my phone is in the car passenger door where I left it.

'See you up there,' I say when Dad hands me the car keys.

Dim lights on the concrete pillars of the car park fill it with shadows. The soles of my sandals ring out as I cross over to the MG.

Without warning, a young guy jumps out from behind a concrete pillar. My height, wiry, his face gaunt. Before I realise what's happening, he grabs the car keys out of my hand. We face each other, my breath tight and shallow, a scream trapped in my throat. He is young and dressed in shiny black tracksuit bottoms, gleaming white trainers and a football strip I don't recognise. His black hair sits lank on his shoulders.

'*Ton sac*,' he says.

'No.' Instinct makes me clutch the strap of my

handbag tight, even though I should hand it over for my own safety.

He steps in, grabs my shirt with one hand and wrestles my bag from my shoulder with the other. My screams echo around the car park, loud and primal. My legs buckle beneath me as terror takes over. His face is close to mine. His breath reeks of cigarettes.

Somewhere in the distance, I register a door slamming.

My next scream is silenced by the man's fingers around my throat. I thrash in his grasp, my air supply severed.

'*Merde*,' he says. His hand releases my throat as he drops to the floor.

'Colette.'

Dad is here. Dad is here and the man is down on the floor.

'You okay?' Dad says.

'He's got the car keys.'

Dad grabs the man's arm and twists it until the keys fall to the floor. 'Not now he doesn't.' He kicks the keys over to me. I pick them up.

The man springs to his feet, turns and attempts a headbutt. Dad ducks away and then punches the man in the face, three times, until he slides to the ground.

'Don't watch,' Dad says.

A hard knot deep in my stomach. I want to stop looking, but I can't. The man tries to crawl away, but Dad pulls him back and hooks an arm around his neck. I see terror in his eyes. Dad's face is twisted and ugly. I don't recognise him.

'*Pitié,*' the man says.

Dad releases his neck and hauls him to his feet. Drags him to the entrance of the car park and shoves him out into the night. '*Casse-toi et ne reviens pas.*'

Fuck off and don't come back.

As soon as Dad slams the door to the garage shut, violent shakes take over my body. Uninvited tears stream down my face.

When Dad returns, wiping his hands on his jeans, his face has settled. He is my father again. 'Hey, kiddo.' He envelops me in a hug. I sag into him, grateful to be safe. My father. Protecting me as always.

'He won't bother us again,' Dad says.

An image of his face as he choked my attacker makes my shoulders tense.

'What is it?' Dad holds my shaking body away from him and searches my face.

'Nothing.'

'You're in shock.' Dad releases me. 'That's all.'

'We should call the police.'

Dad hesitates. 'I'm not sure that's a good idea.'

'But that's two incidents in the block now.'

'And if the police interview me twice in one fortnight, how will that look?'

He's right. I'm not thinking straight. We can't have Dad associated with any sort of trouble.

'Even if the police do by some miracle track the guy down,' Dad says, 'he'll tell them a pack of lies and I'll end up getting charged with assault.'

'You're right,' I say. 'Sorry.'

'Look at you.' Dad puts an arm around my shoulder. 'You're still shaking. Let's get you home and get you a stiff drink.'

33

LYNNE

As soon as Sandy opens the door to his apartment, I fling my arms around him.

'Thank God you're safe,' I say.

A few days ago I could have killed him, but when he phoned this morning and told me about Colette being attacked in the car park last night, I got a fright. What if something had happened to either of them?

He kisses my forehead. 'It's all good. Nothing to worry about.'

'That man could have had a knife. Doesn't bear thinking about.'

'I'm so happy you're here,' he says. 'I've missed you.'

Is he? Has he? I'm still not over seeing him with

that woman and I'm furious he lied to me, but he at least deserves a chance to explain. He is, after all, the kind of man who protects his daughter with no thought for his own safety. A brave and good man. That's why I want to spend the rest of my life with him.

'You look knockout,' Sandy says.

'Well, you did say we were going somewhere fancy.' I chose my khaki silk jumpsuit for the occasion and a pair of Roman sandals I bought from Zara yesterday. I did dither over what underwear to put on but settled in the end for my black lacy gear. Not that Sandy will get lucky tonight. Not with his recent behaviour.

'I've still to get changed,' Sandy says, 'but it won't take me a minute. Come through and say hi to Colette.'

'Can I use the loo first?'

'Of course.'

Inside the guest bathroom, I inspect myself in the mirror over the sink and decide to apply a fresh coat of lipstick. My hands are trembling. There's still a lot of anger in me. A lot of questions buzzing round in my head. Is that woman at the café a prostitute? Is that why Sandy gave her money? No doubt he'd say he was helping her get off the streets, just like that one on the promenade. Who is he? The patron saint of whores? Is that why he won't sleep with me? Too busy getting his end away with some slapper.

Could she be his mistress? Or his ex-mistress? Maybe he had her stashed away in Nice when he was still married to Angie.

In the mirror, my mother's face replaces mine. That knowing look she had. I shake my head until she disappears. Calm down, Lynne, I tell myself. Don't give up on your dreams that easily. Just because you saw Sandy talking to another woman doesn't mean he's sleeping with her.

I take a deep breath in and out. That's better. Tonight, when the time's right, I'm going to tell Sandy what I saw and ask him to put my mind at rest.

* * *

When I enter the living area of the apartment, I find Sandy clattering cutlery as he loads the dishwasher and Colette sitting at the kitchen island, staring at her laptop, a glass of white wine beside her.

'Hello, Lynne,' she says. 'How are you?'

'Never mind me, how are you?'

She reaches for her wine. 'I'm okay.'

She looks tired, bless her. I'm dying to give her a hug, but I'm not sure she'd like it. I stand on the other side of the kitchen island, unsure what to do with myself.

'I feel bad you'll be here on your own so soon after what happened,' I say. 'Why don't you come to dinner with us?'

'I tried to persuade her,' Sandy says, 'but she insists on working.'

'Thanks, Lynne,' she says, 'but I've got a deadline to meet.'

'Right.' Sandy slams the door of the dishwasher shut. 'Better get changed. Won't be long.' He whistles his way out of the room and down the hallway, leaving me and Colette alone.

'Can I offer you some wine?' she says.

'No thanks. Best save myself for later.' She does look weary. 'You were lucky your dad was there last night,' I say.

She glances at her laptop screen. 'Yes. Very lucky.'

'Thank God he knows how to handle himself. What did the police say? Are they going to try to find the guy?'

'Actually, Lynne,' she says, 'we decided not to tell the police.'

I'm surprised at first but when Colette explains why, I understand. 'Yes,' I say, 'your dad doesn't need any more hassle from the police.'

'Exactly.'

'And Christ knows what that Kathy would have to say about it,' I add. 'Having her on your back would be worse than the police.'

Colette takes a swig of wine. 'Quite.'

I glance towards the hallway. No sign of Sandy yet. 'How was your day out last week?' I ask. 'Thursday, wasn't it?'

'Sorry?'

'Your dad said he was taking you out for a drive. Did you go anywhere nice?'

Her bewildered expression suggests she has no idea Sandy lied to me. Did he lie to her as well?

'Hang on,' she says, 'I think... yes, we did drive up the coast a bit last week. I'm sure it was on Thursday.'

I'm not surprised she's covering for him. He is her father. 'Well, it's great you're doing some fun things together.'

'Yes,' Colette says in a high, bright voice. 'It's great. Really great.'

34

LYNNE

Le Plongeoir restaurant and bar is only a fifteen-minute walk from Sandy's flat. To get here, we took a lovely shortcut from Mont Boron all the way down to the port and then headed left. I've never seen anywhere like this place. A restaurant shaped like a boat perched on an outcrop of rock in the water. We had to walk across a wooden jetty to get to it. Our table is next to the metal railings that run around the edge of the restaurant space. Down below is the sea. Aqua with bits of bright jade. So gorgeous I could cry. We've a roof over us, but the restaurant is open on three sides. To my left I can see the port, the roofs of the old town and, in the distance, the Promenade des Anglais.

There's still an hour to go until sunset but the light is all mellow and the rocks below look golden. It's the most romantic place anyone's ever taken me.

'Sandy,' I say, 'it's magical.'

'I've seen worse,' he says with a smile.

Every table is full. No wonder. According to Sandy this is the most iconic restaurant in Nice. Le Plongeoir means diving board and three of them jut out from the back of the restaurant. On the highest one is a gorgeous little sculpture of a woman ready to dive into the water below.

'What do you think of the wine?' Sandy asks.

He ordered us an expensive white I've never heard of. 'Delicious,' I say. It is as well. He'll have to choose the wine for our wedding, that's for sure. It's nice to be thinking about the wedding again. Then I remember the mystery woman and a solid lump of anxiety forms in my gut. Best wait for the right moment to mention her. Don't want to spoil the lovely atmosphere.

'Let's get stuck into this.' Sandy inspects the seafood platter in front of us. I quite fancied the prawn risotto they've got on the specials board, but Sandy was chatting away to our waiter in French and before I knew it, he'd ordered for both of us. 'Have an oyster,' he says.

I've never been a fan of oysters, but I pick up one of the rough shells and fork the rubbery bit attached to it into my mouth.

'Amazing,' Sandy says when he swallows his. Mine lodges in my throat. I wash it down with water.

'Are you sure Colette will be okay on her own?' I ask.

'She'll call if she needs me.'

I feel bad for putting Colette on the spot about her dad, but I had to get my facts straight. 'I thought I'd invite her out for a coffee one morning,' I say. 'Do you think she'd like that?'

'That's a great idea. Hang on.' Sandy wipes his hands on his napkin and takes his phone from the pocket of his black chinos. 'I'll text you her contact details.'

My phone pings in my bag. 'Thanks.'

'I think it gave her a fright, seeing me go for the guy like that,' he says as he puts his phone away.

'I'm sure she was more scared of him.'

'I don't know. She's been a bit distant.'

'She's had a shock, that's all.'

He gazes at me with those beautiful eyes. 'I feel like I'm letting her down. Like she's disappointed in me.'

'Don't be daft.'

'I have nightmares about going back inside. Sometimes I wake up in the night and I think I'm back there.'

'That must be—'

'I couldn't stand it. I couldn't do it again.'

'Hey.' When my hand reaches across the table, he squeezes it tight.

'I'm not a violent man, but I had to do the necessary to survive in there.'

'It's okay. I get it.' I don't really, not fully, but when I was fifteen my dad came home from an all-day drinking session and started having a go at me in the kitchen. When he grabbed me by the hair, I snatched up the bread knife from the kitchen table and threatened him with it until he backed off. My mother watched the whole episode from the kitchen doorway but did nothing to defend me. The next morning, Dad couldn't recall a thing, and Mum pretended nothing had happened. I remembered clearly the thrill of the knife's steel handle in my sweaty palms, and the look of shock and terror on my father's face.

A waitress stops by our table and tops up our wine glasses. Little Miss Chic in her black Capri pants and a black linen shirt. She's all big, flirty eyes and giggles as she chats away to Sandy in French. She's also a slim brunette, just like the woman in the old town. Is that his type? I feel fat and pasty, and I wish my hair wasn't red.

When she finally leaves us in peace, Sandy raises his glass. 'To you, Lynne.' He clinks his glass against mine. 'Isn't this perfect?' he says.

It should be. I'm with the man I love, sitting in a beautiful restaurant, but I can't stop thinking about that woman.

'I saw you the other day when I was wandering round the old town,' I say. 'I wasn't sure it was you, but then—'

'Which day?'

'Thursday.'

'I didn't see you.'

'No. I was—'

'You were following me?'

'No.' My chest is all fluttery panic. Why did I bring this up? 'I was walking, and you were ahead of me and I—'

'Why didn't you shout me?'

'You were with someone. I didn't want to interrupt.'

'Thursday.' He frowns. 'I can't really remember what I—'

'You were with a woman.' I sip my wine but get

only hints of bitterness and notes of paranoia. 'Short. Dark-haired. Sort of—'

'Of course.' He rests an elbow on the metal railing beside us. 'Yes, she's not someone I'd want you to meet.'

My breath catches in my throat. Is he about to tell me something awful? *There's someone else, Lynne. I've been trying to find the right time to tell you.*

'Bit of a sad story really,' he says.

'I'm all ears.'

'The woman you saw is the daughter of a man I went to prison with. I wouldn't say anyone in there was a friend, but this guy had my back a few times.' He grimaces, as if he doesn't want to recall those incidents. 'Anyway,' he says, 'he asked me to check on his daughter.'

'That's what you were doing?' I could cry with relief.

'It took me a while to find her, but I've done what he asked.'

'She looked angry with you.'

'She's angry at her dad. She doesn't want him interfering in her life and she didn't take kindly to him sending a stranger after her.' He sips his wine. 'She's not in a good place. Abusive husband, drugs. It's a mess really.'

'Poor girl.'

'Anyway, it's done now. I won't be seeing her again.'

I feel awful. I should have known there was nothing to worry about. He knows what it means to love a daughter, and he was only helping a friend. He's a beautiful person, inside and out.

'One thing,' he says. 'Don't tell Colette any of this, will you?'

'Why not?'

'When I told her I wanted to help this girl out and give her some money, she made me promise not to get involved.'

So Colette knows this girl exists. Somehow this makes Sandy's version of events even more credible.

'She doesn't want me connected with anyone from prison,' he says. 'I feel awful keeping it from her, but I had to do the right thing.'

'Of course you did,' I say. 'I'll not breathe a word.'

* * *

When we finish dinner and leave the restaurant, the sun is setting. Gold-fringed clouds over the hills to the west of Nice and a pale pink streak over the bay.

'I'll walk you home,' Sandy says, and slips his hand in mine.

Does this mean tonight's the night? Me and Sandy in bed together at last. Oysters are an aphrodisiac, aren't they? We had plenty of those. Good job I shaved my legs earlier and put that nice underwear on. Part of me just wants to get it over with. It's tiring, all this preparation for no result.

We walk around the port, past the bars and restaurants, and then head towards the promenade. Sandy natters on about the city, giving me little snippets of history. I'm so happy. Moments like these are what I dreamed of.

'I'm sorry about earlier,' I say. 'I was silly... about that woman.'

'It's okay,' he says. 'I know you didn't have it easy with your exes. We've all got baggage at our age. Me more than most.'

'I feel bad. I shouldn't have thought—'

'God knows you've got reasons to doubt me. I'm lucky you're even here.'

'I don't doubt you.'

'Are you sure you want to be with me?'

'Of course.' Terror shoots through me at the thought of losing him. I wish I'd never said anything. 'Of course I do.'

'Yes,' he says quietly, 'you're the kind of woman who's in it for the long haul.'

We walk on until we reach what Sandy tells me is Rauba Capeu beach.

'Weirdest looking beach I've ever seen,' I say, following him down a set of steps that leads to a big strip of concrete topped at one end by a huge pile of concrete blocks. Sandy leads me closer to the water, across some proper rocks, my smooth-soled sandals slippy beneath me. Near the water's edge is a wide, flat stone. Sandy stands on it with open arms and I step into his embrace. Sunset is fading, and further out in the bay the water is shiny black.

'I like to come here around sunset,' he says.

'I can see why. It's gorgeous.'

'Lynne,' he says, 'I want to talk about the future.'

I don't know if I'm feeling dizzy from all the wine or because of what he might be about to ask me. Romantic dinner, bringing me here to watch the sunset. Could there be a more perfect spot for a proposal?

'Are you sure you want to be with me?' he says.

'I've never been more sure of anything.'

He hesitates and takes a deep breath. This is it. He's going to drop to his knees and ask me to marry him.

'That's good,' he says. 'That's all I need to know for now.'

'Oh.' I could kick myself. If I'd kept it together and not bothered him with those silly questions, maybe he'd have felt secure enough to ask me. What if he had it all planned, and I ruined it?

'We'll figure it out as we go,' he says.

35

JANE

I cannot stop thinking about Mr James. If that even was his name. Mr James, who could be one of the hundreds of guests I have spoken to over the years. I always show interest in the lives of our guests but share only basic details about myself – I come from the Cotswolds; I studied French and English Literature at university. For most people that is enough. It is an art form, making people feel as though they know you without revealing anything of yourself.

It is Friday, four days since Mr James came to the hotel. Michel and I are talking now but relating to him is difficult. He thinks I am still angry about him confiding in Alazne, but it isn't that.

I am scared. I am, at times, overwhelmed by anxiety. It rises from my solar plexus, and I have to leave whatever room I'm in and find a private place where I can let the tears come. Violent sobbing that moves through me like a storm. When it happened this morning, I was taking Theo to school and, gripped by paranoia, I kept thinking of how this stranger now knew about my son. What if I had put Theo in some kind of danger? I had to stop in the street and cover my face with my hands while I swallowed the sobs down.

Tell Jane I hope to catch her soon.

An innocent comment or an indirect threat from Sandy?

Last night, the same recurring, conflicting thoughts kept me awake. Sandy, I reasoned, would not come looking for me himself. What if he'd hired a private detective to do it? Wouldn't that make sense? No, I thought, don't be ridiculous. Even if he had, he knows nothing about me apart from the name I had then. Both my first name and surname are different now.

But what if?

I am exhausted but working is better than sitting around with my thoughts. Memories long buried are surfacing. Details of the night with Sandy. I remember I was wearing a black, off-the-shoulder top. I remember the first part of my body he kissed was my bare shoulder.

It is lunchtime, and Lili and I are waiting on the tables out in the courtyard. It is hot and still, and every table beneath the plane trees is occupied. Mostly by guests but locals and day trippers also come here to sample Darid's cooking, which has earned him good write-ups on Tripadvisor and other travel websites.

I carry a bowl of lamb tagine over to an Italian lady who is staying at the hotel alone. Early sixties with white cropped hair, she is warding off the heat with pale pink linen trousers and a matching linen tunic. As I set the bowl down in front of her, she drains the last of her rosé.

'This looks amazing,' she says in English, dipping her head to inhale the steam rising from the fragrant lamb.

I point at her empty wine glass. 'Would you like another?'

'Why not, yes? I am on holiday.' She relaxes back into her chair with the contended sigh of someone who has left all their worries behind. Lucky her. The scent from the pots of lavender rises up to meet me but does nothing to lessen that whorl of anxiety at my core.

As I pick up her glass, intending to leave, she asks me how long I have lived here. I prepare myself for the usual guest conversation. It isn't long until she asks me where I come from.

'The Cotswolds,' I say.

'I love that place. You are from one of the beautiful little villages?'

'Bourton-on-the-Water.'

'I know it. Yes. So beautiful.'

Louise Disley from Bourton-on-the-Water.

A memory jolts me. The dark whorl of anxiety sends out a warning flare.

The first time I met Sandy at La Cave à Vin, he was with another man, and they were drinking heavily. Sandy didn't seem too affected by the alcohol, but the other man was shouting and singing and provoking some of the other customers. When Sandy came to the bar to buy the fourth round of drinks, he explained the loud, belligerent man was his brother and apologised for him. Then he introduced himself. *Sandy Gilligan from the fair city of Manchester.*

We shook hands and I did the same. *Louise Disley from Bourton-on-the-Water.*

The sound of glass shattering against the gravel brings me back to the present. The guest's wine glass has slipped from my hand and lies in fragments at my feet.

'So sorry,' I say. 'I'll get something to clear this up and I'll get your wine.'

'It's okay,' she says, looking at me with concern. 'Don't worry.'

I smile as I back away, but I am worried. Very worried indeed.

* * *

It is another half an hour before I can escape lunch duties and return to our silent apartment. Michel has gone canoeing for the day with Jacques and Bastien at the adventure park in nearby Vidauban. I think he was glad of the invitation and the chance to get away from me.

Louise Disley from Bourton-on-the-Water.

If Sandy remembers that exchange, he will know where I come from, as well as my original name. I wish I could go back in time and retract that sentence.

In the kitchen, I sit at the table with my laptop. A quick glance at the clock tells me I need to leave soon to pick up Theo. In two weeks, school will break up for the holidays. How will I cope with my son being around all the time when I'm in a state like this?

Minette pops her head through the cat flap, and it

isn't long before she jumps on to the table and plants her front paws on the laptop keyboard.

'*Non.*' She meows as I pick her up and place her on the floor. '*Non,*' I say when she crouches to jump again. She sticks her nose in the air and eyes me with that knowing look before slinking out of the kitchen.

Could a private detective find me? Up until now I thought I was untraceable on social media, but that certainty is gone. Disley is a common surname in the Cotswolds, but, as far as I know, my family are the only Disleys in Bourton-on-the-Water. It would be easy for someone to track them down and find out the names of my parents and siblings.

With twitchy fingers, I enter into the search engine the name of the only family member I am close to. Ben Disley. A page of entries appears. Ben, two years older than me, is a lecturer in medical history at Exeter University and most of the search results are work-related, but there is his Facebook page too, which is public. I told him a few years ago he should set it to private, but he never listened.

I linger on the most recent photographs. Ben and his wife, Sinead, on holiday in Ibiza. Tanned and loved-up and smiling. Like me, Ben rejected God at an early age, unlike our other siblings. Bonded by our lack of faith, we have always kept in touch.

Back in time I go, until I reach Ben and Sinead's wedding four years ago. They got married on a beach in Crete and only my elder sister Rachel and I attended the unconventional three-day celebrations. So many photographs. I did my best to stay out of them unless Ben insisted. Naturally, he wanted one of him with his sisters. I find the picture. There we are with our arms round each other, sunburned faces glowing.

Mandy, my favourite ex-girlfriend of Ben's, has written a comment underneath the photograph. *Wow! You guys! Jane looks as hot as ever. Where is she these days? Can't find her on Facebook.*

Sandy knows what I look like. If he has seen this photograph, he will know it is me and he will know my first name.

Anxiety bubbles up in me. I force myself to read Ben's reply to her comment.

She hates social media. Lucky bitch lives in Draguignan in the south of France.

If he has seen this photograph, he will know everything.

36

COLETTE

Dad has the TV news on in the living room with the volume up. I'm sitting on my bed with my laptop, trying to work, and all I can hear is indistinct chatter loud enough to be distracting. The noise is driving me nuts. I've got a big job on at the moment – a hotel in Copenhagen that needs copy for a new website done fast.

My phone vibrates on my bedside table. Another WhatsApp from Lynne.

No worries. Another time xx.

She messaged me earlier to invite me out for a

drink, but I used work as an excuse. I wish Dad hadn't given her my number.

She took me by surprise the other day when she asked if Dad and I had gone for a drive last Thursday. As far as I can recall, Dad went out for a couple of hours alone that morning, to have a coffee in the old town and then walk up Castle Hill. At first I wondered why he'd lied to Lynne like that, and I wondered if he'd lied to me too. Where did he go that morning? Was he hiding something? Then I realised he might have told her about the drive we had planned for Saint-Tropez the following Tuesday and she'd got confused. Or maybe he wanted a break from her but didn't want to hurt her feelings. I covered for him as best as I could. I didn't want him to look bad.

Is it me or is the TV suddenly even louder? I go through to the living area and ask him to turn the volume down. He looks up from the sofa and frowns, as if he has no idea how loud it is. 'Just a bit,' I say.

'Sure,' he says. 'Sorry.'

In the kitchen, I pour myself a glass of chilled water from the fridge. The afternoon is hot, thirty-one degrees, and the sea breeze only carries heat with it. Dad is dressed just in shorts, his T-shirt lying on the sofa beside him. When he came back earlier than expected from lunch with Lynne, I was working at the kitchen island, enjoying the peace and the cool lick of the air conditioning. I didn't want to waste my Friday afternoon traipsing to the library in this heat, so I opted to work in my room. I did feel a bit annoyed, but I suppose this is his house. He should be able to sit wherever he likes.

'Make us a tea while you're there, love,' he says. 'I'm gasping.'

His request irritates me. As I fill the kettle, I remind myself he's my father. The man who's always looked out for me. The man who would hurt others to keep me safe.

Yet I still shudder at the memory of what happened in the car park. Dad's arm around the neck of my attacker. The look on the kid's face when he scrambled away.

If we had reported the incident to the police, would they have seen Dad's actions as proof of a violent nature or the understandable reaction of a parent protecting a child? How confusing it is that we condone violence from men in some contexts but not others. Do men feel confused by this contradiction too?

Once I've made Dad's tea – strong, no sugar – I take it over to him.

'Have a break for five minutes,' he says, patting the sofa.

'I've got to get on.'

'Five minutes,' he says. 'Come on, make your old man happy.'

I sit beside him and sip my water while he surfs the TV channels. He rarely watches a programme all the way through, a habit that drove Mum mad. I'm suddenly conscious of his bare chest and back. At his trial, the prosecution showed photographs of his body taken by the police soon after his arrest. He had scratch marks on his back and chest. Marks left by Ella as she tried to defend herself, the prosecution said. Dad's lawyer argued the scratches were merely evidence of passionate sex.

'I spoke to your Uncle Jimmy yesterday,' he says.

'How is he?'

'Mad as ever. He's coming over for a quick visit next month.'

'Great. He can stay in the guest room.'

'Actually, we're going to Monaco for some guy time.'

'Oh.'

'Just for two nights. He'll no doubt cost me a fortune at the casino.'

'I'm sure.' Jimmy coming over is good, isn't it? A sign Dad is getting back into life. Still, I can't help associating Jimmy with that disastrous weekend in Marseilles, not that he was even there when Ella set her sights on Dad. I often wish he'd stayed an extra night. How different our lives might be then.

Dad stops surfing and settles on an all-day news channel. The first words I hear are 'Henri Breton'. With a disapproving expression, the female anchor announces another woman has accused the actor of sexual misconduct. An actress, this time. Her photograph flashes up on the screen. Her name is Hanna Fischer, and she is very pretty. The newsreader says the alleged incident happened eight years ago. Tension from my father's body seeps into the space between us. He sits totally still, like an animal spotted by a predator, hoping it can escape unharmed.

'Haven't we had enough of stories like this?' I keep my tone light and cheerful. 'There must be something better on?' Footage appears onscreen of Hanna walking in a park with her husband and two young sons. She is slight and slender, with a gentle look about her. Ella Watson looked demure in court, but Dad's defence managed to show she was anything but.

'Typical, showing her with her family.' Dad shakes his head. 'Like she's a saint just because she got married and had kids.'

After what happened to him, I don't suppose he

will ever have a balanced reaction to these kinds of stories. I'm not sure I will either.

'Loving wife and mother,' he says. 'As if that automatically makes her a credible witness.'

A snatch of Odette's closing statement at Dad's trial comes back to me.

Sandy Gilligan was a loving husband to his wife, Angela, right up to the end of her life, and he continues to be a loving father to Colette and Patrick. Colette who has been here every day to support him and knows beyond doubt, as I'm sure you will too, that Monsieur Gilligan deserves an innocent verdict.

Those words meant something. They were true.

Dad changes the channel. The screen fills with blue. A shark swims across it.

'I'd better get back to work,' I say.

* * *

An hour later, when I'm sitting on my bed, hunched over my laptop, Dad knocks on the door and says he's going to drive down to the beach and have a swim.

'No, I'm good,' I say when he invites me to join him.

After the front door slams shut, I stare at the last

line I've written. *The Scandic Retreat Hotel offers guests a pillow menu.*

I delete the sentence, put my laptop aside and leave my bedroom. In the hallway, I stand outside Dad's room for a minute, pretending I don't know what I'm about to do.

As soon as I enter his room, I can smell him. Not his soap or his aftershave but his own, indescribable scent. I've known it from birth. Bonded with it in some primitive way. I must have been able to recognise it before I consciously understood who he was.

I go to the chest of drawers and open the one where he keeps his socks. Reaching into the back of it, I pull out the innocuous-looking pair of socks that makes me feel sick every time I touch it. It sounds silly, but I like to check the knife is still there when he leaves the house. This time I take it out and let it rest heavy in my palm. Folded up, it looks innocent. Where did he get it from? Did he buy it as soon as he got out of jail? For the first time, my thumb caresses the groove in the curved bit of steel that is the only visible part of the blade.

I only want to see what it looks like.

The blade unfolds smoothly and swiftly. I picture Dad with it in his hand during the fight with the boy in the car park. He could have flicked the blade out in seconds.

There is nothing to worry about. Dad doesn't want to go back to jail. He'll do anything to stay out of that place.

The blade folds away just as easily. I stuff the knife back into the socks and return them to their hiding place. I linger in the room, examining the scattered objects on top of his chest of drawers. Several receipts, including a recent one for a meal for two at Le Plongeoir. He and Mum went there all the time. Liam and I had dinner there the night before Dad's arrest. I think that was the last time we were ever happy together.

Mum's side of the bed beckons. I sit on it, as if doing so might make her appear and give me a good talking to. *Don't give your dad a hard time. He's been through enough.*

Mum says nothing. I rest a hand on Dad's pillow. It holds a slight dent from the weight of his head. In court, Ella claimed my father held a cushion over her face and she couldn't breathe.

I notice the edge of an envelope sticking out from beneath the pillow. I pull it out. It's a white A4 one, bulky and heavy. The front is blank, and I can't help filling it with my fears. I imagine the name ELLA WATSON printed across the front.

My father has always valued his privacy. As kids we were taught never to look through his things. The envelope has already been opened. Mum is talking to me now, as I slide my hand inside. *Don't you dare, young lady.*

The first item to come out is a sheet of paper with a few lines of printed information on it. *Mrs Durand. Hôtel des Arbres, Avenue de Montferrat, Draguignan.*

A sharp pain low in my belly. Mrs Durand is Ella Watson; I can feel it. He has been trying to find her, and here she is, living in a small town less than two hours' drive from here. Ella Watson with her dark eyes and her long, dark hair. How foolish of me to think she was gone from our lives for ever.

My hands tremble as I remove a photograph from the envelope. A woman with dark eyes and long dark hair looks up at me. A woman who is not Ella Watson.

A sharp intake of breath as I try to process what I'm seeing.

Who the hell is she? And why is my father looking for her?

37

JANE

'I'll have one of those.' I point to the cocktail shaker in Bastien's hand. We are standing in his kitchen, an array of alcohol bottles on the vintage Formica table in front of us.

'Really?' He looks at me, surprised.

'Sure. I'm in the mood.'

'But you don't drink.'

'Jesus, Bastien, just give me a cocktail.'

'Okay. Okay.' He pours me a French gimlet into one of the cocktail glasses lined up next to the bottles. 'They're strong,' he says when he hands it over.

'I'm a big girl.' The first sip makes me splutter. Gin, Saint-Germain liqueur and freshly squeezed lime juice. Strong and sour.

I return to the garden, clutching my cocktail glass, and find Elyna and Jacques have arrived. Jacques, lean and tanned as always, pulls out a chair for Elyna at the long wooden table at the centre of the garden. Elyna, tall with wavy blonde hair down to her waist, gathers the folds of her long floral dress in one hand as she sits down, as feminine and elegant as ever. Hard to imagine that when she was at school with Michel and Bastien, she was their tomboy best friend.

'Hey, everyone,' I say when I reach the table. Michel does a double take when I sip my cocktail.

'Jane?' Elyna says. 'What's going on with you?'

'Maybe I'm in a party mood,' I say.

'You don't drink,' Jacques says.

I shrug. 'Maybe I've started again.'

'Jane's in a party mood.' Nathalie applauds me. She has been pumping the milk from her breasts all day so she can have a drink with us tonight. 'What are we celebrating?' she says.

'Whatever you like,' I say. I am drinking to forget, not to celebrate. I want to forget about Sandy.

The hit from the alcohol is instant. A giddy rush followed by a pleasant numbing sensation. We are speaking French as usual, and I wonder if my grasp on the language might slip after a few drinks.

Bastien appears with a tray of cocktails and puts

them on the table. 'To friendship,' he says when everyone has a glass. All six of us raise our drinks. A muddle of clinking follows. *Santé.* It is a warm evening and the garden at the back of Nathalie and Bastien's townhouse looks magical. The solar fairy lights strung between the trunks of two stone pines are beginning to glow even though it is only eight thirty. A small fountain provides the soothing sound of running water in the background. Bastien inherited the house from his grandparents. A three-storey, ramshackle place, scruffy and quirky and full of love. His parents have taken the kids tonight, so we are all child-free for the first time in ages. Everyone has dressed up – the boys have shirts on with their jeans and Nathalie, like Elyna, is in a long dress, hers black and tight and backless. I have on an emerald-green, full-length skirt and a black vest top. Now we have young kids, this is as close as we all get to going out on a Saturday night.

Our first topic of conversation is the school holidays that start a week on Monday. We all laugh when Elyna confesses she is dreading having her boys home for so long.

'At least you lot are actually having a holiday,' I say. Both couples will take a fortnight's vacation out of Draguignan. Michel and I will be here to deal with the hotel's busiest period. We usually go on holiday in late September.

Michel lifts his nose in the air. 'My God, you two, dinner smells amazing.'

Drifting out from the kitchen is the spicy smell of the lamb curry Nathalie has had in the oven most of the day. As a couple they are brilliant hosts, but I would have preferred to stay home. Last night, I woke at 3 a.m. and stared at the ceiling until dawn. There, in the quiet and silent time, I had to think about everything I can forget in the daytime when I'm busy with Theo or working in the hotel. I thought about Mr James. Is he a private detective or is anxiety getting the better of me?

'Jane, this isn't like you,' Elyna says when I am the first to finish my drink and put my glass on the table. I want to tell her the Jane she knows is not the real one. The Jane she knows is a construct, a fiction. Tonight, I want to be Louise. The wild, reckless person I was for those two months in Cannes before Sandy came into my life.

Bastien goes into the house and comes back with another full cocktail shaker.

'Are you sure?' Michel says when I accept Bastien's offer of a top-up. I silence him with a kiss. Afterwards, he looks at me, confused, as if unsure whether the kiss marks the end of our recent tensions, or the start of new ones. I am not sure what the kiss means either.

We have another round of gimlets. My head is pleasantly fuzzy now, my limbs soft. I tell Nathalie and Elyna they look beautiful, and they laugh.

'I like drunk Jane,' Nathalie says.

Jacques takes out his silver tobacco tin and rolls a joint. He is the only one of us who still buys weed. When he offers the joint to me, I refuse. Louise never liked weed either. Michel takes it, though he rarely smokes these days. Maybe he too is in the mood for forgetting.

I tip my head back and look at the sky. The light is fading. Pink clouds float over my head. Soon there will be stars. Elyna tells us her boys are doing a school project about the 1999 theft of the Rembrandt painting *Child With a Soap Bubble* from Draguignan museum. It is the story the town is most famous for. Patrick Vialaneix, a twenty-four-year-old man, became obsessed with the painting and hid in Draguignan museum overnight so he could steal it.

'Philippe cannot believe this guy lived with the painting in his house for fifteen years,' Jacques says.

Vialaneix was obsessed with the Rembrandt. He kept it hidden from his wife and family and had to secretly take it with him every time they moved house.

'Etienne can't understand how he kept it hidden from everyone.' Elyna accepts the joint from Michel and takes a deep drag. 'He doesn't believe anyone can tell lies for that long.'

Everyone laughs except me. I know what it is like to carry a secret around. I understand the stress Vialaneix lived with for fifteen years.

Fifteen. Can I carry my secret around with me for that long? If I do, will it consume me, like the painting consumed its possessor?

Bastien returns to the kitchen, declares the food ready and we eat it outside at the table. The fragrant lamb is full of flavour, but I cannot stomach it. I take small bites and push the rest around my plate, hoping no one will notice I am not eating. There is red wine with the food, and I take plenty of that. Jane warns me I am drinking far too much and will regret it, but Louise keeps holding out her glass for a top-up. Louise ignores Michel when he says she has had enough.

'Shit.' Jacques peers at his phone. 'Another story about Henri Breton.'

'Yeah,' Bastien says, 'Hanna Fischer. Heard about it yesterday.'

Jacques shakes his head. 'No, this is someone else.'

'Another one?' Nathalie says.

Jacques tells us the actress Audrey Marceau has

accused Breton of inappropriate behaviour and sexual assault on a film set five years ago. Why do all the euphemisms for rape have two words? Does splitting the crime in two make it more manageable? Like cutting a piece of tough meat in half to make it easier to swallow?

'How many more?' Elyna says.

My head is spinning, even though I am sitting very still. *How many more?* The women keep on coming and they are talking and the authorities are taking them seriously. I wonder if Sandy is watching the news tonight. The story has been everywhere since his release; he must have heard about it.

'Let me guess,' Michel says. 'He is claiming it was consensual?'

'Of course,' says Bastien.

Jacques shrugs. 'Maybe she did want to sleep with him.'

Nathalie sighs. 'That doesn't mean he didn't rape her.' I want to hug her for saying the word aloud. For having the guts not to cut it into pieces.

'It's not as simple as that,' Jacques says, in the cool, impersonal voice he uses for his legal work. It was Jacques I pumped for information after Sandy's trial. I told him I was curious about a rape case in the newspapers. How did sentencing work here, I'd asked him?

Would the man's victim be informed when he was released from prison?

'Of course it's simple,' Elyna says.

Jacques shakes his head. 'It's a very grey area.'

I stare at him. Louise knows he is right. Louise might have said the same thing herself. Jane knows it too. She knows what it is like to live in the grey. To walk home from a hotel the next morning not knowing if what happened to you was wrong or right. The act itself is not grey, but rape is clever. It uses shame as camouflage.

'Maybe it would have been better if he'd killed her.' My words come out in English. A bad move. My native tongue might betray me.

'What do you mean?' Elyna says, a shocked look on her face.

'Oh, come on.' I take a swig of wine. 'If he'd killed her, we wouldn't be doubting her. We wouldn't be judging her or tearing her character apart.'

Jacques frowns. 'We are just saying—'

'She would be an angel,' I say. 'People would lay down flowers in the street. They would say she was a beautiful talent taken too soon. They wouldn't dare say she was stupid for getting herself murdered. She would be good and the man who killed her would be evil. Simple.'

Everyone is staring at me.

'She's got a point,' Nathalie says in French, guiding me back to safer territory. 'This woman would be a saint by now if he'd killed her.'

Dizziness washes over me. I grip the table for balance as I get to my feet.

'Back in a minute,' I say.

* * *

Inside the house, I stop in the cluttered, homely kitchen. On the worktop, lying on a wooden chopping board, is a large, sharp knife. I pick it up. I wonder if Sandy is thinking about me. Has he seen the story about Henri Breton and, if so, is he wondering if I might finally speak up? If I did, could he go back to jail?

He has a lot to lose.

So do I. My son.

The knife's steel handle is cool in my palm. Nice is not that far away. I could get a taxi to Les Arcs station now, jump on a train and be there in less than two hours. If I knew where he lived, I could wait nearby and jump out at him with this knife. Not to hurt him. No, only to terrify him as he continues to terrify me. To warn him away from me and my family.

I put the knife back and head for the bathroom on the first floor, almost falling over one of the boys' skateboards on the stairs. I sit on the toilet, but it takes me ages to pee. I forgot that happens when you drink too much. When I'm finally done, I get up and my skirt, which for some reason I have unzipped rather than lifted, falls to my feet.

I step out of it and look at myself in the tall free-standing mirror opposite the claw foot bath. I touch my thighs. The thighs Sandy Gilligan bruised by kneeling his weight on them. Back and front. The alcohol is not helping. It is making me remember. Making everything less grey.

I take off my vest top, followed by my bra and knickers. Naked, I look at my reflection in the mirror. Sandy is all over this body. The neck where he left a bite mark that turned yellow then black. A mark I hid with a scarf for over a fortnight. My nipples. He stroked them gently at first and I enjoyed that. Later, when he had crossed over the line, he twisted them hard enough to make me cry out. A cry of pain, not pleasure.

My hand slides between my legs. My husband and son also claimed this place for their own, but I consented to that. Sandy buried his face here once. While he was down there, I thought of Michel and the superior skill of his tongue and fingers, and I missed him. I told Sandy I'd made a mistake and had to leave. I tried to close my legs, but he forced a knee between them to make way for himself. When he'd had enough, he turned me over and found new territory to explore.

A knock at the bathroom door. 'Jane?'

It is Michel. The door inches open. Didn't I lock it? I must be very drunk.

'Jesus.' Michel steps inside and locks the bathroom door behind him. 'What's going on? Why are you undressed?'

I realise I am standing in my friends' bathroom with nothing on. My husband stares at me and for a moment I fear he can see it all on me. Mine and Sandy's story, as if it is tattooed all over my skin.

I walk over to him and put my arms around his waist. 'Kiss me.'

'You're so drunk. Why are you drinking?'

I stand on tiptoes, pull his face down to mine and kiss him. He yields, his tongue fervent, his nails digging into my bare back.

'Fuck me,' I say. He is getting hard through his jeans. He wants me.

He stops kissing me and grips my elbows. 'Not here.'

'They won't mind.' I can hear my friends on the

patio below. Music and laughter. They will probably cheer us on when they realise what we're up to.

I drop to my knees and unzip his jeans. He moans when I put him in my mouth. I am acting like Louise, and he likes it. Louise will do anything. He could fuck Louise as hard as he wants to. Louise likes that.

'No.' He steps away from me.

'What's wrong?' I wipe my mouth as I look up at him.

He zips up his jeans. 'You're too drunk.'

'Really?' Spite shoots through me, cold and merciless. 'Don't you want to have sex with me unless we're trying for a baby? Is that what's wrong?'

'Stop it.'

'Is that all I am to you? A fucking breeding machine?'

'Please.' His face is white. Are those tears in his eyes?

'I'm ready. I want a baby.' I clap my hands. 'Come on, let's get to it.' Maybe I am ready. Maybe I need to put Sandy out of my mind. If I don't, he will stop me living the life I've worked so hard for. 'Come, on,' I say again. 'What are you waiting for?'

Michel shakes his head. 'Not like this.' He picks up my underwear, my skirt and my top and hands them to me. 'Not like this.'

38

COLETTE

The apartment is silent. Dad has gone to dinner with Lynne. He told me not wait up. I smiled and told him to enjoy himself. I don't want him to guess something's wrong.

Maybe nothing is wrong.

The knife is in its hiding place. I checked it after he went out. I also looked for the envelope with the photographs in it but had no luck. He must have hidden it, and I don't want to search too hard in case he guesses I've been in his room. What a strange role reversal. He's gone out, and I'm the one waiting in. I'm the one worried what he might be hiding in his room.

It doesn't matter that I can't find the envelope.

After discovering it, I used my phone to take pictures of the photographs and information it contained.

It's the first week of July, and I've opened the balcony doors wide. The night air streaming in is warm, but I can't stop shivering. In the silent apartment, I sit on the sofa and scroll through the pictures on my phone. Mrs Durand. First name Jane, nationality British, according to the profile I found in the envelope. Where have I seen her before? Maybe she only looks familiar because she reminds me of Ella Watson.

Maybe my father does have a type.

Revulsion pulses through me. Since finding the photographs, I've felt sick. I had a brief burst of hope when I thought Jane might be the daughter of Dad's prison friend. The one he gave money to. I clung to this explanation until I had to admit Jane doesn't look like a mixed-up young woman in a bad place. She doesn't live in Nice, either, which is where Dad said he was going to meet the delinquent daughter. I've also tried to be grateful he isn't looking for Ella. So far that's failed to make me feel any better.

Everything is murky, apart from one fact. My father is up to something. These photographs look like the work of a private detective. The person Dad was speaking to when I overheard him, I imagine. There was no clue to this detective's identity on any of the photographs or information sheets in the envelope. Could it be someone Dad heard about when in prison? Someone shady?

The pictures, most of them, were taken at a distance with a powerful lens. There is Jane, walking through the old town of Draguignan. There she is in the courtyard of the Hôtel des Arbres, serving lunch to customers. There she is walking down a tree-lined boulevard clutching the hand of her son.

When I first saw the little boy, I wondered if I had a brother I didn't know about, the result of a fling Dad had before he went into prison. When I realised the boy was too young for that, I didn't know whether to be relieved or disappointed.

There's Jane with her husband, sitting on a garden sofa in the courtyard of the hotel, kissing while their son plays nearby. The profile that accompanied the photograph names him as Michel Durand. Jane appears to be a happily married woman with a son. Whoever she is, she has more in her life than I do. If I didn't know she existed until recently, why am I certain I recognise her? It isn't only the resemblance to Ella Watson that unsettles me.

I keep coming back to the final picture. Whoever

took it must have gone inside the Hôtel des Arbres for a drink because the photograph focuses on a bar at one end of a dining room, and Jane is standing behind it, pouring out a glass of red wine.

A memory comes to me, along with a wave of nausea. A bar in Cannes. Dim lighting, booths with scalloped cushions and a long bar counter with stools running along it. A girl behind the bar, dark-haired and pretty.

From the sideboard, I take out the stack of family photo albums. As I flick through, I remember Dad doing the same the morning before our trip to Cannes. There we are. Dad and Mum and Liam and me, standing in front of the Majestic Hôtel. We stayed there six nights. Uncle Jimmy turned up for a couple of days too. Mum was annoyed; she didn't know Dad had invited him. Then Mum had to go home because her father had a mild heart attack. Dad wanted to go with her, but she insisted she had Uncle Brian to help her and there was no point us all losing out on the rest of the holiday. Uncle Jimmy stayed one more night and he and Dad went out on the town. Then Dad, Liam and I had two nights in Cannes together.

I scan every picture but there are none taken inside a bar. What was the place called? I'm sure it was on a side street opposite La Croisette. I flip open my laptop and open Google search. *Best bars in Cannes.* The first result is a Top Ten Bars in the city. What I find at number 7 brings bile up the back of my throat.

La Cave à Vin.

Same bar Ella worked at in Marseilles. La Cave à Vin is a boutique chain; I remember now. One Dad said he liked. I want to stop searching. I want to pretend I never found the photographs of Jane. But what if my search puts my mind at rest? I might find there is nothing to worry about after all.

I click on the website's picture gallery. There is the long bar with the glinting optics. I remember Dad perched on one of the bar stools, a glass of red wine in his hand. I remember sitting in one of the booths with Liam and leaning my head against his shoulder as he took a selfie. Liam. Of course. Out of the two of us, he was the better photographer and usually tasked with taking the snaps when we were on holiday or out with friends. Images I then shared on social media.

For the first time in years, I log into Facebook and reactivate my account. Doing so reminds me of why I abandoned it. The comments my so-called friends wrote beneath the final picture of Dad I posted. *Traitor. Wake the fuck up, Colette.*

I don't look at any of that. Instead, I bring up my

photographs and click back through the years. What if I find what I'm looking for? Do I really want to discover evidence against my own father? Evidence of what?

A hot, uneasy pain at the pit of my stomach.

I avoid the pictures of my wedding. I might still be with Liam if Dad had never met Ella Watson. Did Dad meet Jane Durand? That's what I need to find out.

When I come to the pictures of our trip to Cannes, I find a shot of me clowning about on the red carpet in front of the Palais Royal. There's a selfie of Liam and me on the carousel opposite our hotel. There we are in Le Majestic's ornate lobby, drinking coffee. The next photograph stops my breath – me and Dad sitting in a booth at La Cave à Vin. He's looking into the camera, his hands folded under his chin, elbows on the table. I'm gazing up at him, my arms slung around his neck. In the next picture, I'm with Liam. For the first time, I notice I'm not looking at my husband in the same way I looked at my father.

Then I find Jane. She is in the background of a photograph of Dad sitting at the bar. She is looking up at him through lowered eyelids. Coy. Flirtatious. Or am I imagining that?

I check the photographs on my phone against the

one on my laptop. It is her. Dad and Jane met in Cannes. She was a British barmaid, just like Ella.

The question I don't want to ask buzzes in my brain.

What, if anything, happened between them?

39

LYNNE

This is the life. Friday lunchtime, and I'm sitting at a round brass table outside a bar in the old town, Aperol Spritz in hand. My new favourite drink; it's so refreshing on a hot day like today. Moreish, though. This, my second, is almost done.

Yes, this is the life. Be more fun if Sandy was here. We're seeing each other tonight, but he had to talk to his accountant earlier and now he's got some admin to do. I don't mind. Not really. Isn't this what people do in places like this? Sit and watch the world go by. Soak up the atmosphere. I'm living the dream, aren't I?

Almost.

It's nearly two weeks since that romantic dinner at

Le Plongeoir, and Sandy and I still haven't had sex. We've been for romantic walks along the promenade, had God knows how many lovely meals out, but no sign of any bedroom action. We'll figure it out as we go, he said, as we stood on that beach watching the sunset. What is there to figure out? Why can't we get our kit off and get down to it?

The rest of my Spritz disappears and a giddy numbness spreads through me. I order another. When it arrives, the waiter asks if I want something to eat with it.

'No, ta,' I say. '*Non, merci.*'

It's all my fault. I should never have interrogated him about the woman from the café. No wonder he's keeping his distance from me. Thing is, the longer he waits to make a move on me, the more horrible thoughts creep in. What if he lied to me? What if he is sleeping with that woman and that's why he's in no rush with me? I hate myself for doubting him, especially if what he told me about his Good Samaritan act is true. I want to ask Colette if she knows about the guy from prison and his daughter, just to cross-check what Sandy told me, but I can't risk her telling him I've been prying. Especially if he's telling the truth. How will that make me look?

Halfway through my third Spritz, an idea comes to me. One I've been toying with for a while. Why don't I go to the café and check if the woman's there? Wouldn't hurt to see her up close and see what my intuition tells me. What harm could it do?

* * *

By the time I reach the square where Café Corsica is, my feet are killing me, and the straps of my Roman sandals are digging right into my flesh. I got lost on the way here, the Spritzes impairing my sense of direction. Bit unsteady on my feet too.

Six men cluster round one of the tables outside the café, sipping beers and playing a card game. One of them calls out something I don't hear, but in response a figure strides out of the café.

It's her.

She speaks to the men, nods and disappears back inside. I weave across the square and take a seat at one of the white plastic tables. The men are behind me, but I can tell they're having a good stare. Doesn't look like the kind of place popular with tourists or ladies on their own. I take out my phone and scroll through my photos, trying to look casual.

When the woman comes out again with a tray of beers for the men, she looks taken aback to find me sitting there. Is that because I'm out of place or because she knows who I am? What if Sandy's told her about me?

'Be with you in a moment,' she says, speaking English with a heavy French accent.

I'm trembling all over. My mouth is dry, and I can feel a headache starting up behind my eyes. When the woman comes over to me, I put my phone on the table and try to concentrate, try to take her all in, but the alcohol is really kicking in now, making me woozy.

'What do you want?' she says, her voice low and husky. She appears uninterested in me. Either she doesn't know who I am or she's a good actress. She's a skinny thing, legs and arms on show in a denim miniskirt and a black vest top. Bright green eyes and black hair. Piercings all the way up one ear and a tattoo of a snake on one arm. She's pretty but rough-looking. She could easily be the daughter of a man in prison. A girl from a tough background.

'Black coffee,' I say. 'Please.'

Yes, I think, as she heads into the café. She could be the daughter Sandy told me about. She could also be a bit of rough he's got going on the side.

An awful thought comes to me. What if I wasn't

the only woman visiting him in prison? I saw plenty of girls like this one whenever I went there. Once when I visited Sandy, he told me his cellmate had got hold of a mobile phone and was using it to join dating apps. I laughed when Sandy told me the guy had three women on the go. What if Sandy did the same thing?

By the time the girl brings my order out, rage is swirling round inside me. Something's going on between her and Sandy, I know it.

'Can I ask you something?' I say as she puts my coffee in front of me.

She shrugs. 'Okay.'

My phone pings. A message from Sandy flashes up on the screen. I snatch up the phone and try to focus on his words.

Can't wait to see you later. Missed you today.

His sweet words soothe my rage but leave me itchy with guilt. What would he think if he saw me here now?

'Well?' she says, impatiently. 'What is your question?'

I look up at her hard, beautiful face then down at Sandy's message. I've given up everything for him.

Everything. Do I really want to ruin what we've got with my paranoia?

'Forget it.' I get to my feet, still a little wobbly, and take a ten-euro note from my purse. 'Here,' I say, slapping it on the table, 'keep the change.'

40

JANE

Little things scare me. The vigorous boil of the kettle, for instance. I put it on a few moments ago and, as it rattles on its base, I imagine it leaping into the air and pouring its scalding contents over my son, who is sitting a good distance away at the kitchen table. I stand guard and flick it off as soon as it reaches the required temperature.

I know this is silly. I know I am transferring my fears on to an inanimate object. Knowing this does not make me feel any better.

'Maman.' Theo holds up the lumpy figure he has sculpted out of red plasticine. Red is his favourite colour this week.

'*C'est beau*,' I tell him. What if my son is in danger? At night, when I can't sleep, I think of terrible things. The worst is Sandy hurting Theo in some way or threatening to so I keep quiet. The best-case scenario is that the truth about Sandy breaks up my marriage and Theo is scarred by growing up with divorced parents.

'*C'est un bonhomme*,' Theo says, before pulling the head off his masterpiece. The school holidays have just begun. Most parents I know are stressing about how to keep their kids occupied for six weeks. I am praying that is all I have to worry about.

It is Monday morning, just over a week since I disgraced myself at the dinner party. When I finally staggered from the bathroom back out into Nathalie and Bastien's garden, I found Michel ready to leave, holding my handbag. He told them I wasn't feeling well, and, right on cue, I rushed over to the stone fountain and vomited into it.

My friends were very understanding. The morning after the party, while nursing a killer hangover, I spoke to each of them and apologised. They laughed it off, told me it made a nice change for me to be the drunken mess, but I sensed concern beneath the jokes. Nathalie asked me directly if anything was wrong. I told her Michel and I had discussed having another baby and that this had triggered painful memories. I hated myself for the lie, and her sympathy made me feel worse, but I had to say something. Michel's anger faded a little when he learned I'd confided in Nathalie. He saw this as a positive sign and suggested I make another appointment with Julia Martin. When I rang to do so, she was on holiday. I felt relieved. I am so taut she could break me. What would be the point of telling her everything now? I don't know if my fears are real or imaginary. If I tell her and everyone else about my past for nothing, the hard work of concealing it for seven years will have been pointless.

I make a cup of strong tea and tell Theo we are going to sit in the garden. He resists at first but relents when he remembers he left his collection of toy trucks out there. I usher him out the kitchen door.

'Where is Papa?' he says.

'Working.' This morning Michel gathered his laptop and work folders and announced he would be working in one of the empty hotel rooms for the rest of the morning. He said he needed peace to finish one of his graphic design commissions. The hotel will be busy this weekend with the Bastille Day celebrations in town and he wants to get his work done before then. I think he just wanted to get away from me.

The garden is only a small enclosed patio at the

back of the apartment, but it provides some privacy from hotel guests. Here we get sun in the morning and shade in the oppressive heat of the afternoon. We have decorated the compact space with blue ceramic pots of lavender and sunflowers. I sit in one of the deep wicker armchairs while Theo gathers the toy trucks scattered around the patio. Minette appears at the top of the high wooden fence surrounding us and jumps down to join us, much to Theo's delight. He babbles away to her as he pushes his trucks around. She lies down in a strip of shade beneath the fence, uninterested.

The sun is warm on my face, bees hum among the lavender. A peaceful scene, but I am on edge, wary of more memories ambushing me. My drunken night at the dinner party was supposed to help me forget, but instead, acting like my old self for a night has invited the past back in.

I remember now how Sandy and I chatted away the first of the two nights he came into the bar. The night he was with his drunk and obnoxious brother. He was good company, in no way inappropriate, and we talked mostly about his family. He didn't say much about his wife, who'd apparently been called away on a family emergency, only that she was 'great'. I'd heard enough men talking about their wives to know that meant he was happily married but not totally devoted. He spoke for ages about his daughter. He said they'd always shared a special bond. A lovely girl, so good to her dad. Drop dead gorgeous but no bimbo. She had a great job and a great future ahead of her. He confessed he wasn't keen on her husband but admitted no man would ever be good enough for her in his eyes.

The way he talked about Colette made me warm to him. It also made me jealous. I didn't know what it was to have a father–daughter relationship like the one they shared. His love for her made me feel safe. His love for her made me think I had nothing to worry about.

'Go, go, go,' Theo says, jolting me back to the present. He is ramming one of his trucks against a plant pot. When I ask him to stop, he pushes out his lips at me, petulant.

'Play nicely,' I say. Play nicely? I sound like my mother.

He settles into a calmer game that involves piling the trucks on top of one another. I settle back into my chair. Back into the past.

The second night Sandy came to the bar, the night that changed my life for ever, Colette and her husband were with him. I'd imagined her as a bit of a princess, and I was right. She was beautiful and she knew it. From the adoring way she and Sandy gazed at each other, I could tell they were close. When he introduced us, he didn't use my name. *This young lady here is the best barmaid in Cannes*. I remember Colette gave me a quick, dismissive smile before turning to her father and asking him to recommend a cocktail for her. She didn't look at me again, but I didn't care. When I saw Sandy fussing over her, I had an odd feeling of power. I was only a year older than her, but her father saw me as a woman. Not a little girl he had ownership over. Then again, did he really think that much of her? He raped me in the same hotel she was staying at. In a way, he was violating her too. I don't imagine he would see it that way. He would have us in different compartments. Disrespect for me, adoration for Colette.

When I crept out of his room before dawn, I longed to find out her room number, knock on her door and tell her the truth about her father. I longed to shatter their relationship for good. When I saw her supporting Sandy at his trial, I both pitied and hated her.

A red truck lands at my feet.

'Did you just throw that?' I snap.

Theo looks at me with wary eyes. '*Non.*'

A wheel falls off the truck when I pick it up. Theo wails. I do not have the energy or patience for him today. I think of my own mother, struggling to manage four kids and understand why she often resorted to smacking us.

'Would you like a peach?' I say. His little face brightens. 'I'll get you a peach and Papa will fix your truck later.'

In the kitchen, I take a doughnut peach from the fruit bowl on the windowsill and the paring knife from the cutlery drawer and slice the peach into a red plastic bowl. The peach juice is sticky on my fingers as the knife sinks into the flesh.

I've often heard men say having a daughter changes them. They become better men; they treat women better. That didn't happen to Sandy, but is it possible prison has reformed him? If he is searching for me, maybe he wants to apologise? A nice idea, one I wish I could believe, but that dark whorl of anxiety deep inside me doesn't trust it. Surely, he would do anything not to go back to prison again? This thought turns sinister. *He would do anything.* Fear comes over me, dark and smothering. I look down at the paring knife in my hand.

He would do anything.

'Maman,' Theo calls from the garden, 'come see.'

I wipe the knife down and wrap it in a piece of kitchen towel. My handbag is hanging on the back of a kitchen chair. As I slip the knife inside it, the fear subsides. A little.

41

COLETTE

It is 9 a.m., and I'm sitting at a table outside the Brasserie Le Magenta, glad to be under the awning, away from a sky so blue it feels merciless.

'*Merci*, Paul,' I say as the waiter places my cappuccino on the table. No pain au chocolat today; I'm not hungry. I sip my coffee and watch people hurrying past on their way to work. A group of American tourists on a walking tour wanders through Place Magenta. They must be from the cruise ship anchored in the bay. A mass of beige enthusiasm, plying the tour guide with relentless questions.

The coffee is welcome. Jane kept me awake last night. As I stared at my ceiling, I wondered if she lies awake at night too, thoughts of my father keeping her from sleep. One of the photographs in the envelope showed a villa on a leafy street, another showed a close-up of one of the plaques next to the villa's main entrance. *Julia Martin, Psychologue Clinicien.* Why does Jane need to see a clinical psychologist? What secrets from the past has she shared with this Julia, and is Julia the only person she has shared her secrets with?

Once again, I remind myself there's no evidence of any wrongdoing on Dad's part. All he's done so far is find out the name and address of a barmaid he met in Cannes seven years ago. Whatever he's up to isn't stopping him from sleeping. When I got up in the night for a glass of water, I peeked into his room and found him curled on his side. He now sleeps as well as he did before he went to prison. This morning he was up for a run as usual, and when I left the apartment, he was on his phone, booking rooms at the Hôtel de Paris in Monaco for him and Uncle Jimmy.

My laptop is open on the table in front of me and I'm logged into Facebook. Luckily no one has noticed I'm back. The picture with Jane behind the bar at La Cave à Vin fills my screen. I've been over that night so many times. I remember paying Jane little attention when Dad introduced her to me as the best barmaid in the city. Did she say anything to me? I honestly don't remember. I have so many similar memories of

Dad introducing me to bar staff and hotel reception-
ists and waiters. Male and female. Mum said he was a
social animal who liked to talk to everyone. There
was nothing unusual about him befriending a
barmaid.

The voice of the prosecuting lawyer from Dad's
trial comes into my head. *You befriended Miss Watson at
her place of work, and you did so deliberately as part of a
plan to get her to your hotel room.*

We drank the first round of cocktails sitting at the
bar. That's when I took the photograph I'm looking at
now. I'm sure Dad told Jane that Liam and I were only
recently married, and she congratulated us before hurrying off to serve another customer. Liam and I were
tired. We'd spent the day on a sailing trip and wanted
to get back to the hotel and make the most of our luxurious room. Dad said he didn't mind us having the
evening to ourselves but insisted on taking us for a
drink.

We stayed for a second round and that's when we
moved to the booth. Not long after that, Liam and I returned to our hotel room. We had sex and ate club
sandwiches and chips in bed while watching a film.
The next morning, we had breakfast with Dad at the
hotel. He'd already been out for a run, had a shower
and was reading a copy of the *Financial Times* when we

got to the breakfast table. I can't recall anything odd about him that morning.

The lawyer's voice again. *And the next day you carried on with your life as normal. While Ella Watson was in a police station undergoing invasive testing and questioning you returned to your life as if nothing had happened.*

I search for Liam on Facebook. There he is, still with the same profile picture of him and Amber. The rest of his photographs are closed to me. Reserved for friends only, and he and I ceased to be friends the minute he questioned my father's innocence.

Yet he is the one person I need to talk to.

* * *

I go to the promenade to make the call. Less chance of being overheard. Every chance of being knocked over, however, as tourists on electric scooters speed past me. I feel a surge of a hatred for this relentless city. It feels even busier than usual as it gears up for the Bastille Day celebrations at the weekend. The swimmers and paddleboarders out in the bay look like they're trying to escape.

As I walk past a newspaper kiosk, the *Nice-Matin* headline on the billboard sets me on edge. More information about the Henri Breton case. Did Jane read about Dad's trial in the papers?

After claiming one of the white benches over-looking the bay, I take out my phone and call Liam. I've kept his number in my contacts since we split up. A little piece of him I haven't let go of. What if he's changed it? Even if he hasn't, it's almost 9 a.m. back in London. He's probably already at work.

It rings five times and then he answers. 'Colette?' he says.

My number must still be in his phone. This makes me smile, despite everything going on in my head. I can hear traffic in the background of the call. He must be walking somewhere in London. A pang of home-sickness hits me. We used to go into central London together in the mornings. Catch a train from Denmark Hill to Blackfriars and walk from there.

'Colette?' he says. 'Are you there?'

His voice is familiar and comforting. It's so good to hear him. 'Yes,' I say. 'I'm here.'

'What's wrong?'

It hurts to remember how well he knew me. 'Nothing,' I say, aware he can't be fooled. 'I need to ask you something. About that holiday we had in Cannes.'

'Hang on.' I hear horns beeping and his breathing speeds up. He must be running across a road. 'The one in that big hotel?' he says when he reaches the other side. 'The Majestic?'

'Yes.'

'What about it?'

'Do you remember a bar we went to. With Dad?'

'Christ, Colette.' A sarcastic chuckle. 'Which one?'

His criticism of Dad's drinking makes me stiffen. He never criticised it when Dad was buying the rounds. 'It was called La Cave à Vin and we sat at the bar for a bit then moved to one of the booths.'

'That's very specific.'

'Do you remember?'

He sighs. 'Yeah, I remember. The place where we had a row.'

'Did we?' I don't recall us arguing.

'You said the barmaid was flirting with your dad.'

Did I? 'You remember her, the barmaid?'

'She was just a barmaid.' A pause. 'She was fit, though. I remember that.'

'Why did we argue?'

'You said she was flirting with Sandy, and you didn't like it when I pointed out he was flirting with her.'

This isn't what I want to hear. 'Dad chats away to everyone,' I say, more to reassure myself than to contradict him. 'You know that.'

'That's what you said back then. When I said his behaviour was making me uncomfortable you got pissed off with me.'

I see it now. Me stalking out of the bar, Liam following me. The pair of us sniping at one another until we got back to the hotel room my father had paid for. Liam apologised eventually. Then came the make-up sex. Then the room service food in bed and the movie.

'What's this about?' Liam's voice is sharper now, more serious. 'What's going on?' His tone suggests he is putting pieces together I don't want him to connect.

'Nothing.'

'What's he done now?'

'Nothing.' I'm not lying. As far as I know he hasn't done anything.

'I don't believe you.'

'You never did.' My protective instinct kicks in. I think of all the people who doubted Dad and me, including my own husband. Liam's doubt radiates down the phone; if I'm not careful it will infect me. 'He hasn't done anything,' I say.

What the hell am I thinking, talking to Liam like this? What do a few photographs prove? Am I really going to ruin everything Dad and I have worked for since his arrest? Everything we've both sacrificed.

'Is he there with you now?' Liam asks.

'He's living here, yes.'

'Where else would he be?'

'Where else is he supposed to go?'

'What about you? Where do you want to be?'

My breath catches in my throat. For a moment, I think Liam might ask me to come back to the UK. To come back to him.

'Look,' he says, 'there's something—'

'What?'

'There's... I've been seeing someone. For a while.'

'I didn't think you'd become a monk.'

Nervous laughter. 'No. Her name's Amber.'

Amber with her hair in a bun and her adorable dungarees. If I tell him I already know about her, he'll figure out I stalked his Facebook account. 'Good for you,' I say.

'We're having a baby.'

A hollow sensation deep in my belly. 'Congratulations,' I say, my words tinny and distant. 'I'm happy for you.'

'Colette—'

'Really. So happy.'

'I'm sorry.'

'Don't be. It's the best news.'

'Listen, I—'

'I've got to go.'

* * *

I can't move from the bench. My phone sits in my lap where I dropped it, as if it had scalded me. Below me on the beach, a parent and toddler group stakes its claim. Six mothers playing with their offspring. Could this morning get any worse?

Liam and I planned to have kids one day. I didn't give that any thought when I broke up with him. I never wavered in my decision. Either he was with Dad and me or he was against us. I didn't have time to think about the long-term consequences of the split. I had lawyers to deal with and a trial coming up and Liam had to be pushed aside so I could concentrate on Dad.

Jane Durand has a husband and a child. She has the life I once dreamt of. I tell myself that's a good thing, and that she doesn't look like a woman who's had something terrible happen to her. Maybe she wouldn't even remember Dad if asked about him. He would just be one of many men she served while working at that bar.

I need to stop thinking about this. I'm creating a narrative for Jane that might not even exist. I'm comparing her to Ella, which means I'm comparing her to a lie. Yes, their narratives match at the beginning, but what does that prove?

Desperate to get rid of my doubts, I take my phone from my bag and do a Google search for the Hôtel des Arbres. When I find the hotel's number, I hit the call symbol beside it. Heart pounding, I listen to the ring tone. It could be checkout time there. The staff might be busy. I picture Jane gliding around a busy dining room, handing out pots of tea and coffee and making small talk with the hotel guests.

'*Hôtel des Arbres, bonjour.*'

A woman's voice. A young woman with an impeccable French accent. I can't tell if this is a native speaker on the other end or if it could be Jane. She must speak perfect French after living here so long.

'*Allo?*' the woman says.

In the silence that follows I hear her breathing. A shallow inhale and exhale. I listen intently, as if her breath alone might reveal some truth to me.

'*Qui est à l'appareil?*' The woman sounds uneasy, agitated.

I hang up. A plane takes off from Nice airport and curves up up up, cutting a path through the bright blue sky. Terror grips me. I have the oddest feeling the plane is in danger and could plunge into the sea at any moment. All the precious cargo within it lost and broken and washing up into the bay.

42

JANE

Wednesday morning. Michel and I have escaped breakfast duty at the hotel, ahead of the busy week-end. Instead, we are eating with Theo in our own kitchen.

Theo has abandoned his toast to scrawl on his drawing pad with a thick red marker. Red is still his current obsession. He only has one pair of red under-pants and for the sake of peace I've washed and dried them twice already this week. He has a play date with Lena this morning. Nathalie rang last night and in-vited him and me along to her place. I wondered if Michel had asked her to call.

'Minette,' Theo says as the cat slinks into the room.

He gets down from his chair, and the cat lets him stroke her as she laps at the milk I put out for her.

My handbag hangs over the back of my chair. The knife is still in there. Carrying it around with me brings some comfort. I keep seeing Sandy everywhere. In the few hours of sleep I snatch each night, he is waiting. I see him when I look out of my bedroom window in the morning, a shadowy figure at the gates of the hotel. I see him when I'm taking Theo to the play park or at the Carrefour when I am shopping.

A couple of days ago, I answered the phone at reception to silence at the other end of the line. Probably a wrong number or a bad connection, but for a while afterwards I convinced myself Sandy had called me.

Michel glances over at our son, checking he is fully occupied with harassing the cat. 'More coffee?' he asks me. When I nod, he gets up from the table with the empty cafetière. 'Is it my fault?' he says.

I frown. 'Is what your fault?'

He leans against the worktop as he adds three heaped spoonfuls of coffee to the cafetière. He knows I don't like it that strong. 'Sometimes I think—'

'What?' The icy creep of dread up my spine. *Sometimes I think marrying you was a huge mistake. Sometimes I think Theo and I would be better off without you.*

He flicks on the kettle. It hisses to life within seconds. 'Sometimes,' he says, 'I think you've never forgiven me for splitting up with you that time.'

'That's not true.'

'You know I regret it, right? I told you that.'

'That was years ago. You don't have to—'

'Since then it's like part of you has always been out of reach.'

I look at my husband. This man I love. He has done nothing wrong, but for a moment I hate him for not working out what I have kept hidden all these years. Is he really so stupid? I consider telling him. Surely the consequences of sharing the truth can't be worse than the consequences that might follow if I don't get a grip of myself?

The cat lets out a primal squeal, loud enough to make me and Michel turn our heads. Theo has his hands around her middle and is gripping her far too tightly. His face is scrunched up tight as he tries not to let the wriggling creature out of his grasp.

'Theo, let her go,' Michel says. 'She doesn't like it.'

The kettle is gathering pace. As it hits boiling point, Minette lets out another terrified squeal. I leap up and wrench my son away from the cat. He gasps when I smack both his hands hard.

'*Non*,' I say, 'no, no, no.'

'Jane.'

I glance up and see the shock on my husband's face. Theo bursts into tears. The kettle rages behind us, spouting steam.

'He was hurting her,' I say. 'He can't do that. We can't let him do that.'

Theo opens his mouth wide and screams. Michel strides over, picks up our son and carries him out of the room, whispering soothing words in two languages.

The kettle keeps on boiling.

43

JANE

Late morning and I am alone in the kitchen. Michel has taken Theo to the play date at Nathalie's. He is punishing me for punishing our son. Theo was still sulking with me when he left, his eyes wary as I bent down to kiss him goodbye. I apologised to him over and over. *Maman was wrong. Maman was wrong.*

Maman has been wrong about so many things.

I haven't moved from the kitchen table all morning. Each time my coffee cup empties I refill it. My nervous system is buzzing, my circuitry full of red flashing lights. Warning. Stop. Stop thinking about Sandy.

Earlier, I called my brother, Ben. I thought seeing as I cannot make Sandy disappear, maybe I could disappear instead. Temporarily. For everyone's sake. I told

Ben I was considering a visit to the UK and asked if I could come and see him. No luck. He said he would love to see me, but he and Sinead are going to Italy tomorrow for a three-week walking holiday.

For the first time in years, I wish I got on with my parents. If I turned up at home now, my father would guess I am in trouble. He has always thought the worst of me. Maybe if I could have told him about what happened with Sandy, I might have been able to tell everyone else. He would have declared the attack my fault for putting myself in that position. For being the kind of woman who would go back to a hotel with a married man. I wish he was the kind of father I could talk to. One who would listen to the worst I have to offer and love me anyway. Do fathers like that really exist or do they all want their daughters to be the ideal woman in the same way we want them to be the ideal man? Are we always destined to disappoint each other unless we conceal who we really are?

Early afternoon. I am waiting for Michel to bring Theo back from his play date when I hear my son's voice drifting in from the hotel courtyard. When I move to the bedroom and look out of the window, I see Theo sitting with Michel and his parents in the courtyard. The basket of bread at the centre of the table tells me they are about to enjoy a late lunch together now all the guests have eaten. My stomach knots. Michel has excluded me from the meal. What has he told his parents? *Jane's not feeling so good.* This is how my life would look if I was no longer in it. If Michel and Theo were existing without me.

Anger surges through me. I have worked hard to have the life Sandy could have taken from me, and now I feel he is about to take it anyway.

A movement at the hotel gate catches my eye. A man with silvery-grey hair is standing there. He is too far away for me to see his face, but he is looking in through the metal gates at the hotel. I dash back to the kitchen and snatch up my handbag. By the time I rush out of the apartment door and into the hotel garden, the man is gone.

To avoid my family in the courtyard, I slip out of a side gate and on to a path that leads from the garden to our street. No sign of the man in either direction, but guessing he is more likely to head towards town, I hurry to Boulevard de la Liberté.

The road is busy with traffic as usual. I turn right and head downhill, eyes glancing in all directions. Is

that him? There, heading into the old town down Rue
Frédéric Mireur.

A large truck rattles to a standstill in front of me. I
dart across the road, prompting an angry chorus of
beeps from the Range Rover coming in the opposite
direction. On the other side of the road, men sit at tables outside the Turkish café, nursing small glasses of
coffee. They stare in silence as I pass. One man, older,
with luminous blue eyes and a shock of white hair
looks me up and down, as if appraising me.

'Stared enough, have you?' I say to him in French.
'Get a good look?'

He shifts in his seat, a startled expression on his
face.

'Don't think I don't notice,' I say, emboldened by
the knife in my bag. 'We all notice. We all know you're
doing it.' I turn away and march down Rue Frédéric
Mireur. Where is he? Where is Sandy Gilligan?

There he is, at the end of the street, making his way
into the market square. My heart thrashes beneath my
ribs. He is here. He has come to look for me. My past
has finally caught up with my present. What if he is
here not to stop me talking, but because he gets a thrill
out of stalking me like this? Maybe my years of silence
have made him think I am still easy prey.

Fear clogs up my throat and squeezes my chest

muscles tight. Fear makes me want to run back home, but it also drives me on. I want him to turn and see me. I want him to be the prey for once. I want him to feel as scared as I have all these years. I slip my hand into my bag and feel the sharp presence of the knife through its tissue cocoon.

No market on today but the square still hums with life. Almost all the tables outside Café de Flore are occupied. Music blares out from Bar du Marché to the customers enjoying beers and glasses of cold wine beneath the plane trees.

The man saunters past the bar as if he has nothing to hide. As if he is just any man enjoying a day trip to Draguignan. I should call out his name, here, in front of everyone. Where there are witnesses.

I open my mouth, but nothing comes out. All I can think about is Sandy holding the cushion over my face and the panic that rose within me as his weight made it impossible to cry out. Impossible to breathe.

The man lifts an arm and waves. At the far end of the market square a woman waves back. When he reaches her, they embrace, laughing when her oversized sun hat almost falls off.

Is it him? If so, who is he with? If I confront him now, I will be outnumbered.

When they turn and walk up Rue des Marchands, I

stay put, too scared to follow in case they see me. Before long, they are out of sight.

I walk back through the market square in a daze. Was that Sandy Gilligan or was it a man out for a pleasant day trip with his wife or girlfriend? What would I have done if it was him? Nothing. Fear would have consumed me, just like it did in that hotel room. Pathetic. Even if he is only a threat in my head, I don't have the strength to get rid of him there.

I walk up Rue Frédéric Mireur, past the Turkish café where the men are still nursing their coffees. A sob rises in my chest.

Traffic rattles down Boulevard de la Liberté. If I can't make Sandy disappear, maybe I am the one who needs to vanish. A delivery truck speeds towards me, techno blasting out of the open window. I lift one foot off the kerb and close my eyes. Only to see what it feels like. Only to see.

'Madame.'

Strong hands grab my shoulders and pull me back from the road. When I stumble, wiry arms catch me and help me upright.

It is the man I shouted at earlier. The man with the bright blue eyes. Looking into them, I find only kindness and concern.

'Ça va, Madame?' he says.

44

LYNNE

It's a hot one tonight. I stand at the open windows of my apartment, looking out on to Boulevard Jean Jaurès. The pavements are busy. Locals and tourists going this way and that. Loads of traffic, too. It's only Wednesday, but it looks more like a Friday night out there; the old town will be heaving. Sandy says it's because Nice is gearing up for the Bastille Day celebrations on Saturday. He's invited me to watch the fireworks from his apartment.

We were going to try the Thai at the end of Rue de la Boucherie for dinner tonight, but after our big day out, I suggested we stay in and have takeaway pizza. Sandy's gone to get it now.

Tonight could be the night. When I asked Sandy if

he minded us staying in to eat, he said, 'I think staying in is a very good idea,' and he gave me a look that made my legs go all soft. I've had a freshen up just in case, and underneath my black linen dress are the navy silk pants and matching bra I bought on impulse when we were out today.

The tram slides past. Ding, ding. The bell sounds sultry and seductive tonight, rather than miserable. As if it's announcing the start of something.

Down below, I see Amira on her way to the super-market. When I call her name, she looks up and actually waves. God, I love this place. I feel right at home here now. Can't imagine myself back in Colchester.

Today's been so lovely. Sandy took me for a drive to the town his grandfather came from. A good sign, I thought, showing me his family history. Thank God I never said anything to that woman at Café Corsica. Makes me shudder, how close I came to spoiling everything. I've not been back there since, and I don't intend to. Not if I want more days like today.

The first bit of the drive, up the coast, was lovely. All these gorgeous little bays with villas clinging to the rocks. Then we turned inland and that was a bit dull. Lots of low tree-covered hills and industrial estates, but Draguignan was all right when we got there. Nothing fancy, like Nice, but it felt real. Normal people getting on with everyday lives. The old town was pretty. We explored it for a bit together and walked up to an old clock tower that had a fab view over the whole town. Then Sandy said he wanted to find the house his grandfather grew up in. I offered to go with him, but he said he didn't want to tire me out tramping around when he didn't know exactly where the house was. I said I didn't mind, but he got a bit huffy, so I left him to it and said I'd look round the shops. He can be a moody beggar sometimes, but he has been through a lot.

The shops were all right. I found a lingerie boutique just off the market square and that was a hoot. Me with my Google Translate trying to discuss bra sizes with the shop assistant. She was about my age, tanned and glamorous, and we had a good laugh trying to get me sorted. Then I had a quick glass of rosé in a bar in the square, waiting for Sandy to text. When he turned up, he said he hadn't found the house, but he'd had a good time anyway.

'A trip down memory lane?' I said.

He nodded. 'Something like that.' We walked a bit more round the old town, but Sandy turned ever so quiet. When I offered him a penny for his thoughts, he said he was thinking about the past. How not everything was the way you remembered it. I thought maybe his childhood memories of the town didn't match what he could see around him.

Here he is now, coming from the direction of Rue de la Boucherie, pizzas in one hand, bottle of red wine in the other. He looks up at me and smiles. There's a hunger about him tonight. I can sense it.

Another tram glides past and this time the bell makes me go tingly all over.

* * *

The pizzas are delicious and so is the wine. After we finish eating, we carry on drinking. Sandy tells me his brother, Jimmy, is coming to visit him soon.

'That's lovely,' I say. 'Will I get to meet him?'

'Not sure. He's taking me to Monaco for a couple of nights.'

'Oh. Okay.' A boys' trip to Monaco. I don't like the sound of that. I never had to worry about Sandy out with the lads when he was in jail.

Steady, Lynne. Tonight's the night. Don't blow it.

We're almost through the bottle of wine when Sandy suggests we watch TV. 'Just to wind down a bit,' he says. He's picking at the frayed material on the arm of the sofa. Bless him. If tonight is the night, he's obviously nervous about it.

'I've got a much better way to wind down,' I say, resting a hand on his thigh.

He looks down at my hand and places his own on top of it.

'Lynne,' he says, 'I think I—'

Before he can finish his sentence, I hoist myself on to his lap.

He laughs nervously. 'Bold move.'

I kiss him. 'I'm not taking no for an answer tonight.' I keep on kissing him. It takes him a while to get into it but then his hands grip me tight around the waist. A bit too tight, but I don't mind. Not really. Soon I feel him hard beneath me. He groans when I rock myself back and forth along the length of him. 'Someone's excited,' I say. 'What are you thinking about?'

He holds my face in his hands. 'I'm thinking about all the things I could do.' He pulls me towards him and softly bites my lip. 'All the things I want to do.'

Breaking away from him, I stand up and hold out my hand. 'Let's go to bed.'

When we get to the bedroom, he unzips my dress at the back and pulls it over my head. While he takes off his clothes, I crawl on to the bed in my underwear and lie on my side, sucking my stomach in. Wish I hadn't had that last slice of pizza.

Sandy strips down to his boxers and lies beside

me. 'God, you're hot,' he says.

Is he commenting on my appearance or my body temperature? It is ever so warm in here. 'Hang on.' I clamber out of bed and switch on the fan in the corner of the room.

'That's better,' he says as I get back into bed and lie beside him. Sweat rolls down his forehead. Heat or nerves? As his fingers brush across my stomach, I think about our visits together in that tiny prison visiting room. The locked doors, the thrill of getting caught. I can't help wishing we'd had sex then.

'Are you sure you want this?' he says.

'Yes.' I can't wait to get him inside me. It's the last bit of distance between us, and I want it gone.

'Really? Are you sure?'

Poor bloke. After what he's been through, he doesn't know whether he's coming or going. Whether I'm up for it or not. 'You can do anything you like to me,' I say, my hand pressed against the crotch of his boxer shorts. 'I'm all yours.'

He gives a little groan and kisses me, but something is wrong. I can tell from the rapid deflation in his underwear. I slip a hand into his boxers and try to coax him back to life, but it doesn't work.

'Lynne,' he says.

'Sorry.'

'It's not your fault.' He rolls away from me. 'Christ, that's embarrassing.'

'Don't be daft.' I wait for him to say something obvious like, *this has never happened to me before*, but he just stares at the ceiling. Noise filters in from outside – whining scooters, angry car horns and raucous singing.

I rest my head on his chest. 'I love you.'

He sighs and strokes my cheek with his thumb. 'It's all these feelings I've got going on in me right now,' he says.

His love for me is too much, that's the problem. That and the fact the last woman he had sex with had him arrested. No wonder he's struggling.

'Forget about that lying cow,' I say. 'There's nothing you could do to make me treat you like she did.'

'I'm not thinking about her.' He kisses the top of my head. 'Honestly, love, I'm not thinking about her at all.'

* * *

I thought he'd go home as usual but, after we'd cuddled for a while, we both started yawning and he asked if he could sleep over. I was so happy. Maybe that's what we needed to do, I thought. If we snuggled up to go to sleep, with the pressure off us, something might happen. He fell asleep right away and now, three hours later, I'm still wide awake, body buzzing and desperate for his touch.

He doesn't snore; that's something. Both my ex-husbands snored like fiends and the second one thrashed about all over the place in his sleep. Sandy's so quiet I've even checked on him a couple of times to make sure he hasn't snuffed it.

Restless, I get up and go to the bathroom. I wee with the door shut so I don't wake Sandy. Afterwards, I spend a while looking out of the window. Still a few drunk people navigating the old town's twisting streets.

Back in the bedroom, I slide into bed as carefully as I can. Sandy has thrown the sheet off him, and even in the dim light filtering through the curtains, I can see he's fully aroused. Should I wake him by taking him in my mouth? Would he like that?

He turns on to his side, facing me, eyelids twitching as his dreaming eyes rove around beneath them. He mutters something I don't catch, so I edge a little closer, until my lips are almost on his.

'Jane,' he says, 'Jane.' His breath is hot and stale. His body shudders. 'Jane,' he says again.

Jane? Who the bloody hell is Jane?

45

COLETTE

I wake with a start and find my father sitting at the end of my bed.

'What is it?' I say. 'What's wrong?'

He smiles. 'Nothing, sleepyhead. Thought I should wake you before the day passes you by.'

My mouth is dry, my eyes gritty. According to the bedside clock it's almost eleven thirty. 'Shit.' I haul myself up to sitting. 'Sorry. I was awake most of the night. I must have fallen asleep around five.'

'What kept you up?' He looks concerned. 'Is it because I stayed out for the night? Were you worried?'

'No, it wasn't that. Really.' I was awake because of a night in Cannes seven years ago and what might have happened then. I need to speak to him. We've always been able to talk about everything. Surely if I ask him what's going on with Jane Durand he will tell me the truth and it won't be as bad as I think.

'I got you something.' He reaches to the floor and produces a Galeries Lafayette gift bag, the handles tied together with black chiffon.

'What for?'

'Do I need an excuse to treat my girl?' He hands the bag over. 'I walked past the store on my way back, and I couldn't resist going in.'

I untie the black chiffon ribbon and pull out a package wrapped in tissue paper. Inside is a Zadig & Voltaire dress. Pale blue silk with an asymmetrical frill on the right-hand seam.

'It's beautiful,' I say. It is. Dad's always had good taste in clothes and knows what suits me. 'Thank you.'

'I've booked us in at the Negresco bar for lunch,' he says. 'Why don't you have a cup of tea and a shower, stick that dress on and we'll go out and have some fun.'

I fold the tissue paper back over the dress. 'You don't have to apologise for spending the night with Lynne.'

'The dress isn't an apology.'

'Did you have a nice day with her?'

'We went for a drive. I wasn't going to stay the night, but she—'

'It's okay if you like her.'

Suddenly I really want him to like Lynne. I want him to like her so much he loses all interest in the past and whatever happened there.

'Nothing happened,' he says.

'It's none of my—'

'I stayed the night, but nothing happened.' His shoulders hunch in an awkward shrug. 'I'm not sure there's that kind of chemistry between us.'

To my surprise, I feel sorry for Lynne. 'She's really into you,' I say.

Dad fiddles with my bedcover. 'Like I said, I never made her any promises. She knew the score before she came over here.'

'You must have thought there could be something between you?'

'After last night I think we both know it's just a friendship thing.'

I find it hard to imagine Lynne seeing Dad as just a friend. 'Did you end it with her?'

'No. No. Not yet. It's not the right time. I'll let her down gently.' He sighs. 'I guess in the end, she's not really my type.'

What is his type? Younger, sexier? Less available?

'Come on, kiddo.' He gets up and opens my curtains, letting in a flood of harsh sunlight. 'Let's get this show on the road.'

The first time Dad took me to the Hôtel Negresco, I was nine years old. I thought the white belle époque building with the famous pink dome looked like a fancy cake. Mum loved the grandeur of the place and, after that, every trip to Nice included a visit to the city's most famous hotel.

I haven't been here since Dad was arrested. Now he sits opposite me in a low armchair, with a round, marble-topped table between us. He is smart in a pale blue linen shirt and black chinos. His skin is as tanned as it was before he went to jail. Apart from the change in hair colour, I could look at him and pretend prison had never happened.

Our surroundings couldn't be more different from his prison cell. The walls of the bar are panelled with dark wood. White columns decorated with gold leaf rise up to meet the high ceiling, which is painted deep red. Ornate tapestries hang on the walls, most of them filled with angels and cherubs. Outside the heat is fierce but in here the air conditioning is set to keep us cool but not raise goosebumps. All around us, well-dressed people engage in murmured conversations. Wealth whispers here. At a table next to us, a silver-haired woman stands out in a pair of scruffy grey tracksuit bottoms and a creased white T-shirt. She's probably the wealthiest person in the room.

'To us,' Dad says, raising his glass of Bollinger. I raise mine. We clink. Beads of condensation roll down my glass. The champagne has a sour, unpleasant taste. Maybe it has always tasted like this beneath the bubbles, and I never noticed.

Dad picks up his phone and points it in my direction. He asks me to smile and I oblige. His happy daughter in her designer dress with a glass of champagne in her hand. Playing the role he's chosen for me.

'That dress looks the business on you,' he says.

The dress is a size too small. It nips at my waist and restricts my stomach. He bought the size he thinks I should be, not the size I am.

Our lunch arrives. Tasting plates of tuna ceviche, goat's cheese tart and mushroom ravioli. It looks lovely, but my stomach is a hard knot of doubt and fear. Watching Dad tuck into the food reminds me that until recently, sitting here with him would have been a dream. An impossibility. I want to relax and enjoy the moment, but I sense the invisible presence of Jane, urging me to ask about the photographs and find out what's going on.

'Dig in, kiddo,' Dad says.

I pick up a side plate and put a slice of the tuna ceviche on it along with some of the goat's cheese tart. After a few mouthfuls I put the plate down again.

'What is it?' Dad says.

The dress is crushing my ribs. I long to undo the long zip at the back and let myself spill out. Tears lurk, hot and prickly in the corners of my eyes. As if the dress is squeezing them out of me.

'Hey.' Dad puts his food down. 'What's wrong?'

'Nothing.'

'Colette?' Dad looks right into me, as if sensing my doubts.

'It's Liam,' I say, unable to face asking the questions I need to.

Dad sighs. 'What's he done now?'

The same question Liam asked about my father. I say I found out via a mutual friend that Liam is about to have a kid.

'I am sorry, love,' Dad says. 'That must feel pretty shit.'

'It does.'

Our waiter, a young, tall guy with a shaved head, appears at the table to top up our champagne flutes.

'If you ask me,' Dad says, once the waiter has backed away, 'you did the right thing breaking up with Liam. You couldn't have kids with a man who didn't trust us as a family.'

'I know.' Did I make the right choice? What if Liam was right all along? What if my father is not to be trusted?

'You deserve someone who's got your back no matter what.'

I think of Dad defending me over the theft of that ring when I was five years old. How he promised me the truth would come out eventually. After all these years of sticking by him, am I really going to give in to doubt now? What if there's a good explanation for his behaviour?

'Liam was spineless,' Dad says. 'I wish I'd never let you marry him.'

Before my wedding, my best friend Holly asked why I was letting Dad give me away during the ceremony. I shrugged and said it was tradition. She said my father didn't own me. It had never occurred to me I wasn't his to give away. When the day came, and Dad walked me down the aisle to the altar, he turned to me and winked. A wink that said he had no intention of really letting me go, and I winked back to let him know I was in on the joke. This was just a ceremony, and I wouldn't let him give me away if he tried.

'I'm not sure what I deserve,' I say.

At that moment of my wedding ceremony, Dad's presence comforted me. Whatever happened in the future, even if things went wrong with Liam, I would always have one man who would love me unconditionally. One man who was better than any others I might meet. I'm not sure I could have got married without that knowledge.

What if my father isn't that man? What then?

Dad takes a sip of champagne. 'I've got something to tell you.'

For a moment I think he might produce the pictures of Jane and explain why he's trying to track her down. *She was this barmaid I met once years ago, lovely girl. She wrote to me in jail and told me her son is seriously ill. I want to give her some money so he can have a life-saving operation. You don't mind, do you?*

I swallow a mouthful of champagne. It still tastes sour, but I need something to numb myself with.

'I've still got a few useful contacts,' Dad says. 'Business ones.'

Unsure where this is going, I give an encouraging nod.

'This bloke I used to deal with in London is married to a Frenchwoman,' he says. 'They live in Paris now. Anyway, their daughter, who's a bit older than you, works for an advertising agency in Paris and she says they're looking for someone to work with the British and American clients. Someone fluent in French, of course.'

'I'm not really—'

'You could do this, Colette.' His eyes are on mine. Intense, searching. 'You've done so much for me, and I really want you to get your life back on track.'

I stare into my champagne and watch the bubbles trapped beneath the surface. 'But this is my life.'

'C'mon, love. We both know you've got to move on sometime.'

When he tells me the name of the agency, I look up, startled. 'You're kidding?'

His smile is a satisfied one. 'Does that mean your old man did good?'

'Good?' The agency has a global reputation and offices all over the world. 'Dad, that's amazing.' A sudden lightness fills me. The feeling that all is well with the world, or could be.

'I said you'd need time to consider it,' Dad says.

Paris. I could walk away from all this now and get on with my life. I wouldn't have to think about Jane again. Now, at this minute, Dad is the man I've always known. Looking out for me. Wanting me to have the best.

'What about you?' I say. 'Would you stay here?'

'I'm almost done with Nice. I fancy a fresh start.'

'Where?'

'Who knows. I might go off travelling for a while.' He swigs his champagne. 'Your mum always wanted to go to Brazil for some reason. I feel I should see it on her behalf.' Tears spring to his eyes. 'Sorry.'

'It's okay.'

'I know Australia won't let me in, but maybe Patch would come and meet me somewhere else. I'm sure if we meet in person, I'll get through to him.' He rubs away tears with the heel of his hand. 'He's my son. I love him.'

A rush of positive thoughts lifts my heart. What if everything will be okay? What if we can heal as a family and move on with our lives? What if there really is an innocent explanation for Dad tracking down Jane Durand? Maybe she's one of many past conquests he wants to contact to check if he hurt her in any way. What if he's working his way through a whole list of them in an attempt to be a better man?

Dad waves our waiter over and asks him to take a photograph of us.

'Of course.' The waiter takes Dad's phone and steps away from the table. 'Okay, ready?' he says, holding the phone out in front of him.

Dad and I raise our glasses and smile. I want us to stay in this moment for ever. I want to keep all these positive feelings, all this hope.

'Can I have a look?' I say to Dad when the waiter hands him the phone back.

'Sure,' he says, passing it to me.

I stare at the photograph, keen to see us the way the outside world does. Doting father, loving daughter. I see now that the blue of my dress matches the blue of his shirt. We look happy. I sense Jane looking over my shoulder, telling me the image is an illusion. I want her to leave us alone. I zoom in on Dad's face, as if seeing him up close will tell me what to believe and what to ignore.

As I press the screen, the photograph vanishes, and Dad's photo library appears. I see a picture of him and Lynne standing somewhere elevated, terracotta tiled roofs spread out behind them.

I show him the picture. 'Is this where you went yesterday?'

'Yes.' He takes the phone back. 'Your nan had a cousin who lived there.'

'Where?'

'A small town inland a bit. You wouldn't know it.' He lifts the champagne bottle out of the ice bucket. 'Draguignan.'

46

LYNNE

Sometimes, you can't beat a bottle of cheap plonk. Vino Collapso, as my dad used to call it. The Pinot Grigio I'm knocking back now came from the Carrefour. Sandy wouldn't be seen dead drinking it, but he's not here. I carry my full glass over to the long windows and look out over the boulevard. Nearly three in the afternoon, and it's still stinking hot. Too early to be this drunk, but who cares?

'Cheers.' I lift my glass in a toast to no one. A man strolling past below looks up and shakes his head. I didn't mean to get drunk today, but who can blame me? This morning, before Sandy left, he apologised again about his performance, or rather the lack of one.

I told him it didn't matter, but it does. Really. Especially if this Jane is why he couldn't get it up last night.

She is the reason; I'm sure of it. I'm also sure Jane is the woman from Café Corsica. If I confront Sandy, will he tell me I'm imagining things? My second husband had me convinced for years his affairs were all in my head, but I was right about every one of them.

What about Sandy's trip to Monaco with his brother? I bet the whole thing's a ruse so he can get a couple of nights away with Jane.

Ding, ding.

'Shut up,' I shout at the miserable tram, smug and smooth on its rails. I hate this city. I want to be back in Colchester in my quiet little flat. Away from all this traffic noise and all these people. Earlier I went to the beach, intending to have a swim on my own – sod waiting for Sandy – but there were signs forbidding swimming due to pollution. You never get that on Clacton beach.

When I turn back to the living room, the mess I made earlier confronts me. Sandy's letters are strewn all over the coffee table. Shortly after opening the wine, I started reading through them again. Did he mean the promises he made about spending our lives together, or is he just full of crap? I think about all the Friday-night invitations I turned down so I could stay in and write letters to him. The money I spent on phone calls and on prison visits. I could have dated other men and Sandy wouldn't have known. I didn't, though. I take my commitments seriously.

My Vision Book is lying on the living-room floor. I slump down beside it, open it up and gaze at all my hopes and dreams. My favourite pale pink dress. I do so want to wear it one day. What if I'm the problem? Sabotaging everything like I usually do. Maybe the truth is he just doesn't fancy me. Christ, that might be even worse than him cheating on me.

My phone buzzes. Sandy? I snatch it up from the coffee table and find a text from Colette.

You at home? I'm in the old town. Thought I might drop in and say hi.

Colette? What does she want? Her text is all chummy, as if we hang out together all the time. As if it's quite normal for her to pop by of an afternoon.

What if something's happened to Sandy?

My anger vanishes. Hands shaking, I type a reply with my address and tell her to come on up. I drain the rest of my wine. What if Sandy is ill? Seriously ill. Suddenly, all I want is to see him again.

Minutes later, my buzzer sounds, and I let Colette into the building.

'I needed a walk after lunch,' she says when she gets to the front door of the flat, 'so I thought I'd stop by and say hello.' She's wearing a beautiful dress and a black, Chanel handbag hangs off her bony shoulder. So elegant. She looks knackered though, the skin beneath her eyes dark and puffy.

'Is Sandy okay?' I say. 'Has something happened?'

'He's fine. He's at home.'

I usher her inside, apologising for the state of the flat. 'Sorting through some old stuff,' I say, mortified by the mess. I'm not much better in my creased linen trousers and my white T-shirt with sweat stains under the arms. Clutching an empty wine glass like a drunk. 'Have a seat.' She perches on the edge of the sofa and rearranges her fancy dress over her legs. 'Would you like a cup of tea?'

'I'll take some of that if there's any,' she says, pointing to my wine glass.

'Of course.' Luckily, I bought two bottles from the supermarket. I drain the last of the first bottle into my glass and open the new one for her. 'I'm afraid I've had a few already,' I say, handing her a glass filled to the brim.

'Well, why not. When in France.' Her voice is too

bright. Too cheery. The way people talk when they're trying not to cry.

'Is everything all right?' I say.

'Yes, of course.' She sips the wine, unable to disguise the slight wrinkling of her nose as she swallows it. Fussy madam. It occurs to me she might feel strange about Sandy having stayed the night. What if she wants to talk to me about it? What will I say? I know what I want to say. No need to worry, love, nothing happened with your dad because he's too busy shagging the tart from Café Corsica.

Steady, Lynne.

'You must be looking forward to your Uncle Jimmy coming over?' I say.

She knocks back some wine. 'Yes, it'll be good for Dad to see him.'

'You're not going with them?'

She shakes her head. 'Boys only.'

Like hell it is. 'Jimmy will come to yours on the way, I assume?'

She frowns. Probably wondering why I'm so interested in the Monaco trip. 'Dad's picking him up from the airport and they're driving straight there.' She glances at the letters on the coffee table. 'He might stop in on the way back.'

'Well,' I say, 'that's nice.' If Uncle Jimmy is even coming to France.

'Did you have a nice day out on Wednesday?' she says.

'Day out?' My fuzzy, wine-addled mind doesn't click what she means at first.

'Dad took you to Draguignan.'

'That's right, yes.' I kneel on the floor on the other side of the coffee table. 'Your great-granddad was from there, wasn't he?'

She looks confused. 'You mean my nan's cousin?'

'Sandy definitely said it was his grandad.' My next gulp of wine sloshes around my stomach. I feel very hollow. Did I eat lunch?

'What did you do there?' she says.

'Just wandered around, had a look at the old town.'

'I should really visit there one day. Are there a lot of nice hotels?'

'I don't know.'

'You didn't see any?'

'Not in the old town. When Sandy went off for a wander, I—'

'Where did he go?'

'To try to find his granddad's old house.'

'You didn't go with him?'

'He said he'd find it quicker on his own.'

'How long was he gone for?'

'Hard to say. An hour, maybe.' What's with all the questions? She's making me feel woozy. 'Can you excuse me a minute?'

With the help of the coffee table, I get myself up off the floor and stagger to the bathroom. At first, I think I might be sick but, after bending over the toilet for a few minutes, the wooziness disappears. 'Get a grip, Lynne,' I mutter.

I need to pee, so I sit on the loo. Afterwards, I wash my hands and splash cold water on my face. I need to keep myself together in front of Colette. While she's here I should suss out if she knows anything about this Jane.

I return to the main room to find her still sitting on the sofa, my Vision Book in one hand and a letter of Sandy's in the other. 'Oh,' I say and stand there, unsure what to say. She doesn't even look up. No apology for snooping around in my belongings. Isn't reading another person's mail a crime?

'He says here he wants to marry you,' she says, her eyes roving over the letter.

'Yes. He said he wanted us to spend the rest of our lives together.'

'"I never thought I'd be up for marrying again,"' she says, reading from the letter, '"but now I've met you, I feel differently. I want to spend the rest of my life with you, Lynne. I promise you that, and I promise you'll never regret it."'

'I cried when I read that,' I say. 'He's got a way with words, your dad.'

She puts the letter aside and turns the pages of my Vision Book. Embarrassment floods my cheeks as she observes my little scraps of hope. I see myself through her eyes, and it isn't pretty. A middle-aged woman chasing the impossible.

'You must think I'm ridiculous,' I say.

Her eyes are wet. Is she about to cry? 'No,' she says. 'You're not ridiculous. Not at all.'

Is she being kind, or does she pity me? Hard to tell. I watch as she closes the scrapbook and puts it back on the coffee table with the letter on top.

'I'm sorry for looking at your private things without asking,' she says, 'but I needed to know.'

'Know what?'

'Do you want to marry him?' she asks.

'I'm in love with him.' Still, despite my doubts. I want to marry the Sandy who wrote that letter to me. 'He hasn't asked me yet.'

'The thing is...' She looks at me with her sad eyes. 'What?'

She hesitates. 'I'm sorry, Lynne.' She gets up and smooths down the front of her dress. 'I really am.'

What for, I wonder? 'You don't have to go,' I say.

'I've got things to do.' She picks up her handbag and walks into the hallway.

'Who's Jane?' I say.

When she turns, the look of fear on her face makes my stomach drop. She knows. She knows something.

'Who's Jane?' I say again.

She steps towards me. 'Why are you asking me that?'

The urgency in her voice makes me back away.

'Tell me,' she says.

I tell her the truth. I explain her father said the name aloud in his sleep several times. 'I just wondered who she is.'

'That's all?' she says. 'That's why you're asking?'

Why does she look so relieved?

'He's always talked in his sleep,' she says. 'It used to drive my mum nuts.'

'So, you don't know any Jane?' I say.

She opens the front door. 'I am sorry, Lynne,' she says.

47

LYNNE

Nearly five in the afternoon, and I'm camped out on the opposite side of the square from Café Corsica. Been here nearly half an hour. I know Jane's here because now and then she comes out with plates of food for the men at the outside tables.

What does Sandy see in her? She's... what's the word? Grungy. Today she's got on a pair of denim shorts and a black halter-neck top. I can see her skanky tattoo from here.

I'm sitting on a step in a tenement doorway. The smooth stone is cool beneath my dress. I got changed and put my face on before coming here. No way I'd let her see me looking a state.

I don't care what time her shift finishes; I'm not going anywhere.

After Colette left, I returned to the living room and picked up my Vision Book. I thought about the look on Colette's face when I asked about Jane. She knows something. She'd lie for her father, no doubt about it. Thick as thieves the pair of them.

I looked again at my scrapbook and all my pathetic dreams and hated myself. After another glass of wine, I tore each page out of the book and ripped my dreams to shreds. Then I put those shreds in the shower cubicle and set fire to them before washing the ashes down the plughole. I did consider destroying Sandy's letters, but I couldn't do it. I couldn't destroy my past with him until I was sure we didn't have a future.

That's when I left the flat and came here to face Jane. I stopped at a bar on the way and made myself bold with a vodka shot. Then I made myself bolder with another.

Suddenly she appears in the doorway of the café, denim jacket knotted round her waist and a handbag over her shoulder. She's leaving. She waves goodbye to the customers as she walks away, cigarette hanging from her lips.

She's coming in my direction. I shuffle back on the

step, trying to hide in the doorway. Has she seen me watching her? I take out my phone and pretend to type a text as she approaches. When she passes me, I see tanned feet in a pair of cheap flip-flops. Her red toenail varnish is chipped. Jane, the woman who has wrecked my dreams, has chipped nail varnish. What a travesty. I get to my feet, my legs rubbery with booze and from sitting too long.

'Hey,' I say.

She keeps on walking. I follow her. She must hear my footsteps because she glances over her shoulder before flicking ash from her cigarette and carrying on.

'I want a word with you.'

I'm sure she's speeding up. Has she recognised me from my visit to the café the other day? I bet she knows damn fine who I am.

We're the only people in the street. I break into a run, but before I can reach her she stops and wheels round.

'What do you want?' she says.

I pull up sharp.

'You,' she says, coming closer to me. 'What do you want?'

'I know who you are,' I say.

She takes a moment to process the words. 'You know me?' she says, eventually.

'Stay away from Sandy.'

Her green eyes narrow. 'What do you know about him?'

'You're sleeping with him, aren't you?'

'What?'

'You are having sex with him.' I speak slowly for her benefit. I don't know the words in French, and I don't have time for Google Translate.

She laughs. 'No. I am not having sex with this man.'

'Don't lie to me.'

'It is true. I—'

'I saw him with you at the café. He was giving you money.'

'You have spied on me?' She jabs the cigarette into the space between us. 'Are you crazy?'

'I know you're sleeping with him.'

'Who the fuck are you?'

'I'm his fiancée. Almost.'

'Look.' She glances around the empty street, as if scared someone will overhear. 'Sandy is a friend with my father. They met in Baumettes. My father, he is worried about me. He told Sandy to find me and one day there is Sandy at the café.'

Exactly what Sandy told me when I questioned him at Le Plongeoir. 'I see you've got your stories straight,' I say. 'He told you, then, that I was on to you?'

'What are you talking about?' She takes a drag from her cigarette and exhales smoke into my face. 'I borrowed some money from a bad person. I was in trouble and when Sandy turned up and gave me money it was for me a huge help. He even came back another time and gave me more.'

'You're a good little liar, I'll give you that.' Tears prick my eyes. 'Sandy and I are in love,' I say, 'we're meant to be getting married.'

'You have this all wrong.' She shakes her head. 'I don't have time for this.'

'You don't fool me, lady,' I say as she walks away. 'I wasn't born yesterday.'

48

COLETTE

Monday morning. The train carrying me to Draguignan is the Marseilles service. The same one I sometimes took when visiting Dad. The train has just left Saint-Raphaël, and the coastline is changing. Grey and white limestone giving way to red, jagged rocks.

I almost wish Dad was still locked away. At least I didn't have these doubts then. They are only doubts. I don't know anything for sure yet.

Do I want to? If my worst fears are true, he could go back to prison. How would I feel then?

As I got dressed this morning, I told myself I might not even speak to Jane. That didn't stop me picking out my smartest pair of linen trousers and a white blouse.

I also applied full make-up, put on my most expensive jewellery and completed my outfit with my Chanel sunglasses. An armour of sorts.

When the train approaches Cannes, a sour taste fills the back of my throat. I think of the Majestic Hôtel. If something did happen between Jane and my father, did it happen there? He wouldn't do that to me, would he? Not in the same hotel.

This morning, an item on the news brought me a spark of hope. Dad was in the shower, getting ready to go to the airport and pick up Uncle Jimmy, but he'd left the TV on, loud as usual. I came through to the living area just in time to hear the end of a story about Henri Breton in the news. Two actresses he's worked with recently have spoken up to support him. They claim his behaviour with them was always appropriate.

This news item gave me an idea I'm clinging to now as the train pulls into Cannes station. What if Dad and Jane had an enjoyable, consensual fling, and he wants her to support his version of events with Ella? Maybe he's trying to clear his name, and he'll tell me about it once he has all the evidence together. He might be scared to tell me because he knows I'll be upset about him cheating on Mum.

If so, why didn't he ask Jane for help during his trial? If she has a different story to Ella's, wouldn't he have told his lawyer about it?

Ella Watson in the witness box, her dark eyes fixed on me.

When the train stops, the family across the aisle get up and bundle out of the doors, the father laden with beach bags. I close my eyes and don't open them again until Cannes is behind me. Before long, the train swings inland. Low hills, flat fields. Industrial estates and garden centres displaying huge, brightly coloured sculptures of animals and comic book heroes.

Yesterday, after leaving Lynne's flat, I walked about in the late afternoon heat for ages, thinking about the letter from Dad. *I want to spend the rest of my life with you, Lynne. I promise you that...* So much for not making her any promises. Poor Lynne. Either he's been lying to her or to me. Or to both of us.

The defendant, Monsieur Gilligan, is a manipulative character. Used to getting what he wants, in business and in his personal life.

That scrapbook with all the wedding pictures in it made me want to cry. Lynne's not my kind of person, but she doesn't deserve to be treated badly. It made me sad to see her so drunk and unhappy. From the way she asked about Jane the other day, it's obvious she thinks Dad might be cheating on her. If only that's all it was. She didn't come to the apartment to watch the Bastille Day fireworks on Saturday. She said she had a migraine, but I bet she was avoiding Dad.

When I finally returned to the apartment yesterday, Dad had gone for a run. Out of habit, I checked the knife and found it still in its hiding place. After leaving a note for Dad explaining I needed a nap, I took to my bed and stayed there, refusing his offer of scrambled eggs for supper.

In the early hours of the following morning, still wide awake, I crept into his room. I stood at the side of his bed, watching him sleep. I thought about him calling out Jane's name in the night. I waited there for a long time, hoping he would speak and give something away, but he remained silent. I knew then that to find out more I would have to go to Draguignan. I would have to speak to Jane.

* * *

The taxi journey from Les Arcs station into Draguignan takes twenty minutes. I ask the surly driver to drop me off on Boulevard de la Liberté. I've already looked at a map of the town and know where I need to go.

La Liberté is busy with cars and vans and scooters. It is almost half past twelve and the relentless heat reflects off the roads and pavements. Draguignan, from what I saw in the taxi, is small and provincial. Not a typical place for an English person to settle. Did Jane come here for love, or did she have other reasons for wanting to hide herself away?

In less than five minutes, I'm standing outside the Hôtel des Arbres. Beyond the plane trees and the cypresses, I can see the hotel building and the courtyard outside it.

A tall man comes out of the hotel with a child in his arms. Jane's husband and son; I recognise them from the photographs. Michel fetches a football from a corner of the courtyard and encourages his son to take a kick. I wonder if she's told him anything about my father. Not that I know if there's anything to tell yet. That's why I'm here.

Jane emerges from the building, as if I've somehow summoned her. She is wearing practical clothes – a loose linen dress to protect her from the heat and a pair of white trainers. Shielding her eyes from the sun, she watches her family for a moment. Her son waves at her, and she blows him a kiss. She says something I can't hear to her husband. He nods but doesn't turn around. Seeing her with her family makes my chest ache. She seems to have everything. Surely that means whatever happened between her and my father can't have been that bad? And if it was, shouldn't I let her get on with her life and leave the past untouched?

49

JANE

I sit at the hotel reception desk. The numbers on the computer screen before me blur and distort. I am supposed to be checking a bill query for the trendy young couple from Paris standing in front of me, but my concentration is all over the place.

'You charged us for two bottles of wine at lunch on Saturday, but we only had one,' the husband says. His wife leans her head on his shoulder. She looks bored and tired. Monday-weary after their weekend away.

'Right. Yes. I've got it.' I spot the mistake, amend the bill and print them a copy. Alazne comes into reception just as the husband hands over his Visa card to pay. She hovers by the reception desk, tidying up the display of leaflets for local attractions. I can tell she has something to say to me. Michel must have told her about me smacking Theo and about my general erratic behaviour. After my near miss with the truck on Boulevard de la Liberté on Friday, I walked around in a daze for several hours. When I returned home, I claimed to have a migraine. I went to bed and slipped into a blank, black sleep for fourteen hours. I spent most of the weekend in bed, avoiding everyone.

As soon as the couple leaves reception, Alazne turns her warm smile on me.

'I hope you don't mind,' she says, 'but I've made you a doctor's appointment this afternoon. At one thirty.'

'I'm fine. I only had a migraine.'

'No, Jane.' Her voice is firm. 'You need to see someone.'

'I feel fine now.'

'Please,' she says, 'he might give you something to help. Something temporary.'

Medication. I can't blame her for thinking I need it. Maybe I do.

'Please, Jane,' she says, 'we only want to help.'

* * *

Michel and Theo are in the courtyard playing football. I stand and watch them. When Theo sees me, he waves, and I blow him a kiss in return. He seems to have forgiven me for smacking him. Whether he has forgotten is another question. Michel has done neither, and I can't blame him.

Would I really have stepped in front of that truck? I don't think so, but how can I be sure? What if that man hadn't pulled me back from the kerb? Perhaps this visit to the doctor is a good idea. Some medication might stabilise me. The thought I might have harmed myself and left Theo without a mother is terrifying. Once I have myself under control, I will make my relationships with my husband and son a priority.

When I tell Michel about the doctor's visit, he nods and says he will drive me there. Is that a good sign or does he just want to make sure I go? He tells me to be ready to leave in half an hour.

The phone at the reception desk rings. I hurry inside to answer it. '*Bonjour*,' I say. Silence greets me. '*Allo?*'

A sharp intake of breath on the other end of the phone. 'Jane?'

A woman's voice. A cold tingling sensation spreads across my chest. 'Yes.'

'Jane, my name is Colette Gilligan.'

50

COLETTE

I'm standing outside a launderette on Boulevard de la Liberté, where Jane instructed me to wait. My heart hammers in my chest. Every atom of me wants to run.

Too late. There she is, further up the street, hurrying towards me with her head down. I adjust my sunglasses, glad of their protection. Not from the fierce glare of the sun but from her gaze and what it might tell me. As she approaches, I see she is wearing sunglasses too.

'Colette?' she says, even though she must know it's me.

I nod, unsure what to say. She's clutching the strap of her handbag so tight her knuckles are white.

'Did he send you?' she asks.

I shake my head. 'I just want to talk to you.'

'Fine.' She looks behind her. 'Come with me.'

* * *

We cross the busy road. She leads me past a Turkish café where silent men sip coffee and smoke cigarettes. One of them, an older man with white hair, calls out to her and says hello. She waves a hand in greeting but keeps going. We hurry down a narrow street and come out in a market square. We stay silent. I want to look at her face, but she stays a few steps ahead of me.

As we cross the market square, she glances around her, as if worried about seeing someone she knows. This makes me think she has something to hide. Something she hasn't told anybody yet. Is that good or bad?

'Where's your car?' she says. 'You didn't park by the hotel, did you?'

'I came by train.'

'Good. Don't come near the hotel again.'

Yes, she's a woman with something to hide.

We exit the square up another narrow street with yellow and pink tenement buildings on either side. We both jump when a lanky girl with braided hair leaps out of a doorway. It's unbearably hot. My blouse is sticking to my back.

'There's a park by the old clock tower,' Jane says, 'we can talk there.'

She strides on. Every now and then she slips a hand into her bag, as if checking for something. I could dart away right now, down one of the many streets branching off from this one. I could get back to the train station and return to Nice and forget everything I've discovered so far.

I keep following. She takes me through an archway at the bottom of an ancient stone tower then up a steep street lined with dilapidated buildings. For a moment I wonder if I'm safe. What if she wants to do me harm?

Glancing up, I see an old clock tower on top of a rocky outcrop. We wind our way towards it, past two-storey yellow and ochre buildings with green shutters.

'It's not much further,' she says.

At the side of the clock tower is a tall metal gate. Beyond it, three young boys chase each other round a small grassy park. When I follow Jane inside, I see the boys' mothers sitting on a low wall. The small radio beside them blares out French pop music. One of the mothers is plump and blonde, the other skinny with dyed blue hair in pigtails. The skinny one has a baby on her lap. Both women are sipping from plastic water bottles that appear to be filled with red wine. They shoot Jane and me threatening looks, as if daring us to criticise them. Despite their unwelcoming attitude, I'm glad of their presence. Glad not to be with Jane alone.

Jane sits as far back from the women as possible, on another low wall beneath two olive trees. I sit further along the wall and place my handbag between us as a barrier.

We sit in silence. When she takes off her sunglasses and turns her face to me, I see her properly for the first time. She is without doubt the barmaid from my holiday photographs. The same dark, alluring eyes and full lips. The same thick dark hair. Compelled to meet her gaze, I remove my glasses. She flinches and fear flits across her face.

'You're so like him,' she says. 'I'd forgotten.'

In the distance, a bell tolls once. Soon afterwards the bell in the clock tower beside the garden echoes the single toll.

'Has he said something about me?' Jane says.

'No.'

'Then why are you here?'

How little I've thought this through. Of course, she was going to ask me this.

'Have you known all along?' she says. 'Have you been lying for him?'

'No. God, no.' I should tell her about the private detective, but I'm torn between defending myself and defending Dad.

'What do you know?' she says.

It's what I don't know that scares me. 'I found your name and address. I wondered who you were.'

'Has he been looking for me?'

The boys shriek. Both mothers yell at them before returning to their wine.

'You remember me, don't you?' Jane says. 'From the bar in Cannes.'

'It was a long time ago.'

'You're still defending him?' Jane shakes her head. 'How did he find me?'

'I did some detective work of my own.'

'No.' She clutches her bag close. 'He hired a private detective, didn't he?'

My silence gives him away.

'I knew it,' she says, 'but I told myself I was being crazy.'

'I want to know what happened.' I don't want to know any of it.

'I keep seeing him everywhere. Has he been here? Is he looking for me?'

'No. I don't know.'

Telling the truth about Dad still feels like a betrayal. I need to hear her side of the story. I'll know straight away if she's lying. I'm sure of it.

51

JANE

I am not sure which of us is more terrified. My body is tense, alert, ready for flight. Being this close to her is triggering the same fear I get when I think about her father. As if my body is recognising their shared DNA. Their shared blood.

My hand dips into my bag. My pulse slows a little as my fingers brush against the knife. I am not going to use it. I just want to know it is there.

'I want to know what happened,' she says again.

I have been waiting seven years for someone to come along and wreck the life I have built. Now I know I must take control of the narrative. It is my story to tell.

I close my bag and start at the beginning. I tell her

about the first night I met Sandy with her uncle. I tell her about the second night and what happened at the bar after she left with her husband. I don't leave anything out. I confess that when he offered to buy me a drink, I told him to take me for one after my shift.

'You knew he was married, but you flirted with him anyway?' she says.

Heat crawls up my neck. She can't accuse me of anything I haven't blamed myself for already. Maybe I shouldn't continue. Maybe my story is not worthy.

'You're married,' she says. 'What if someone did that to your husband?'

Michel. He will be searching the house, wondering where I am. After Colette's call, I returned to our apartment, telling him I was getting ready for the doctor's appointment. I grabbed my handbag, left the house without being seen and escaped the hotel through the side gate. What will I say when I see him next? I have a feeling that this day, this meeting will change everything.

'And then what?' she says. 'You knew he was married but you went back to his hotel room to sleep with him?'

The shame I have carried around for seven years threatens to overwhelm me. Then I think of Ella. Sandy's lawyer tried hard to shame her into not speaking. She didn't let that happen, and it is time I didn't either.

'He didn't force you to go to his hotel room,' Colette says. 'You chose to go.'

'Yes, I did. But I didn't consent to what happened later.'

The nearby radio switches to a new song. 'Good Times' by Chic. Did Sandy and I dance to this one? Shame clogs my throat, but I must push through it. I must speak the truth.

Colette keeps her eyes straight ahead as I describe the hotel room and what happened in it. The champagne, the kissing, Sandy between my legs and the moment I thought about Michel and changed my mind. The moment I told Sandy I wanted to leave, and he said I wasn't going anywhere, and I would enjoy myself if I stopped being an uptight bitch and relaxed.

'Stop,' Colette says when I get to the part where Sandy held a cushion over my face. 'That's enough.'

52

COLETTE

'What happened to me was almost identical to what happened to Ella,' Jane says.

I rest my arms on my legs to stop them shaking. Her calmness is unnerving. Her calmness makes me think she is telling the truth.

If she is telling the truth, then so was Ella Watson.

I don't want to think about that. I don't want to think about Dad at breakfast in the Majestic Hôtel, the morning after Jane says he raped her. How normal he seemed, as if nothing unusual had happened. The same way he behaved after returning from his weekend in Marseilles.

'Why didn't you say anything?' I ask. 'You've had

years to say something.' Part of me still wants her to be to blame.

'I know how it seems,' she says.

Dad is a ghostly presence between us. The reassurances I should give Jane – it wasn't your fault, you have nothing to be ashamed of – stick in my throat.

'If you're telling the truth,' I say, 'then you could have stopped it happening to someone else.'

She turns to look at me, her face drawn. 'You helped him too. You spoke up for him in court, you stuck with him through everything.'

She's right. I helped him in so many ways. His unwitting accomplice.

'We've always had each other's backs,' I say, unable to summon my usual pride in this fact.

'Do you still?'

A flush of disgrace crawls up my neck.

'It must be hard hearing all this,' she says.

The pop music stops. The plump woman picks up the stereo, the skinny one balances her baby on her hip. They gather up their sons and leave, the flurry of activity making the baby wail. Soon it is just me and Jane, with the heat and the truth oppressive around us.

'Have you told anyone else?' I ask.

She shakes her head. 'No. Not even my husband.'

What about the psychologist she visits? What

does she talk about with Julia Martin? What mental health issues does she have that might make her unreliable? If she reports Dad to the police and there's an investigation, what will they uncover?

With horror, I realise I'm thinking like him. He must have had similar thoughts when he hired a detective to find her. I glance around the empty park. The two of us, alone. What if Jane ceased to exist? Wouldn't that solve Dad's problem?

'We're both his victims,' she says.

Dad loves me. How can I be his victim? The idea is appalling, but it also offers an unexpected chink of light. A possibility of escape I didn't know I was looking for.

'What if he does it again?' she says.

This thought has been hovering in a dark corner of my mind since our conversation began. 'He won't,' I say, without conviction.

'What if he comes here, looking for me?'

'I don't think that's—'

'Am I in danger?'

'I'm sure he—'

'What about my son? Would he hurt my son?'

'No, he would never—'

'Really?' Her face twists with fear. From the direction of the old town comes the tolling of a bell. 'I need to go.'

'Wait,' I say, but she's already on her feet and crossing to the other side of the park, the opposite direction to where we came in. I follow her and see she's heading for a set of twisting stone steps that lead down into the old town.

'What are you going to do?' I say.

She stops on the steps and looks up at me. I imagine her falling and breaking her neck on the rough stone. An accidental death that would solve everything.

'I don't know yet.' She looks deep into my eyes. 'What about you, Colette? What are you going to do?'

53

JANE

Colette will not do anything. Every sip of brandy I take makes me more certain of this. Fifteen minutes ago, after leaving her in the park, I ran back through the old town and made my way to this bar on Rue de l'Observance. A quiet, basic place she will not walk past and where no one I know would ever come. Apart from two old men reading newspapers in the corner, I am the only person in here. The other customers are sitting outside, under the awning. In here, a lazy overhead fan does nothing to dispel the heat.

I am so tired. I never could have imagined that the first person I told my story to would be the daughter of the man who raped me. Isn't sharing the truth supposed to set you free? I don't feel free. Fear crawls through me, as acute as before.

Sandy did hire a detective. Colette's silence told me that. I think he came to Draguignan too; I think it was him I saw with that woman in the square.

I check my phone and find another missed call from Michel and another text.

Where are you? Please call.

I am so tired. I want to go home and climb into bed and forget everything that just happened, but I can't. This is not over. This is not the end.

I shiver, despite the heat seeping in from outside. The next sip of brandy burns my throat as it goes down. I don't think Colette did know the truth about Ella, or about me. I don't think she lied for her father deliberately, but I don't believe she will do anything useful with the truth. When I got to the worst part of my ordeal, when I described Sandy putting the cushion over my face, she begged me to stop.

My story must have been hard for her to listen to, but why come here if she wasn't prepared for what she might find? Do I really believe she has any authority over Sandy? No. Nor do I believe she would support me if I went to the police with my story.

We've always had each other's backs.

The police. Could they do anything? What evidence do I have? The concierge who saw me at the hotel that night probably doesn't work there now, and I doubt the hotel keeps CCTV footage for seven years. Even if her uncle remembered me, he wouldn't speak out against family. I should have told her to give Sandy a message. To offer him a deal. Stay away from me and my family and I will stay silent.

On my phone I look up the timetable for trains to Nice. Colette has just missed one and will have to wait an hour at the station for the next train. I could get in a taxi and go there now and give her the message. Would she pass it on? Could she and Sandy carry on as they are with the full knowledge of what he has done?

I suspect she would ignore my request and create whatever narrative she needs to keep things as they are. An impulse I understand better than most.

Ella. What would Ella do?

What if I made my offer to Sandy in person, with Colette as a witness? He couldn't hurt me then, could he? I picture myself getting to the train station and staying out of sight so Colette cannot see me. I will get on the train and when it arrives, I will follow her from the station to where she lives. I will wait until I see her and Sandy together and then confront them. Even if I lose Colette on the way, I know the area they live in. I will track them down, even if it takes a little while.

I check inside my handbag. I have my purse, my phone and, at the bottom of the bag, the knife.

I am the one who has to tell him, I think. It has to be me.

PART IV

54

COLETTE

When Dad arrives back from Monaco on Tuesday evening, just after seven thirty, I greet him with a glass of champagne.

'That's my girl.' He drops his overnight bag on the sofa and takes the glass from me. 'What are we celebrating?'

'Do we need a reason?'

'For champagne? Never.'

I lead him out on to the balcony. Pre-dinner snacks await him on the table. Olives with pimento and artichokes.

'Thanks, love,' Dad says. 'This looks amazing.' A shrill ringtone interrupts us. He pulls his phone from the pocket of his navy shorts. 'It's Lynne.' He sighs. 'If I ignore her, she'll only keep ringing.' He puts the phone to his ear. 'Yup. Hello. I've only just got back.' He hurries indoors and disappears into his bedroom. I hope he doesn't notice anything out of place. Last night, I searched his room and found the envelope with all the information about Jane hidden inside a stack of towels in his wardrobe. I've put it in the boot of my car for safekeeping.

Five minutes later, Dad returns to the balcony and settles himself into a chair.

'All good?' I ask.

'She sounded drunk. She insisted on coming here to talk to me, but I told her you and I were having dinner together.' He squeezes his eyes shut and opens them again. The skin beneath them is dark and puffy.

'Late night?' I say.

He picks up one of the cocktail sticks I've laid out and spears himself an olive. 'You know Jimmy.' I thought the two of them might stop in on the way back to the airport so I could see my uncle, but Dad said they didn't have time.

'You had fun, though?' I say.

Dad laughs. 'As I say, you know Jimmy.'

A shudder of revulsion runs through me. I gaze out at the bay. The silvery-blue water is calm and still. 'How was the hotel?' I ask.

'Pricey, but you only live once, right?'

'What did you get up to?'

'Few drinks, some nice meals, a bit of blackjack in the casino.' Dad helps himself to an artichoke and tuts as a spot of oil lands on his black linen shirt.

'Did you win?'

'You know me.' He dabs at the oil with a napkin. 'I always get lucky.'

Did you get lucky afterwards, I wonder? Did you spend your winnings in a bar somewhere and chat up a young barmaid with dark hair and dark eyes.

What if he does it again?

'What's for dinner?' he says. 'I'm starving.'

'Roast chicken and salad.'

'You're too good to me. I don't deserve you.'

Since returning from Draguignan, I've been busy getting everything ready. *What about you, Colette? What are you going to do?* On the train journey back to Nice, I couldn't stop thinking about Jane. When I was boarding the train, I glanced back at the station and saw a dark-haired woman by the ticket machine and thought for a moment it was her. I knew it was my conscience getting to me and, as the train pulled away from the station, I realised I had to face the truth about my father. Somewhere between Cannes and Saint-Raphaël, I knew exactly what I had to do.

'You're right,' I say to my father, 'you don't deserve me.'

'That's what I told Jimmy.' Dad leans over and rubs my arm. An affectionate gesture that makes me stiffen. 'You've always been there for me. Not just these past five years but when your mum died as well. I couldn't have survived that without you.'

What would Mum think of me now? Sitting here believing terrible things about my father. Plotting to discover the truth, whatever the cost. Then I remember one of the last conversations I had with her in the hospice. I promised her I'd look after Dad when she was gone. I thought she'd be glad to hear that, but she managed a weak laugh and said I had no idea what it took to look after a man like Dad. No idea at all.

A tense yapping interrupts us. Ramona. Dad looks down into the garden.

'Evening, Kathy,' he says, raising his glass.

Kathy holds Ramona to her chest as she looks up at us. 'Hello, Colette,' she says. For the first time, I realise she's looking at me with concern, not hatred. I want to tell her not to worry. I want to tell her I have a plan.

'More champagne?' I ask when Kathy disappears into the block.

'Why not?'

In the kitchen, my hands shake as I lift the champagne bottle from the fridge and fill up Dad's glass. I think of the fear on Jane's face.

Am I in danger? Is she? I need to know.

I open a kitchen drawer and take out a small white envelope. On the front is my father's name. It took me a while to disguise my handwriting. To be certain he wouldn't know the note was from me.

'By the way,' I say when I take his full glass out to the balcony, 'this was lying on the doormat when I came in earlier. Someone must have dropped it off.'

'Oh. Odd.' He frowns as he examines the envelope.

'I'm just going to get dinner sorted.'

'Great. Thanks, love.'

I head indoors. From the kitchen I watch him open the envelope and take out the note inside. His face betrays no emotion as he reads it.

I'm in Nice. I know you've been looking for me. We need to talk about what happened in Cannes. If I don't hear from you, I'll come to your house again. 07818 454331. Text only.

The rotisserie chicken I bought from the deli earlier is still warm beneath the tinfoil wrapping. Shame we won't get to eat any of it.

I'm severing the legs from the main carcass with a carving knife when Dad comes in from the balcony. He fetches his phone from the pocket of his linen jacket and returns outside.

The carving knife doesn't need to do much. The flesh of the leg is tender and pliant and falls away from the bone with ease.

It isn't long before the burner phone I bought with cash from a shop near Nice-Ville train station vibrates silently in the pocket of my jeans. 'Just going to the loo,' I say. Dad nods but doesn't look up from his phone.

In the bathroom I lock the door and take the phone from my pocket. As my calm veneer dissolves, I press my throbbing forehead against the cool, tiled wall. Several minutes pass before I can bear to look at the phone and read my father's text.

Who is this?

I don't want to use Jane's name. I don't need to. He knows exactly who these messages are meant to be from. With trembling hands, I type my reply.

You know who I am. I want to meet tonight.

How did you find me?

Same way I imagine you found me.

I leave my forehead pressed against the cold tiles as I wait for his reply. Tears cluster in my eyes. I want a miracle. I want him to somehow redeem the situation and for us to go back to how we were before.

Was there ever any before? My father was an illusion, but surely that illusion is better than reality?

Meet me at Rauba Capeu beach. Steps by the sea wall. Half an hour.

A sharp pain in my chest. His response is still not an admission of guilt but my excuses for him are running out. The place he wants to meet her is public but also, at times, deserted. Secluded spots can be found if you clamber out on to the rocks.

I flush the toilet. Run the cold tap and splash water over my face. When I step out into the hallway, I almost bump into Dad.

'Everything okay?' I say.

'I need to pop out for a bit.'

'What's happened?'

'Bit of a Lynne situation I need to deal with.'

'She's been on the phone again?'

'Yup.'

'Is she okay?'

'Nothing to worry about.' Forced laughter. 'Bloody women.'

He goes into his bedroom and closes the door. I hover in the hallway, recoiling at his lies. Horror fills me as I hear the noise of drawers opening and closing.

When I open the door, he has both hands in his underwear drawer.

'Have you lost something?' I ask.

'No.' He takes out a pair of socks, squeezes them, puts them back in the drawer.

He won't find the knife. I took it and hid it in my room earlier.

When he turns to look at me, I don't recognise him. He looks the same, he sounds the same, but he is not the man I thought was my father.

'Sorry,' he says, pushing past me. 'I've got to go.'

55

LYNNE

I'm in a taxi on my way to Sandy's. We're winding our way up Boulevard du Mont Boron. Not far now. When I phoned him earlier, he said he'd see me tomorrow, but I can't wait until then. I'm going to tell him I know about Jane, and I'm going to give him a piece of my mind.

'Sorry,' my driver says as he brakes on a sharp bend. 'Crazy, twisty road.'

The car's jerky motion makes my stomach drop. I've been on the Aperol Spritz since lunchtime. They say alcohol numbs, but it's done nothing to numb my anger.

I could kill Sandy.

Monaco with Jimmy my backside. I did a bit of surveillance on Café Corsica when Sandy was away, and I didn't see Jane once. The two of them were together, I'm sure of it.

Honestly, what is it with me and men? Sandy may be innocent of committing the crime he was jailed for, but he's guilty of shafting me, that's for bloody sure. My eyes blur with tears. I should have known it was too good to be true.

He must be in my bad books because I look a right wreck and I don't care. Hair tangled, a creased old sundress on and my face and chest all blotchy from too much sun.

As we approach his block of flats, I fumble in my handbag for my purse. When I look up again, I see him on the pavement ahead of us, looking at his phone.

'Pull over,' I say to the driver. 'Pull over.'

Tutting, the driver obeys and parks behind a black Peugeot 208. I slide down in my seat a little but can still see Sandy. He puts his phone in one of the pockets of his shorts and pulls a piece of paper from the other. He stares at it for a moment before ripping it up. Then he crosses the street and shoves the paper shreds in a dustbin. I sit up again and watch as he disappears down the same set of steps we used when we took that shortcut to Le Plongeoir. He's heading for the port.

He told me he was having dinner with Colette and staying in all night. Lying little sod. Bet he's off to see Jane. I'll catch him up and have it out with him. I grab a handful of euros from my purse, but before I can pass them to the driver and get out of the taxi, Colette appears in the street.

At first, I think Sandy must have forgotten something and she's about to chase after him, but at the top of the steps she hesitates, craning her neck as if she's looking to see how far ahead he is.

Is she following him? What the bloody hell's going on?

'Take me down to the port,' I say to the driver. 'Quick as you can.'

56

COLETTE

When I reach the port, some of the day's heat is draining away, along with the light. The sun won't set fully for at least half an hour, but already a pearly sheen has spread across the bay. Layers of rose-pink and gold tint the sky over the western hills.

The port is noisy. Clashing music from the various bars mingles into one distorted melody. Despite the noise, the terrace tables outside the bars are only half full, as if the city is having a breather after the weekend's Bastille Day celebrations. Turning my head to the left, I catch a glimpse of a dark-haired woman ducking into a bar. Once again, my conscience turns her into Jane, as if reminding me why I need to confront my father.

I cross the road in front of the marina and see him striding ahead of me along Quai Lunel. I keep his black shirt in sight as I follow him. My handbag is slung across my body. Inside it I have my own phone, as well as the burner phone. In the right-hand pocket of my jeans is the switchblade knife. I wanted to bring it as evidence. To show him his secrets are not safe with me.

I turn on to Quai Rauba Capeu and stop. There, ahead of me, is Dad, hurrying down the stairs that lead to the beach. When I reach the same stairs, I see him standing on the rocks on the right-hand side. He's looking at his phone and doesn't see me descend to the beach.

On the strip of concrete facing the water, a homeless man lies unconscious on top of a sleeping bag, an empty vodka bottle beside him. To my left, in the distance, three teenage boys clamber over the concrete tetrapods.

As I walk towards my father, he looks up and sees me. He stumbles a little as he takes a step back on the rocks.

'Hello, love,' he says when I reach him. 'What are you doing here?' He slips his phone into the pocket of his shorts. 'Were you out for a walk?'

'No.' My heart punches at my ribs. My mouth is dry.

He glances up at the steps, his face drawn and anxious. A cornered animal.

'I thought you were going to see Lynne?' I say.

'I stopped for a look at the view.'

How easily the lies slip out of him. How convincing he is. Or was. 'You shouldn't have strung Lynne along.'

He frowns. 'I haven't. I never promised—'

'You promised to marry her. I know. I read your letters.'

'What? When did you—'

'Did you mean any of it, or were you just using her?'

'What's with all the questions?'

'Answer me.'

'Okay. Jesus.' A wave splashes over the rock. 'Lynne was great while I was in prison, but now I'm out, I can see it's not going to work.'

'That's convenient.'

'I'm in a better place now, and I can do better than Lynne.'

He doesn't deserve Lynne. He doesn't deserve anyone.

His eyes flick to the steps again. I remember Jane's

words. *What about you, Colette? What are you going to do?*

'Waiting for Jane, are you?' I say.

He looks at me, startled. 'What? How did you... Who's Jane?'

With a sigh I take the burner phone from my bag. 'I messaged you on this and pretended to be Jane.'

'I don't understand.' He doesn't. He is utterly bewildered. As he begins to comprehend, his expression changes from confusion to anger. 'Let me see that,' he says, holding out his hand for the phone.

I slip it back into my bag. 'No.'

'What do you think you're playing at?' he says.

I've always hated making him angry, but right now I don't care. Gone is my usual urge to make his anger stop so he will go back to loving me and making me feel special. I don't need to be the centre of his universe.

'Christ, Colette. I can't believe you did this.'

He can't believe I outsmarted him. Does that mean he's never thought me capable of much? 'I went to Draguignan,' I say. 'I talked to Jane Durand.'

He assumes an authoritative air. 'I'm not sure what's going on and what you think you know, but I can tell you that this woman—'

'I found the envelope with all the photographs of

her. All the information about who she is and where she lives now. I've taken it and put it somewhere safe.'

'You had no right to—'

'Did you hire a detective?'

'That's none of your business.'

'I remember her from Cannes. She's in my photographs from that holiday.' Photographs that might be useful evidence for Jane if she decides to report my father. Evidence at least that they met. 'She told me what you did.'

'She's lying.'

'Just like Ella Watson?'

'Yes.' A note of desperation in his voice. 'They're both lying.'

'You admit to sleeping with her, though? When Mum was alive. When you were supposedly happily married.'

'A stupid mid-life slip-up. That's all it was. Meaningless.'

'How many other women have you done this to? How many other "slip-ups" have you made?'

'This is ridiculous.'

'Why are you looking for Jane? I know you went to Draguignan. Lynne told me.'

'Listen.' He reaches for me, but I step away. 'What happened with Ella really shook me up. I knew I hadn't done anything wrong, but I thought about... I remembered Jane, and I wanted to know it was okay.'

An explanation I would have believed before, but now I don't. Unless he really is guilty of ignorance and nothing else.

'So, you asked her to meet you here so you could find out?'

'I didn't expect her to come looking for me.'

Behind him, to the west, ember-bellied clouds are rising over the hills. The blue above us deepens as the light fades further.

'I wanted to protect you,' he says. 'You've already had enough to deal with.'

His eyes widen when I take the switchblade knife from my pocket. 'You were looking for this to bring with you,' I say. Why?'

'What the... That's my personal property. You can't invade my privacy like that.'

His indignation makes me want to laugh. He seems to think he still has some authority.

'Why did you want to bring it?' I say. 'What were you going to do with it?' The handle is cool and smooth in my palm. One small movement from my thumb and the blade would come out of hiding.

'Jesus, Colette. I wasn't... I had no intention of hurting her.'

'Why did you want to bring it?'

'What, you think I was going to kill her? Here, in public?' He gestures to the homeless man, who appears to be slipping in and out of consciousness. The teenagers are clambering up the tetrahedrons and on to the sea wall. They will soon be gone.

'Why did you want to bring the knife?' I ask.

'Protection.'

'From Jane?'

'She might have brought someone with her.'

'If you didn't do anything wrong, you've nothing to be scared of.'

'Enough.' He presses the heels of his hands against his temples. 'You don't get over being in prison straight away. I had to be on my guard there the whole time. I had to look after myself.'

'You're not in prison any more.'

'Aren't I?' His eyes are wild. He looks unhinged. 'If Jane has her way, I could go back there again. Is that what you want?' He stretches out his arms, as if to embrace me. My thumb presses the handle of the knife. The blade flicks up and glints between us. 'For God's sake,' he says, 'that thing's lethal. Stop playing with it.'

'If what Jane says is true, you deserve to go back to prison.'

'We had sex,' he says. 'She wanted it. She wanted it

and then she decided she didn't like it. I'm not going back to jail for that.'

'It was rape.' The word flies out of me, dark and true.

'Why didn't she say anything?' he says. 'She's had years to report me, and she never did. Did she know about Ella?'

'Why does that matter?'

'I bet she read about the trial. If she really thought I was some kind of monster, why didn't she come forward?'

So many reasons. Reasons he isn't capable of understanding. He's asking the same questions I asked Jane when we met. Questions I'm now ashamed of.

'She's just another woman out to wreck our lives,' he says. 'Can't you see that?'

I jab the blade into the space between us, forcing my father closer to the edge of the rock. 'The only person who's wrecked my life is you.'

His expression hardens. 'I've been a good parent to you.'

'You destroyed my world. My marriage, my career, my friendships.'

'I've given you everything.'

'You've used me for years. You knew you were guilty, and you let me defend you. You made me your accomplice.' I have hated the woman he abused. Disparaged other women with similar stories. Failed to believe and support them.

'I'm your father,' he says. 'Of course you defended me.'

'I'm done with protecting you.' The handle of the knife so cool and smooth in my palm. 'If Jane decides to press charges against you, I'll give the police all the evidence I've got. I'll back her all the way.'

'What about loyalty?' He edges towards me, eyes flashing with anger. 'What happened to that?'

'Your criminal record means the police will have to take Jane seriously.'

'No.' He lunges forward and grabs me by the throat. 'You need to stop this.' Before I can fully register the shock of his powerful grip, the shock of his violence, my hands shoot out to push him away.

It's only when the blade pierces his flesh that I remember I'm holding the knife. Only when he gasps do I realise the blade has slipped between his ribs, deep into the right side of his body.

He stands absolutely still. As if the shock of the penetration has frozen him in place. We are so close I can smell him. That indescribable father scent, tinged with something new. Tinged with fear.

Panic fills his eyes. We stare at one another for

what feels like a very long time. My body is shaking. For a moment I wish he would hug me. I wish I could recapture the feeling of safety his arms have always given me.

He lets out another sharp gasp as I pull the knife out of his body.

'No,' he says, 'leave it.'

Too late. The knife falls from my grasp on to the rocks. We both look down at it, but he moves first. With a groan he stoops down, picks it up and throws it behind him, into the sea.

'It was an accident,' he says. 'We both lost control. We weren't thinking straight.'

'Yes.' A strange calm in my chest. I must be in shock. I glance behind me. The homeless man is still passed out. The teenagers have gone. There is no one looking down on us from the sea wall.

My father presses one hand against his shirt. Against his wound. His face is very pale. 'We need to call an ambulance.' He takes his phone from the pocket of his shorts, but when he tries to dial with one hand it falls on to the rock.

This time I move first, pouncing on the phone and backing away from my father.

He groans again. Sweat beads on his forehead. He looks different. Small. Pathetic. 'Call for help,' he says.

'Hurry.' His voice is weak and wretched. He sounds as if he's crumbling, and I realise I've been holding him up all this time. 'We don't have long,' he says.

I touch my neck. I wonder if his fingers have left marks there. The strange calm spreads throughout my body. I look at him, waiting to feel something – panic, pity – but I am numb. I wonder if this is how he felt when he committed his crimes? Maybe I've inherited this ability of his, and I never knew it until now.

What about you, Colette? What are you going to do?

Jane is with me. So is Ella. So are all the other nameless women who have suffered because of men like my father. I rub my throat. What would he have done to me if the knife hadn't been in my hand? If it had only been my inferior physical strength against his superior one? If I was just a woman fighting off a much stronger man?

'Please.' He takes his hand away from his shirt. His palm is covered in blood.

I put his phone in my handbag. 'You and I are finished.'

'I never meant to hurt anyone.' He presses his bloody hand against his ribs again. 'Especially not you.'

'I don't believe you.' I turn my back on him. 'I don't believe a word you say.'

57

LYNNE

My stomach's in knots as I crouch behind the sea wall, handbag clutched to my chest. Crouching isn't easy at my age, but I can't risk Colette spotting me. I still can't believe what I've just seen. Or what I think I've seen. When I got the taxi to drop me off at the port, I had no idea the night would end up like this. After I stumbled out of the car, I couldn't see Sandy anywhere. I was sure I'd missed him, but then I saw Colette. I started following her and soon spotted Sandy. He had no idea his daughter was following him.

Before long, we were here, at Rauba Capeu beach, the three of us.

There's Colette now. I shrink back against the wall

as she appears at the top of the steps. The light's fading fast, but if she looks to her right, she might see me.

She walks with her head down, hands in her pockets. She walks fast and she doesn't look left or right.

As soon as she's a good distance away, I haul myself up and hurry to the steps. Looking down, I see a homeless man crashed out on a sleeping bag. Straight ahead of me, on the rocks, is Sandy, lying on his side.

I rush down the steps, bag hanging over my shoulder. When I get to the rocks, I take my time. Don't want to slip. I pause for breath. The sunset is almost over now. In the distance, the street lamps are on all along the promenade, making it all sparkly, the opposite of what this moment is.

'Lynne?' Sandy's voice is low and croaky.

Such a gorgeous view, but it's like I'm looking at it for the last time. Nice is only a holiday destination now, not somewhere I'll be spending the rest of my life.

'Lynne, is that you?'

'The one and only.'

'How did you... Why are you here?' He moans in pain as he pushes himself up to sitting. 'Never mind. Just call me an ambulance. Hurry.' The hand pressed against his ribs is slick with blood.

'Got yourself in a pickle there,' I say.

'Are you drunk?'

'A little. Probably a lot.'

'Lynne, please get help. I need you.' He glances at the fresh blood oozing between his fingers. 'I need something to stop the bleeding. Have you got a scarf?'

'Nope.'

'Christ's sake, you must be the only woman in the South of France not wearing a scarf.'

Odd how when I left the flat earlier, all I wanted was to know the truth about Jane. Right now, I don't care about her. Much more pressing matters to deal with.

'What were you arguing with Colette about?'

He looks up at me, his face ghost-white. 'You saw us?'

'I saw everything.'

'It was an accident.'

'Which bit? You grabbing your own daughter by the throat?'

'You don't understand, she—'

'What kind of man attacks his own daughter?' An easy question to answer. Men like my father. I thought Sandy was a liar and a cheat, but I'd never have put him in that category. Until now. 'Why was she so angry?' I ask. 'What on earth would make her threaten you with a knife?'

'She... she was confused about something.' He clutches his ribs, his face twisting with pain. 'It was an accident,' he says.

'It was self-defence. You attacked her, she didn't have a choice.' I gaze up at the darkening sky. 'I wish I'd had the courage to finish my dad off. Would have made my life a damn sight easier.' I think of him grabbing my hair in the kitchen that time and me threatening to stick the bread knife in him. What stopped me? Fear or misplaced loyalty?

'It wasn't Colette's fault,' he says again.

'Oh, I know that. You've brought this all on yourself, Sandy Gilligan.' He doesn't need to worry about his daughter. My mother never protected me, but I'll look out for Colette.

'Please,' he says, 'can we talk about this later? I really need an ambulance.'

'Relax. Enjoy the sunset. Might be your last.'

'Not funny, Lynne, I'm running out of time. Please... get help.'

'No, I don't think I will.'

Gasping and groaning, he gets to his feet. He tries to grab my phone, but I back away, too quick for him. He collapses to his knees, and the pain makes him cry out. I look back at the homeless man, but he's still out of it. I spot two figures by the sea wall, but they're joggers and they keep going, and they've probably got headphones on and even if they do look this way it's too dark for them to see us clearly.

'Lynne.'

He's on his knees in front of me. As if he's about to propose. How often have I fantasised about such a moment? That night, after Le Plongeoir, I even thought he was going to do it here, on this beach. What a mug.

'No, Sandy,' I say, wanting to know how it would feel to refuse him. 'I won't marry you. I wouldn't marry you if you were the last man on earth.'

It feels satisfying. That's me done with romance. For good.

He collapses on to the rock and curls into a foetal position, facing the sea. This is where he will die, bleeding into the Bay of Angels.

'I could never love a man capable of harming his daughter,' I say.

'Lynne,' he whispers, 'please.'

'Screw you, Sandy Gilligan,' I say. 'Screw you.'

58

COLETTE

I've always liked October in Nice. Fewer tourists, less traffic; the sun still shines and the temperatures range from the mid-teens to as high as twenty. A good time of year for my last visit to the city.

I arrived in Nice two days ago to oversee the final stages of the sale of the apartment. The retired couple who bought the place asked for the furniture with it, but everything else had to go. Yesterday, I supervised the removal company as they packed up what remained of my personal stuff, as well as the family mementos I had shipped over when I sold Riverbank Cottage. I've arranged for everything to join the rest of our family's belongings in storage back in England. Patch and I are in no hurry to claim any of it.

Unsure what to do with Dad's clothes and valuables, I asked the removal company to pack those too.

I'm staying at the Beau Rivage Hôtel, not far from
the Promenade des Anglais. This morning, I woke at
6 a.m. Unable to get back to sleep, I put on my running
gear and jogged along Boulevard Jean Jaurès and
across the back way to Mont Boron. I needed a final
look around the apartment on my own before I hand
in my keys to the estate agent. For the past five weeks,
I've been in a rental flat in Paris, waiting for this apartment sale to complete so I can finally be free.

The balcony doors are open, letting in a brisk
breeze and optimistic birdsong. I'm sitting on the
white sofa, looking around me at the almost bare
apartment. Only three months ago, Dad was still here,
sitting where I am now.

Hard to believe he is gone.

I take in the bare walls of what was once my
prison. Whenever guilt comes for me, and it does, I tell
myself I've served time for my crime already.

Dad is gone, and I'm going to live for myself now.

How quiet it is without him. Without the TV
blaring in the background. In the weeks after his
death, when the police investigation was still ongoing
and the authorities were still pretending to be concerned about the murder of an ex-prisoner, I had to

stay here in the apartment. I had to play the role of the concerned daughter, pushing the police for answers, for justice, knowing all along I was the culprit they never once suspected.

Throughout it all, that strange calm inside me. As I listened to myself lie to the police, to Lynne, to my brother, I wondered again if I'd inherited my father's worst abilities. The difference between us is I can admit my crimes to myself.

After leaving him on the beach that night, I headed back to the apartment. On the way, I removed the SIM card from the burner phone, snapped it in half and disposed of each piece in a different rubbish bin. The phone I dumped in a skip by an apartment block fifteen minutes from here. I'd considered calling the police and telling them the truth. Dad attacked me and I stabbed him in self-defence. But what if they didn't believe me? When the police turned up at the apartment at four the following morning to break the news of Dad's death to me, it didn't take them long to start snooping around. They found his phone where I'd left it, plugged into the charger in his bedroom. Even if I'd disposed of it somewhere, the police could have examined his phone records. I told them Dad had left the apartment in a rush the previous evening and must have forgotten it.

When they quizzed me about the anonymous text messages, I wiped the ever-present tears from my eyes and claimed to have no idea who they could be from. They wanted to know if Dad had been in contact with anyone from Baumettes. Even early on they wanted to connect his death to his past in jail. One ex-convict embroiled with another. An obvious explanation and the easiest one for them.

To make sure they stuck to this theory, I had to let Jane know about Dad's death as soon as possible. I couldn't have her going to the police with her story and telling them I knew about my father's past crimes. I used a burner phone, from a different shop this time. Our final conversation was a difficult but necessary one. I had to forget about Jane, and I hoped she would soon forget about me.

I also had Lynne to deal with. When the police interviewed her, I was nervous but nothing came of it. She was so kind to me after Dad's death. For the first week, she stayed at the apartment with me, insisting I shouldn't be alone. She was there when I phoned Patch to break the news to him and promised to keep an eye on me until he could get to France the following week. She even accompanied me to the mortuary and waited for me while I identified Dad's body. He looked so pure and peaceful in the viewing room, so like the

Dad I once loved, that I feared I'd made a terrible mistake. Then I remembered Patch saying two versions of our father existed, and I knew I'd killed the monstrous one, leaving the good one to die in peace.

When Lynne was here in the apartment with me, she spent a lot of time weeping and drinking wine. She insisted Dad was the love of her life, and she would never love again. At one point, I considered telling her I thought Dad was guilty of raping Ella, in order to lessen her grief, but I couldn't risk dropping my devoted daughter act, and I thought I should at least leave her illusions intact. A few weeks after Dad's death, she returned to the UK. We made the usual promises to keep in touch, but I think we both knew that wouldn't happen.

After locking up the apartment for the final time, I decide to take the shortcut down to the port. As I cross the road and walk down the steps, past the villas and apartment blocks, I can imagine Dad striding ahead of me, setting the pace. When I get to the foot of the steps, I zip up my fleecy hooded top against the breeze and begin to run.

That's good, kiddo. Let's get the blood moving.

As always, I sense Dad beside me as I run, urging me on. Since he died, I've been running almost every day, carrying on his routine. The therapist I've been seeing in Paris has encouraged me to separate the different parts of him. Which parts do I still love and need? What parts did I want to die with him?

The worst parts of him have been useful to me these past few months. I don't think I'd have survived without them.

Down at the port, the marina is crammed with boats that will stay moored until next summer. The cafés are still serving breakfast outside. In a month or so, they will have their outdoor heaters on.

I take a familiar route, along Quai Lunel and on to Quai Capeu. When I get to the sea wall overlooking Rauba Capeu beach, I stop. My heart skips beats beneath my ribs. My breathing is short and shallow.

This isn't the first time I've been back here. In the end, Patch and I brought Dad's ashes to this beach and scattered them in the sea. Patch thought it fitting to dispose of him in the place he'd met his end. My brother, like the police, believes Dad had a run-in with another ex-convict, a low life who has so far avoided detection. Once the newspapers identified Dad as the man stabbed to death on Rauba Capeu beach, I wondered if the private detective he used would come forward or the homeless man who'd been there that night. Nothing so far.

I gaze down at the rocks where my father died. A trio of drunk British men found his body around midnight and called the police. I try to imagine his last moments. How alone he must have felt. I try to imagine, as I often do, alternative outcomes to our argument. What if I hadn't stabbed him? I would have had to live with the real version of him and with his crimes. I might have had to give evidence against him to the police. Worse still, I might have been tempted to forgive him. I might have discovered how weak I could be.

I wouldn't be free like I am now.

A plane soars into the sky over the bay. Tonight, I'm flying from Nice to Paris and from there to Bangkok. I'm going to travel in Thailand for a few weeks and then go to Sydney to stay with Patch and Jenny and meet my nieces. I've spoken to Jenny often since Dad died. She's been kind to me. I misjudged her. I misjudged a lot of things.

My plans for the future are still vague. At least I don't have to worry about money. Patch and I are wealthy now, the money Dad and Mum worked so hard for is ours. I still don't know what to do with my share, but I'm going to give most of it away to a good cause. One that will benefit women who've suffered like Ella and Jane have.

It's not at all what Dad would have wanted.

59

LYNNE

Dear Barry,

Thanks for your letter. I hope you're having a good week in there. Can't believe it's mid-October already. Feels like autumn's really here now. Did your poetry class go ahead on Wednesday? It seems you're doing as much as you can to keep busy on a daily basis and to work on your long-term goals too. I'm so impressed you've started an English Literature degree! I was never one for studying. You'll have to recommend me something good to read. I love how you're doing something positive with your life sentence. Most people facing twenty-five years in jail would give up living, but you haven't. Positivity is such an attractive quality.

So is honesty. I appreciate you being honest about how you ended up in prison. I do understand. Don't get me wrong, the world would fall apart if we all took the law into our own hands, but I can see why you wanted to teach the man who beat your brother to a pulp a lesson. Like you say, what happened was a terrible accident. Anger and alcohol are not a good mix. Circumstances can get out of control so quickly after a few drinks, can't they? All I know is it's not up to me to judge anyone else for their mistakes.

Thanks for all your kind words about Sandy. His death was a lot to deal with. Some days I still can't believe what happened. It was tough on his daughter too; they were very close. I think about her often. She was a lovely girl, and I hope she's happy now, whatever she's up to.

Coming back to England after it happened was hard. I thought about trying to get my old job at Colchester General back, but, once everyone there heard about Sandy's murder and knew the truth about his criminal record, there was no way I could go back there. Not everyone's as open-minded as us, Barry.

That's what brought me to Wakefield. That and the job at Pinderfields Hospital. When I first moved up here, when I didn't know a soul, I drove past the prison every day on my way to work and I thought I bet there's someone in there just as lonely as me. I'm glad I took the chance to join the prison's pen pal scheme and even more glad it led me to you.

The poem you wrote for me made me cry. I loved the line about how when you wake up in the morning and look out of your cell window it makes you happy to know we are looking at the same sky. So romantic. After Sandy, I thought I'd given up on love, but I've decided not to let his death take that from me.

In answer to your question, yes, I do enjoy writing these letters and I'm glad you do too. That said, if you would like to speak on the phone sometime, I'd be up for that too. Or, once you feel ready, I could come and visit. Next month, maybe, or is that too soon? If it is, just say. I won't mind. Not really.

60

JANE

It is just after 10.30 a.m., and Michel and I are coping with another busy day at the hotel. I'm in one of the first-floor rooms, getting it ready for the next arrivals. One of our housekeepers is off sick today, and I was happy to help. Pierre is on reception and Alazne helped me with the breakfast shift. The open window of this room overlooks the courtyard, and I can see Michel pottering amid the plane trees, clearing up some of the debris from last night's thunderstorm. The first one of October, but probably not the last. There are loose branches and leaves scattered about and several lanterns have fallen from the trees. As Michel sweeps leaves into a pile, he glances across at our son, who is playing with Lena. Nathalie asked us to mind her for a few hours while she takes Nicole to a play-group. Theo and Lena are pushing his toy trucks over fallen branches, lost in a world of their own.

The guests who checked out of this room this morning have left it tidy. It doesn't take me long to clean out the shower and put out new toiletries. As I'm hanging up fresh towels on the heated rail, a rush of dizziness forces me to stop and take a few deep breaths. Now I'm almost three months pregnant, the morning sickness is easing off, but I'm not free of it yet. I put down the lid of the toilet, sit on it and wait for the dizziness to pass.

Three months. Has it really been that long since Sandy died? It is hard to think back to that time, to remember how scared and paranoid I was. Hard to remember my confrontation with Colette, when I learned I had good cause to be frightened. I was so lost. So out of control.

I never went to Nice. After leaving the bar on Rue de l'Observance, I hurried back to the market square, intending to catch a taxi to Les Arcs station at the bottom of Boulevard de la Liberté. That's when Michel found me. He had been searching all over town. As soon as he put his arms around me, I broke down. Speaking to Colette had unlocked me, and, as much as I wanted to, I could not keep my secrets any longer.

Looking back, I can see the breaking point was always going to come.

Michel brought me home. We lay on our bed together and I told him that seven years ago, in Cannes, a man had raped me, and that this past trauma was haunting me in the present. I did not tell him Sandy's name; I was not ready to hear it in his mouth. Michel held me close while I shared some of the details of that night. He passed no comment. Made no judgement. After I had finished that part of my story, I promised I would tell him more once I had slept. I was so very, very tired. Alazne got her doctor to come to us. He gave me a tablet that made me sleep until lunchtime the next day.

When I woke, I found Michel had asked his parents to take Theo to their house so we could be alone. He hadn't told them anything. He knew that decision was mine alone. We talked again. It was hard to make him understand why I had kept my secret from him for so long, but he eventually accepted my silence was not a reflection on him. I had kept the rape to myself because I did not want it to define me.

I wanted to stop my story there and not tell him about Ella in case I spoiled the fragile tenderness between us, but I had to carry on. I found several news articles about Ella's case online and showed them to him. I admitted to attending the trial and to being ashamed of not speaking out. Michel, his expression shifting between shock and anger as he tried to process my confession, told me I was not responsible for Sandy's actions and could not blame myself for what happened to Ella. Hearing him say Sandy's name made everything real. I could no longer hide from what I had to do.

I had to go to the police with my story to prevent Sandy attacking another woman, but I needed a few more days to prepare for what would come. The endless questions, the disruption to our lives, the possibility of not being able to make my charges stick.

Thank God we waited. Colette's call changed everything. I can still remember every word of that conversation.

'Hôtel des Arbres,' I said when I answered the phone. I was covering reception for an hour while Michel took Theo for a walk.

'Jane?' Colette said.

'Yes.' My breath clotted in my throat. 'It's me.'

'He's dead.' She started sobbing. 'He's dead.'

I did not have to ask who she meant.

'Someone stabbed him,' she said. 'Two days ago.'

A pause. A space for me to say how sorry I was for her loss. I said nothing.

'The police think it was probably someone he knew in prison,' she said. 'I can't believe it. I know he did some terrible things, but he didn't deserve that.'

No one deserved it more, I thought. As I listened to Colette crying, I wondered how she could be so upset at his loss, knowing everything he had done. Was she still in denial about him?

'Why are you calling me?' I said.

'It's going to be in the papers tomorrow, but I wanted to tell you myself. I thought you'd want to know.'

Relief washed through me. I had to suppress the urge to laugh.

'You're safe, Jane,' she said. 'It's over.'

Once the dizzy spell has passed, I move from the bathroom to the bedroom and strip the bed. After putting a clean sheet on the mattress and wrestling the duvet into its fresh cover, I sit down and pause to catch my breath. The pregnancy brings waves of fatigue as well as nausea at this stage. I rest my hand on my stomach and smile at the thought of the new life growing there. We don't want to know the baby's sex, but I have a feeling this one is a girl.

With Sandy gone there was no need to go to the police. Michel said he was sorry I would not get my chance for justice. I did not tell him I now had all the justice I needed. Some stranger might have put the knife into Sandy, but I had wished him dead more than once. Maybe Ella had too. I hoped wherever she was she would find out Sandy was gone.

That night, Michel and I had the kind of close, loving sex Sandy had held me back from for so long. Three weeks later, I discovered I was pregnant. Thanks to the stress of recent events, I had probably forgotten to take my contraception regularly. A very happy accident.

* * *

'Lena. Throw to me.' My son's happy voice drifts in through the open window. I return to work, manoeuvring the pillows into clean pillowcases and plumping them up. My pulse flutters as my hand sinks into their soft, feathery bodies and for a moment I cannot breathe. I drop the pillow and tap my fingers over my face and forehead in the sequence Julia Martin showed me in my last session. I see her once a week now, and as well as talking, we practice techniques for relieving the symptoms of trauma when they appear.

'Jane.'

Michel is calling me. When I reach the window, I

see Alazne laying a tray of coffees on one of the court-yard tables. Michel beckons me down for a break.

'Coming,' I say.

When I get to reception, Pierre leaves the desk and comes out into the courtyard with me, clutching his copy of the local paper. We settle into our chairs and Alazne hands out our coffees. Mine, the only one I will have today, is weak and milky. Theo and Lena thank Alazne for their orange juice but soon return to their games. Michel sits beside me, one arm across the back of my chair. Minette appears and winds herself around my legs for a moment before darting off to the other end of the courtyard, busy with important feline matters.

When Pierre lays his paper on the table, I see the headline is about Henri Breton and his upcoming rape trial. While reaching for the sugar bowl, Pierre turns the paper face down to hide the story. He, like everyone else, is trying to make my recovery from the past as easy as possible. I am so lucky to have them. After Sandy's death, I told Alazne and Pierre every-thing. I was the 'good girl' no longer, but it didn't mat-ter. My family here accept the real me, as do my friends. Nathalie, Bastien, Elyna and Jacques have been fantastic. Michel and I would not have survived this so well without such good support.

As for my own parents, I am not sure I will ever tell them. My sessions with Julia have shown me this is my story, and it is up to me who I share it with. I still have guilt about not reporting the rape at the time, but I cannot change the past. I think about Henri Breton and his upcoming trial. The scandal has been in the news constantly. An ugly saga. I am amazed by all the women voicing support for him on social media sites; it makes me despair. It sometimes seems as if so many women are sharing their stories of assault and abuse and yet nothing is changing.

As we drink our coffee, we discuss hotel matters – staff rotas for the next few days, what to do about the broken bed frame in room 11. Theo and Lena get to their feet and chase one another around the thick trunk of the plane tree at the centre of the courtyard.

'Be careful, Theo,' I say. 'Go slowly.'

'Okay, Maman.' He creeps around the tree and Lena follows him. Today he is in denim shorts and a red sweatshirt. He no longer obsesses over colours the way he used to. A relief in some ways, but I can't help missing each phase as he grows out of it.

Michel's fingers knead my knotted shoulder muscles as he tells his father about the new graphic design project he is working on for a theatre company in Aix-en-Provence. Despite the joy of the pregnancy, the past few months have not been easy on us as a couple. We still have a lot to mend, individually and together, but I am okay with that. I want us to live our reality now, not some romantic version of it.

When I first started therapy for the rape with Julia, I thought recovery would mean getting my old self back, the me that existed before Sandy. Now I know recovery is going forwards, not backwards. Sharing my story may not have changed the world, but it has changed my world. Instead of destroying the life I have built, speaking the truth has given me a new beginning.

Michel places a hand on my belly. I rest a hand on top of his.

'How is the little one today?' Alazne asks.

I smile. 'Behaving.' She and Pierre are so excited about the baby, although not as excited as Theo is about having a little brother or sister.

A high-pitched squeal grabs our attention. Lena has fallen over, on to her hands and knees. Alazne scrapes back her chair and stands up, but before she can get to Lena, Theo is there. He helps his friend to her feet and gently brushes the dirt from her hands.

'Good boy, Theo,' I say. 'Good boy.'

ACKNOWLEDGMENTS

To my agent, Charlie Brotherstone, much gratitude as always for your support of my writing and for your work on its behalf. To the wonderful team at Boldwood Books, huge thanks for backing my stories and for working so hard to share them with the world. Special thanks must go to my editor, collaborator and plot-fixing genius, Tara Loder. Working with you is a joy!

To the tutors and writers at The Novelry, thanks are due again for helping to get *The Ideal Man* up on its feet. I'm especially indebted to Louise Dean, Jack Jordan and Tash Barsby for their brainstorming skills... and the wonderful shout line! Heartfelt thanks also to Lesley Glaister for insightful comments on an early draft.

This novel would not have come together without the people who helped with my research. Stuart Gibbon, thanks for once again answering police procedural questions. Muriel Ponsolle, thanks for being my woman on the ground in Nice, for sharing your own invaluable contacts and for introducing me to Le Plongeoir restaurant! To lawyer and fellow author, Lia Middleton, gratitude for your legal expertise. Big thanks to Anna-Karin Faccendini for your advice on French criminal law, without which I would have really struggled. Thanks to Laurene Huck from the French Institute in Edinburgh for checking and correcting my inadequate French! Thanks once again to Dr Mark Flynn for help with character psychology and to Matt for honest answers to questions about men and women. As always, any errors in this work are mine alone.

To Dad, Susan, Charly and Billy – so much love to you always and huge thanks for all your support.

Susie and Mary... another novel down! You're the best and none of this would be possible without you and the inspiration you bring to my life. Thanks for everything and for being brilliant people to go on a research trip to the South of France with!

MORE FROM T.J. EMERSON

We hope you enjoyed reading *The Ideal Man*. If you did, please leave a review.

If you'd like to gift a copy, this book is also available as an ebook, digital audio download and audiobook CD.

Sign up to T.J. Emerson's mailing list for news, competitions and updates on future books.

https://bit.ly/TJEmersonNews

The Perfect Holiday, another twisty psychological thriller from T.J. Emerson, is available now.

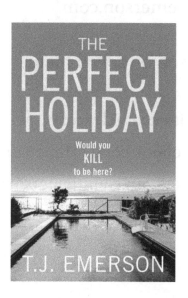

ABOUT THE AUTHOR

T.J. Emerson's debut psychological thriller was published by Legend Press and received brilliant reviews. Her short stories and features have been widely published in anthologies and magazines, and she works as a literary consultant and writing tutor. She lives in Scotland.

Visit T.J. Emerson's Website:

http://www.traceyemerson.com/

Follow T.J. Emerson on social media:

twitter.com/TraceyJEmerson

facebook.com/TJEmersonAuthor

instagram.com/tjemersonwrites

THE *Murder* LIST

**THE MURDER LIST IS A NEWSLETTER
DEDICATED TO SPINE-CHILLING FICTION
AND GRIPPING PAGE-TURNERS!**

**SIGN UP TO MAKE SURE YOU'RE ON OUR
HIT LIST FOR EXCLUSIVE DEALS, AUTHOR
CONTENT, AND COMPETITIONS.**

SIGN UP TO OUR NEWSLETTER

BIT.LY/THEMURDERLISTNEWS

Boldwood

Boldwood Books is an award-winning fiction publishing company seeking out the best stories from around the world.

Find out more at www.boldwoodbooks.com

Join our reader community for brilliant books, competitions and offers!

Follow us
@BoldwoodBooks
@BookandTonic

Sign up to our weekly
deals newsletter

https://bit.ly/BoldwoodBNewsletter

Lightning Source UK Ltd.
Milton Keynes UK
UKHW041302220223
417454UK00026B/702